THE CUTTING

JAMES HAYMAN

St. Martin's Paperbacks

This is a work of fiction. All of the characters, organizations, and events portrayed in this novel are either products of the author's imagination or are used fictitiously.

THE CUTTING

Copyright © 2009 by James Hayman.
Excerpt from *The Chill of Night* copyright © 2010 by James Hayman.

Cover photograph by Herman Estevez.

All rights reserved.

For information address St. Martin's Press, 175 Fifth Avenue, New York, NY 10010.

EAN: 978-0-312-38953-6

Printed in the United States of America

Minotaur edition / July 2009
St. Martin's Paperbacks edition / June 2010

St. Martin's Paperbacks are published by St. Martin's Press, 175 Fifth Avenue, New York, NY 10010.

10 9 8 7 6 5 4 3 2 1

For Jeanne

ACKNOWLEDGMENTS

There are many people I wish to thank for their help and encouragement in writing this book. Among them, in no particular order, are:

Detective Sergeant Tom Joyce, who once held McCabe's job in the Portland Police Department's Crimes Against People unit and who now teaches Criminal Justice at Southern Maine Community College. What I got right is due to Tom. What I got wrong is entirely my own fault.

Dr. George "Bud" Higgins and Dr. Bob Kramer of Maine Medical Center and Dr. Bob Zeff of the Iowa Heart Center for their knowledge and insights about medical practice in general and transplant surgery in particular.

Portland attorneys Brenda Buchanan, Ron Schneider, and Elizabeth Burns for their insights on criminal and family law.

Bruce White, Transplant Co-Ordinator at Maine Med.

Jim Ferland of the Office of Chief Medical Examiner of Maine for showing me where and how autopsies are done.

Jane Hayman Abbott, Cynthia Thayer, Lewis Robinson, Kate Sullivan, Mike Kimball, Shonna Humphrey, Brenda Buchanan (again), Jane Slovan, Richard Bilodeau, and Eleanor Lincoln Morse, fine writers all, who were kind enough to read the manuscript and offer ideas and suggestions that improved it enormously.

Laima Vince, whose writing workshops helped get me

started down this road, and Cevia Rosol for proofing and copyediting the early drafts.

Charlie Spicer, Yaniv Soha, and Andy Martin of Minotaur Books for their unstinting support and encouragement.

Meg Ruley, a good friend and, without question, the best agent a first-time novelist could ever hope to find, and Suzy Kane, a fellow islander, who introduced me to Meg.

Finally, my children, Kate and Ben, and my wife, Jeanne, for their love and encouragement every step of the way.

PROLOGUE

July 1971

He pressed the terrified creature firmly against his body. He was a sturdy boy, tall for his eight years, with dark hair and a long, thin face. After more than a month of summer sunshine, his normally fair skin had turned quite brown. He could feel the rabbit, just weeks old, shivering, and he felt a sense of rising excitement, anticipating the adventure that lay ahead. The boy resisted an urge to run toward the secret place. He feared tripping over a bit of protruding ledge or a branch buried in last fall's rotting leaves. His prize might fall loose and scamper away. Even as the boy walked, his breathing quickened. He lightly stroked the bunny's soft fur, trying to calm its beating heart and, perhaps, his own as well.

It took him nearly twenty minutes to reach his destination, a kind of natural cave formed by arching tendrils of bittersweet vines as they reached upward to grasp and wind around the young white pine and birch trees that surrounded the place. The boy had filled in the lower walls, layering spruce branches atop the bittersweet. He had also cut away the growth from the interior and brought in armfuls of dead leaves and pine needles to form a kind of floor. The entire space measured about four feet in diameter and at its center was no more than three feet high. Shafts of sunlight entered from above, projecting a pattern of brightness and shadow on the ground.

The boy crawled into the cave, securing the rabbit with one hand against his chest. Moisture from the ground soaked through the knees of his jeans and felt cold against his skin. Once inside, he laid the animal on the ground, holding it by its ears. Its black button eyes were fixed on the boy, who saw what he sensed was both terror and resignation. It was a feeling that the creature knew—and in its way accepted— what the boy had so carefully planned and prepared for. This seemed to the boy to be as it should be.

With his free hand he withdrew the folding knife from his back pocket. He had sharpened the three-inch blade to razor fineness on his father's stone, and he took care not to cut his finger as he worked it open.

He forced himself to wait a few seconds, enjoying the anticipation. He could feel his heart pounding as he placed the point of the blade just below the creature's neck. He pushed hard and then sliced down toward its stomach, open- ing the animal up. The creature's screams pierced the air. So like the high-pitched shrieks of pain that came from his infant brother when the boy played with him. He didn't let the sound distract him from his task. He was quite sure no one could hear.

He had no words for the feeling that shook his body as he gazed upon the rabbit's beating heart and held it for an instant in his hand before the beating stopped and the crea- ture died. He only knew it was something he wanted to ex- perience again and again.

1

Portland, Maine
September 16, 2005
Friday. 5:30 A.M.

Fog can be a sudden thing on the Maine coast. On even the clearest mornings, swirling gray mists sometimes appear in an instant, covering the earth with an opacity that makes it hard to see even one's own feet on the ground. On this particular September morning it descended at 5:30, about the time Lucinda Cassidy and her companion Fritz, a small dog of indeterminate pedigree, arrived at the cemetery on Vaughan Street to begin their four-mile run along the streets of Portland's West End and the path that borders the city's Western Promenade.

The cemetery was one of Portland's oldest and was surrounded by a chain-link fence, now falling into disrepair. The gates on the Vaughan Street side were locked to keep out neighborhood dog walkers. The earliest gravestones dated back to the late 1700s. On most of these stones, dates and other specifics had faded to near illegibility. Those that could be read bore the names of early Portland's most prominent families, Deering, Dana, Brackett, Reed, Preble. These were old Yankee names, many of which had achieved a measure of immortality, having been bestowed upon the streets and parks of a young and growing city. More recent stones marked the graves of Irish, Italian, and French-Canadian immigrants who came to Portland to work in the city's thriving shipbuilding trades or on the railroads in the last half of the nineteenth century. Today, however, no more of the dead would be buried here, regardless of ancestry or influence. The place was full, the last remains having been interred and the last markers erected in the years immediately following World War II.

When the fog moved in, Lucy considered canceling her run, but only briefly. At age twenty-eight, she was preparing for her first 10K race. She had more than enough self-discipline not to let anything as transitory as a little morning fog interfere with her training schedule. It was tough enough getting the runs in, given the long hours she worked as the newest account executive at Beckman and Hawes, the city's biggest ad agency. In any case, Lucy knew her route well. The fog wouldn't be a problem as long as she took care not to trip on one of the sidewalk's uneven pavers.

The air was cool on her bare legs as Lucy performed her stretches—calves and quads and hamstrings. She pulled off her oversized Bates College sweatshirt, revealing a white sports bra and blue nylon shorts, and tossed it into her car, an aging Toyota Corolla.

She saw no other joggers or dog walkers and thought she and Fritz might well have the streets to themselves. She slipped off his collar to let him run free. He was well trained and wouldn't go far. She pulled a Portland Sea Dogs cap down over her blond hair, stretching the Velcro band down and under her ponytail. She draped the dog's lead around her shoulders and set off along Vaughan Street at a leisurely pace, with Fritzy first racing ahead and then stopping to leave his mark on a tree or lamppost.

Lucy liked the quiet of the early morning hours in this upscale neighborhood. Passing street after street of graceful nineteenth-century homes, she glanced in the windows and imagined herself living in one or another of them. The image pleased her. She saw herself holding elegant dinner parties. The food would be simple but perfectly prepared.

The wines rare. The men handsome. The conversation witty. All terribly *Masterpiece Theatre*. Ah well, a pretty picture but not very likely. She was not, she knew, to the manner born. She watched Fritz scamper ahead and then turn and wait for her to follow.

Lucy moved through the damp morning air, bringing her heart rate up to an aerobic training level. She thought about the day ahead, reviewing, for at least the twentieth time, details of a TV campaign she was presenting to the marketing group at Mid-Coast Bank. She'd worked her tail off to land this new client, but they were turning out to be both difficult and demanding. After work, she planned a quick trip to Circuit City to pick up a birthday present for her soon-to-be twelve-year-old nephew Owen. Her older sister Patti's boy, Owen told her what he "really really wanted" was an iPod, but he wasn't optimistic. "We don't have the money this year," he added in grown-up, serious tones that had Patti's imprint all over them. Well, Owen was in for a big surprise.

After that it was back to the Old Port for dinner with David at Tony's. The prospect of dinner at Tony's pleased her. The prospect of sharing it with her ex-husband didn't. He was pushing to get back together, and yes, she admitted, there were times she was briefly tempted. God knows, no one else even remotely interesting was waiting in the wings. Yet after a couple of dates, she was surer than ever that going back to David wasn't the answer for either of them. She planned to tell him so tonight.

She ran along Vaughan for a mile or so, climbing the gentle rise of Bramhall Hill, before turning west across the old section of the hospital toward the path that lined the western edge of the Prom. The fog was thicker now, and she could see even less, but her body felt good. The training was paying off, and she felt certain she'd be ready for the race, now ten days away.

Suddenly Fritz darted past and disappeared into the mist, barking furiously at what Lucy figured was either an animal or another runner coming up the path in her direction.

Then she saw Fritz run out of the fog, turn, and stand his ground, angry barks lifting his small body in an uncharacteristic rage. Instantly alert, Lucy wondered who or what could be getting him so agitated. Usually he just wagged his stub of a tail at strangers.

Seconds later a runner emerged from the fog about fifteen feet in front of her. He was a tall man with a lean, well-muscled body. Had she seen him jogging here before? She didn't think so. He was unusually good-looking with dark, deep-set eyes that would be hard to forget. Late thirties or early forties, she thought. Fritz backed away but kept barking.

"Quiet down," Lucy commanded. "It's okay." She smiled at the man. "He isn't usually so noisy."

The tall man stopped and knelt down. He extended his left hand for Fritz to sniff, then scratched him behind the ears. He smiled up at Lucy. "What's his name?"

Lucy registered the absence of a wedding band. "Fritz," she said.

"Hey, Fritz, are you a good boy? Sure you are." He scratched Fritz again. The dog's stubby tail offered a tentative wag or two. He looked up. "I've seen you running here before. I'm sure I have."

"You may have," she said, though she was sure she would have noticed him. "I'm here most mornings. I'm training for a 10K."

"Good for you. Mind if I run along? I'd enjoy the company."

She hesitated, surprised at the man's directness. Finally she said, "I guess not. Not as long as you can keep up. I'm Lucy."

"Harry," he said, extending a hand. "Harry Potter."

"You're kidding."

"No, I was christened long before the first book came out, and I wasn't about to change my name."

They took off, chatting easily, laughing about the name. Fritz, no longer barking, kept pace.

"You live in Portland?" she asked.

"No, I'm here on business. Medical equipment. The hospital's one of my biggest clients."

"So you're here quite often?"

"At least once a month."

They picked up the pace and turned south down the western edge of the Prom.

"Normally there's a great view from up here. Can't see a damned thing today."

A dark green SUV sat parked at the curb just ahead of them. "Could you excuse me for a minute?" Harry pointed and clicked a key ring. The car's lights blinked; its doors unlocked. "I need to get something."

He leaned in, rummaged in a small canvas bag, and then emerged from the car holding a hypodermic and a small bottle. "I'm a diabetic," he explained. "I have to take my insulin on schedule." Harry carefully inserted the needle into the bottle and extracted a clear liquid. "Only take a second." Lucy smiled. Feeling it was rude to watch, she turned away and looked out over the Prom. The fog wasn't dissipating. If anything it seemed to be getting thicker. She performed a few stretches to keep her muscles warm while they waited.

She sensed more than saw the sudden movement behind her. Before she could react, Harry Potter's left arm was around her neck, pulling her sharply back and up in a classic choke hold. Her windpipe constricted in the crook of his elbow. She couldn't move. She wanted to scream but could draw only enough breath to emit a thin, strangled cry.

Frantic and confused, Lucy dug her nails into the man's flesh, wishing she'd let them grow longer and more lethal. She felt a sharp prick. She looked down and saw the man's free hand squeezing whatever was in the hypodermic into her arm. He continued holding her, immobile. She tried to struggle, but he was too strong, his grip too tight. Within seconds wooziness began to overtake her. She felt his hands on the back of her head and her butt, pushing her, headfirst, facedown, into the backseat of the car.

Turning her head, Lucy could still see out through the

open door, but everything had taken on a hazy, distant quality, like a slow-motion film growing darker frame by frame and seeming to make no sense. She saw an enraged Fritz growling and digging his teeth into the man's leg. She heard a shout, "Shit!" Two large hands picked the small dog up. She tried to rise but couldn't. The last thing Lucinda Cassidy saw was the good-looking man with the dark eyes. He smiled at her. The slow-motion film faded to black.

2

The summer crowds in the Old Port had thinned now that Labor Day had come and gone, but the air was warm, and Exchange Street bustled with energy. Shops and restaurants were open late and busy. Packs of teenagers in varying states of grunge—some with piercings and tattoos and some without—spread themselves across the sidewalks, forcing middle-aged tourists out onto the narrow streets.

Detective Sergeant Michael McCabe and Kyra Erikson walked in step, side by side, holding hands. Seeing them absorbed in each other's company, chatting happily, it would have been easy for a passerby to conclude, correctly, that they were lovers.

Tonight they were heading for Arno, the city's latest northern Italian hot spot. As usual, it was Kyra's choice. McCabe's restaurant habits were as predictable as they were unadventurous. He pretty much always ordered the same thing: a rare New York strip steak, preceded by a single malt Scotch—no ice—and accompanied by a couple of bottles of cold Shipyard Ale.

Kyra, on the other hand, was a real foodie. She was looking forward to one of Arno's specialties, "duck-meat ravioli, served," she recited, practically drooling, "in a light brown sauce with thin slices of rare grilled duck."

McCabe considered their differing approaches to dining a minor incompatibility. He had no problem indulging her passion for haute cuisine. After dinner they planned to go back to his apartment and watch a movie, John Schlesinger's *Billy Liar*, with Tom Courtenay and a young, very sexy Julie Christie. An old favorite from McCabe's former life in film school at NYU. He'd never told Kyra she reminded him of Christie in this role. She had the same curly blond hair, the same liquid eyes, the same full, almost pouty lips, except, thank God, Kyra almost never pouted. The resemblance was one of the things that first attracted him to her. He wondered if she'd appreciate the comparison.

They paused by a young street musician seated on the pavement, his back against the brick wall of a small jewelry shop. He was playing a beautifully polished violin. A hand-lettered cardboard sign, propped against the wall, identified him as a JUILLIARD DROPOUT. They listened for twenty or thirty seconds. Then, before walking on, McCabe dropped a couple of dollar bills into the man's open violin case.

"You're in a good mood."

"Why not? It's a beautiful night. I'm with a beautiful woman. He's a good player and I like the piece. Mozart. Violin Concerto." McCabe paused, but only for a second, searching his memory. "Number Three."

It wasn't that he knew a lot about classical music. He didn't. He knew nothing of music theory or the styles of various composers. He only occasionally listened to it. It was just this weird mind of his. Once he had seen or heard something—anything—he almost never forgot it. They walked on, the silken, sensuous notes of the violin fading behind them.

McCabe knew Kyra had found it unsettling when she first discovered he could repeat, verbatim, lengthy passages from a book or an investigation report he read months before. She assumed what he had was a photographic memory. He said not. "There is no such thing," he told her. "Nobody's ever been able to prove that a brain can 'photograph' an image and then 'see' it again."

"You remember everything?"

"Only if it interests me. I've got something called an eidetic memory. My brain is just unusually efficient at organizing stuff and filing it away where it can lay its hands on it."

They continued up Exchange Street. They passed a black-and-white patrol car pulled into a space marked with A NO PARKING sign. A young, round-faced female cop sat behind the wheel. She smiled as she spotted McCabe with someone so obviously his girlfriend. "Hey, Sergeant, how ya doin'?" she called out.

He smiled back. "Keeping an eye on the delinquents?"

"Yeah, you know, Friday night. Another few hours the drunks'll start pouring out of the bars."

Arno, as expected, was crowded and noisy. Two or three groups stood by the door waiting for the hostess to notice them. Since their own reservation wasn't for another fifteen minutes, McCabe and Kyra wandered into the small bar, where squadrons of young business types, male and female, jockeyed for position. He noticed the distinctive squat shape of a Dalwhinnie among the bottles at the back of the bar. It was one of his favorite malts and not always available. He signaled the bartender and ordered a double, neat, for himself and, without having to ask, a Sancerre for Kyra. Glancing over, he saw she was chatting with one of her art contacts, Gloria Kelwin, a gallery owner he'd met a couple of times before. McCabe brought the drinks over and handed Kyra her wine.

"Why, hello, Michael," Gloria purred, bending forward to brush McCabe's cheek with her lips. "Caught any bad guys lately?" She spoke in a mannered way McCabe found consistently irritating. Not waiting for his response, she turned her attention back to Kyra. Kelwin's gallery, North Space, carried Kyra's paintings and prints, and Kyra was hoping to schedule a solo show. McCabe watched Kyra's face, animated and alive, as she described a new series of figure studies she was working on, small oils of young dancers, bodies abstracted in fluid athletic poses. He found her quite irresistible, watching her when she didn't know he was watching. In the end, he was happy shutting out the words and concentrating instead on the smooth peaty burn of the Scotch as it traced its way down his throat, wondering for the hundredth time how he'd managed to attract this sensual, sensitive woman.

As he sipped, McCabe felt his cell phone vibrate in his pocket. He pulled it out in time to see the call was from Maggie Savage. While a chance encounter with an overbearing gallery owner couldn't spoil the evening, McCabe knew Maggie's call might. Placing his nearly empty glass on the bar, he excused himself and stepped out onto Exchange Street. The air felt fresh, and he could smell the sea. He leaned against the building and waited a moment before calling her back. Then he punched in her number.

Maggie was the number two detective in McCabe's Crimes Against People unit. Technically, as the unit's leader, McCabe wasn't supposed to have a partner, but he'd stretched the rules, and they'd worked together since his arrival in Portland three years ago. Back then, she hadn't been shy about letting him know she resented the "so-called star" from the NYPD, sweeping in and taking the job she felt she'd earned for herself. In her view, the department passing on her application was nothing more than simple sexism. The fact this was the first time they'd ever brought in a senior detective from outside, regardless of expertise or experience, reinforced her conviction. Nevertheless, McCabe knew that in the process of working together, he'd earned her respect—and she his.

Maggie picked up on the first ring. "Hate to interrupt a night on the town, McCabe, but we've got kind of a mess here."

"What's up?"

"A teenaged girl's body was found in that scrap metal yard off Somerset. Looks like it could be the Dubois kid."

Katie Dubois had disappeared more than a week ago. "I gather the body's pretty cut up," she continued. "Maybe a sex thing. I don't know. You're the murder expert."

"Aw, shit." He let the idea sink in. Portland wasn't New York, and murder wasn't all that common. Hell, there'd been only nineteen homicides in the whole state the previous year. Just two in the city of Portland.

"Alright, I'm at Arno. Y'know, the new place on Exchange? Pick me up here. I'll run in and apologize to Kyra."

The noise level in the bar had risen to a din, and McCabe didn't want to shout to make himself heard. He tapped Kyra's shoulder and led her over to a marginally quieter corner near the coat room. "I have to go," he said.

"Oh, no," she said, disappointment spreading across her face. "It's taken us weeks to get this reservation."

"Someone's been murdered. A teenage girl."

Kyra closed her eyes for a moment, then opened them and nodded. "Okay. You go. I'm sure I can join Gloria." She looked up and kissed him softly on the lips. "Don't worry. It's what I get for falling in love with a cop."

"I'll see you at the apartment?"

She nodded, smiled, and turned to go back into the bar.

Maggie was waiting at the curb in an unmarked Crown Vic when McCabe emerged. He slid into the passenger seat. "Any more background?"

"The body was found by a homeless guy. Drunk. Possibly disturbed. Other than that, nothing. No ID. No wallet. No clothes. Nada. The uniforms on the scene are pretty sure it's Dubois."

They rode in silence for several minutes.

"So how's the food at Arno?" Maggie asked. "As good as everyone says?"

"I dunno."

Maggie peered at him in that owlish way she had. He'd

seldom seen a cop who looked less like a cop. "I forgot," she said. "You only eat Scotch and steak."

"The Scotch was great, but I never got to the steak. We never even got to the table. Kyra's probably just sitting down now with a gallery owner we ran into in the bar."

"Well, I am sorry to have dragged you away."

"Not your fault."

It took less than five minutes for McCabe and Savage to reach the scene. There were a couple of black-and-white units, blue lights flashing, blocking access to the area. Maggie pulled in behind one. They got out. McCabe grabbed a Maglite and a pair of latex gloves from the trunk.

The area was a small industrial wasteland slated for eventual development. Maybe two or three acres, no more than that. Most of it was surrounded by a deteriorating chain-link fence. Yellow crime scene tape stretched across the openings in the fence and back another thirty or so yards. Piles of rusting scrap metal littered the landscape. A few clumps of weeds struggled for life in the stony hardpan. Other than that, just dirt, a lot of trash, and a dead body. Identity would have to be confirmed, but as they moved closer, McCabe became certain it was Katie Dubois.

Even in the empty grayness of death, he could see Katie once had a pretty face. Round with chubby cheeks. Shoulder-length blond hair tied in a ponytail. Eyes open and clouded over, revealing none of the horror one expected in the eyes of someone facing imminent slaughter— and slaughter it was. She'd been sliced practically in half by a deep cut that angled from just below her neck to just above her navel. The flaps of skin were folded neatly back into place. Circular burn marks were visible on her breasts and on her thighs near her genitals. There might be others hidden from view.

The girl was naked. She lay on her back, knees up, legs spread, one arm angled straight back as though she'd been reaching for something overhead. Or maybe doing the backstroke. McCabe was sure she hadn't fallen this way. Someone had arranged the body in this position.

He stood for a couple of minutes, scanning the corpse, remembering the details of the case. Katie Dubois was sixteen years old. She'd gone missing Wednesday before last. A junior at Portland High School and a star soccer player, she hadn't come home from a night out with her friends. She was last seen in the Old Port, hanging out with five other teenagers. Flyers with her photograph were stapled to telephone poles all over town. Tom Tasco and Eddie Fraser were the lead team on the case. They were experienced detectives, and they worked it hard. McCabe read their investigation reports and found them impressively thorough.

None of the other teens had any idea where Katie might have gone. Her boyfriend, Ronnie Sobel, told detectives he was talking to some friends and when he turned back, Katie was gone. One of the girls said that wasn't quite how it happened. She claimed Katie and Sobel were arguing. She thought it had to do with Ronnie hooking up with another girl, but she wasn't sure. Anyway, she said, when Ronnie walked away from her, Katie stormed off. Most of the department as well as dozens of friends, family, and volunteers had been looking for her ever since. They'd combed the city. The nearby Scarborough marshes. A lot of people thought she might turn up in the harbor. She hadn't. She'd turned up here.

McCabe felt a familiar rage growing within him. Murder in Maine tended to be a family affair, husbands killing wives, friends killing friends. As often as not they called the cops themselves as soon as they realized what they had done—but this was different. This had the random, brutal anonymity of the big city, and McCabe allowed himself a moment to mourn a universe where one human being could do this to another, especially to a teenager. Then he put these thoughts away and let the cop side of his brain kick in, inspecting the corpse, inspecting the ground where the girl lay, trying to figure out if there was anything he should be noticing. Anything that would give him a better idea of what happened to Katie Dubois and who was responsible for it. He saw signs of duct tape adhesive across her mouth and ligature marks on her wrists, ankles, and neck. Her clouded eyes revealed no signs of pinpoint hemorrhaging, suggesting that mutilation, not strangulation, was the immediate cause of death.

Standing here in a scrap yard in Portland, Maine, McCabe suddenly had the feeling he was back in New York. It wasn't like he was imagining it. Or remembering it. It was like he was really there. He could hear the rush of the city. He could smell the stink of it. A hundred bloodied corpses paraded before his eyes. His right hand drew comfort from resting on the handle of his gun. Mike McCabe, once again lured to the chase. He knew with an absolute certainty that this was his calling. That it was here, among the killers and the killed, that he belonged. No matter how far he ran, no matter how well he hid, he'd never leave the violence or his fascination with it behind.

McCabe stepped back from Katie's body, careful not to trip over Maggie who was kneeling a few feet behind him, writing her notes. He approached the uniformed officer who'd found the body. He remembered the man's name. Kevin Comisky. "Kevin," he said quietly, "what do we know?"

"Not much. I was on patrol. Quiet night. I just made the turn off Marginal onto Franklin when this drunk comes running out, waving his arms around. He's screaming something about murder, but he's pretty incoherent, so I put him in the car, which, by the way, he stinks up pretty bad. I ask him to tell me where he saw whatever he saw. He manages to direct me here. I see the body. Call Dispatch. They send Kennerly as backup. Then they call you guys."

McCabe used his cell to call police headquarters at 109 Middle Street. Two evidence techs were currently on duty. He told both he needed them at the scrap yard ASAP. Then he called Deputy ME Terri Mirabito. Portland, with a population a little over sixty-five thousand, wasn't big enough to have its own medical examiner's office. Normally whoever was assigned would have to drive down from the state lab in Augusta, a good hour and some away, but Mirabito lived in town, and if she was home she could get here a lot faster. She answered on the first ring and said she'd be right over.

"Where's the drunk now?" he asked Comisky.

"Still in the unit," said the cop. "It's gonna take more than a paper pine tree and a squirt of Lysol to get the stink out of that baby."

"Either of you guys touch anything or move the body around?" McCabe addressed both uniformed officers.

Both responded negatively. One said, "It's tough enough just looking at her."

"Okay. I'm going to wander around, see what I can see. Then I'll want to talk to your friend in the car, so please make sure he doesn't go anywhere."

He turned to Maggie. "Where are Tasco and Fraser? I thought this was their case." He knew he was sounding irritable, but tough shit. A detective should never lose track of his case.

"Mike, they've been putting in eighteen-hour days for over a week. Anyway, Tom's on his way in. I couldn't find Eddie."

McCabe nodded. "Find him."

He turned away and used his cell to call home. Casey answered. "Hey, Case, how're you doing?"

"Hello, Daddy dearest. I'm fine," McCabe's thirteen-year-old daughter said in a playfully proper tone. "Are you still eating dinner?"

"We never got to dinner. I'm working." He wondered if Casey had known Katie Dubois. They were both soccer players. Probably not, he decided. Casey was still in middle school. Eighth grade. "I'm going to be late. What are you up to?"

"I've got some friends over. Do you want to talk to Jane?"

"Oh, really? Who's over?"

"Gretchen and Whitney." They were two of Casey's best friends and lived nearby on Munjoy Hill. "We're kind of in the middle of something." Doing her best to put on an aristocratic British accent, she added, "I don't want to go into it. I'll fetch Jane."

"Okay," he laughed. "Fetch Jane. As long as you're not doing something you're not supposed to."

"Dad, I'm not a baby, y'know."

"Okay. Get Jane. I love you."

"Love you, too."

McCabe could hear Casey shouting, "Hey, Jane, it's Dad," the single syllable drawn out, "Da-aaad!"

Jane Devaney was a sixty-year-old retired nurse and high school sex education teacher McCabe employed on a part-time basis to look after Casey. She also rode a Harley. Casey found that indescribably cool. So did McCabe.

Jane's voice came on. "Hiya, Mike."

"Everything good there?"

"Oh yeah, we're fine. Kids are fooling around. Girl stuff. I'm deep into *Supernanny.* Keeping tabs on the competition. I take it you're working late?"

"It looks that way."

"Want me to spend the night?"

"Not necessary. I'm not sure when I'll be home, but Kyra should be there as soon as she finishes dinner."

"Well, if you decide you want me to stay, just let me know. It's not a problem."

"Thanks, Jane. I appreciate it."

McCabe closed the phone and returned it to his pocket. He pulled on the surgical gloves he'd brought from the car. Pointing the flashlight at the ground, he started inspecting the area where the girl's body was lying. Senior evidence tech Bill Jacobi and his partner would arrive soon enough, but McCabe wanted to have a more thorough look around first.

McCabe figured the girl was most likely killed somewhere else and the body dumped here later. If so, he'd find little in the way of evidence. He saw no blood on the ground, and the blood on the body was dried and old. A greenish cast of decomposition was beginning to show on her abdomen. Katie Dubois had been dead a while. McCabe guessed at least forty-eight hours.

The ground was stone hard, so he doubted he'd find any footprints or tire tracks, but he watched where he walked and looked anyway. Also, he saw nothing to suggest the body had been dragged the thirty or so yards from the street. No bent clusters of weeds. No visible scrapes of dirt around the girl's heels or head or shoulders. He figured the killer carried Katie to where he dumped her. No great feat. She couldn't have weighed more than 110 pounds even before she lost most of her blood. The killer would have gotten some of that blood on his clothes. Possible evidence unless he burned them.

He played his light over the girl's body, inch by inch. The cut down the middle of her chest looked as careful and clean as if it had been made with a razor or possibly a surgeon's scalpel. The burn marks were recent and deliberate. In the lobe of her right ear he found a small gold earring with a dangling heart-shaped charm. He moved the light to the left ear. The lobe was torn, and the mate to the earring, assuming there was a mate, was gone. Accidentally caught on something? Maybe. Roughly pulled out? Possibly. Taken as a trophy? More likely. Her navel was pierced with a silver-colored semicircular bar with tiny metal balls at either end. A blue tattoo that looked like a Chinese or maybe Japanese character adorned the skin above her left hipbone. A twenty-first-century teen.

The crime scene techs arrived and began drawing their diagrams and taking their pictures. McCabe pointed out the remaining earring and asked the senior tech, Bill Jacobi, to make sure to check for both prints and DNA. Jacobi gave him a "So what do you think, I'm stupid?" look in response.

"Looks like somebody started the autopsy without me." McCabe turned at the sound of a woman's voice. Deputy State Medical Examiner Terri Mirabito stood behind him, looking at the body. "I think I resent that," she added, "both on her behalf and mine."

"Good to see you, Terri. Glad you're here." McCabe had worked with her on half a dozen cases over the past three years and valued her skills.

After photographing the body from several angles, Mirabito knelt down for a closer look. "How long do you think she's been dead?" McCabe asked.

"A while. She's out of rigor. Only slight lividity." With gloved hands, she gently pulled back the fold of tissue on the left side of the girl's chest. McCabe could see what appeared to be grains of rice inside the cut. Only the rice was moving. Maggots.

"Judging by the activity in there, I'd say she was killed forty-eight to seventy-two hours ago. Maybe a little longer depending where the body was kept." Terri pulled the skin back a bit further. "Well, sonofabitch, will you look at that?"

"What? What is it?"

Terri looked up, a grim expression on her face. "Her heart's gone."

"What do you mean, gone?"

"Just what I said, McCabe. Gone. As in not there." Terri was shining a small high-intensity light into the girl's exposed chest cavity. "Some creep opened her up, cut through her sternum with a saw, and removed her heart. I couldn't have done it cleaner myself."

Neither said anything for a moment. "Ritual murder?" he finally asked.

"Beats the hell out of me. Whoever did it, though, knew what he was doing."

"You're assuming it was a he?" asked Maggie.

"I am." Terri rubbed her gloved finger gently along the severed bone. "After he cut the sternum, like any good surgeon, he most likely used a retractor to spread her ribs and get at her heart. I'm not sure how much more the autopsy will tell us, but maybe something. If we can get positive ID by tomorrow morning, I'll do the procedure in the afternoon. We've got nothing else scheduled." There was an unsettled edge to Terri's normally cheerful voice. "You and Maggie want to join the party?"

"Just leave word what time you want us there."

Terri turned back to the body and continued her preliminary examination. McCabe glanced over to the black-and-white Crown Vic with the flashing lights and the Portland PD slogan, PROTECTING A GREAT CITY, emblazoned in gold on its rear fender. Some days, he thought, we keep that promise better than others. A dirty-looking man of indeterminate age was leaning against the back door. A uniformed officer stood nearby. Satisfied he wasn't going to find anything else useful, McCabe walked over to join them. After a last look back at the body, Maggie followed.

"This is the guy who found the body," the cop told them. "Says he'd be happy to tell us more about it if maybe we could come up with a little whiskey for him."

"Oh, really," said McCabe. "Well, I guess we'll have to think about that."

The man steadied himself against the car. He was a skinny little guy. Maybe five feet four. His eyes darted between McCabe and Maggie. Clearly he had no love for cops.

"What's your name?" McCabe asked.

"Lacey. Dennis Patrick Lacey."

"Got any ID, Dennis?"

The man handed McCabe a Maine driver's license. It had expired three years ago. Lacey was fifty-five years old. McCabe would have guessed ten years older. He handed the license back.

"Wrestling fan?"

"Huh?"

McCabe pointed toward Lacey's T-shirt. A picture of a grimacing wrestler and the letters WWE adorned the front.

"Christ, no. They give you this crap at the shelter. It's stuff nobody else wants."

Lacey seemed coherent enough. McCabe glanced at Maggie, who flipped open a mini recording device.

"This is Detective Margaret Savage, Portland, Maine, Police Department. The time is 9:54 P.M., September 17, 2005. The following is an interview recorded in a vacant lot off Somerset Street, Portland, Maine, between Detective

Sergeant Michael McCabe, also of the Portland PD, and
Mr. Dennis Lacey, residing at . . . Mr. Lacey, can you tell
us where you live?"

"Wherever I can doss down."

McCabe began. "Would you tell us what you saw tonight?"

"I didn't have nothing to do with it."

"We don't believe you did," McCabe said as gently as he
could. "We just need to know what you saw to help us find
whoever did do it."

Lacey looked at McCabe as if trying to gauge to what
degree he could be trusted. He finally shrugged and began speaking. "Aw, jeez, it was awful." McCabe could
hear traces of a brogue under the man's slur, its lilting
rhythms reminding him of his own Irish grandparents.
"Warm nights like this," Lacey said, "I sometimes sneak
into the scrap yard. Just to sit. Look at the stars. Have a
few drinks. Read a few poems. If I can afford it, maybe I
bring something to eat."

"You read poems?" Maggie asked. "What poems would
those be?"

Lacey reached into his back pocket and pulled out a dirty,
well-worn paperback copy of Yeats. He handed it to Maggie.
"I'm a sailor," he said, slurring his words only a little. "Able
seaman . . . or I was. Not so able anymore. I spent lot of
nights at sea staring at the stars, did a lot of reading."

"You read Yeats?" she asked.

"Him and a few of the other Irish poets. I like the sound
of the old words," he said. "These days, I'm all alone, y'know,
and words are my only company. Nobody bothers me here
or tells me to shut my yap."

Lacey began to recite, stumbling over only a few of the
words.

*"I will arise and go now, and go to Innisfree,
And a small cabin build there, of clay and wattles
    made:*

*Nine bean-rows will I have there, a hive for the
    honey-bee,
And live alone in the bee-loud glade . . ."*

As the words came out, the cops all stared at Lacey. McCabe, too. Maybe McCabe most of all. When the old sailor paused, searching his memory, McCabe waited a moment and then filled in Yeats's next line.

*"And I shall have some peace there,
    for peace comes dropping slow . . ."*

"So you know old William Butler, do ya?" said Lacey. "Unusual for a cop."

McCabe smiled. "Unusual for a sailor. Now, can you tell me when you first saw the girl?"

"I didn't see her at first. Didn't see nothin'. Not till I got up to take a leak, which I did against that pile of scrap over there. I was just zipping up and I noticed something a little ways off. I walked closer and there she is. All cut up. It's a terrible thing, y'know. A terrible thing."

"How long were you there before you had to take your leak?" asked McCabe.

"Not long. Twenty minutes." Lacey shrugged. "Maybe less."

"So you got here around eight thirty?"

"Aw, jeez, I dunno. I don't have no watch or nothin'. It was dark."

"Did you see anything else near the body?"

"Something else? Like what?"

"Like maybe a knife or a razor?"

"Nah. Nothing like that."

"Or maybe some jewelry?"

"What kind of jewelry?"

"Any kind. Like maybe a gold earring you thought you could get a few bucks for?"

"No. I didn't see nothing. Or take nothing. I just wished

I had something to cover her up with. She was lyin' there exposed to the whole world."

"You didn't touch her?"

"No, I didn't touch her or nothing else either." He pulled a pint bottle of whiskey from the sagging pocket of his pants. "D'ya mind if I finish what little's left here?" There was perhaps an inch of amber liquid in the bottle.

McCabe silently nodded assent. He wouldn't have minded a little himself. "What kinds of cars were parked nearby?" McCabe gestured to the curb, where the techs were checking for tire tread marks and other evidence.

"Didn't see no cars. Maybe some driving by, but none that were parked."

"Any that slowed down? Any you could identify?"

"Just cars going along. You couldn't see what kind of cars they were."

"Thank you, Mr. Lacey." McCabe looked up and noticed a couple of reporters had arrived, including a crew from the local NBC affiliate.

"Hey, McCabe. Remember me? Josie Tenant, News Center 6. We heard the Dubois girl was found murdered here. Can you give us a statement?"

"Not at the moment." McCabe turned away.

"C'mon, McCabe. Is it Dubois in there or isn't it?"

Media relations weren't McCabe's strong suit. He turned to face her. "Look, Josie, this is an active crime scene. I'm not entirely sure how you got here so fast, but it would really be helpful if you kept your folks on the other side of Somerset. We're still trying to collect evidence." Tenant and her cameraman reluctantly retreated to their van. The other reporters followed.

McCabe turned to Comisky, the cop who'd found Lacey. "Kevin, would you take Mr. Lacey down to 109? If Detective Sturgis is around, see if he'd be kind enough to take the rest of Mr. Lacey's statement. Otherwise, I'll do it when I get back." To Lacey he added, "Make sure you let us know where we can find you. Here's a card with my number on it. We may have to talk to you again. Do you understand?"

"Aye, aye, Captain." He threw McCabe a shaky salute and staggered toward Comisky's car. "Canadian whiskey's not so bad, y'know," he said, looking sadly at his now empty bottle. "It's not Irish, but it's not bad." The homeless man climbed unsteadily into the back of the car.

Before Comisky could follow, McCabe said softly, "Make sure you check his pockets for a gold earring or anything else he might have picked up here."

The patrol officer nodded, slid behind the wheel, turned the key, and opened all four windows before starting off.

Bill Jacobi and Terri Mirabito were completing their tasks. There didn't seem to be much more McCabe could do. He approached one of the other uniformed patrol officers. "Keep the reporters out until the body's picked up and the area's clear—and don't listen to any of their bullshit."

"Don't worry, Sergeant. I've heard it all before."

McCabe and Maggie Savage got into Maggie's Crown Vic for the short ride back to the office. "Do you want to join Sturgis interviewing Lacey?" McCabe asked.

"No. There's no way he's the killer. I'm sure Carl can get whatever else there is to get. I just hope he doesn't start doing his bullying Carl shit. Lacey's got enough problems already."

"Well, Maggie, that's very thoughtful of you. Maybe, instead of interviewing Lacey, we should just get him a bottle of Jameson's and ask him to read us some more Yeats."

Maggie didn't laugh. "You know, McCabe, I love you dearly, but sometimes you're really an asshole," she said. "Anyway, I called Katie's mother and stepfather when I saw the news van pull up. I didn't want them hearing about their daughter's death from News Center 6. So I told them, as gently as I could, that I thought we'd found her and that we needed to talk to them again."

"How'd they take it?"

"About what you'd expect. The mother broke down sobbing. Couldn't talk. Just wanted to know if I was sure it was Katie. I told her I was, and she put the stepfather on the phone. He was quieter. They agreed to come downtown and talk to me when I told him how important starting fast could be on cases like this. We'll see if maybe they can remember anything new."

"Okay. Just drop me off. I want to take another look at the missing persons file on Katie. Then I'm going to hit the computer. See if anybody's reported anything similar."

Maggie pulled into the curb in front of 109 Middle Street, the PPD's small headquarters building on the edge of the Old Port.

"You've got the world-famous memory. Anything ring a bell?"

McCabe didn't answer. He just sat staring out the windshield. A few raindrops were splattering against the glass. Why the hell would anybody neatly and precisely cut a girl's heart out of her body? Sexual nutcase? Some kind of anatomical collector filling his trophy case?

"McCabe?"

He looked at her and nodded, almost imperceptibly. "I do remember something," he said.

"D'ya want to share it?" she asked.

"Let me check it out first. I also want to set up appointments with a couple of the cardiac surgeons up at Cumberland Med. Find out what it takes to cut out somebody's heart."

"Think this could be the start of a serial string?" Maggie asked as McCabe exited the car.

McCabe turned back and leaned in the open window. "I don't know. It's sure got the earmarks."

The streets were emptier now. As McCabe walked toward the building, he could feel that the air had become noticeably cooler, the first hint of the coming autumn and the dark winter that lay beyond.

3

Two foam cups partially filled with cold coffee greeted McCabe at his desk. He checked his messages. There were two from his boss, Lieutenant Bill Fortier. In the first, Fortier delivered fair warning that Chief Tom Shockley was going to take a personal interest in this case. In the second, he asked McCabe to set up a detectives' meeting for the morning to organize the investigation. Finally, there was one from the great man himself, Portland Police Chief Thomas H. Shockley. "Hey, Mike. It's Tom Shockley. We need to talk about Dubois ASAP. I'm giving a speech at a fund-raiser tonight. I can fend off the press until tomorrow, but then I need a complete update. Meantime, don't talk to the media. I'll handle that. Give me a call at home tomorrow A.M. You've got the number."

McCabe knew Shockley liked making any and all public statements on major cases himself. He thought he was better at it than anyone else in the department, and that was probably true. Shockley was a political animal, and McCabe knew that could be useful even in a small city like Portland. Still, it amazed him how much the chief loved looking at himself on the tube.

As usual, McCabe's desk was a chaos of paper, none of it critical and all of it irrelevant to the Dubois case. He swept it, in a batch, into the left-hand drawer of his desk. The important stuff, files from a couple of ongoing cases, was already locked safely in the right-hand drawer on top of a pair of Casey's ski mittens. The background on the Dubois case wasn't among it.

He pulled the missing persons file on Katie Dubois and brought it back to his desk. He'd read it once, but he wanted to go over it more carefully now that he knew for sure her death was a homicide. As he sat, he glanced at Casey's mischievous face, age seven, beaming up at him from within the confines of a metal picture frame. The simple fact that Casey was now just a couple of years younger than the girl dumped in the scrap yard somehow made this case more personal. Not more important. Just more personal.

McCabe opened the file. Right up front were three digital photos of Katie Dubois, alive. The first was a family shot from her last birthday. He checked Date Of Birth on her personal info data form. The birthday was two months earlier, July 14. In the picture Katie looked even prettier than he'd thought. She was sitting in front of a big white cake with two candles on it in the shape of a one and a six. Sweet sixteen. Her lips formed an exaggerated pucker, mugging for the camera, ready to blow out the candles. He wondered what she'd wished for. Whatever it was, it wasn't what she got.

The second picture was the one they posted around town and gave to the media. A formal close-up, it had a Sears Portrait Studio look about it. The third one showed Katie, wearing a Portland High School soccer uniform, standing on the field with her mother. Probably just after a game. Other players and fans could be seen in the background. Both mother and daughter were smiling a little stiffly as if someone had asked them to say "cheese." Katie's mother, Joanne Ceglia, looked younger than McCabe expected, probably under forty. Reddish blond hair. Freckles. He checked the file for her maiden name. O'Leary. He thought as much. A McCabe will always recognize an O'Leary. She had the same shaped face and mouth as Ka-

tie. There was a similarity in the eyes as well, but the ener-
getic, fresh-faced prettiness of the daughter was gone from
the mother.

He put the photos back and skimmed the file summary
of the missing persons report. He'd read it before, and
there wasn't much that stood out. Katie was Joanne Ceglia's only child. Katie's father, Louis Dubois, was a commercial fisherman who'd drowned ten years back when the
trawler he was working on capsized in an ice storm off the
Georges Bank. All hands were lost, Dubois's body never
recovered. Two years later, in 1997, Joanne married Frank
Ceglia. Ceglia made a good living as a union pipefitter,
probably forty dollars an hour or more. The only thing to
notice about him was the AutoTrack report Tom Tasco had
recorded showing Ceglia had done a little time for petty
drug dealing when he was a kid, followed by a couple of
years on probation. He'd been clean ever since.

McCabe skimmed Tasco and Fraser's interview sum-
maries and case reports. They'd done a thorough job. They
conducted scores of interviews. They grilled her boyfriend,
Ronnie Sobel. They gamely followed up on every tipster's
call, and there'd been dozens. Despite these efforts, the
department hadn't come close to finding Katie or prevent-
ing her death.

McCabe put the reports back in their jacket. He tapped
the computer to life and Googled the name "Elyse Andersen," getting 437 hits. He found the one he was looking for
on page two. An article in the *Orlando Sentinel*, dated
April 2, 2002. McCabe remembered reading it on a flight
from Orlando back to LaGuardia.

He'd taken Casey down to Disney World for spring break.
The idea had been to cheer her up after he and her mother,
Sandy—the beautiful Cassandra, Casey's namesake—had
divorced. McCabe hadn't thought about Sandy in a long
time. The familiar refrain, "selfish bitch," came instantly
to mind. He supposed Sandy's new life, married to an in-
vestment banker, commuting between a fancy house in the
Hamptons and a nine-room co-op on West End Avenue,

suited her better than being the wife of a cop ever had. Still, McCabe wondered how comfortable she was having walked out not just on a failed marriage but also on her only child. She told McCabe the banker didn't want to be burdened with kids. At least not somebody else's kids. He'd forced Sandy to choose between having money and having a daughter. McCabe wasn't surprised she'd chosen money. That's just the way Sandy was. There was nothing anybody could do to change it. He wasn't bothered for himself, but he'd never forgiven Sandy for what she'd done to Casey.

The news story sprang back to life in McCabe's mind as he read.

A construction crew working for the D. J. Puozzoli Construction Company of Orlando yesterday unearthed the decomposed remains of a nude woman, later identified as 26 year-old Elyse Andersen of Winter Park. Ms. Andersen, a sales representative with Mulvaney Real Estate in Orlando, was reported missing three weeks ago by her husband, Martin Andersen, also of Winter Park. An unnamed source at the Orange County Medical Examiner's office told the Sentinel that the cause of death had been the 'surgical' removal of Ms. Andersen's heart.

McCabe closed out the page. He remembered the rest of the article pretty much verbatim. Orlando police were following several leads. There was no mention of additional wounds, but the article did include the name of the lead detective on the case, Sergeant Aaron Cahill. McCabe looked through the rest of the hits on the Google search and found one follow-up article. Apparently Sergeant Cahill's leads led nowhere and the case went cold. McCabe decided to wait until after the autopsy, when he would know more about the manner and cause of Katie Dubois's death, before contacting Sergeant Cahill of the Orlando PD.

He printed out the article and slipped it into a brand-new

murder book. Then he picked up the coffee cups and walked them to the small kitchen at the back of the bullpen. He poured the dregs down the sink. One of McCabe's detectives, Jack Batchelder, stood nearby making a fresh pot.

"Hiya, Mike. Bad night, huh? At least that's what I heard." Batchelder was a balding, overweight man of fifty. In McCabe's view, Jack was pretty much a burned-out case, putting in time, padding his pension with a few more years, before calling it quits.

"I guess you heard right, Jack. Anything else going on?" McCabe asked.

"The usual Friday night mayhem. A couple of domestics. A kid got beaten up in a brawl down by the ferry terminal. Oh yeah, there's another missing persons report. Woman named Cassidy Works for an ad agency here in town, Beckman and Hawes. Her ex-husband called it in about eight o'clock."

McCabe looked up. That was about the same time he and Kyra were arriving at Arno and Lacey was sneaking into the scrap yard. "Who took the call?"

"Bill and Will. They should be talking with the ex now." Detectives Bill Bacon and Will Messing had been universally known by their rhyming first names since McCabe teamed them up a year earlier.

Carl Sturgis joined them by the sink. "Hey, McCabe," he said in that shrill terrierlike bark of his, "that homeless guy they brought in? He didn't have shit to say. He was just sneaking into the scrap yard for a couple of snorts. Found the body. Started running around screaming till he found Comlsky. End of story. Except he was pissed I didn't offer him a drink. Big joker. Says you promised him some booze. I told him it was up to you to keep your own promises. I mean, you didn't really do that, did you?"

"Don't believe everything you hear," McCabe said, pouring himself a fresh coffee, "but thanks for asking." He tossed a dollar into the can next to the coffeepot. "Where is he now?"

"I got a uniform to drop him off down by the shelter. I

told him to let us know where we could find him. Fat chance."

McCabe took the coffee back to his desk and called Bill Bacon's cell. It looked like it was going to be an even longer night than he'd thought. Bacon picked up. "Hiya, Mike."

"Where are you guys?"

"In the car. You heard about our missing person? We just finished with her ex-husband. Says he's very upset. I personally think he's full of shit. Anyway, we're on our way to her apartment."

"Back it up, Bill, and give me the two-minute drill on this."

"Missing woman is named Lucinda Cassidy. She's twenty-eight years old. Works for an advertising outfit on Free Street, Beckman and Hawes." Bacon sounded like he was reading from his notes. "Young management type. She was supposed to meet her ex-husband for dinner at Tony's at six thirty. Guy named Dave Farrington. They've been divorced less than a year. She's not there when he arrives. He orders a drink and waits. By seven she still hasn't turned up, which he says is very unlike her. He orders another drink and starts making calls. First he tries calling her numbers. There's no answer either on her landline or her cell or at the office. So next he looks up her boss's home number and reaches him. The boss, a John Beckman of Beckman and Hawes, says she never showed up for work this morning. He's pissed 'cause she missed some big meeting or something. Tells Farrington he thought maybe she was sick or maybe there was a family crisis, but when she didn't answer her phone, he didn't know what to think. Naturally, the schmuck doesn't think to call us."

"You said you thought the ex was full of shit? You think he had something to do with the disappearance?"

"I wouldn't say that. Not yet, anyway. I just think he's a slick-assed jack who's a little too full of himself. Anyway, Farrington next calls Cassidy's sister, his ex-sister-in-law. She hasn't heard from Lucinda in a couple of days. So now he's really worried. He calls 911 about eight. Wants to know if there've been any accidents reported or if anyone brought her into any of the local hospitals. The answer is no. Dispatch routes the call to us. First thing, we go to Tony's, talk to Farrington, who's still there, having another drink. Then we go with him to her apartment to see if maybe she's home and just not answering the phone. She's not. At least, there are no lights on and she's not answering the door either."

"Is that it?" McCabe asked.

"Not quite. Will checks her vehicle and plate numbers and sends out an ATL just in case she's on the road somewhere. About an hour later we get a call from a unit on the West Side. Connie Davenport. Cassidy's car's been found. Beige '99 Corolla. Parked on Vaughan Street by the old cemetery. Neighbor tells Davenport the Corolla's been there all day. Turns out Lucinda's a jogger. She runs every morning, usually on the West End. Farrington told us she was training for a 10K." Bill Bacon stopped talking, and there was silence on the phone.

"What are you thinking, Billy?"

"Mike, I've got a bad feeling about this one," he said finally. "I just called the evidence techs to check out the scene on Vaughan. Then I want them to flatbed the car to 109 and check it for prints, blood, fibers, the works."

"Busy night for the techs."

"Yeah. I guess for all of us. Like I said, we're pulling up to the apartment now. Landlord's meeting us here with a key. If she still doesn't answer the door, he said he'd let us in." Another pause. "I'll call you back."

"Is Farrington still with you?"

"No. I got a uniform to take him down to the station to give us a set of prints. We'll check for matches both in the apartment and in the Corolla, but I'll bet he can prove he's been in both places before."

"I'll wait for your call," McCabe said and then hung up the phone.

Next, McCabe called Lieutenant Bill Fortier at home. Fortier's wife, Millie, answered. She went to get him. In the background McCabe could hear sounds of the Sox game. "Yeah, Mike, what's up?"

McCabe filled him in on what was going on at the scrap yard and what Bacon had told him about Lucinda Cassidy.

"You think she just took off?"

"Leaving her car sitting there on the street? Doesn't seem likely."

"You think it's the same guy?" Fortier asked. He sounded like he was munching on something crunchy.

"Seems like the timing's all wrong, but who the hell knows? Our boy would have to finish with one vic and right away go pick up another. Most freaks don't work that way."

"Yeah, doesn't one killing usually satisfy the lust for a while?"

"It's supposed to," said McCabe, "but all these sadistic whack jobs have their own little quirks. Anyway, nobody's killed Cassidy yet. At least as far as we know. Let's not hurry her along."

"You think I should come in? Get everybody together tonight?"

"I'd rather have our people on the street tonight than sitting in a conference room. They know what they're doing, and I can coordinate by cell. If the same guy's responsible, we ought to get a jump on it. Besides, there's not much to report yet, and, like I said, Cassidy may still be alive."

"Alright—but we better make quick progress, or the wrath of Shockley will come down on all our heads."

As he hung up the phone, McCabe looked up to see Maggie leaning against his desk. Nearly six feet tall, she was a lean, slightly gawky-looking woman with bright, searching eyes. McCabe always thought she looked more like a college professor than a cop. "So?" he asked.

"Parents think the boyfriend's to blame," she said. "According to Tasco's report, he and Katie were seen arguing just before she walked off and disappeared."

"He's got a solid alibi. Isn't that right?"

"True. There were five other kids in the group. They all

say he stayed with them for at least two hours after Katie left, which would have made it about midnight. After that, he says he went home to bed. His mother says he got home around twelve thirty. She was still up."

"What did her parents say about him?"

"They don't much like him. They see him as being pretty much an operator. Stepfather says Katie came in drunk a couple of times after dates with Sobel, and she was out all night more than once."

"Having sex?"

"The mother thinks so. Says Katie had a prescription for birth control pills, and she told her always to carry condoms. 'Don't depend on the guy to carry condoms.' That seems to have been the sum total of her motherly advice."

"It's pretty good advice."

"Yeah, but it shouldn't end there," said Maggie. "Not for a sixteen-year-old."

"C'mon, Mag, you know as well as I do Sobel as the murderer just doesn't figure. You don't acquire the skills to neatly remove a human heart cutting up frogs in biology class. Plus, if he did kidnap her, where does he keep her for a week before he kills her? Under his bed at home?"

"Yeah. I know."

"Where are the parents now?"

"On their way home. I paid for a cab." Maggie paused, waiting for McCabe to react. He didn't.

"I'm putting in for it," she said. "I expect to be reimbursed."

"Did I say anything? Fortier's the Scrooge around here. Not me."

"Don't pull that Mr. Innocence stuff with me, McCabe. Fortier's afraid of you. He'll do whatever you tell him to do."

"What makes you think he's afraid of me?"

"You're smarter than he is and he knows it. Plus that memory thing of yours. Always calling up little-known facts out of thin air. That really makes him nervous. He always thinks you're going to show him up in public. Or, even worse, around Shockley."

"How much was the cab?" asked McCabe.

"I gave them ten bucks. I don't expect the Ceglias will send back any change."

"Ten bucks!" McCabe exclaimed in mock alarm, but before Maggie could react he added, "Sure, put in for it. By the way, another shoe just dropped."

"What sort of shoe?"

"We've got a brand-new missing person."

"Oh, Jesus. Already?"

McCabe filled Maggie in on Lucinda Cassidy's disappearance.

"Are we assuming it's the same guy?" Maggie pulled her own desk chair across to McCabe's desk and sat down. She produced a big bag of Rold Gold pretzels, poured a mound of them on the desk, put her feet up, and started munching.

"Definite possibility. Whoever arranged Katie's body so artfully out there in the scrap yard was showing off. He's preening. Wants us to notice him. I'd love to minimize the media feeding frenzy and deny him that pleasure."

"I don't think that'll be possible. We've got the gruesome murder of a teenage girl. Add in Cassidy's disappearance and they'll be all over it."

"Shockley will be thrilled." McCabe's phone rang. He checked his watch. It was after midnight. Bill Bacon was on the other end. "What did you find?" He silently signaled Maggie to pick up on the other line.

"Not much. It's a four-unit house on Pine Street. Cassidy's got a one-bedroom on the top floor. Place is a mess. Bed's unmade. Lipstick and mascara and other girl stuff scattered around the bathroom. Panty hose over the shower rail, that sort of thing. There's one dirty dinner dish in the sink and the remains of a frozen pizza in the trash. Her briefcase is on the couch in the living room with papers from her office scattered around. Her laptop's there, too. She was probably working at home last night."

"Getting ready for the big meeting Beckman was talking about?"

"Kind of looks that way."

"Anything else?"

"Yeah. Farrington said she had a dog. Small mongrel named Fritz. There's dog stuff around the apartment—dog bed in her bedroom, food bowl in the kitchen—but there's no leash and no dog. He also said she was a runner, but I don't see any running shoes. My guess is she took the dog for a run this morning and never made it home. She was supposed to be at work at eight thirty, so it had to be early."

"What time did the neighbor spot the car?"

"She said first thing, around seven."

"Okay. Let's get as many people as we can scouring areas where people jog, starting on the West End where we found her car." Without being asked, Maggie left to begin making the necessary calls. "Any photos of her in the apartment?"

"Yeah, plenty, and Farrington gave me one. He was still carrying it in his wallet."

McCabe told Bacon to meet them on the Western Prom and hung up.

Maggie was back in less than five minutes. "I've managed to round up half a dozen uniforms plus a couple of detectives from across the hall. Bill and Will make ten. You and me make an even dozen. I think that's about it. At least until morning. What about Tasco and Fraser?"

"They're working the neighborhood around the scrap yard. Let's take Batchelder. If nothing else, the walk will do Jack good. We'll leave Carl here. Somebody should be manning the phones, and I don't think I can bear spending the night listening to Carl whining about how wet he's getting."

Ten minutes later McCabe and Maggie joined a dozen wet cops combing Portland's Western Promenade and adjacent neighborhoods for any trace of Lucinda Cassidy. They'd broken up into teams. McCabe and Maggie along with Jack Batchelder and Officer Connie Davenport were moving along the western edge of the Prom itself. The rain was heavier now, and McCabe knew it might be washing away evidence.

About fifteen minutes after they'd started, Officer Davenport called out, "Hey! I think I've found something! Look at this."

She was shining her flashlight on a wet Sea Dogs baseball cap. It had been partially hidden by weeds protruding from the edge of the steep drop-off that bordered the far side of the Prom. "Could be hers," said Connie. She knelt above the cap and poked a ballpoint pen under the little Velcro strap in the back. She slid the cap into an evidence bag. If the cap was Cassidy's, there might be more evidence nearby. McCabe peered over the drop-off. "I'm going down to have a look."

He handed Maggie his gun and holster. He figured that was a sensible precaution against accidentally shooting himself, should he slip and fall on the way down. "I'm supposed to be management, you know," McCabe wisecracked to the others. "I'm not supposed to be doing this shit." Nobody laughed.

The only response came from Jack Batchelder. "Don't break your leg," he said. "It's dark, and the rain's made that sucker slippery."

"Thanks, Jack. I'll do my best." McCabe stepped backward over the edge and began working his way down the wet, weedy embankment. Rivulets of water trickled past him, cutting small indentations in the soil. He had no rain gear, and water was soaking through his thin jacket to his skin. Drops of rain slid behind the collar of his shirt and traced their way down his back. Holding the flashlight in his right hand, he created handholds with his left wherever he could find them. He crisscrossed the slope, shining his flashlight left and right, not quite sure what he was looking for. He was breathing heavily, a little surprised how tricky the descent was proving to be. He made himself a promise to cut down on the Scotch and to hit the gym at least three times a week. Well, two anyway.

About fifty yards from the top, a small rock outcropping McCabe was using as a toehold gave way, and before he could stop himself, he slid a good ten feet on his chest through muddy, stony soil. He came to a painful stop against a tree root. His flashlight landed about three feet to his right. It was still on. About ten feet beyond the flashlight, reflected in its flickering beam, two black eyes stared back at him. He lay perfectly still, slowing his breathing, carefully watching whatever it was that was watching him. He could hear the voices of the others shouting from the top. "Hey, Mike, are you alright?" "Did you hurt yourself?"

He didn't shout back for fear of startling the animal or whatever the hell it was. A cat? Maybe a big rat? With his left hand he scooped up a small handful of wet soil and tossed it in the direction of the eyes. Nothing. He gingerly nudged his body a foot or so toward the light. Still nothing. He slid another foot. Then another. He wrapped his hand around the barrel of the light and lifted it up. Still no movement. The shouts from the top grew more insistent. He pointed the light directly at the eyes. They shone back brightly. Now he could see the shape of a face. A white muzzle. A black nose. He crawled toward it. Not wanting to shout, he pulled out his cell and hit Maggie's number. "Are you okay?" she asked.

"I'm okay," he told her. "I found her dog. It's dead."

4

The throbbing beat of a headache provided the accompaniment to Lucinda Cassidy's slow return to consciousness. She was alive. She was certain of this, but she wasn't sure where she was or why. She opened one eye. Then the other. She was looking straight up into bright overhead lights that forced her to squint until her pupils adjusted. She was lying flat on a bed with raised sidebars in a small, nearly bare room. Practically everything in it seemed white except for the hospital gown she was wearing. It was the kind that opens at the rear with little blue flowers printed all over it. Hospital bed. Hospital gown. She supposed that's where she must be. In a hospital. Had there been an accident? She couldn't remember. The headache didn't make it easier.

The room didn't look like any hospital room she'd ever seen before. There was no TV or telephone. No privacy curtain hung from the ceiling. No buttons or buzzers to summon a nurse. Nothing but the bed, a small bedside table, and a single chair that stood against the wall near the door. Lucy tried to lift her hand, wanting to rub away the throbbing pain behind her eyes and in her temples, but her hand wouldn't move. She pulled harder and realized that what she thought were bandages wrapped around her wrists and ankles were, in fact, restraints tying her to the bed. Both her hands and her feet were secured with canvas straps. No. Not a hospital. A prison. She wasn't a patient. Someone was holding her prisoner. But who? And why?

Slowly, as grogginess receded, she began to remember. She remembered the fog. She remembered running along the Western Prom, and meeting the man with the hypodermic, the one who called himself Harry Potter. With a kind of despair, she remembered Fritz.

The man must have brought her here. Wherever here was. Okay, that was who. The why, she supposed, must have something to do with sex. It certainly couldn't be ransom money. Sex slavery? Jesus Christ. That happened to girls from the Ukraine. Not Bates graduates with good jobs in New England ad agencies.

She supposed Harry Potter would rape her. The juxta position of the name and the act made it seem ridiculous. To be raped by an adolescent fictional wizard. A British adolescent fictional wizard. "Officer, it was 'Arry Potter what done me wrong."

"Oh, no, miss, it couldn't be, he's such a nice little fellow."

Ridiculous. Terrifying. She began to laugh. A little hysterically. She was certain he would rape her. When rape is inevitable, lie back and enjoy it. Isn't that what all the assholes say? Bullshit. She'd fight the sonofabitch every step of the way. Given half a chance, she'd pull a Lorena Bobbit and bite his cock off. The idea of defiance made her feel a little better. Was it possible he'd already raped her while she was conked out? She didn't think so. Even unconscious, she was sure she'd have some sense of it if that had happened.

If he raped her, what happened afterward? She knew what he looked like. He wouldn't let her go with a promise not to tell anyone. Maybe he'd keep her for a repeat performance. Or a bunch of repeat performances. Like anything else, though, rape would get old. Then he'd kill her. A knife? A gun? He had a hypodermic. Her mind played with the words "lethal injection."

Never had she imagined life ending this way. She began

to cry. Not in great heaving sobs but softly, quietly. This happened to other people. Not to strong, competent people like her. "I won't let it." She mouthed the words, a ritual to build conviction. "I will not let this happen." She didn't know what she could do—but something. Was this denial? When facing imminent death, isn't one's first reaction always denial? What follows in that famous litany? Fear? Anger? Acceptance? She couldn't remember. Well, if it was fear, she'd just zipped past denial in a hurry. Because now all she felt was deathly afraid.

How long had she been unconscious? Hours? Days? When she didn't turn up at the office, Charlie Roberts or John Beckman would have called her apartment, called her cell phone. They knew she wasn't someone who just didn't show up for work, especially with an important meeting on tap. Would anyone from Beckman and Hawes have called the police? She didn't know. Maybe she'd already missed dinner with David. She was ravenously hungry. David would have called, wouldn't he? David would have reported it, wouldn't he? David was such an asshole, he might have thought she was standing him up and walked out of Tony's in a huff. Why did she marry him in the first place? Probably for the sex. He was very good at sex. Don't be stupid. Nobody gets married for sex these days.

Would people, even now, be watching reports of her abduction on television? She imagined pictures of herself flickering on the screen. "A Portland woman, Lucinda Cassidy, was reported missing today. Ms. Cassidy was wearing blue jogging shorts and a white sports bra." No, they wouldn't know any of that, would they? She remembered that girl a couple of years ago who vanished from some club. Some creep had shot her. Buried her down in Scarborough. Of course, just last week that high school soccer player, Katie something, disappeared. They hadn't found her yet, either dead or alive.

Lucy remembered feeling righteous anger sitting safely in front of her TV listening to reports of missing women. She'd never realized how far she was from understanding the awful reality of the thing. How far from understanding the fear that was gnawing at her and wouldn't let go. Lucy closed her eyes and tried to suppress a rising panic.

"Control this." Almost pleading with herself. "Don't give in to it. The only way out is to stay calm, to think clearly." She breathed deeply and slowly just like Rebecca taught her in yoga class. She tried to picture herself in a different place. She concentrated on slowing the beating of her heart. She listened. There was no sound but the distant hum of what might be an air-conditioning system.

She looked around the room again, studying the details. It was a small room, windowless, maybe twelve feet square. The walls and ceiling were white. Both seemed to be covered with some sort of acoustic tile. Lucy supposed, hopefully, that the purpose of the tile was to soundproof the room. That might mean there was someone outside the room who wasn't supposed to hear what was going on inside. Who wasn't supposed to hear her if she screamed. There was a door. It looked solid and heavy. Possibly made of steel or some other metal. It had a silvered knob and a button lock. Above the knob was a dead bolt. She supposed it was bolted, but the opening in the door was too narrow to know for sure.

Then she became aware of another sound. Breathing that wasn't her own. Slow shallow breathing from behind the bed. She held her own breath to listen. Yes, definitely breathing. She was afraid to say anything, afraid to move. In the end she began crying again. "Who are you?" she sobbed. "What do you want from me?"

His face, the face from the Prom, came into view. He was holding a hypodermic. He rubbed her arm with an alcohol swab. "I'm sorry, Lucinda, but I'm not quite ready for you yet."

He plunged her back into darkness.

5

It was nearly dawn when McCabe, muddy, bruised, and hurting in more places than he cared to think about, turned into the parking area behind the large white Victorian on the Eastern Prom. He pulled the lovingly restored cherry red '57 T-Bird into parking space number three. McCabe and Sandy had scrimped and saved to buy the car the first year they were married. He sat for a minute, nursing his pain, holding on to the wheel, not knowing why those days came to mind. Days of innocence long since lost. There was nothing he and Sandy loved more than cruising around Westhampton Beach on a summer Saturday with the top down. Guys making twenty times as much as the two of them put together—brokers, bond traders, network producers—would walk slowly around the parked car, gazing in admiration both at McCabe's vintage T-Bird and at McCabe's wife from every angle. He smiled bitterly at the memory. Michael McCabe, twenty-four years old. Hot shit extraordinaire. Hot car. Hot woman. Hot times.

Then the hot times came to an end. He always found it funny—painful but funny—that when Sandy finally ran off with one of those guys, it was the car she wanted to keep. Not the daughter they conceived on a blanket in the Westhampton dunes on a moonlit night one of those very same weekends. Knowing Sandy, she might have brought up custody of the car in court if her lawyer had let her. "Let's see. I'll trade you one forty-year-old classic convertible for one little girl. Even-up trade. No draft choices. No players to be named later. Well, fuck you, Sandy. I've got them both, and no, you can't have them back."

McCabe opened the driver's side door and gingerly climbed out. It had stopped raining. He could see stars in the eastern sky over the bay and the first hints of red on the horizon. He climbed the three flights up to the three-bedroom condo he shared with Casey and, as often as possible, with Kyra.

Taking off his muddy shoes, he left them in the hall and went in. He opened the door to Casey's room. He knelt by the side of her bed and watched her sleeping face. "Have I lied to you?" he asked silently. "Have I encouraged you to believe there's safety in a world that knows no safety?" Of course he had, but it was a loving lie. Harsh truths would intrude soon enough. He could only hope they wouldn't come in the brutal way they had for Katie Dubois. He brushed a strand of dark hair from over her eyes and gave her a kiss so soft he was sure it wouldn't wake her.

Her lids flickered open, and her blue eyes, so like Sandy's, looked up at him. She was bathed in the faint pre-dawn light of an autumn morning. "What happened?" she asked. "You look really awful."

"It was kind of a rough night," he whispered. "I'm sorry I woke you."

"I was sort of awake anyway. Are you okay?"

"You should see the other guy," he smiled.

"You were in a fight?" She sat halfway up to get a better look at him.

"No, I'm only kidding. Go back to sleep. I'll tell you about it in the morning."

She looked out her window at the thin red line slowly widening in the eastern sky. "It pretty much is morning."

"There's time for more sleep." He kissed her again. She

put her arms around his neck and pulled him down to give him a hug, "Don't," he said, "you'll get all muddy."

"That's okay," she said, releasing him. "Kyra's here. Jane went home."

He smiled. "Good night, sweetie. I'll see you in the morning."

He went to his own bedroom.

Kyra's sleepy voice rose from the bed. "I'm glad you're back. I was beginning to worry."

"Is everybody in this house an insomniac? A man can't sneak into his own bedroom without causing a commotion?"

She flipped on the brass bedside lamp. "You don't look so good."

"I kind of fell over a cliff."

"In the line of duty? Or just for the fun of it?"

He took off his torn jacket, let it fall to the floor, and sat in the birch bentwood rocker in the corner of the room. "We found the Dubois girl."

"I heard. It was on the eleven o'clock news."

"Any details?"

"Not really. Just that she'd been murdered and maybe raped."

Kyra was lying on her side, looking at him, head propped up on one arm. She was covered only by a thin cotton sheet that revealed the curves of her long, slender body, and in spite of his weariness McCabe found himself wanting her. In fact, needing her.

"You'd better take a shower," she said, sensing his desire. "I'm not making love to anybody who looks like he finished on the wrong side of a mud wrestling tournament."

She slipped out of the bed, naked, and walked to him. "Here, let me help you," she said.

She pulled him to his feet and began unbuttoning his torn shirt. He let her undress him, holding out his arms like a child so she could unbutton his sleeves and pull off his shirt. She unzipped his trousers and, along with his underpants, they fell to the floor. He stepped out of them. She ran her fingers, teasingly, up and down, along the underside of his erection. He reached for her.

She backed away. "No way," she said. "Not till you're clean."

They got in the shower together. The hot water played over them and stung the scraped, reddened skin on his chest and arms. She gently washed his body and then his hair, commenting, as always, on how many more gray hairs there were than the last time. Then he washed her. After that they just stood for a while in the hot water and stroked each other.

When they had dried, McCabe lay on his back on the bed and Kyra climbed on top of him. He entered her and they made love, slowly, sweetly, silently, for what seemed like a long time. Then he fell asleep, watching the horizontal patterns of light and shadow play against both floor and walls as the new morning sun shone through the slats of the wooden blinds.

He woke around seven thirty. His bruises hurt, and he was disappointed that the other side of the bed was empty. Kyra must have gotten up early and gone off to her studio. He wanted her here. He hadn't yet had his fill of her. He pushed the sheets back. He was still naked, and with the windows open the morning air coming through the blinds felt soothingly cool on his scraped skin. He grabbed a pair of ancient red sweatpants that lay in a heap on the floor behind the bentwood rocker and pulled them on. The words ST. BARNABAS TRACK running down one leg represented the last remnant of Mike McCabe's less than heroic career as a middle distance runner on his high school squad. He walked to the window and pulled the cord to open the blinds further. He stood, looking out at Casco Bay and the islands. That view and the fact that it was less than a mile's walk to police headquarters were the primary reasons he'd paid more than he could afford for the three-bedroom condo when he signed on, three years earlier, as chief of the PPD's Crimes Against People unit

It was one of those golden September mornings. Not the kind he would have chosen either for investigating a murder or attending an autopsy. Cool air and a good breeze. He watched the down-bay ferry chug toward Portland and a small sailboat, its yellow-and-red-striped spinnaker billowing, move left to right across his field of vision. Absentmindedly he fingered the old scar that ran seven inches across his abdomen, a souvenir from his days as a newbie, still wearing a uniform. He'd been careless making a collar, and a drugged-out teenager slashed him with a four-inch switchblade. He hadn't seen it coming, but he didn't shoot the boy. He was proud of that. He brought the kid in. He was proud of that, too, but he'd vowed never to be so careless again.

There was a knock at the bedroom door. "Yeah," he called.

Casey came in and flopped down on the bed. "You looked pretty beat up when you came in last night."

"I was pretty beat up."

She positioned the tattered remains of Bunny, a stuffed animal she'd had since she was a baby, on her lap. It was now little more than a fuzzy rag with ears, but she refused to give it up.

McCabe lay down next to her. "Did you have a good night?" he asked.

"It was okay. Gretchen and Whitney were here till about eleven. We just messed around till Whitney's mom came and got them. Kyra came in about ten thirty. She's gone?"

"I think she went to her studio."

"Are you going to marry Kyra?" Casey asked, a serious expression on her face. She was fiddling with Bunny's ears.

"I don't know. Maybe, but not right now." He had no idea where this conversation was going. "How would you feel about that?"

"Is that important?"

"How you feel? Yeah. It's real important."

"I dunno. I like Kyra. Would that make her my mom?"

"Your stepmother."

"You think I look like Mom? I mean my real mom?"

"Yes, you do. Your mother's a beautiful woman. You will be, too."

He looked down and was surprised to see that Casey was holding a picture of Sandy. In the picture, Sandy was wearing cutoffs and a bikini top and leaning against the T-Bird. The black hair. The ice blue eyes. The face the camera loved.

"Where did you find that?" He hadn't seen the picture in years.

"I've had it," she said. "I brought it with me from New York."

"Really?" This was news to McCabe. "Do you have any others?"

"A couple. This is the best one." They sat quietly for a moment, neither quite knowing what to say next.

"Do you want to see your mother?" he finally asked with more than a little reluctance.

There was another silence. Longer this time. "No. Not right now. Why were you so late last night?"

"We were investigating a murder." McCabe wondered how much he should tell her about it and decided to offer an expurgated version. She'd see it on the news soon enough anyway. "A girl was killed," he said, "not much older than you."

"She was murdered?" There was shock in Casey's voice. She found it hard to believe such a thing could happen to someone her own age. "That's horrible. Was she that soccer star, the one in those posters they had up all over town?"

He nodded. "Yes."

"God, she was actually murdered?" Casey fussed with Bunny, pulling at his ears, not saying anything for a minute and then playing with the word "murdered," repeating it softly to herself once or twice to make it real. Finally she asked, "Do you know who did it?"

"Not yet."

"But you're gonna catch them?"

"Yeah." He sat on the bed beside her, pulled her up onto

his lap, and gave her a long, hard hug. "It's an awful thing, but there are awful people in the world. That's why I do what I do. That's why you never talk to strangers. We'll catch him. C'mon . . . this is supposed to be quality time." Teasing each other with the words "quality time" was one of their private jokes. "Let's get dressed and I'll take you down to the Porthole for a cheese omelet. Then I've got to go back to work. Jane'll take you to soccer."

"Okay." Casey said, smiling. She loved riding on the back of the Harley. She ran down the hall to her room to get dressed.

As McCabe watched her go, he recognized the small knot of fear that began to grow in his stomach. A fear that was as real and hard as a fist. A fear that one day, perhaps soon, he might no longer be able to protect this child whom he loved and for whom he would so readily lay down his own life.

6

McCabe headed for Middle Street right after dropping Casey off at the apartment. He checked to find what, if any, progress had been made on the two cases during the hours he'd been away. That didn't take long. Basically, there'd been none. An e-mail from Terri Mirabito informed him the Katie Dubois autopsy was scheduled for 3:00 P.M. Maggie had been copied. He hit "Reply All" and told Terri they'd both be there. There were two phone messages from Bill Fortier, who sounded nervous. Before returning them he called Tom Shockley's home number.

"Tom. It's Mike McCabe."

"Mike. I heard about the Cassidy woman." Shockley sounded juiced up, excited. McCabe ran down the current status of both cases for Shockley. Much of the information the chief had already heard from other sources. "I'm talking to the press at eleven. I want you with me."

"Chief, press conferences aren't really my thing."

Shockley was in no mood to be dissuaded. "Mike, I'm just asking you to give me an hour. The press has to be briefed."

Knowing Shockley, McCabe imagined it'd be a real circus. "Maybe so, but I don't think we ought to give away too many details. For one thing, it gives the killer what he craves: publicity and attention. For another, it might give ideas to would-be copycats."

"McCabe, we've just had a horrible murder of an innocent teenaged girl. On the very same day, another young woman is kidnapped. The public has a right to know what's going on. What we're doing to catch the killer. The media expects you to be part of the briefings, and so do I. Cases like these don't happen in Portland—at least not very often—but they're part of the reason I pushed back against both the union and department tradition to offer you a job. Don't worry. I'll do most of the talking. All you have to do is stand there and look professional."

For a moment McCabe just stared at the picture of Casey on his desk and said nothing.

"Mike, are you there?"

"What time does the party start?"

"Eleven. Outside City Hall."

"Alright. Just do me one favor, Chief. A case like this is going to bring the nutcases out of the woodwork. So let's not give out too many details." Knowledge of the details was exactly what they could use to separate genuine informants from the fakers.

"Fair enough," said Shockley. "How about we don't mention the earring or how the body was arranged?"

"How about we don't say anything about her heart being cut out either. That's the big one."

Shockley didn't respond. He knew the details about Katie's heart would really turn the media on. McCabe figured he was reluctant to give that up.

"Alright," he said finally. "We'll keep the heart to ourselves."

"That's the right decision," said McCabe. "I'll be there. So will Maggie."

"Good," said Shockley. He hung up.

McCabe stared angrily at the dead phone in his hand. He knew it wasn't the need for a press briefing that was bugging him. That was a given. Part of the game. What was really pissing him off was his feeling that, deep down, Shockley saw Katie Dubois's murder as an opportunity to generate headlines that'd make him look good, headlines that might even lend traction to his rumored run for governor. Especially if it was Mike McCabe, the cop from away, the cop Shockley hired over the objections of many in the department, who cleared the case. That's what was pissing him off.

McCabe forced himself to put Shockley's press conference out of his head. He pushed the button to boot up his computer and Googled "Cumberland Medical Center," "Portland," and "heart surgery." On Cumberland's Web site he learned its cardiac unit, the Levenson Heart Center, was the jewel in the hospital's crown, named one of America's top one hundred cardiac facilities three years running. A little more digging told him a Dr. Philip Spencer headed up the cardiac unit and was, apparently, its superstar surgeon.

He clicked on Spencer's name, and his bio popped up on the screen. Tufts University Medical School, 1988. Residence in cardio-thoracic surgery, Bellevue Hospital, New York City, '88 through '92. Advanced training at the Brigham in Boston in heart transplant procedures, '92 through '96. Came to Maine in 1996, nine years ago, to start Cumberland's transplant program. Spencer's list of honors ran for several paragraphs. Obviously, if anyone knew how to remove a human heart and who else in Maine had the skills to do it, Spencer was the guy.

He called Spencer's office at Cumberland, but the doctor wasn't there. To McCabe's surprise, his home number was listed. He lived on the West End near the hospital. McCabe tried the number. A woman answered.

"Mrs. Spencer?"

"Yes?"

"This is Detective Michael McCabe, Portland police. Is Dr. Spencer at home?"

"No, I'm afraid he's not. I think he's gone out for a run."

"Could you ask him to call me when he returns?"

"May I ask what this is in reference to? We've already given to the Children's Fund." Her voice and manner were pure Yankee blue blood.

"Mrs. Spencer, this is not about a donation. We're investigating a homicide, and Dr. Spencer may be able to help."

"Oh, I see. It's about that poor girl, isn't it? Do you have any suspects yet?"

"Mrs. Spencer, I'm sure you'll understand, I'm not at liberty to discuss the case."

"Of course. I'll have Philip call you."

McCabe gave Spencer's wife his cell number. He looked up and saw Tom Tasco and Eddie Fraser standing by his desk. They looked tired. Normally Eddie had a kind of jumpy energy. He couldn't stand still. Right now he was standing still.

"We may have a witness," Tasco said.

McCabe hung up the phone. "Go ahead."

"Eddie and I were canvassing all the commercial properties in the area to see if anybody saw or heard anything," said Tasco. "There's a moving and storage company on the other side of Somerset? Richard A. Morgan Van Lines?"

"I know the place."

"Seems they've got a night security guy. Student at USM. Name's Mark Shevack."

"How long has he worked there?"

"About a year," Fraser said. "He got the job when he started over at the U. last September. My guess is he mostly snoozes or listens to his iPod, but he occasionally has to wander around and check things out. Says he thinks he saw a car stop and park on Somerset on a line with where the vic was found. It stayed there about ten minutes, then took off."

"When?"

"Thursday around midnight."

"That works okay with time of death, but it means she was lying there for nearly twenty-four hours before anyone spotted her."

"Not many people go in there."

"Did Shevack get a decent look at the car?"

"Not really," said Tasco. "He says it was a dark-colored SUV. Couldn't tell what kind. Thought it might be European. Curvier look than a Jeep or Explorer. He couldn't make a color or plate number either. He says it was pretty dark and he really wasn't paying much attention. He's only responsible for checking the warehouse. He only noticed it because cars don't stop on Somerset very often. Almost never that late."

"Is that it?"

"No. There was a security camera, too," said Fraser.

"That's good news."

"Yes and no. Unfortunately, it's mostly pointed on the warehouse area, but on a corner of the frame, it picked up what might be part of the car in the background."

"Might be?"

"Yeah. It's time-coded, but way the hell out of focus. You can see a dark car-blob stop where Shevack said at eleven forty-eight. A human-blob gets out of the car-blob and goes to the rear, where, as best we can tell, it unloads what might possibly be the body and carries it into the yard. Then the human-blob comes back without the possible body-blob, gets in the car, and drives away. It's eleven fifty-nine."

"Eleven minutes?" McCabe considered how long eleven minutes could be. Too much time just to carry the body to where it was dumped, arrange it to his liking, and walk back. So what's he doing in there for eleven minutes? Admiring his handiwork? Jerking off? That's some cocky bastard.

Eddie Fraser was trying to get his attention. "Mike, it's gotta be our guy. It's gotta be. Starbucks is trying to computer-enhance the image now. C'mon, let's see how he's doing."

McCabe and the two detectives went downstairs to the small cubicle where the PPD's resident brainiac sat in front of a computer setup far more sophisticated than McCabe's. He was a Somali kid named Aden Yusuf Hassan. When he started working for the PPD a few years earlier he was instantly nicknamed Starbucks by the cops, more for his addiction to strong coffee than for any resemblance to the Melville character.

Starbucks had arrived in Portland at age fifteen back in 2000, in the first wave of Sudanese and Somali refugees who came fleeing genocide in their own lands. Shockley hired him part-time while he was still in high school, part of a brief flirtation with building racial diversity in the department. The kid had never touched a computer in his native country, but he learned fast. He was a natural. One of the best McCabe ever saw. He could teach himself the basics in complex programs in just a couple of hours, mastery in a few days. Without question, he was the number one computer geek in the department, maybe in the whole city. Starbucks sat hunched in front of a flat-panel monitor, his dark brown face scrunched up in concentration.

He looked up as McCabe and the others approached. His face exploded in a huge smile. "Good news, Detectives!" He said it emphatically, practically shouting out the word "Detectives" with only a trace of a Somali accent, his only language until age fourteen. "I make the car as definitely an SUV. Maybe a Lexus. Maybe a BMW. A 2002 model, maybe 2003." Starbucks traced an index finger along the back edge of the blob that, thanks to his efforts, now looked more like a car. "See? Follow the rear roofline? Now look." A second, more recognizable SUV popped up on the screen next to the still-blurry shot from the security camera. "Here is a known 2002 Lexus SUV. Same position. Same angle. You can see the line's the same."

The outlines seemed nearly identical. Then the Lexus image was replaced by another similar one. "Now here's a BMW," said Starbucks.

Again a similarity to the blob. Not quite as close. Without taking his eyes off the screen, McCabe said, "Eddie, can you guys check DMV for all '01 through '06 Lexus SUVs registered in Maine? Check BMWs as well while you're at it, and throw in New Hampshire. Then see if you can cross-check ownership against a database of male MDs. Especially surgeons and pathologists. Maybe biologists or biology teachers. Eliminate anyone over the age of sixty. Our guy's not that old. Starbucks, can you do anything to tell us more about the guy who gets out of the car?"

Starbucks advanced the tape frame by frame searching for an image of the man that might provide additional information. McCabe watched. Just as the man-shaped object reached the back of the vehicle, he paused and turned toward the road, maybe to check if he was being watched, but he never looked right at the camera. At best, it was a one-quarter to one-third profile, more side than front. Still, it was something.

Starbucks's fingers worked his keyboard, and the image on the screen became more of a man, less of a blur. "Starbucks," said McCabe, "keep a record of exactly what you're doing to enhance this image. If the tape's ever going to be admissible in court, you're going to have to be able to repeat and verify every single thing you do."

"No problem, Sergeant. I'm keeping notes, and I'm recording each step on a nonerasable CD. Repeatable and verifiable. How much it will tell us about the bad guy is less certain." Both McCabe and Starbucks knew that even if the tape led them to the killer, by itself it wouldn't be sufficient to positively identify the guy or prove he did it. They'd need more.

The young Somali zoomed in, isolating the portion of the frame where the man-blob could be seen in direct relation to the car. "Since we know the height of the car and the height of the fence, we can see the man is quite tall. By simple triangulation I estimate his height at six foot one or, at most, six two."

"Anything else?"

"His face is mostly turned away, and the source material is of poor quality. However, he has broad shoulders, appears to be Caucasian, and is wearing a baseball cap. Even from this angle we can see he has quite a long face. Maybe a big nose, but that's less certain."

"A tall, thin-faced white doctor in a cap. Well, that narrows things down some," said Tasco.

McCabe watched as Starbucks played with the keys again. He advanced the image to the scene where the man-blob lifted the tailgate and unloaded his cargo. Starbucks advanced the scene again and stopped it. Now the tall white doctor was carefully carrying his trophy in his outstretched arms into the scrap yard. A groom carrying his bride over the threshold. In the middle of a busy city. The guy was clearly a risk-taker. Maybe that was part of the thrill.

Starbucks moved the scene forward and back a number of times, finally stopping on the frame that provided the best view of the bundle. It seemed to be wrapped in a light-colored fabric. Starbucks zoomed in on the image. "Well, from the shape it certainly could be Katie," said McCabe. "Or maybe just a bundle of trash from some guy too lazy to go out to Riverside."

"Strange shape for trash," said Tasco. "Besides, Jacobi's team didn't find anything else out there remotely similar."

"Just Katie."

"Yeah, just Katie."

They ran through the portions of the tape where the car was parked. Two other cars drove by during the eleven minutes, but there was nothing else that seemed revealing. "Let's put out some publicity on this," said McCabe. "See if we can find one or both of the drive-bys. Maybe they'll remember something useful about the parked car."

"I'll continue working with this," said Starbucks. "By altering the individual pixels I think I can improve resolution. Give us a better idea of what the guy looks like. What he was wearing. However, as I said, the quality of the source material is poor."

McCabe checked his watch. Almost time for Shockley's press conference. "Okay. I'll check in with you guys later. Right now I've got to attend a command performance for the GO." "The GO" was the squad's nickname for Chief Shockley, a.k.a. "the Great One."

7

The press conference began on schedule on the broad granite steps of Portland's hundred-year-old beaux arts City Hall. The event was, as McCabe expected, perfectly stage-managed. Camera crews and reporters from the local network affiliates plus reporters from all of Maine's major daily papers stood in a crowd at the bottom of the stairs, looking up at Shockley. Among them McCabe saw a face he recognized as a stringer for one of the New York tabloids. There were probably others.

The mayor and several city council members flanked Chief Shockley. Close to a hundred of the merely curious were also in attendance. Shockley wore full-dress blues for the occasion. McCabe and Maggie Savage positioned themselves behind him and slightly to his right. At least, McCabe mused, there were no musicians on hand to start things off with a rousing chorus of "Hail to the Chief." Probably only because Shockley hadn't thought of it.

"As most of you know, a brutal murder was committed in our city within the last forty-eight hours." As Shockley began to speak, McCabe's eyes scanned the crowd. The one real benefit of this sort of circus was that it might just draw "a person of interest." One by one he began recording the faces in his memory. He wouldn't forget them.

Shockley continued. "A young woman, not yet out of high school, was killed and possibly raped, her body left in a vacant lot off Somerset Street. I can assure you this crime will not go unpunished. All the resources of this department are focused on finding the killer or killers. Our investigation is already well under way and is being led by Detective Sergeant Mike McCabe, formerly one of New York City's top homicide detectives"—Shockley graciously gestured in McCabe's direction; McCabe graciously nodded back—"who now heads up our own Crimes Against People unit. You can rest assured he and his team will leave no stone unturned in their efforts to apprehend the killer or killers of Katie Dubois. I'll take your questions now."

Half a dozen reporters waved their hands. Luke McGuire of the *Press Herald* got the first question. "Chief, can you tell us if you've developed any leads and, if so, what they indicate?"

"Thank you, Luke. Yes we have developed several leads and are following up on them now . . ."

McCabe and Maggie exchanged glances. Exactly what leads was Shockley referring to? He didn't know about the video.

". . . but I'm sure you'll all understand that we can't yet reveal these to the public."

Toni Taylor, an attractive woman in her forties, a reporter for the local ABC affiliate, was next. "Chief, we heard another woman was reported missing yesterday. Are the two cases in any way related? What can you tell us about that?"

"Yes, that's true, Toni. A local businesswoman named Lucinda Cassidy was reported missing last night about the same time Katie Dubois's body was discovered. At this point we have no reason, other than the coincidence of timing, to believe the two cases are related."

The questions and answers continued in a set-piece pattern for about ten minutes. McCabe was getting antsy. He wanted to get moving on the case. Then a reporter Mc-

Cabe didn't recognize was called on. "Chief, you've said some nice things about Sergeant McCabe. Could the sergeant tell us more about his background and career experience?"

McCabe eyed the man, wondering what, if anything, he might know. Before he could open his mouth, Shockley fielded the question as smoothly as a big league shortstop. "Let me respond to that, Charlie." Okay, the man's name was Charlie, and it seemed Shockley knew him.

"Sergeant McCabe is a modest man who, I suspect, won't do justice to his own accomplishments, but I'll touch on a few of the highlights. In just ten short years Michael McCabe rose from rookie patrolman to head of the homicide desk at the NYPD's Midtown North precinct, one of the top homicide jobs in the country." As Shockley continued, McCabe could feel his toes curling inside his shoes. He suspected he might be blushing and hoped he wasn't scowling. Maggie gave him a slightly amused smile.

"During his three years at Midtown North," Shockley continued, "McCabe was credited with clearing more than sixty murders with a conviction rate of better than ninety percent, one of the best in the history of the NYPD. The guilty included a number of gang leaders and drug kingpins and, importantly for our present circumstances, at least two high-profile serial killers." Shockley rattled on for a while, and McCabe was relieved Charlie didn't ask any follow-up questions. He didn't seem to know about TwoTimes. McCabe didn't need all that coming back to haunt him now.

He went back to scanning the faces in the crowd. One stood out, an exotic-looking woman around forty, expensively though casually dressed. More Saks Fifth Avenue than L.L.Bean. To McCabe, she seemed anxious, edgy. Her fingers kept opening and closing the metal clasp on her leather shoulder bag. Her eyes blinked frequently. As Shockley spoke, she seemed to focus on McCabe, but, like a shy schoolgirl, she looked away the instant he glanced in her direction. This happened two or three times, and McCabe knew she was more than a passerby, more than a voyeur attracted by the cameras. She had something to tell him. He needed to find out who she was and what she was doing here.

She must have sensed what he was thinking, because even before Shockley finished speaking, she suddenly turned and hurried away. He watched her cross Congress Street and start down Exchange. He paused, perhaps too long, but then, playing back his brother Tommy's words— *You've got good instincts, Mike. Follow them*—he ran down the crowded steps of City Hall, taking them two at a time.

He could hear Shockley's voice behind him. "Thank you, ladies and gentlemen. As you can see, it seems Sergeant McCabe is wasting no time picking up the investigation." The crowd laughed appreciatively.

Dodging oncoming traffic, almost getting hit by an ancient Chevy pickup, McCabe crossed Congress Street and ran onto Exchange. Too late. She was out of sight. He hurried down the street, looking left, looking right, checking building entrances, a fancy dress shop, a small Chinese takeout. Maybe she'd slipped into one of the shops. He peered in the windows. She couldn't be far. Across the street an old brick building housed the *Press Herald* offices. He knew a security guard manned a desk near the entrance. He entered the building, holding his shield at eye level. He pushed past two men and a woman on their way out. "Sorry. Sorry. Excuse me."

He leaned around a woman signing in with security. "Excuse me," he asked the guard, "did you see an attractive, well-dressed woman, brownish hair, maybe forty? Kind of in a hurry?" The security man looked bewildered. "Did you see her come in here? A minute ago?" The guard shrugged and wordlessly shook his head.

"Chasing a suspect, McCabe?" The voice came from the stairwell beyond the security station. It was Preston Summerville, one of the paper's editorial writers. "Looks like you lost her. A well-dressed woman, brownish hair?" Summerville's well-honed reporter's instincts were kicking in. "What's she done? Maybe I can help—"

"Did you see her go out the back?" he asked just as Josie Tenant burst in the front door, cameraman in tow.

"Hey, McCabe, what's going on?" she called out.

McCabe sighed. Hunter chases fox. Hounds chase hunter. Hounds catch hunter. Fox gets away. It wasn't supposed to work that way, was it?

"Sorry," said Summerville. "Didn't really notice." McCabe went out the door that led to the parking lot. He scanned the cars in the lot but knew it was over. If she came out here, she was gone. If she didn't, if she continued down Exchange Street, she was still gone.

8

It was 3:00 P.M. and McCabe and Maggie Savage were both present in the autopsy room at the Maine State pathology lab on Hospital Road in Augusta. Terri Mirabito entered, clad in her blue scrubs, pulling on a pair of surgical gloves. "Good afternoon, everybody," she called out. "Shall we begin?" Terri was short, perhaps five-one or five-two, a trifle plump but definitely cute, with a round, sunny face and a mop of curly black hair. Before he met Kyra, McCabe seriously considered asking her out on a date. Though he did imagine dinner-table conversation between a homicide cop and a forensic pathologist might tend toward the ghoulish.

McCabe watched in silence as she took the case chart from Assistant Pathologist Jose Guerrera and began reading aloud. "Today is September 17, 2005. This is case number 106-97-4482. Katherine Dubois. Caucasian female. Sixteen years old. Date of birth, July 16, 1989. The body has been positively identified by the deceased's mother, Joanne Ceglia of 324 Dexter Street, Portland, Maine. Height 5'3½". Weight 106 pounds, 45.2 kilograms." She continued reviewing the preliminaries, recording additional findings on the file as she proceeded. She checked the photographs Guerrera had taken earlier and found them acceptable.

Terri then began a close examination of the body that

had once been Katie Dubois. She identified nine second-degree circular burns, each about half an inch in diameter, that had been randomly inflicted, six on Katie's chest, three on her inner thighs.

"Was she burned postmortem or ante?" asked McCabe.

"Ante," said Terri. "Postmortem tissue doesn't redden like this."

Why on earth did he burn her? McCabe wondered. Why did he have to do that, too? Was it punishment for defiance? Lying there on the autopsy table, Katie seemed so slight, her barely developed body so childlike, so vulnerable in death, McCabe found it hard to imagine that she'd been anything but terrified, anything but compliant.

McCabe watched Terri closely as she worked. She was humming an old Beatles song, "Hey Jude," tunelessly, probably mindlessly, to herself. She painstakingly checked every millimeter, looking for hairs or fibers that weren't Katie's, for anything that might provide a clue to where the girl had been and whom she'd been with. She found nothing. Terri checked both fingernails and toenails for traces of skin or hair that might have been scratched from an attacker during a struggle. As he watched, McCabe noticed Katie's toenails were painted an assortment of bright colors, each toe a different color, a smiley face drawn on the big toe where someone, probably Guerrera, had earlier hung an ID tag identifying Katie as case number 106-97-4482. McCabe hadn't seen the nail polish in the gloom of the scrap yard and chided himself for carelessness. Again Terri found nothing. "Clean as a whistle," she murmured more to herself than to the cops.

Terri then swabbed Katie's vaginal and anal cavities for traces of semen. Though he'd attended dozens of autopsies of women who had been sexually attacked, this time, for the first time, McCabe felt he was intruding in a place he shouldn't go. He imagined Casey's body laid out like this on a stainless steel autopsy table, exposed under bright lights to faceless cops and probing pathologists, and he wished he were somewhere else. He forced the image from his mind. He knew he had to be here both for himself and for the girl—in a way, for Casey, too. Terri spoke for the record. "There is severe vaginal and anal bruising indicating rough sex or possibly insertion of a dildo or other foreign object. The subject may have been raped multiple times prior to death."

Guerrera reported that the swabs came up negative for semen. "Either he used a condom or maybe he was just as happy playing with toys." He spoke with a soft Castilian accent that seemed somehow out of place in this cold sterile room.

Terri looked up at McCabe. "Are you alright?" she asked. "You don't look so good."

"Yeah, I'm okay." He didn't elaborate.

Terri nodded and then went back to her work. She examined the incision that had been made in Katie's abdomen. She carefully removed the small ornament that decorated Katie's navel. Using a scalpel, Terri then cut diagonally from each of Katie's shoulders down toward the opening that already existed in her chest and abdomen. She continued the cut down beyond the navel to the pubis. She reopened the already sawn sternum and began removing, examining, and weighing each of the girl's organs, excepting, of course, her missing heart. With the body opened, the stench of decomposing flesh filled McCabe's nostrils, and he felt a rising nausea. This was the moment in each autopsy where, for McCabe, the corpse lost its connection with the living, its human identity becoming once and for all time a memory. McCabe's mind let go of Katie and now shifted to planning the next steps in the Dubois investigation. At the same time, he found himself wondering if Lucinda Cassidy might still be alive and, if she was, how on earth he'd ever find her before she, too, ended up on a table like this.

An hour later the autopsy was over. Terri, removing her gloves, walked McCabe and Maggie to the door. She looked at McCabe. "Like I said last night, someone surgically removed this girl's heart. Underline surgically. Removing a heart is not a difficult procedure, especially if you don't care if the patient—victim—dies, or if you actually want the patient to die."

"How could you remove someone's heart and not have the person die?" asked Maggie.

"It's done all the time," said Terri.

"What do you mean?" Maggie was genuinely confused.

"It's called a transplant. A sick heart is removed from a person and a healthy heart put in. In most cases, the patient who receives the heart goes on to live a perfectly normal life. At least for some period of time."

A transplant was something McCabe hadn't considered. He found the notion intriguing. He looked at Terri. "Do you think that's even remotely possible?" he asked. "That Katie's heart was removed as part of a transplant procedure?"

"I suppose it's possible, but damned unlikely. There's certainly a shortage of hearts available for transplant. Someone might even kill for one. Many have died for want of one. The thing is, a successful transplant can't be done outside a modern OR, and I can't imagine any American transplant center accepting a donor heart without knowing exactly whose it was or where it came from. It just wouldn't happen.

"Even so," Terri continued, "this extraction was done skillfully. The incision was clean, most likely made with a scalpel. I'd guess the sternum was cut with a Stryker surgical saw. Like the one I use for autopsies. Hard to find outside a hospital. Or someplace like this. Anyway, I'd say you might—underline might—be looking for a murderer who trained as a doctor. Probably, but not necessarily, a surgeon. Possibly, but not necessarily, a cardiac surgeon. Again possibly, a pathologist. That's the best lead I can give you. Katie Dubois was alive, her heart was beating, when the surgery—and I'm going to call it that—began. The removal of her heart was the immediate cause of death. What I'm really curious about is whether or not she was either anesthetized or brain dead at the time the heart was removed."

"If not?"

"If not, she would have suffered horribly."

Maybe our boy got off on that, thought McCabe. "Your blood tox results will tell you that?" he asked.

"Yes. I'll let you know as soon as I do. It'll be a while, but I'll try to hurry the lab along as much as I can."

9

McCabe's cell phone rang on the return trip from Augusta. "This is McCabe."

"Sergeant McCabe? This is Dr. Spencer. Phil Spencer. My wife said you called?"

"Yes, Dr. Spencer, I was hoping you could spare me half an hour."

"Hattie said you wanted to talk to me about the Dubois girl," said Spencer. Without waiting for a response, he continued. "I'm not sure how I can help, but I'll be happy to talk with you. I keep an office in the hospital, in the Levenson Heart Center. It's one of the luxuries the hospital affords me. If you can come up in an hour or so, say seven o'clock, I can spare you some time. I should warn you, though, I may have to run out midconversation. I'm waiting on a harvest."

"A harvest?"

"Yes. We're harvesting a heart. For a transplant. Or, more accurately, a surgeon in New Hampshire is harvesting a heart."

"You call removing a heart 'harvesting'?" McCabe found the term a little creepy.

"Yep. Organ recovery is more politically correct these days, but I've said harvesting for fifteen years, so I guess I always will. Anyway, once I get word the heart's on its way, I won't have much time to talk."

McCabe glanced at his watch. Five after six. He could make it by seven if he drove straight through to the hospital. "See you at seven," he said.

It was a warm, pleasant evening, and he drove with the Bird's retractable hardtop down, catching as much of the sunset as he could. There wasn't much traffic, and he picked up his speed, taking 95 to 295. He reached the Congress Street exit for the hospital with time to spare.

He pulled the Bird into the crowded visitors' parking lot and headed for the hospital. An oversized revolving door led into the main lobby. Spotting an information desk manned by elderly volunteers, McCabe lined up behind a gaggle of other visitors and, as he waited, studied the comings and goings of a wounded humanity. An old woman, legs wrapped in bandages, hobbled painfully toward a bench, where she sat heavily. A girl, no more than fifteen, perhaps as young as Casey, rode in a wheelchair, a dazed expression on her face, a newborn in her arms. An aide was pushing the chair toward the exit. A middle-aged couple, the girl's parents, McCabe supposed, walked behind. White-coated students and residents scurried importantly around them, stethoscopes stuffed in pockets, badges pinned to chests.

Finally an elderly woman sporting a fluffy halo of white hair smiled up from behind the desk. "May I help you, sir?"

"I'm here to see Dr. Spencer. Dr. Philip Spencer."

"Yes, of course," she said. Her tone suggested Spencer was someone she held in high regard. "Dr. Spencer's office is in the Levenson Heart Center in the Harmon Wing. Is he expecting you?"

"Detective Michael McCabe." He opened his badge wallet. "Yes, he is expecting me."

She phoned to announce McCabe's arrival. She nodded, apparently to the person at the other end of the phone, and looked up again. "Walk down this hall as far as you can go, take a left, and then your first right. Take the elevator to the seventh floor. You'll see the sign for the heart center. They'll direct you from there. Shall I draw you a map?"

"No, thank you, ma'am. I can remember your directions."

McCabe found Spencer's office without difficulty. At seven o'clock on a Saturday evening no assistants manned the outer office, but Spencer's door was open. McCabe poked his head in and gently knocked. Philip Spencer was on the phone. Smiling, he waved McCabe in and directed him to a wing chair at the side of his mahogany desk. Covering the bottom of the phone, he mouthed the words, "Just take a minute."

McCabe nodded and sat down. The furniture was conservative and expensive. Standard issue, he supposed, for senior executives of every stripe including, it seemed, the medical stripe.

Spencer looked even younger than McCabe expected and handsome enough to play a doctor on TV as well as in real life. He was tall and slender, his straight dark hair beginning to turn gray. His face and manner exuded WASP breeding. His deeply tanned skin suggested a lot of time spent either outdoors or in tanning salons, and McCabe didn't see him as a tanning salon kind of guy. He was dressed in surgical scrubs.

McCabe glanced around. There was nothing out of place. The items on Spencer's desk were precisely arranged. Medical journals on the coffee table were stacked in date order, no untidy edges sticking out. Photographs of Spencer, sometimes alone, sometimes with others, lined one wall. In several he was wearing scrubs, as he was today, standing with people McCabe assumed were grateful patients, happy to be leaving the hospital alive, new hearts beating, their leases on life, at least for the moment, renewed. In one photo Spencer was dressed in black tie and flanked by former president George H. W. Bush, Barbara Bush, and Maine's Senator Olympia Snowe. A banner behind them indicated they were celebrating the twenty-year anniversary of the Levenson Heart Center.

To McCabe, the most interesting of the photos showed Spencer, maybe ten years younger, dressed in climbing gear, posing for the camera with a group of three other men all about the same age. A hand-lettered sign in front of them read DENALI SUMMIT. ALT: 20,320 FEET. WE MADE IT! Three of the climbers were smiling proudly into the camera, but Spencer's face was turned away. He was standing second from the left, his eyes focused on the man standing next to him. McCabe thought there was something unexpected about Spencer's expression. He couldn't quite figure out what it was.

He scanned the rest of the framed photos. Interestingly, there were no shots of the doctor's wife. None of family vacations. None of Spencer children, if any such children existed.

McCabe turned away from the photos and looked through the windows behind Spencer's head. Far in the distance, he could see the distinctive triangular shape of Mount Washington silhouetted in the last of the sun's setting rays. "Pretty spectacular, isn't it?" Spencer said, hanging up the phone. "One of the rewards of being on the top floor."

He pushed some papers into a folder, flicked on his desk lamp, and leaned back in his chair. The light accented the shadows of Spencer's deep-set, nearly black eyes as they studied McCabe. "Sorry about the delay," he said. "Now, how can I help you, Detective?"

"What do you know about Katie Dubois's death?"

"Not much. Basically what I read in the paper last week after her disappearance. Katie Dubois was a sixteen-year-old high school girl from Portland. She was a good athlete. A pretty blonde. She vanished after a night out in the Old Port. Last night Tom Shockley told me she'd been murdered."

McCabe stiffened. "How do you know Shockley?"

"We go to the same parties. That's where we were last night. At a fund-raiser for Kids with Cancer at the Pemaquid Club."

The Pemaquid Club was a tony in-town watering hole for Portland's rich and well connected. It was housed in an elegant redbrick Georgian mansion on the city's West Side. McCabe doubted there were many cops among its membership rolls.

"What else did he tell you?"

"Not much. We were having a drink together at the bar when he got a call about the murder. I could only hear his end of the conversation, so I asked him what'd happened. He said the girl's body was found in that scrap yard on Somerset. Naked. Cut up. Maybe raped. Then he took out his phone again and called you and left a message. He said you'd be running the investigation and that he had a lot of confidence in you. That's it. All I know."

"Did you watch Shockley's news conference this morning?"

"Afraid not."

"What I'm about to tell you is confidential."

"I understand."

"Katie Dubois died because her heart was cut out of her body." As he spoke, McCabe watched Spencer's face for signs of reaction. All he saw was a mild curiosity.

"Removing the heart was the cause of death? It wasn't done postmortem?"

"No." McCabe told Spencer most of what Terri Mirabito had said about the cause and manner of Katie's death, leaving out any mention of ligature or burn marks. Or of rape.

"Dr. Mirabito's right. Removing a heart is not that difficult. Not if you've got the proper tools—a scalpel, a reciprocating saw to cut the sternum, a retractor to spread the ribs. Pretty much any surgeon could do it, certainly any cardiac surgeon."

"Why do you think the murderer—whoever it was— might have wanted to cut out her heart?"

"Me? I haven't a clue. We both know there are all kinds of crazies in the world. I suppose some of them could be doctors. It was probably something sexual. From her picture, Katie was an attractive girl. People express their sexual fantasies in strange ways, but psychiatry's not my field of expertise."

"You're a transplant surgeon, right?" asked McCabe. "You remove hearts for a living?"

"Not exactly. I'm head of the transplant program here at Cumberland. The goal is to give people new hearts. In each case to save a life. That's what turns me on. Harvesting—organ retrieval—is more often than not somebody else's task."

"What's it like? Cutting a heart out of a living human being? For a heart surgeon, is it simply all in a day's work, or is it something somebody might get off on?"

"You mean sexually?"

"Yes."

"I don't know. I can tell you it's never all in a day's work. Even when you know the heart will be used to save another life. On one level, the human heart is nothing more than a muscle that works like a small pump. Weighs less than a pound. Only a little bigger than your fist. Yet it beats a hundred thousand times a day. Pumps a couple of thousand gallons of blood. Unless we go out of our way to screw it up, it will, most likely, keep on doing that every day for seventy, eighty, even ninety years, often without routine maintenance. Show me another machine that can do anything like that." Spencer sounded genuinely excited.

"You said on one level. What's the other level?"

"The other level is spiritual. Ancient people believed the heart was the seat of the soul. Some of us still do. When I do remove a heart, sometimes I hold it in my hand for a minute or two knowing it will give new life to a dying patient. An extraordinary feeling. Today, though the legal definition of death is death of the brain, some people still believe the soul resides, at least partly, in the heart."

"Are you one of them?"

Spencer smiled. "That, Detective, is my secret."

"You'll be doing a transplant tonight?"

"Yes. I'm waiting for a heart to be harvested in a hospital in New Hampshire sometime this evening. When it gets here, I'll be putting it into the body of a forty-five-year-old high school teacher with a wife and two children. Without the transplant, he'd be dead before the end of the year."

"Do you think Katie Dubois might have been killed to harvest her heart for a transplant?"

Spencer looked up. "You mean as part of some sort of black market in organs?"

"Yes."

"The answer is no."

"Why not?"

"Couldn't be done."

"You said yourself removing a heart wasn't that difficult."

"It's not. Any reasonably well trained surgeon or pathologist can do it easily. Harvesting the heart isn't the problem."

"So what is the problem?"

"There are a lot of problems. For starters, there isn't a transplant facility anywhere in this country that would accept a harvested heart without knowing precisely where it came from and under what circumstances the donor died, or without the participation of an organization called the United Network for Organ Sharing, which works through various regional OPOs—organ procurement organizations."

"That's where you get your harvested hearts?"

Spencer seemed relaxed, on his own turf. "That's where we *have* to get them. No choice. The OPOs have a monopoly. There are a couple of dozen of them in the United States. They divvy up the country geographically. Cumberland is the only hospital in Maine doing heart transplants, and all our hearts come through the New England Organ Bank in Newton, Mass."

"How does it work?"

"When a heart becomes available, let's say somebody is injured in an auto accident, they're taken to the nearest hospital, which is probably not a transplant center. Then a

lot of ifs come into play. If the patient dies and if the heart
is healthy. Or if the patient is brain dead and if the heart is
healthy. If the hospital's trauma team can get permission
from the victim's family to harvest the organs. If all those
ifs fall into place, the hospital informs the New England
Organ Bank and prepares to harvest all usable organs, including the heart."

"Who decides who gets the heart?"

"On any given day, the New England Organ Bank has a
backlog of approved transplant patients waiting for hearts
or, in some cases, for a heart-lung combination. Those
who'd die first are at the top of the list. Geography is also a
consideration. You don't want the heart traveling any farther than it has to. Time in transit is an enemy to a successful transplant. When that's all sorted out, the heart's offered
to the highest-priority patient with the right blood type and
compatible tissue located in the nearest transplant center.
Right now, today, there are over twenty-five hundred very
sick people in the United States waiting for hearts. Many if
not most of them will die waiting."

"An ideal situation for a black market, wouldn't you
say?"

"For the sellers, sure."

"Also for the buyers," said McCabe. "You just said yourself a lot of people die waiting. Wouldn't a few of them be
willing to pay a substantial amount for a chance to jump
the queue?"

Spencer paused for a minute, studying McCabe. "I'm
sure they would," he said in a considered voice, "but who's
going to perform the transplant, and where? Any recognized transplant center would be crazy to even think about
it. So would a qualified surgeon. The operation can't be
done by a surgeon acting alone, no matter how skilled or
experienced, and it can't be done on a kitchen table. When
I transplant a heart, there are ten to twelve specialized
people in the OR. All critical to the procedure. Plus a lot of
sophisticated equipment. Most important is a heart-lung
machine and a perfusionist to run it. The heart-lung ma-

chine circulates and oxygenates the patient's blood and keeps him or her alive between the time the sick heart is removed and the healthy heart goes in and begins beating."

"What else is required?"

"What else?" Spencer shrugged. "A diagnostic lab to perform pre-op and post-op tests. A well-stocked blood bank. A facility for postoperative recovery and one-on-one care for at least a few days. You need an array of monitors. You need someone to prescribe and administer antirejection drugs and to watch the patient for signs of infection due to a compromised immune system. You need to be able to follow a fairly rigid postoperative protocol. I just don't see how some kind of rogue surgeon could put all that together on his own."

"How long is a living heart viable after it's harvested?"

"Not long. Four or five hours. Our heart in New Hampshire will be placed in an iced saline solution in an ordinary picnic cooler, put on a helicopter, and flown directly here. While that's being done, we'll remove our patient's diseased heart and attach him to the heart-lung machine until he receives his new heart. It's all very tightly coordinated."

Four or five hours. Terri Mirabito estimated Katie's time of death as forty-eight to seventy-two hours before Lacey found her in the scrap yard. Since her body was found around 8:00 P.M. Friday, a transplant would have to have taken place sometime between 8:00 P.M. Tuesday and 8:00 P.M. Wednesday. Twenty-four hours. A big window.

"How long does a transplant operation take?"

"Depends how complicated. Anywhere from four hours to a whole day."

McCabe resisted the temptation to ask Spencer where he was between Tuesday night and Wednesday night. Or Thursday while the body was being dumped. He had no evidence whatsoever that Katie Dubois's murder was anything other than a random attack by a sexual sadist. McCabe found Spencer's manner annoyingly arrogant but he had nothing aside from the fact that he was a cardiac surgeon to implicate him one way or the other.

"How many other surgeons are on staff here at Cumberland? How many other cardiac surgeons?"

"There are twelve of us in the cardiac unit. Another hundred or so in other specialties or practicing general surgery. I'm not sure of the exact number."

"How many do transplants?"

"Myself and two others. James Puccio and Walter Codman."

"Could you get me a list of the other surgeons' names and contact info? Or shall I get that from a hospital administrator?"

"Detective, I seriously doubt any surgeon on the staff of this hospital is leading a double life as a sadistic killer of teenaged girls. We're pretty damned careful about who we bring on board."

"I appreciate the sentiment, Doctor, but the evidence suggests we're looking for a surgeon, and this is one of the places surgeons work. Especially surgeons with an interest in the heart. I'll also be checking with other hospitals."

Spencer pursed his lips. "Very well," he said after a moment. "I'll have my assistant get you a list of the names."

"Thank you. I'd also like bios and résumés."

"Sorry. I'll give you names, but that's it. No CVs or other personal information. There are serious privacy issues involved. If you want to know more, you'll have to talk to each of the doctors individually."

As Spencer spoke, an image flashed in McCabe's mind of Lucinda Cassidy, strapped to an operating table, Philip Spencer leaning over her, ready to cut. "Dr. Spencer, time is critical here," he said. "The more we spend chatting with your staff, the colder the trail will get. It would save us a lot of time if you would help."

"Sorry. No."

"I can get a court order, if I have to." McCabe wondered if the doctor knew he was bluffing. Getting a court order from any judge to go rummaging through the personal backgrounds of more than a hundred respected doctors might be a tall order.

"Then that's what you'll have to do. I'm not giving you access. You can always try HR, but I don't think you'll have any better luck there."

He thought about the murder of Elyse Andersen. "Any of your surgeons move here from Florida in the last couple of years? Orlando maybe?"

"You're starting to annoy me, Detective."

Spencer's patience was wearing thin. McCabe decided to drop the issue, at least for now, and try another tack. He glanced again at the Denali picture and again was struck by Spencer's expression. What was it?

"I see you're a mountain climber," he said.

"I've done some climbing, yes. Denali, as you can see. Logan in Canada, El Pico de Orizaba in Mexico, Katahdin here in Maine."

Was Spencer relieved to be changing the subject? McCabe wasn't sure. "Those other guys are friends of yours?"

"Old friends. We all went to medical school together. We did residencies together. All but one in cardiac surgery, then transplant surgery. At the time, we called ourselves, a little arrogantly I suppose, the Asclepius Society."

"Asclepius?"

"Yes. After the Greek god of healing. Asclepius was so skilled a physician he could actually bring the dead back to life. That's what we thought we would be doing as transplant surgeons. Bringing the dead back to life."

McCabe remembered the story from classics class at St. Barnabas. Instead of being pleased with the healer, Zeus became so angry with Asclepius for co-opting the ability to bestow immortality that he slew him on the spot. Seared him with a lightning bolt, like an ancient Tony Soprano.

"How about you?" asked Spencer.

"How about me what?"

"Are you a climber?"

McCabe thought back to his muddy descent down the slope of the Western Prom. "No. I'm definitely not a climber," he said. "It's not anything I've ever thought about doing."

"Maybe you should."

"I can't imagine why."

"Well, I could give you a lot of rigmarole about healthful exercise, but I've always thought the best answer to why anyone climbs mountains was George Mallory's. Mallory was a British climber who tried an ascent of Everest back in 1924. He wanted to be the first man to reach the summit. When people asked him why he was determined to make a climb most considered impossible, and some thought suicidal, his answer was 'Because it's there.'"

"That's why you climb? Because it's there?"

"That's why any serious climber climbs. Climbing is physically demanding. It can be dangerous. It can't be called fun in any conventional sense of the word. It forces me to push myself further than I ever thought I could. Test myself. Find out how good I am. To me, and others like me, pushing the limits of our skill is what makes life worth living. It's always exhilarating. Either hanging from a precipice twenty thousand feet up or cutting open a human being and replacing a heart in an operating room. That sense of exhilaration is what led me into transplant surgery."

The word "risk-taker" popped unbidden into McCabe's mind, and he wondered again where Spencer was at the critical times. "I gather Mallory didn't make it," he said. "Edmund Hillary and Tenzing Norgay were the first to climb Everest."

"Yes. Thirty years later. In 1953. A New Zealand beekeeper and a Nepalese Sherpa. Mallory tried and died in the attempt. The equipment available to him in 1924 wasn't up to the task. Everest is easier today because of modern equipment. Not easy, but easier. I'm curious. Isn't there anything you do to test your own limits? To see if you can? Because it's there?"

McCabe shrugged. "I chase murderers. Like Everest, they're there—and catching them *can* be challenging."

Spencer smiled. "You're joking, but I'm serious. You know, I'll be going up to Acadia in a few weeks for a training climb up the Precipice. It's a fairly easy climb, but it does have a few tricky patches. Short, steep verticals that can be tough for a beginner. Would you like to give it a try?"

McCabe was surprised by the invitation, wondered why it was offered. "I don't think so."

"Why not? You look reasonably fit. I know you don't lack courage. Tom Shockley told me you ran into the Twin Towers and saved someone's life on September 11."

"Tom Shockley's got a big mouth." McCabe wasn't surprised Spencer knew Shockley. Portland was a small town. He supposed he shouldn't be surprised, either, by Shockley's indiscretion. It was the nature of the beast. "Anyway, it wasn't something I planned. Like an ascent of Everest. Or Denali. I happened to be in a meeting at police headquarters on Centre Street that morning. It's about a five-minute drive from the Towers. When the first plane hit, we all rushed over to see if we could help."

"But *you* ran into the building?"

"Only because that's where help was needed. Look, Dr. Spencer, I'm a cop. What I did a lot of other cops did, too. I was just luckier than some. I made it out alive. It wasn't fun. Or challenging in the way you mean. It's also personal, and I have to tell you I don't appreciate Shockley talking about it. To you or anyone else."

"How does he know about it?"

"He didn't hear it from me."

"Interesting."

"If you say so. Did Shockley say anything else?"

"Just that you were a top New York homicide cop who'd gone through a nasty divorce. That you came to Portland because you wanted a safer, more wholesome environment to bring up your daughter."

Spencer's beeper went off. He glanced at the screen. "Detective, I'm afraid I have to run out on you. They've started harvesting my heart." As he stood up he added, "I'll be happy to read Dr. Mirabito's autopsy report and talk to her about whether the wounds on the body were consistent with a harvesting procedure. From your description I suspect they were. As to whether or not a black market in hearts for transplant is even remotely possible, and I don't think it is, you might want to talk to our transplant coordinator here at Cumberland. She can tell you far more about the logistics than I ever could."

Spencer put his hand on McCabe's elbow and led him toward the door. They passed the Denali photo. Looking at it close up, McCabe was struck even more than before by something in Spencer's expression, something in the attitude. He still wasn't sure what.

"I've enjoyed meeting you, Detective. Good luck in catching whoever it was who cut up that girl. Please let me know if there's any other way I can help."

McCabe interrupted Spencer's dismissal. "Just one last question," he said

"Okay, but make it quick." Spencer headed toward the elevator bank.

McCabe followed. "You know that Denali picture? Who are the other three guys?"

"I told you, old friends from medical school. Why do you want to know?"

"Are they all transplant surgeons?"

"So that's it. Listen, I told you this murder was not about heart transplants." Spencer pushed the down button harder than he need have.

"But those men are transplant surgeons, aren't they?"

"Yes, two are, not that it's any of your business."

"Not all three?"

"One's dead."

The elevator arrived. McCabe followed Spencer in. Spencer pressed five for himself and the lobby for McCabe. "What are the names of the two who are alive?"

"Oh, for God's sake, this is ridiculous."

"Humor me."

The doors opened at five and Spencer stepped out. McCabe followed. Spencer stopped and turned to face him. "You're not going any farther."

"What are their names? I can find out on my own. It'll just take longer."

Spencer didn't say anything for a minute. He just stared at McCabe with distaste, as if he had eaten something unpleasant. "The man on the left, next to me, is DeWitt Holland. He's at Brigham in Boston. The one on the far right is Matthew Wilcox, who's at UNC in Chapel Hill."

"Who's the dead guy? The one you're looking at in the picture?"

"His name was Lucas Kane." Spencer's attitude softened. "A tragic, tragic loss. In some ways Lucas was the most talented of us all."

"How did Kane die?"

"Lucas was brutally murdered about four years ago. Now, if you'll excuse me." Spencer turned his back and walked away.

"Just one last question, Dr. Spencer," McCabe called after him, the image of Peter Falk's Columbo popping into his mind. "Where were you around midnight last Thursday night?"

Spencer turned. "At home. In bed."

"Your wife was with you?"

"Yes. We usually share a bed."

McCabe rode alone to the ground floor. He passed through a swirl of people in the lobby without noticing them. He left the building and headed toward the Bird. A gaggle of smokers, mostly hospital workers, stood clustered in the corner of the parking lot sucking on their weeds. McCabe was tempted to see if he could bum a smoke from one of them. He'd been a two-pack-a-day smoker for years, and burning tobacco still smelled good to him. He only broke the habit after Casey was born.

10

It was nearly eight thirty when McCabe got back to the condo. He was carting a plastic bag filled with frozen dinners and wondering if Casey had managed to scrounge up anything to eat. Before he could fish the keys out of his pocket, the door swung open. Kyra stood on the other side, a concerned expression on her face.

"What's the matter?" he asked

"Your wife called," she said.

"My wife?"

"Your ex-wife, if you prefer." She took the bag of groceries and went to the kitchen. "You know?" she called out. "Cassandra? The drop-dead gorgeous one in the picture Casey showed me." Kyra stuck the food in the freezer, took out a cut crystal highball glass, and poured him three fingers of Scotch. She put the bottle back, then paused, took it out again, and poured herself a short one, diluting it with ice and a little water.

"Oh," he said, "that ex-wife. Did she say what she wanted?"

"She's flying up here. She wants to see Casey."

He stood quietly for a moment, absorbing the information. "When?"

"The end of the week."

"Does Casey know?"

"Yes. She took the call. They talked for a couple of minutes." Kyra handed him his drink, sat down on the couch, and sipped her own. He'd never seen her drink hard liquor before.

"How did she react?" he asked.

"From what I could hear on this end, she pretty much blew Sandy off. Said she didn't want to see her. Sounded cool. Hung up after a minute or two. I asked her who it was on the phone. She told me."

"She okay?"

"I don't know. Abandonment isn't easy to come to terms with."

McCabe sat on the broad window seat and gazed down at a million lights shining across the bulk of an enormous white cruise ship as it pulled out of Portland harbor. The *Princess* something. Kyra flipped off her sandals and stretched her legs out on the couch. She looked very much at home.

"Where's Casey now?" he asked.

"I gave her some dinner and drove her to Sarah Palfrey's house. Presumably to watch TV and do some homework. Aside from anything else, that gives you a chance to sort out how you feel before you discuss it with her."

McCabe was hit by a sudden surge of anger. "I know exactly how I feel," he said. "Sandy's got no right to suddenly drop back into Casey's life. Not after three years of silence."

"You've never told me much about your relationship with Sandy."

"You never asked."

"I'm asking now."

McCabe sighed. The anger ebbed. He didn't like talking about his failed first marriage, but maybe it would help— and maybe Kyra did have a right to know. He sucked in a breath, held it for a minute, let it out slowly, and then began to talk.

"My relationship with Sandy was different in just about every way from what we have between us. It was built on lust, not love. That was true at the beginning, even truer at the end. For the last few years there was nothing between Sandy and me but sex. That never stopped. She could always turn me on, and she loved proving it. My emotional life focused on Casey—and, I guess, on my job. You know how I am. When I get involved in a case I can't just turn it on and off. It consumes me. Sandy couldn't deal with that. She hated it."

McCabe swirled the Scotch in the Waterford glass. A wedding present from his sister Fran. One of a set of four. Sandy had taken two to her new life. He'd broken one in the move to Portland. This was the last.

Kyra watched him as he finished the drink. "Didn't you love her in the beginning?"

"I thought I did. Unfortunately, Sandy didn't have much use for my love. She loved herself more than enough for both of us. In the end, any feelings I might have had for her withered away."

"Why didn't you split earlier? File for divorce?"

"I thought about it."

"What stopped you?"

"Fear of losing Casey. In most divorce proceedings the mother gets custody. The father gets to visit. I wasn't about to let that happen. I was totally in love with my daughter from the instant she was born, and I wanted her with me." McCabe rose from the window seat and went to the kitchen to pour himself another Scotch. He held up the bottle. "You want another?"

"Not for me. I'm not sure you should have one either."

"I'm all right," he said. He poured the Scotch and returned to the window. "In the end, Sandy solved the problem for me. She started screwing around with some rich banker. Not her first affair, by the way. Just the first who asked her to marry him. She walked out and never looked back."

"Then you got Casey. The perfect solution, right?"

"Not quite perfect. I assumed at the time that Sandy would want to see her daughter occasionally. Y'know, one day a week, one weekend a month, alternate school vacations, whatever."

"She didn't?"

"No. She didn't. She hardly even bothered to call. She was always too busy shopping. Or getting a pedicure. Or whatever the hell else it is that Sandy does with her time. Casey was ten years old and in an emotionally fragile place, and here was her own mother telling her she didn't care enough to take a cab across town or even pick up the phone to talk to her. I found that unforgivable at the time. I always will."

"Did you ever talk to Sandy about it?"

"I tried. Maybe not hard enough, but I did try. Unfortunately, every conversation with Sandy ultimately ended up being about Sandy. How busy her new life was. How difficult it was adjusting to a new husband. Especially one who doesn't want children. How she wasn't sure she was ready emotionally to be a mother again. Sandy just went on and on. I can repeat each of those conversations verbatim. Each time it would get to a point where I couldn't listen anymore and I'd slam down the phone in a rage. It would take me weeks to work up the energy to try again."

"There's been no contact at all in three years?"

"No. Just some expensive Christmas and birthday presents. The last one didn't even come with a card. It just arrived. We figured it was from Sandy because we didn't know anyone else who'd send her something from Tiffany's." There was an edge in his voice again, the anger coming back like an old familiar friend.

McCabe walked to the kitchen to pour himself another Scotch. Then he decided not to. The last thing Casey needed if she wanted to talk about any of this was for him to be incoherent. He rinsed out the Waterford glass and put it on a high shelf where it wouldn't get accidentally bashed. Then he sat down again by the window.

"You know, when the job came up in Portland, I told people—myself included—living in a smaller city would be healthier for Casey. The job would be less demanding. I could spend more time being a father. It was all true, but I was also using distance to help Casey rationalize Sandy's neglect. I figured being three hundred and fifty miles away might soften the impact of having a mother who didn't care enough to ever find out how she was doing."

"Do you think it worked?"

"Not really. When Casey showed me Sandy's picture this morning, it was obvious having a mother was something she's been thinking about. I asked her if she wanted to see Sandy again. She said no. Then she asked me if we were getting married. You and me. She wanted to know if that would make you her mother."

"What did you tell her?"

"That we might be someday, but we weren't there yet."

"That was the right answer."

"Are you sure?"

"Yes. For now, anyway. Let me ask you something else. You might find this hurtful, and you can always tell me to shut up and mind my own business—but since you're talking about us getting married, I guess it is my business. You just said moving away from Sandy, moving to Portland, was all for Casey's benefit. Wasn't it, at least a little, for yours as well?"

He wasn't sure where this was going. "How so?"

"After the divorce, wasn't there some small part of you that rejoiced? Some small part that shouted, 'Whoopee! I get the prize. I get to keep this beautiful little girl and Sandy doesn't. I get all of Casey's love and Sandy doesn't get any'? By packing up and moving six hours away, weren't you trying to make sure it stayed that way?"

"No."

"No?"

"No. Absolutely not." McCabe spoke quietly. "Am I glad Casey's living with me and not with Sandy? Absolutely, but if you're asking if I'm happy my thirteen-year-old daughter feels abandoned by her own mother and, as a result, more dependent on me, the answer is no. No way. Not then. Not now. Not ever."

"Okay, if that's true and the answer really is no, shouldn't you welcome Sandy's efforts to reconnect? Seems to me Casey's got a right to get to know her mother. You said yourself that might have been what she was asking to do when she showed you the picture. What an amazing coincidence it is that Sandy calls up the very same day. I realize, if they do see each other, it won't make up for what's already happened, but don't you think it might be a start?"

McCabe stared into Kyra's eyes and said nothing. Maybe she was right. She probably was. Yet, for now, there was still too much anger, too much hurt for him to admit it.

Finally Kyra stood up. "Okay. I'm going back to my own place now. Sarah's mother said she'd bring Casey home. When she gets here, try not to react purely emotionally. Think hard about what you say about Sandy and how Casey should react to the idea of seeing her again. Think how it will affect your relationship with your daughter. Not just now but for a really long time." She leaned down and kissed McCabe on the lips. He barely noticed. Then she left.

McCabe dialed Sandy's number in New York. She picked up on the second ring. He was a little surprised she was home on a Saturday night. "Hello, McCabe," she said. "I thought I might be hearing from you." She spoke in that smooth, throaty growl he knew so well and once found irresistible. Like a young Lauren Bacall leaning against the door in *To Have and Have Not*. "You know how to whistle, don't you, Steve? You just put your lips together and blow."

"How are you, Sandy?"

"I'm very well, thank you, and yourself?"

"Couldn't be better. Thank you for asking."

"What can I do for you, McCabe? I mean, now that we've established that we're both feeling fine. We are feeling fine, aren't we?"

"Not entirely. I don't think you should come up to Portland. At least not now. Casey doesn't want to see you, and neither do I. Aside from anything else, I'm in the middle of a major murder case."

"I know. It even made the New York papers. Banner headlines in the *News* and *Post*. MURDER IN MAINE. TEEN-AGED GIRL RAPED AND MUTILATED. Quite Gothic. Your boss certainly has a way with words. I'm not sure Casey wouldn't be safer here in Manhattan. All we have is your common garden-variety crazies."

"As I said, Casey doesn't want to see you."

"Did she tell you that?"

"She did, in fact. Even before you called."

"Well, we may have a problem with that, McCabe. In case you've forgotten, I am Casey's mother, and I intend spending some time with my daughter before any more time passes."

"Your daughter? You have the brass to actually call her that after walking out because Daddy Big-Bucks didn't want to 'raise other people's children.' That was the phrase, wasn't it, Sandy? 'Raise other people's children.' You know me. I never forget a phrase—or anything else, for that matter."

"Let's not let this get nasty, McCabe. As Casey's mother I have a perfect right to see her and spend time with her. I don't want to have to go to court to protect that right, but I will, and thanks to Peter—or Daddy Big-Bucks, as you so charmingly call him—I can afford the best lawyers in the business. So please let Casey know, if you don't mind terribly, that I'll be coming up Friday and taking her down to Boston for the weekend. She and I have a lot of catching up to do."

McCabe hung up the phone, poured himself another Scotch, then poured it down the sink. He reached for the phone again and called Bobby.

Estelle answered. "McCabe residence." He should have been prepared for Estelle's shrill greeting. She'd worked for McCabe's brother for ten years. Somehow he never was.

"Hi, Estelle."

"Michael, darling, how are you?" Her piercing tones assaulted his eardrums.

"I'm doing okay. How are you?"

"Aside from my gallbladder, not bad."

McCabe decided not to ask about her gallbladder. "Is Bobby there?"

"I'll see if he can talk." Bobby was a hotshot personal injury lawyer and McCabe's older brother. His only brother since Tommy had been killed.

"What's up, Mike?" Bobby always got right to the point. There was a moment of silence.

"Sandy called."

"Okay, so Sandy called."

"She wants to come up to Portland and see Casey."

"A fairly normal desire for a child's mother. I'm surprised she hasn't called earlier."

"I just want to know if there's any way I can stop her." Bobby didn't do divorce work, but he was tough and smart and usually knew the right answers.

"Stop her? I don't think so. At least not legally. We're talking visitation here. Not custody. Am I right?"

Jesus. Custody. McCabe hadn't even considered that possibility. "Custody hasn't come up," he said.

"Well, it seems to me no judge in his right mind would try to keep a mother from seeing her child. What did the divorce decree say about Sandy's rights to see Casey?"

"Not a lot. The phrase was 'reasonable contact on reasonable notice.' But you've got to remember Sandy never contested the divorce. It was just something the judge felt ought to be in there."

"Okay, so now, after three years, your ex-wife wants to reconnect with your daughter. I don't necessarily see that as bad for Casey. Neither will any family court judge. It might be different if she posed some kind of physical threat to Casey."

"Emotional threats don't count?"

"Maybe if the mother was provably psychotic, but even there you probably have to establish a reasonable likelihood of physical harm."

"Provably self-centered, uncaring, and narcissistic just doesn't cut it, huh?"

" 'Fraid not. A weekend visit is 'reasonable contact,' and she's giving you 'reasonable notice.' If I were you, I'd just take it as a positive sign that Sandy wants to see Casey and leave it at that. I think it'll be good for Casey to get to know her mother, warts and all."

"What if she does decide to seek custody?"

"Cross that bridge when you get to it."

"Maybe I should just kneecap the bitch."

"Watch your mouth, asshole. Anybody hears a gunslinger like you even whisper threats like that and you not only lose Casey, you could also lose your job. By the way, speaking of mothers, Thanksgiving's at my house this year. Mom's getting too old to do all that work. I'm assuming you and Casey will be there. You can bring your girlfriend if you want. What's her name again?"

"Kyra. Her name is Kyra. Try to remember it. Anyway, we'll try to get there. How's Mom?"

"Fragile. Getting a little forgetful. I keep thinking about Aunt Joy's Alzheimer's and wonder if it's in our genes. Weird in your case. Like, what do you get when you cross a photographic memory with an Alzheimer's victim?"

"Beats me."

"I don't know. How about somebody who never forgets all the things they can't remember? Forget it. Not funny. Anyway, you're coming?"

"Assuming I'm not up to my ass in dead teenagers."

"Yeah, I heard about that. Scumbag actually cut her heart out?"

"Jesus H. Christ. You heard that on the news?"

"Yep. Your boss is giving interviews. 'We will leave no stone unturned to find the killer or killers.' " Bobby was doing a passable job of mimicking Shockley's public persona. "Sonofabitch ought to be on Mount Rushmore. I take it you were trying to keep the heart thing quiet."

"Trying to. Though I don't know if it really matters."

"Anyway, we have people for dinner. Give my love to Casey and to, uh . . . and to, uh . . . what did you say your girlfriend's name was?"

"Good-bye, you asshole."

11

Maggie stopped by McCabe's desk. She was wearing black jeans, a black T-shirt and black high-top Keds, accessorized with a black holster and sidearm. There were circles under her eyes.

"You alright?" asked McCabe.

"I was out late last night. Didn't get much sleep."

"New boyfriend?"

"Yeah." She paused. "Maybe." Another pause. "Could be." She shrugged. "He's a nice guy—but it was only our second date."

"How's he feel about dating a woman who wears a gun?"

"Apparently fine," she said. "Unlike Ryan, I think he's secure enough to handle it. Anyway, I got a call from Terri Mirabito."

McCabe waited.

"She won't have the final tox report for a while yet, but the initial screening indicates no trace of any anesthetic drugs in Katie's body. Or any other drugs, for that matter. Just a little alcohol. If that holds up, and Terri thinks it will, Katie was fully conscious and her heart was beating when our freaky friend started cutting her up."

McCabe winced. "Shit," he said.

"My sentiments exactly."

"How much alcohol?"

"Not much. Apparently it was part of her last supper. He treated her to beluga caviar and champagne just before killing her. They found traces of both in her stomach."

"A little farewell party?"

"I guess. Also, they're pretty sure he had sex with her multiple times both front and rear."

"Anything else?"

"Nothing critical. We'll have to ask Terri when she's less pissed off. Right now she's very pissed off."

He imagined Katie, battered and sexually abused, being forced to eat caviar and champagne as a prelude to her own death. It was hard not to share Terri's anger. "I want to call a cop in Orlando," he told Maggie. "It's that thing I mentioned in the car. I'll see you in the conference room in about fifteen minutes." McCabe had scheduled a meeting of the detectives involved in the two cases.

"I'll be there."

He called the Orlando, Florida, police department as soon as Maggie left.

"Sergeant Cahill," he said to the voice on the other end. "Aaron Cahill."

McCabe found himself wondering if Cahill was still a cop, wondering if he was still in Orlando, wondering if there was a chance in hell he might have come to work early on a Sunday morning. If not, he'd try to get a cell number. Waiting, McCabe drummed his fingers on the surface of the desk. He glanced at the picture of Casey.

"This is Cahill." A deep, Johnny Cash–like voice with traces of the Florida panhandle boomed over the phone line. Apparently Cahill had come to work.

"Sergeant Cahill? This is Sergeant Michael McCabe, Portland PD."

"Two oh seven? Is that Maine or Oregon?"

The Johnny Cash–like sound was uncanny. McCabe half expected Cahill to burst into a chorus of "I Walk the Line."

"Maine."

"What can I do for you?"

"Elyse Andersen?"

"What about her?"

"We've got one of our own."

"No shit? Same MO? What do you know about the Andersen case?"

"The MO's not identical, but close enough. What I know is what I read in the *Sentinel* coverage."

"Which is?"

"Your vic's nude body was accidentally discovered by a construction crew about three weeks after death. That part's not similar. Our body was dumped in a scrap yard in the middle of town. The part that is the same is that the cause of death was the removal of the girl's heart, and in both cases the ME says whoever removed the heart knew what he was doing."

"Yeah, the medical examiner felt pretty strongly that the heart was removed by a doctor, most likely a surgeon."

"Exactly what our ME said."

"Okay," said Cahill, "let's talk, but just to make sure you are who you say you are, I'm going to call you back."

"Don't you have caller ID?"

"I do, but for all I know there could be a whole bunch of spare phones at the Portland PD."

"So call me back. Ask for Detective Sergeant Michael McCabe. You want the number?"

"I'll look it up."

McCabe hung up and waited. Less than a minute later, his phone rang. "Cahill?"

"Yeah, it's me. Tell me about your case."

McCabe ran down the basic facts surrounding the discovery of Katie Dubois's body and what Terri Mirabito had reported, including that Katie died in excruciating pain.

"Sounds like it could be the same guy," said Cahill, "but why would he bury the vic in one case and dump her in the middle of town in the other? Getting lazy?"

"No. Our body wasn't just dumped. I think he was presenting it to us. Maybe taunting us with it. I think he likes taking chances, gets off on it."

"Well, that part's sure as hell different. Our guy was trying to hide the body. Only pure chance we ever found her. She was buried in a piney woods section of Orlando that was slated to become a new golf course. If construction took place as planned, we never would've found her. She would've been six feet under the ninth hole, probably forever."

"Sounds like Jimmy Hoffa under the fifty-yard line at Giants Stadium."

"Same idea," said Cahill.

"So how'd you find her?"

"The guy had no way of knowing it, but the architects decided to change the plans. They put the clubhouse where the ninth hole was going to be."

"So they sent the diggers in?"

"You got it. Right in the middle of digging the foundation, the backhoe comes up with a load of mucky soil, and smack in the middle of it, there's Elyse Andersen. At least what was left of her. The backhoe driver doesn't notice her at first and drops the whole load into a dump truck. He finally sees one of the workers jumping up and down and pointing at the truck."

"Must have been a bit of a shock."

"I guess. But at least they were smart enough to know something serious was going on and call us immediately. She was mostly in one piece when we found her, except of course for her heart. She'd been dead three, maybe three and a half weeks. Naked. Badly decomposed. We might not have noticed that the heart had been removed except that the breastbone had been cut with a surgical saw and spread." There was a pause. "You guys check VICAP for other cases where a heart's been removed?"

"We're waiting on their report now."

"We didn't find anything similar back then, but if it is the same guy, maybe Andersen was his first."

"You found Andersen by accident. There could be

dozens of others who were never found," said McCabe, "and never will be. Unless we find the bastard and he leads us to them."

"So if it's the same whacko—and that's a big if—he suddenly switches MO and dumps her in plain sight. That's because?"

"I don't know. He's a risk-taker. Maybe, like a junkie, he keeps needing a bigger and bigger hit to get the same high. Just killing them and cutting them up doesn't do it for him anymore. He's got to taunt us with them now."

"So how do we find him?" asked Cahill.

"If he's itchy to get noticed, maybe he'll find us. I assume you checked the local hospitals, surgeons, cardiologists, pathologists, nurses with OR experience, and so on?"

"For weeks. My guys did over six hundred interviews. Anybody and everybody we could think of who might have had the skills and access to the tools to pull this off. All we got is a big fat goose egg. Zero. Not a damned thing."

"Anyway, can you find out if any of your local surgeons have since moved to Maine? Or New Hampshire? Or even Massachusetts?"

"We can take a crack at it."

"Tell me about Andersen. How did the guy get his hands on her?"

"It wasn't random. He targeted her. She was a local real estate agent. The whole scam was pretty simple. I'm surprised it doesn't happen more often. Unknown male calls her office. Asks for Andersen by name. Another saleswoman asked who was calling. He says his name is Harry Lime."

"Harry Lime? You've got to be kidding."

"Yeah, I know. The character in *The Third Man.* Apparently the woman's not a movie buff, and the name doesn't mean a thing to her. Anyway, our so-called Harry Lime tells her he's a potential buyer and Andersen was specifically recommended to him. He wants Andersen to show him a house. So she routes the call to Andersen. Notes on Andersen's desk indicate the guy also tells her his name is

Harry Lime. Said he was looking for a house in the eight-hundred-thousand to one-million range. He asks her to show him a specific house in a new subdivision. She agrees to meet him there. She never returned from the appointment. The house was locked up. Lockbox in place. No fingerprints anywhere. Not even hers. Her car was found in the driveway, but not in the center. Way over to the right. Like there'd been another car parked next to it. My guess is as soon as they go in, he jumps her, knocks her out or ties her up, then loads her in his car and drives off."

"Once again the risk-taker. Anybody could have seen him. I gather nobody did."

"Nope. All the houses around the one she was supposed to show him were empty. It was the middle of the day, and there wasn't a soul around," said Cahill.

"Well, that part sure fits with dumping a body in the middle of the city at eleven o'clock on a Thursday night. I assume you did a major search for her before the body turned up?"

"Full-court press. We even had a couple of hundred National Guardsmen looking for her. Came up with zip."

"Did you check to see if his name might really be Harry Lime?"

"We checked. AutoTrack came up with six Harry Limes. Two in L.A. One in Chicago. One in New York City. One in Georgia. One here in Florida. All came up negative. We think he was yanking our chains with the name."

"When did all this happen?" asked McCabe.

"More than a month before she was found."

"She was dead three to four weeks when you found her. Which means he kept her for what? A week before he killed her?"

"Based on the fact that she was buried about five feet down and the kind of bugs they found in the body, that's what the ME figured, but it's still a guess. You know as well as I do we can't pin it down exactly, specially when you're looking at decomposed remains."

"Even so, it's about the same time frame we have here."

One week. He wondered if that's all the time they had to find Cassidy. One week. It wasn't much. "What about the phone call?" he asked.

"It came from a pay phone outside a 7-Eleven. Nobody there remembered anybody using the phone around the time the call was placed."

"Anything else I should know about Elyse Andersen?"

"What do you want to know?"

"What was she like? I saw her picture in the *Sentinel*. Good-looking woman."

"That she was. Twenty-six years old. Blond. She was a competitive triathlete. She'd been training for an upcoming event."

"That's interesting." McCabe said. "Dubois was young, blond, and an athlete. High school soccer player. Prospect for all-state this year."

"Could be a coincidence," said Cahill.

"Maybe," said McCabe. "Or maybe he likes blondes with firm muscles and healthy hearts." McCabe told Cahill about the disappearance of Lucinda Cassidy. A blonde and a runner. Training for a 10K. Andersen. Dubois. Cassidy. Three young blondes. Three athletes. Coincidence? McCabe didn't think so. Neither did Cahill.

"I'll e-mail you the case files, but I want you to promise to keep me in the loop. Specially if you find something. I'll reopen this case in a minute if I think you can give us something to go on."

"That's a deal."

All of McCabe's detectives plus a few others on loan from the Crimes Against Property unit were crowded into the small fourth-floor conference room. Some were standing against the wall, others sitting. Most were sipping coffee from paper cups, eating bagels and doughnuts, and basically bullshitting when McCabe arrived. Bill Fortier was hunched silently at the head of the table with a worried look on his face. Tom Tasco was reading the *Press Herald* coverage of the Dubois murder. A detective from the other side of the building was peering over his shoulder. Mc-Cabe's picture, taken at the press conference, was on the front page next to images of Shockley and Katie Dubois. The photographer had caught him off guard, a questioning scowl on his face. He seemed to be looking into the distance, and McCabe guessed it was snapped just as he had seen his mystery woman take off. Maggie, who was leaning back in her chair, long legs propped against the side of the table, quipped, "Nice shot, McCabe. Makes you look like you not only want to catch the bad guy, you want to eat him for lunch."

"Yeah, Mike, you've gotta learn to smile for the camera," added Bill Bacon.

Ignoring the hazing, McCabe poured coffee for himself from the urn just outside the door before sitting down.

Fortier began. "Okay, let's start with Dubois. What leads do we have? What leads was Shockley talking about?"

"Shockley was mostly blowing smoke for the media, Bill," said Tom Tasco. "The only thing that remotely qualifies as a lead is a surveillance video of a vehicle that arrived in the right place at what we think may be the right time." He filled the others in on what the moving company's security camera had recorded and what Starbucks had built from it.

"I've got the DMV reports." Eddie Fraser was waving a batch of printouts with one hand and eating a chocolate-covered doughnut with the other. There were bits of chocolate around his mouth.

"That was fast," said McCabe.

"That's 'cause we're good," said Fraser. "Like we agreed, we covered all of Maine, all of New Hampshire, and we threw in Massachusetts north of Boston as a wild card. Owners of late-model Lexus or BMW SUVs who are doctors, surgeons, pathologists. We added biologists at the high school and college level, figuring they ought to be good at cutting up frogs and mice, if not people. We came up with four hundred and sixty-two names."

"If we're talking about people who're good at cutting up

animals," asked Will Messing, "why not check butchers? They cut up animals all day." The others looked at Messing as if he'd descended from another planet.

"Butchers?" said Maggie. "You mean like grocery store butchers? You think a butcher could have done this?"

"Why not? They're good at cutting meat, and who says a butcher can't be a freak?"

"It's a hell of a leap from a surgeon to a butcher," said Tom Tasco.

"Use your imagination," Messing persisted. "My brother-in-law's a butcher. You should see him butterfly a leg of lamb. It's like an art form."

"C'mon, Will, for Christ's sake, we're talking about a teenage girl here. Not a leg of lamb," said Carl Sturgis.

"You want to make your brother-in-law a suspect?" Tasco laughed.

"I think we're getting a little off track," said Maggie.

"Okay, okay." Messing shrugged at them. "Just trying to think outside the box." Clearly he felt the others didn't recognize creative thinking when they heard it.

"Anyway," Eddie Fraser continued, "I cross-checked the DMV list with AutoTrack. Numbers went up to four ninety. Obviously we've got to run down that list. Separate the probables and possibles from the impossibles and the unlikelys. We've already started, but with four hundred and ninety names we're going to need some help."

"Well, you should be able to disqualify a lot of them right off the bat," said McCabe. "Bill, can you assign some additional detectives and patrol officers to help Tom and Eddie run down the list?"

Fortier nodded. "No problem. Anything else?"

"Yes," said Tasco. "We're reinterviewing Katie's friends at school. Plus her teammates on the soccer team. We want to see if any of them remember anything they didn't want to tell us when they thought she was still alive. Sometimes kids hold stuff back they think their friends wouldn't want cops to know."

Maggie said, "I'm sorry, but that whole scenario just

doesn't work for me. I don't buy that the kids she was with had anything to do with this. My bet is talking to them won't get us anywhere. So let's start with what we do know. We've got a sixteen-year-old high school girl. No Goody Two-Shoes, but not a bad or a wild kid either. Good athlete. Okay student. Anyway, Wednesday night she's out cruising around the Old Port with a group of friends. She has a fight with her boyfriend and storms off. The others figure she's just blowing off steam and they'll run into her later—"

"Which they never do."

Maggie continued. "So is she heading for home? We don't know. If so, how does she plan to get there? We don't know. She doesn't have a car, and Jack's checked every taxi company in town and come up empty. It's three or four miles to her house. Walkable but still a pretty good hike. Plus she never got there. So what the hell happened to her?"

"Somebody grabs her off the street, shoves her into his car, and off they go," said Tasco.

"Unlikely in the Old Port," said McCabe. "Too many people around. Maybe farther out, or maybe she hitches a ride."

"Only if she knew the guy," said Maggie. "Her mother insists she'd never get in a car with a strange guy, assuming her mother knows what she's talking about."

"Her parents told you they were home from 6:00 P.M. on, so they would've heard her if she ever arrived?" asked Fortier.

"Yeah. It's the same thing they told Tom and Eddie. We have no reason to doubt it."

"Okay," said McCabe, "let's say she knew the guy at least well enough to accept a ride from him. So who does she know who also has the skills to be the freak? Her doctor, maybe?"

"I got the name of their PCP from Katie's mother," said Maggie. "It's a female doc at the family health place on India. Dr. Annabelle Blum. We haven't had a chance to interview her yet."

"Okay," said McCabe, "let's scratch Dr. Blum. At least for now. How about a biology teacher at the high school?"

"Portland High has three biology teachers," said Fraser. "The department head's a gray-haired sixty-one-year-old woman named Angela Kovaleski. Katie was in her class last year. Got a B. Teacher number two is younger but also female—"

Sturgis interrupted. "We seem to be excluding people because they're female. Do we know for sure the killer's not a female?"

"Not for certain," said McCabe, "but sexual sadists are almost always male. Unless we have a compelling reason to believe otherwise, I say we're looking for a guy."

"The third biology teacher is a guy," said Fraser. "Name's Tobin Kenney. We haven't interviewed him yet. He's in his twenties. This is his third year at the school. Came here from Norway—"

"The town or the country?" asked McCabe. Norway, Maine, was about fifty miles north and west of Portland just fifteen miles beyond Poland.

"The town," Fraser replied. "One more thing. He's also the assistant girls' soccer coach."

"Okay," said Maggie. "That means Katie knew him. Probably trusted him."

"She was on the team?" asked Fortier.

"Oh yeah," said Tom Tasco. "Big-time. Best sophomore they had last year. Kenney certainly knew her, and potentially Kenney's got the skills to be the freak."

"Is he on your Lexus list?" asked McCabe.

"Nope," said Fraser, leafing down the list of names. "We don't know what he drives."

"That doesn't exclude him," said Maggie. "No way it excludes him."

Though she spoke in even tones, McCabe sensed Maggie was getting excited. Like a hound who picks up a scent and is just aching to be let loose to follow it. Well, he'd been there a lot of times himself. So far it seemed a slim connection, but maybe the scent would lead somewhere. "Okay," said McCabe. "Maggie and I will track down Mr. Kenney later today."

"Anything else?" asked Fortier.

"Yeah. A couple of things," said McCabe. "First, Maggie got the autopsy report."

Maggie spoke in measured tones. "Terri Mirabito says there was no trace of any anesthetic drug in Katie's body when she was cut open. She was wide-awake. Probably tied down and gagged when the bastard started cutting."

Everyone at the table winced. Nobody said anything. Fortier broke the silence. "You said there were two things. What's number two?"

"I talked to a detective in Orlando, Florida. Looks like Katie wasn't our friend's first victim." McCabe filled them in on his conversation with Aaron Cahill. He told them that, like Katie Dubois and Lucinda Cassidy, Elyse Andersen was young, blond, and athletic. "I'm not a big believer in coincidence. I think if we find Katie Dubois's killer, we find Lucinda—but we don't have a lot of time. Katie was killed roughly a week after she was abducted. So was Andersen. Cassidy was taken Friday. You do the math.

"First, let's cross-check for overlaps between Katie and Cassidy. Where they exercised. Where they bought their clothes. Where they went for pizza. Doctors they visited. People who might have come in contact with both of them. Anything or anyone they might have in common.

"Also, because we don't know how many mutilated bodies might be buried out there, I want to check all missing person reports for young blond athletic females, say between fifteen and thirty, who disappeared between 2002 and now. Jack, you take that. Check our own records first. Then check every other department in New England. See what the FBI can offer through VICAP, and the RCMP."

"Dubois was from Portland," Maggie said. "So's Cassidy. If it is the same guy who did Andersen, maybe he left Florida and moved north. So let's check HR records in hospitals for surgeons, including residents, who've moved here from Florida in the last three or four years. Then maybe broaden it to other docs."

"There are privacy issues," said McCabe. "We may need subpoenas to get access to their personnel files. I already had a run-in with a Dr. Spencer at Cumberland on that issue."

"Shockley can help make that happen," said Fortier. "I'll develop a list of doctors and hospitals and have him find us a judge who'll authorize the subpoenas. Meantime, what do we know about Cassidy?" Fortier was ready to move on.

"We're going full speed ahead," said Bill Bacon. "We have search teams out all over the place. Will and I and two teams from other units have been canvassing the neighborhood and the hospital to see if we can find anybody who might have seen her jogging. Her employer, Beckman and Hawes, is putting up a ten-thousand-dollar reward for any information that helps us find her."

"Dead or alive?" asked Fortier.

"They didn't specify. One other thing. We don't know if she was currently in a relationship. Her ex-husband and her sister say no, but it's always possible she had somebody with her Thursday night or Friday morning. Bill Jacobi's taking her car and apartment apart for signs of a boyfriend or anyone else being present. The baseball cap and her dog's body are up in the state crime lab for DNA analysis. There was blood on the dog's teeth—"

"Which means maybe the freak was bitten," said McCabe.

"We think so. We'll have DNA results on the blood in a couple of days. All we need is a suspect to match it against."

Fortier's pager went off. He looked at it. "Oh, Christ. Shockley's here."

"And he wants to see you this minute?" said McCabe, underlining the words "this minute" in an almost perfect imitation of Shockley's public persona.

"So what else is new?" Fortier stood up and looked around the faces at the table. "I know you're all working your butts off. Keep at it. We're not gonna worry about overtime on these two. Mike, you said you wanted to work both cases. If it is a single perp, that makes sense. Anyway, the GO says that's your call." Fortier collected his notes and left.

12

Once again, Lucy began the long uphill journey back to consciousness. Her brain felt gauzy and uncertain. The headache was back, its throbbing constant, though duller and less insistent than before. She let her mind wander, in a kind of fugue state, through the rooms of her apartment. The sun shone through the oversized south-facing windows, lighting a million dust motes. Fritzy, on his back, feet in the air, wriggled with pleasure in the warm patch where the sun struck the floor. Her laptop waited where she'd left it, open on the couch. She reached for it. There was so much to do. Her hand wouldn't move. Odd, she thought, and tried again. Still it wouldn't move. Only then, with a sudden rush, did she remember where she was. She opened her eyes. The room was dark. Beyond dark. Utterly black. He must have known she was afraid of the dark, must have known she always left a small light burning even when she slept. He must have known.

The panic rose like a living thing, up through her body and into her throat, where it came bursting out in a long scream, uncontrolled and uncontrollable. She thrashed against the restraints, up and down, side to side, yanking and pulling until she could feel her wrists and ankles begin to bleed. None of it helped. No matter how loudly she screamed or how fiercely she struggled, the blackness closed in from every side.

13

When McCabe got back to his desk, the phone was ringing.
"This is McCabe."

"Detective McCabe?" An older woman's voice, harsh
with a smoker's rasp.

"That's right. How can I help you?"

"It's about that girl who was murdered. I may have seen
her."

"May I have your name and address?"

Maggie was at her desk, and he signaled her to listen in
on the call.

"Annie Rafferty. I live at 22 Hackett. That's off Cumberland on the East Side."

"I know the street. Can you tell me what you think you
saw?"

"I know what I saw. I'm getting older now—seventy-four,
seventy-five in November—but my eyes are still good. The
thing is I don't sleep so good anymore. I get these pains in
my legs. When it's bad, I get out of bed and sit and look out
the window. Well, the other night—the night the girl went
missing—I was sitting there wishing the pain'd just go
away. Across the street the front door opens and this girl
who looked like the one they're showing on TV, well,
she's standing in the doorway yelling and screaming at

somebody. Then she takes off, fuming mad. I got a good look, and I tell you it was the Dubois kid."

"Can you remember what she was screaming about?"

"Oh, you know, f-ing this and f-ing that. I'm no prude, and I cursed out more than one jerk in my time, but I wouldn't want to repeat what I heard her screaming. Even to an Irish cop who I'm sure has heard it all before. All the while, she's standing there wearing this tiny little miniskirt, showin' off her cute little ass and swearing like a sailor."

"Do you remember what time it was?"

"About eleven thirty. The clock said eleven fifteen when I got out of bed, and not much time'd passed."

"Who lives in the house, the one across the street?"

"Well, that's what was so surprising. It's this nice young man. Always real polite. Shovels my steps for me when it snows, brings me groceries—"

"Mrs. Rafferty, can you tell me his name?"

"He's a teacher over at the high school."

"His name? Please."

"Yes . . . his name. It's Kenney. Tobin Kenney."

"Well, whaddyaknow!" Maggie mouthed the words both silently and loudly, if such a thing were possible. She smiled and gave McCabe a thumbs-up.

"Mind if we stop over, Mrs. Rafferty?"

"Annie."

"What?"

"Call me Annie."

"Okay, Annie then. Please don't go anywhere or talk to anybody about any of this till we get there."

Hackett was a short street, running just two blocks along the northern edge of Munjoy Hill. Small frame houses built around 1900 for the families of merchants and tradesmen lined both sides. Like much of the Hill, Hackett Street had fallen on hard times in the sixties and seventies as a generation of younger families fled Portland for the city's growing suburbs. Many of the houses were broken up into small apartments. Others simply deteriorated. Now, after decades of decay, gentrification was taking root, and some of the houses were being restored by young urban home-steaders. As McCabe and Maggie pulled up, it was easy to see Annie Rafferty's wasn't one of them. The house had long ago abandoned its middle-class pretensions, and no-body was fixing it up. The dark green asbestos siding, probably put up forty years ago, was deteriorating. The trim was badly in need of paint. Drooping lace curtains, once white, had turned a dusky gray.

Maggie rang the bell. As they waited, they noted that Tobin Kenney's house stood directly across the street and that the car in the driveway was a Subaru. She rang again. Finally Annie Rafferty, wearing a stained polyester house-coat, dark blue and decorated with big pink flowers, an-swered the door. From the way the thin fabric clung to her bony body, McCabe could tell she had nothing on under-neath. While Mrs. Rafferty hadn't bothered to dress for their visit, she'd definitely made up her face. She wore lipstick that was bright red and freshly applied. Pink blusher shone from the hollows of her cheeks. Her thinning hair was colored a shade of red McCabe had never seen before. At least not on a human head. She smelled of cigarette butts.

"Mrs. Rafferty?" asked McCabe.

"You must be Sergeant McCabe," she said. "You aren't Tessie McCabe's boy, are you? From Windham?"

"Sorry. I'm Rosie McCabe's boy. From the Bronx."

Rafferty glanced at Maggie and then back to McCabe. "I thought you said you was comin' alone." She winked at him. "Too bad you didn't."

In spite of himself, McCabe blushed. Then, feeling slightly ridiculous, he introduced Maggie. "This is my partner, De-tective Margaret Savage." Maggie nodded. She didn't look happy. McCabe guessed she was imagining how a jury might react to the flirtatious Mrs. Rafferty on the witness stand. Well, at least she wouldn't be wearing the clinging housecoat. "May we come in?"

"That's why you came, isn't it? But I already told you

everything I know on the phone." She turned and headed back into the living room.

McCabe and Maggie followed her in. The living room, like the woman, smelled of stale smoke. Mrs. Rafferty signaled McCabe and Maggie to sit on a worn green sofa, not unlike one McCabe's parents had purchased from a Sears store off Bruckner Boulevard in the seventies. McCabe wondered if his mother's sofa would look as shabby as this one to a pair of cops entering her house today. He was sure it wouldn't look as dirty.

The room was filled with junk. Piles of old newspapers and magazines lay against the walls. Knickknacks and souvenirs of vacations taken decades earlier covered every surface. McCabe noticed a framed photograph on the wall. Two overweight men were flipping steaks at a backyard barbecue and clowning for the camera. "The one on the left is my husband, Dennis," said Mrs. Rafferty. "He dropped dead of a heart attack just a coupla weeks after that picture was taken. Nineteen eighty-five."

"I'm sorry," said McCabe.

"Don't be," she said. "Dennis was a nasty sonofabitch. He used to beat me silly every chance he got. I like to think God spared me a bunch of black eyes and maybe a few broken bones when he gave Dennis that heart attack. So," she added, "what else you wanna know?"

"I'd like to look out the window where you saw Katie Dubois. If you don't mind."

"No, I don't mind. Not if you don't mind the mess in the bedroom."

The three of them climbed the stairs to a small bedroom at the front of the house. Mrs. Rafferty was right about the mess. The bed was unmade. Clothes were piled on the chair by the window. The old woman collected the clothes and tossed them on the bed. McCabe sat and looked out the window. He had an expansive view of the house and porch across the street. Of course, at five foot two Annie Rafferty would never have seen as much of Kenney's house as McCabe at six foot one. He scrunched down to approximate Mrs. Rafferty's height. Even at that level, he had a direct line of sight to Tobin Kenney's front steps. It would have been easy for her to see the girl's face as she turned, even in the dark. Unless, of course, the girl was silhouetted by light shining behind her from Kenney's house. That was possible. A defense lawyer might try to make something of that. Still, even if Mrs. Rafferty's testimony was bulletproof, it didn't make Kenney a murderer. All the old woman saw was an angry girl leaving Kenney's house alive. It seemed to McCabe that Kenney as a suspect was beginning to feel considerably cooler. Maggie asked Mrs. Rafferty if she'd mind coming down to police headquarters and repeating her story in an official interview. She said she wouldn't. They set up a time. Then they left.

14

After leaving Annie Rafferty's house, the two detectives walked directly across the street. Nobody answered the doorbell, so they wandered around back, where they found Tobin Kenney up a ladder applying varnish to the side of an old wooden sailboat mounted on scaffolding.

Like a lot of young guys losing their hair, Kenney shaved his head in an effort to look cool instead of bald. McCabe figured he was twenty-eight, maybe twenty-nine, lean and muscular with a flat stomach. No hint of a paunch. He wore round wire-rimmed glasses. His jeans were torn at the knees and stained with varnish. His gray T-shirt was adorned with a picture of a football and the words UVM. UNDEFEATED SINCE 1974. McCabe wondered if he was the kind of guy a teenage girl might find sexy.

"Pretty good record," said Maggie, as Kenney stepped down from the ladder. She was gesturing at the T-shirt.

"Oh, that," said Kenney with a smile. "That's a UVM joke—'74's the year Vermont dropped football. I suppose you're cops, aren't you?"

McCabe ignored the question. "That's a beautiful boat you're working on," he said.

"It surely is that," said Kenney. "She's a 1936 Alden sloop. Kind of rare. They don't make boats like this anymore."

"Yours?"

"I wish. There's no way I could afford anything like this. Rich people buy these boats and hire people like me to fix them up. Like I asked before, you guys are cops, right?"

"That's right," said Maggie. "I'm Detective Margaret Savage, Portland PD." She held out her shield and ID. "This is Detective Sergeant Michael McCabe. If you're Tobin Kenney, we'd like to talk to you."

"Yeah, that's me. I guess you want to talk about Katie? Jesus, what a terrible thing that was." He walked away from the scaffolding that held the boat, across the small yard, and up three steps to a wooden deck at the back of the house. Maggie and McCabe followed. "Anybody want a beer? Or an iced tea or something. You probably can't drink alcohol if you're on duty."

"No thanks, we're fine," said McCabe.

Maggie sat at a small round patio table near the kitchen door. McCabe leaned against the railing. Kenney seemed edgy, but that wasn't strange. People talking to cops in a homicide investigation were usually edgy, even when they didn't have anything to hide. Kenney emerged from the kitchen. He was sipping a bottle of Geary's and carrying a bag of potato chips. He slipped into the chair next to Maggie. "So what do you want to know?"

"Tell us about Katie," said McCabe. "Everything you can think of, even if it doesn't seem relevant. We're going to record the conversation."

"Oh yeah? Why's that?" asked Kenney.

"Let's just say we're not real good at taking notes." Maggie put the small digital recorder on the table and turned it on.

"That's okay. I'm not much of a note-taker myself." He focused his attention on Maggie instead of McCabe. Maybe he found her attractive. Or maybe just less threatening.

"What can I tell you about Katie?" He shrugged. "She was a good kid. Smart. Real good player. I guess you know, I'm assistant coach of girls' soccer. I met Katie coaching the freshmen my first year in Portland. For her age, she was about as good a player as I've ever seen. Small but fast. Great moves. If this hadn't happened, she had a good shot at making all-state this year. She was already getting some interest from Division I schools, and she's only a junior. *Was* only a junior," he corrected himself.

"You played at UVM?" asked Maggie.

"Yeah. Three years varsity. Mostly second string. I was okay but no great shakes."

"Was Katie popular with the other players?"

"I think so. She never acted like a big star. Just tried to fit in. Pretty girl. Big smile. Always seemed lighthearted. Except on the field. There she was totally different."

"What do you mean?" asked McCabe.

"She was an aggressive, competitive player who couldn't stand losing. She pushed herself harder than the other players—harder than the coaches—ever did. It was like she was trying to prove something. Y'know, it's hard to believe she could actually be dead. Who the hell could do something like that?"

"Somebody bad," said McCabe. He paused, watching Kenney and letting the silence hang to see if it would provoke a reaction. It didn't. Kenney just sipped his beer, looking from one detective to the other, waiting for the next question. Finally McCabe asked, "Did you ever see anyone hanging around at practice sessions that maybe shouldn't have been there? Guys particularly. Anyone that made you suspicious?"

"You know, when she went missing, I thought about that. Occasionally we get scouts from college teams. Mostly we get to know them, but there were a few this year I didn't recognize."

"Any of them seem particularly interested in Katie? Interested enough to talk to her? Get to know her?" asked Maggie.

"Sure. They all wanted to talk to Katie. Pitch their schools. Like I said, she was our best player by far and still only a junior. It's gonna be a tough year without her."

"Do you usually talk to them?" asked Maggie.

"They're supposed to let us know they're there. Sometimes they don't. Y'know, now that you mention it, one day after practice, the same week she disappeared, I saw Katie talking to some guy I didn't recognize."

"What about him in particular?"

"Just that she seemed real excited. Nodding and smiling a lot. After he left I asked her who he was. She said a scout from a school down south. That surprised me. Our players—even the good ones like Katie—don't usually attract a lot of interest outside New England. She didn't tell me his name."

"Remember which college?"

"Yeah," Kenney said thoughtfully. "I'm trying to remember what she said. University of Southern Florida . . . Western Florida . . . something like that."

Florida again. McCabe asked, "Can you describe the guy?"

"I didn't get a good look at him. Mostly from the rear."

"How about his size?"

"Big. I'd say around six foot two. Built like an athlete. Trim. Broad shoulders."

"Hair?"

"Well, he had hair. Unlike yours truly." Kenney flashed a smile at them. "Dark, I think. He was wearing a cap, so it was hard to tell. Back of the hair was trimmed short and neat. Conservative. They talked for a while, then he got in his car and left."

"What kind of car?"

"Oh, Christ." Kenney paused. It came to him. "An SUV. One of the expensive ones."

"Color?"

"Dark. Green, I think."

"Did you notice the plates?"

"Didn't even glance at 'em."

"What was he wearing?"

Kenney closed his eyes as if trying to relive the moment in his mind. McCabe found it frustrating other people couldn't visualize scenes as easily as he could. "Cowboy boots," he said finally, "black cowboy boots. Not many people in Maine wear 'em. Jeans, I think. A long-sleeve black polo shirt. A baseball cap."

McCabe found it hard to imagine Spencer in cowboy boots, and he didn't have broad shoulders. "Anything else you remember?"

"Just that I told Katie not to talk to any more scouts, especially guys, without letting one of her coaches know. That it wasn't smart."

"How'd she react to that?"

"Practically rolled her eyes. Like any kid, she thought nothing bad could ever happen to her."

"Any word what the school's doing as a result of her death?" asked Maggie.

"Not yet. My guess is the principal will declare the day of the funeral an official day of mourning and let the kids take time off to attend whatever service the family's planning. That's what I'd do."

"When was the last time you saw Katie?"

"At practice. The day she disappeared. Wednesday before last."

The answer seemed honest enough. Without Annie Rafferty as a witness, McCabe might have accepted it as the whole truth. Of course, McCabe knew, Rafferty might have made the whole thing up. A tired old woman, possibly dozing, in front of a bedroom window? Any defense lawyer worth his salt would jump on that and suggest that Rafferty was asleep and dreaming. Even if Rafferty was wide-awake and telling the truth, how were they going to prove the girl she saw on Kenney's front porch was actually Katie? McCabe had to push harder. Get Kenney himself to provide the corroborating evidence. "You teach biology?" he asked.

"Yeah, sophomores and juniors. Never had Katie in class, though." He was on his way into the kitchen.

When he returned with another beer, Maggie said, "I guess you've done a lot of dissecting, being a biology teacher and all?"

Kenney looked at her strangely. "Dissecting? Sure. A zillion frogs. Sometimes fetal pigs. Sometimes things a little bigger. Why?"

McCabe wanted to see what would happen if he put on a little pressure. "Pretty good with a scalpel, are you?" he asked. If Kenney was the killer, the question might rattle him, maybe make him think they were onto him.

"What the hell is this all about?" asked Kenney.

"Maybe you want to tell us, Tobin?" asked McCabe.

"Whoa. Wait a minute. Let's just back up here. Are you telling me I'm a suspect in all this?"

"Suspect? Nobody said anything about suspect," said Maggie. "We're just having a little conversation. Checking on the whereabouts of the people who knew Katie. The people she trusted."

"Am I under arrest or something?"

"Come on, Tobin. Relax," Maggie said softly. "Like I said, this is just an interview, a little chat. That's all."

"So maybe you can tell us what happened that night," McCabe said. It was his turn now.

"What night?" Kenney sounded worried. Defensive.

"Well, the night Katie disappeared, of course."

Kenney's eyes darted back and forth between them. He didn't say anything. McCabe figured he was thinking about lawyering up, and that'd be the end of the interview. If he was really innocent, though, he might keep talking just to prove it. "You got a girlfriend, Tobin?"

"No . . . yeah. Well, not really. There's this woman I see from time to time," said Tobin. "I don't know what that has to do with any of this."

"Were you seeing her that night?"

"The night Katie was killed?"

"No. Not the night she was killed." McCabe leaned in toward Kenney, forcing the younger man to look up at him. "We can talk about *that* night later." He was speaking quietly. Calmly. One friend to another. Aware of the recorder and its little green light, there was no threat in his voice. All the threat was in his eyes, which bore in on Kenney.

"Why don't you just tell us about the night she disappeared? Where you were. What you were doing."

Kenney slid his chair back an inch or two away, avoiding McCabe's gaze, looking out toward the boat in the yard. "Jesus, I don't know." Pause. "Let me think. No. Wait." Pause. "I do remember what I was doing. Yes, I do. I remember the teachers talking about Katie's disappearance the next day at school when she didn't show up. When she didn't show up for practice, that's when I got really worried. I knew she might cut her classes, but Katie would never miss practice. Never. Not unless something was really wrong. The night before," Kenney said, "I went to the movies."

"The movies?" asked Maggie, with just the slightest touch of well-practiced disbelief in her voice.

"Yes. The movies."

"Alone?"

"Yes. Alone—but I can prove I was there. I ran into some people I know. Another teacher at the high school, Ellen Bodine, and her husband. I've probably still got the ticket stub." Kenney seemed relieved by his response. It was as though he'd solved a difficult problem and now things were going to be alright.

"What did you see?" asked McCabe.

"You mean the movie? *Cinderella Man.*" There was no hesitation.

"How'd you like it?" asked Maggie. "Is it as good as they say?" The irrelevance of her question confused Kenney, which, McCabe knew, was Maggie's intention. "Is Russell Crowe as good as they say?" she continued. "And Renee Zellweger?"

"Yeah. It's good," said Kenney. "They're good." His eyes were darting between them.

"What time was the show? What time did it let out?" McCabe asked.

"I don't know. It probably started at seven or seven fif-teen."

"So it let out around nine?"

"Yeah. Around then." A drop of sweat rolled down one

of the lenses on Kenney's glasses. He took them off, pulled up a dry bit of T-shirt, and wiped off the moisture.

"So what did you do then?" asked Maggie.

"I came home. Had something to eat. I picked up a pizza at Torrelli's on India Street. I graded papers for a while."

"All by yourself?"

"Yes, of course, all by myself."

"Then what?" asked McCabe.

"Then I went to bed."

"Alone?"

Kenney looked at McCabe and didn't say anything.

"You went to bed alone?" McCabe asked again.

"Yes, alone."

McCabe decided to take a chance. If Kenney lawyered up, then fuck it. "Y'know, Tobin, I really don't like it when people bullshit me. I . . . really . . . really . . . don't like it."

Kenney looked up. "I'm not bullshitting anyone."

"Y'know what, Tobin? I think you are. Y'know what else? I think I can prove it."

There was fear in Kenney's eyes. "Prove what? You can't prove anything."

"You weren't alone that evening, were you, Tobin? In fact, I've got a witness who says as much. In fact, my witness will swear to it. Maybe you started out grading papers all by yourself, but then somebody stopped by a little later. Didn't she, Tobin? Somebody named Katie Dubois? Isn't that right, Tobin?" McCabe was using Kenney's first name over and over, hitting him with it, like a boxer jabbing lightly to the face. It was a technique he'd learned a long time ago. Sometimes it worked. Sometimes it didn't. "Tobin? Are you listening to me, Tobin?"

Kenney sat still. He was clearly frightened. He didn't say anything for a minute. Finally he asked in a small voice, "What sort of witness?"

"A witness who saw and heard Katie Dubois leaving this house the night she disappeared. Now why don't you just come clean and tell us about it, Tobin."

Kenney sat stone still except for a little nervous fluttering of his eyelashes.

"Maybe Katie was a little upset when she arrived?" McCabe started in again. "Maybe she told you her boyfriend was cheating on her? Maybe you figured she needed a little comforting? Is that what happened, Tobin? Hey, there's nothing wrong with that. You're a nice guy, isn't that right, Tobin? Comforting pretty little sixteen-year-old girls is right up your alley, isn't it? A little comforting? Then maybe a little hugging?" Then McCabe's voice dropped the teasing tone and became hard. Cold. "Who knows? A little hugging might just lead to a little fucking, too. Isn't that right, Tobin? Isn't that what happened? You fucked her and then you killed her?"

In his mind's eye McCabe saw Kenney with his arms around Katie Dubois. Kissing her, his hand running down her back, slipping under her skirt, pulling her pants down—but it wasn't Katie he saw Kenney kissing and fondling. It was Casey, and he had to close his eyes and force the image from his mind.

"That's not true!" Kenney's voice was nearly hysterical. "I didn't fuck her! I didn't kill her! That's not how it happened!"

Maggie asked, softly, "That's not how what happened, Tobin?"

"Oh, I'll bet you're just one hell of a horny dude, aren't you, Tobin?" said McCabe, his voice quiet, his eyes full of threat. "The kind of guy who maybe thinks with his dick instead of his brain? Now why don't you stop the bullshit and tell us what really happened that night."

"Yes. No." Kenney's voice came out a hollow whisper.

"Look at me, Tobin," Maggie said, as gentle as a mother, her face near his. "If you tell us what happened, we can help you. If you don't, then we can't."

"Yes, she came over," Kenney said, "but, no, no, no, I didn't kill her."

"You didn't kill her?"

"No, I didn't kill her. I didn't kill her."

"You didn't kill her?" McCabe was in his face now. "You just fucked her, is that it? Fucked her to comfort her? Fucked her to make her feel better about her boyfriend screwing her over? Is that what happened, Tobin? Hey, Tobin, you know as well as I do, fucking a sixteen-year-old student can land a teacher in a whole pile of shit. Did you panic? Is that what happened, Tobin? You fucked her and then you killed her because you panicked?"

"I didn't fuck her," said Kenney, his voice a soft wail, "and I didn't kill her." He was rocking back and forth, his arms wrapped tightly around his chest.

"Well, why don't you tell us exactly what you did do, Tobin? Because I can promise you, one way or the other, we're gonna find out, and when we do, we're gonna fry your ass."

"I didn't kill her. I didn't kill anyone. I've never killed anyone. She came over and she gave me a blow job and then she left and that's all there was to it! That's all! She gave me a blow job!"

McCabe was about to speak again, but Maggie caught his eye. She gave him a look that said, "Back off." McCabe nodded and moved to the end of the deck. He leaned back against the wooden railing and waited. Kenney was still rocking forward and back in his chair, still holding himself.

Maggie spoke softly. "Tobin? Why don't you just tell us straight out what did happen that night."

Kenney glanced over at McCabe. "Don't worry about him," Maggie said. "Just look at me. Look at my eyes. He won't ask you any more questions. Just tell me what happened between you and Katie so we can finish this up and we can leave you alone and you can get some rest."

The assistant girls' soccer coach sat there for what seemed like a long time, saying nothing. Then he began to speak. His voice was flat. Toneless. Without affect.

"After the movies, I picked up a pizza from Torrelli's, like I said. I got home about ten. I got a beer from the fridge and ate a couple of slices. I had a bunch of papers to grade. I usually grade papers on the sofa. I put the graded ones on the coffee table, the ungraded ones next to me on the couch. That's how I organize them.

"A few minutes after I started grading, the doorbell rang, and it was Katie. She was all sweetness and 'Gee, can I come in and talk for a while?' But she looked a little weird, like she'd been crying. Like she was stressed out. So I let her in. I asked her what the matter was. She sees I'm drinking a beer and says, 'Can I have a beer, too?' I tell her she's too young, that we could both get in trouble. Then she takes my hand and starts stroking it and says, 'Oh, come on, Mr. Kenney.' She actually called me Mr. Kenney. 'Please. I'm not going to tell anybody.'

"Right there, I should have put her in the car and driven her straight home, but I didn't. I was feeling lonely, and one part of me wanted her to stick around. So, like a jerk, I got her a beer. She takes a swig, and we sit down on the couch where I was grading the papers. She's wearing this tiny little miniskirt and it's riding up over her crotch. She asks me if I think she's attractive. I say yeah, she's very attractive. Then she asks me if I think she's sexy. I don't answer—but I don't get up, either. Then she says, 'If I were your girlfriend, would you go screwing around with other girls?' I say, 'No, I wouldn't.' Then I say, 'Get up, I've got to take you home.'

"But she doesn't get up. She lies down and puts her head in my lap. She takes my hand and she puts it on her breast, and I'm thinking to myself, 'Holy shit, what's this all about?'

"She asks me again if I think she's sexy. By this time, I've got an incredible hard-on, and I know she can feel it 'cause she's got her head in my lap. God help me, I really do want to fuck her, but I know I can't. So I ask her what happened with Ronnie Sobel. He's her boyfriend. She says Ronnie's an asshole and she doesn't give a shit about Ronnie and don't I think she's sexy? I say sure she's sexy, but I'm a teacher and she's a student and we shouldn't be even thinking stuff like this, but then she rolls onto her front and I'm looking down and she's unzipping my fly.

"Look, Margaret, or whatever your name is, I know I sound like a jerk. Your buddy over there thinks I'm worse than a jerk. Maybe he's right. I'm twenty-six years old and she's sixteen. Even worse, I'm her coach—her teacher—and there she is, opening my zipper. I've got this fucking hard-on that's ready to explode. Then she's got her mouth on it and boom, like in ten seconds flat, it's all over. I'm coming all over her face and all over my pants and the couch and whether you believe it or not, Margaret, I feel like the biggest asshole in the world. You know something else? I still do. But I did not fuck her and I did not kill her." Kenney just sat there for a while, looking nowhere, saying nothing.

"What happened next?" asked Maggie.

Kenney looked at her. "She left."

"Just like that?"

"No. After I came, I'm thinking to myself, holy shit, what have I done? I got up and got her a towel to wipe her face. Then I told her to get in the car. I'm going to drive her home. She says she wants to spend the night. I tell her she can't. She gets angry, and we argue about it for a while. Then she slams out the door and she just stands there on the front steps, screaming at me through the screen that I'm an asshole. She just gave me a great fucking blow job, she says, and I won't even let her spend the fucking night. She calls me a bunch of names. Tells me to go fuck myself.

"Then she was gone." Kenney looked up. "Just like that she was gone. Ran off into the night, and that's the truth of the matter. I didn't kill her and I didn't fuck her. Maybe that sounds like Bill Clinton. 'I didn't have sex with that woman'—but it's the truth."

"Why didn't you come in and tell us this when she was reported missing?" asked Maggie.

"I picked up the phone about a hundred times, but I couldn't do it. I knew it would cost me my job, and I guess I convinced myself that she'd just run off and would come home after a while. Pretty stupid, but who knew she was going to go out and get herself killed? If I'd just pushed her in the car and driven her home, none of this would ever have happened."

Maggie believed him. In spite of his anger, so did McCabe.

"Is this going to get me arrested? Statutory rape?"

"You screwed up, big-time, Tobin," said McCabe. "In Maine, any sexual act between a teacher and a student under eighteen is a crime. Doesn't matter who started it. Maybe, if you're real cooperative, real contrite, they'll let you off with a suspended sentence. Maybe not. Either way, you better go find yourself another career. Another life. There's no way you're working with kids anymore. Not now. Not ever."

Later, in the car, before driving away, McCabe sat there thinking about what Kenney'd told them. "Why do you think he talked?" he asked Maggie. "It would have been so easy for him just to stonewall the whole thing."

"Guilt."

"You think?"

"Sure. He's just a kid himself. Probably not a bad kid. He was already feeling guilty about the blow job. Then when Katie turned up dead, it got a whole lot worse. You heard him. He was blaming himself. He had to tell somebody. So he told us. Which leaves us with the question, what do we do now?"

"I don't know. Try to find some dude from Florida with cowboy boots and a fancy SUV. If he really is from Florida. I'll see if Cahill will do a doctor/Lexus cross-check down there. We should also get some people talking to the girls on the soccer team again. See if any of them remembers him. Maybe he talked to more than one kid. Or maybe they saw him talking to Katie."

15

Purely on impulse, McCabe picked up the Bird and drove to
the West Side. There was still plenty of light, and on a Sunday evening crossing from one end of the city to the other
took less than ten minutes. He drove west on Spring Street,
passing Mercy, Portland's smaller hospital, on his right.
Covering the same distance in New York could take an hour.

He slowed as he passed 24 Trinity Street and then rounded
the corner. McCabe parked where the Bird wouldn't be seen
and walked back. Philip and Harriet Spencer's home was a
private place, a sizable property surrounded by an ancient
wrought-iron fence, free from rust and in perfect repair. A
glance at the house and grounds told him that if Spencer
was somehow involved in Katie's Dubois's murder, money
wasn't a motive. The house itself was a century-old redbrick
Georgian with a slate roof and black shutters. Graceful and
classically proportioned, the work of a well-schooled, if unadventurous, architect. The solid oak front door was polished a lustrous brown. It looked easily capable of deterring
the efforts of any unwelcome visitors, at least any not
equipped with a battering ram.

McCabe pushed the bell. Chimes pealed inside. He
hadn't planned the visit and found himself hoping Spencer wasn't home. He wanted to talk to the doctor's wife.

Failing that, he hoped, at least, to get a sense of how the man lived. As McCabe waited, his eyes took in the lush grounds.

Every corner of the neat, nearly secret garden was meticulously planned and planted. Even late on a cool mid-September afternoon, the perennial beds were a mass of summer color. Clumps of Montauk daisies vied for attention with asters, hollyhocks, foxgloves, and purple coneflowers. The names of plants and flowers recalled from another Sunday, one spent with Casey, roaming the grounds of the New York Botanical Garden in the Bronx. Even the Latin names would stay etched forever in his memory. McCabe rang again. Still no one answered.

He moved to the left of the front door. There, two tall windows had been left open, he supposed to admit the fresh breezes of this cool early fall day. Open windows suggested someone was home. McCabe squatted down and peered into the room. It was furnished as an informal library or sitting room. Inside, near the window, not far from his nose, the *New York Times* Sunday magazine lay abandoned on a small cherry side table, the crossword puzzle half completed, in pen. Built-in bookcases covered the two far walls. Squinting, McCabe could make out some of the titles. To the left, recent fiction, memoirs, gardening books, their bright jackets lending a splash of color to the otherwise brown room. The shelves on the right presented a more somber aspect, books with plain, academic gray or green covers. McCabe couldn't make out the titles but assumed they were medical texts. Philip's books. Philip. The superstar surgeon. The man who climbed mountains and transplanted hearts. To test himself. To see how far he could push the limits. *When I do remove a heart, sometimes I hold it in my hand for a minute or two knowing it will give new life to a dying patient. An extraordinary feeling.*

Still no one answered the door. McCabe gave it up and walked around to the right of the house. A black Porsche Boxster waited on the white and pink gravel driveway. A tiny trunk. No one could carry a corpse, not even a diminutive corpse like Katie, in that. Beyond the Porsche, behind and to the right of the main house, stood a sizable unattached building. Probably once a carriage house. Today, he guessed, a garage. It had double-wide sliding barn doors, each with a row of glass windows.

He walked back. He looked around, saw no one, decided to have a peek. The windows were a little higher than he imagined and a little grimier. He stood on tiptoes and blocked the reflective light by cupping his hands. The interior was surprisingly dark. There was room for three cars. Only one was there. A Lexus SUV. A 2002? A 2003? He couldn't tell. Couldn't be sure about the color either.

"Are you looking for something?"

McCabe turned from the window. A tall, lanky blonde was looking at him, a pair of lopping shears at the ready. She seemed prepared to use them. The *Press Herald* would love it. PORTLAND POLICE DETECTIVE LOPPED TO DEATH BY IRATE HOUSEWIFE. Even in her faded gardening jeans and baggy sweatshirt, she was the kind of woman whose stance and attitude exuded old money. "Are you Harriet Spencer?" he asked.

"I am. Who are you, and why are you peering in my garage?"

McCabe held up his shield and ID. "Detective Sergeant Michael McCabe. We spoke briefly on the phone yesterday, and actually I was looking for you."

"In the garage?"

"Well, I tried the front door and no one answered. So I thought you might be in there."

"I don't normally hang out in the garage, Detective."

"I'm sure you don't, Mrs. Spencer. I was also prepared to look around the grounds."

"Well, now that you've found me, what can I do for you?"

"I was wondering if I could ask you a few questions."

"If it's about that murder, I'm not sure how I can help you. Did my husband return your call?"

"He did. He and I spoke yesterday afternoon. Can we go

into the house? It shouldn't take more than a couple of minutes."

Harriet Spencer thought about that for a moment, then led McCabe through a rear door that led directly from the back garden into the kitchen. She directed him to a red oak farmhouse table. "Would you like some coffee or a cold drink?" she asked.

"Only if you're having some," he said.

"I am." She took out a black bag of coffee beans and began preparing a pot. "I only noticed you by the garage because I was coming in for coffee anyway."

He looked around the large kitchen while she measured out the coffee and water. If he expected something out of *Architectural Digest,* he would have been sorely disappointed. No Sub-Zero refrigerators or Viking ranges here. The appliances and the décor were plain and functional, the cabinets old-fashioned wood, painted white with glass fronts allowing one to see inside. There was a butler's pantry off to one side. McCabe guessed the kitchen had last been updated sometime after the end of the Second World War. The Spencers, it seemed, weren't the kind of people who made a competitive sport of cuisine. Perhaps only the newly rich played those games. Mrs. Spencer handed McCabe a mug of coffee and a spoon. She put a small jug of milk and sugar on the table and sat down. "I'm a private person, Detective, so I'm warning you in advance, I may decide not to answer your questions."

"That's your privilege, Mrs. Spencer, but any information you can offer could be helpful on this case. How many cars do you and Dr. Spencer own?"

Her expression betrayed a sense that this was not the kind of question she expected. "Three. Why do you want to know?"

"The Porsche in the driveway?"

"Yes. That's Philip's toy."

"The Lexus in the garage?"

"That's mine."

"How about the third one?"

"Philip has a BMW he drives when he's not fooling around in the Porsche. Once again, why do you want to know?"

"Does Dr. Spencer ever borrow your Lexus?"

"Occasionally, when he needs to haul something or other."

Like the remains of dead teenage girls or kidnapped joggers, McCabe thought. "He takes the BMW to work?"

"Only when he has an appointment away from the hospital. Or if it's raining. Otherwise he walks."

"Do you recall if he used your Lexus last Thursday or Friday?"

"I don't know. He may have. No. Actually I lent it to a friend. I was away. From Wednesday morning to Friday. Visiting my mother in Blue Hill. She's quite ill, and I try to get up there as often as possible. I took Philip's BMW. I prefer it to the SUV on long trips."

McCabe's mind went back to the photograph on Spencer's wall, and finally he knew what bothered him about it. "Do you know a man named Lucas Kane?" he asked.

She looked at him oddly. "How on earth do you know that name?"

"Your husband mentioned it."

"Lucas Kane was someone I knew a long time ago. When I was growing up. His parents had a summer place not far from ours."

"In Blue Hill?"

"Near there."

"Did you know him well?"

"No. Mostly our parents were friends. I lost track of Lucas after we both started prep school. Then, eight years later, he turned up in Philip's class at medical school. I introduced them, and they became good friends. They did their surgical residencies together in New York."

"Kane was a surgeon?"

Harriet Spencer examined McCabe's face before answering. "No. Lucas never practiced. He lost his license."

"Why?"

"You'll have to find that out on your own. But you're a detective, aren't you? It shouldn't be hard."

"Did you consider Kane a friend?"

"A friend?" McCabe saw the hint of a smile flicker across her face. "No, I never would have called Lucas that."

"When was the last time you saw him?"

"I haven't seen Lucas Kane in more than fifteen years."

"Where is he now?"

"Dead. Murdered. In Florida. I believe that's where he lived."

Florida again. "Did you go to the funeral?"

"No. Philip went. I had no interest."

"Can you tell me why?"

"I don't think it's any of your business."

"What friend?"

"I beg your pardon?"

"You said you lent the Lexus to a friend. Last week. What friend?"

"Alright, either you tell me why you're asking these questions or this conversation stops here and now, and you can just pick yourself up and leave my house."

"Mrs. Spencer, have you ever heard the name Harry Lime?"

"No."

McCabe paused, visualizing the Denali picture. Philip Spencer and Lucas Kane. What was it? Admiration? Affection? No. More than that. In the end, the question asked itself. "Mrs. Spencer, were your husband and Lucas Kane lovers?"

"That's it, Detective. It's time for you to go. I don't like being questioned like a common criminal. If you have any further questions, you can ask them through my attorney."

"Were they? Lovers, I mean?"

"Get out." Harriet Spencer stood, walked to the kitchen door, and opened it. "Get out now," she said, "and don't come back."

McCabe went to the door and left. Descending the two steps, he looked across to the garage and thought about sneaking in. He wanted a closer look at the Lexus. He knew it was a stupid idea. He didn't have a warrant, and Harriet

Spencer certainly wouldn't give him permission to conduct a search. If he was seen, anything he found would be compromised as evidence.

Could he get a warrant? Maybe. The Lexus matched the vehicle in Starbucks's surveillance video. Philip Spencer was the right height and had the necessary skills to "harvest" Katie Dubois's heart. Harriet Spencer was away from Wednesday until Friday. The Lexus was here. She lent it to a friend, she said. Also, Philip Spencer's whereabouts during the critical hours were unknown.

Where were you around midnight last Thursday night?

At home. In bed.

Your wife was with you?

Yes. We usually share a bed.

A demonstrable lie. A heart surgeon, young enough and tall enough, alone with a Lexus. Was that enough? Probably not. Tasco and Fraser had barely started checking on the list of other surgeons with Lexuses. Let alone those whose wives had Lexuses. There might be dozens young enough and tall enough who had no alibi during the critical hours. Even so, he wanted the crime scene techs to examine the Spencers' vehicle for trace evidence of Katie. Or Lucinda. Or both. Plus he wanted to examine the house as well. He just had a feeling about this man.

16

Harriet Spencer, Hattie to her friends, stood by her kitchen door. Through the double-glazed panes, she watched Mc-Cabe descend the back steps, pause to look over at the garage, then turn and walk down the gravel drive toward the front of the house and out of sight. Hattie hurried through a darkened hallway to the living room, the room Philip liked to call the drawing room, where she stood by a window and watched the detective leave through the front gate. The bright afternoon had faded to twilight, the sun, deep in the west, lighting the street in a red-orange glow, casting long shadows, as the detective turned right and walked away. She wondered why there was no car parked nearby. Perhaps he'd walked. For a minute or two, even after he was out of sight, Hattie stayed at the window, looking out, standing as still as she could, hardly breathing, as if movement, any movement at all, might upset the proper order of things. An order that once upset would be gone forever.

Finally, in the growing darkness, still dressed in her gardening clothes, she walked to the walnut drinks cupboard that stood against the far wall. She found a lead crystal water goblet and a bottle of Tanqueray. She filled the glass nearly to the top and left the room.

Sipping warm gin, Hattie climbed the broad staircase

that rose in a graceful curve from the center hall toward the second floor landing and the bedrooms beyond. She walked to the end of a long hall, entered the large master bedroom, and, without turning on the lights, sat down in a striped silk tub chair by the window. She noticed the bed wasn't made. The rumpled sheets kicked to the bottom of the queen-sized four-poster, the thin summer blanket fallen to the floor. Still another sign of disarray? Was it worth it? Worth the lies? The secrecy? Yes, she thought, it was. Hattie sipped her gin and looked out the window. A fly buzzed on the ceiling. A car passed by on the street below. The room grew dark.

The idea that her feelings for Philip could ever have been described as love seemed distant and alien. She remembered meeting him, senior year at Brown, in a study room in the Rockefeller Library, the Rock. They sat across from each other three nights in a row before he asked if she wanted to go and have a coffee. Such a serious young man. Good-looking, intensely involved in his studies, always analyzing, always taking things apart. Very smart. More than a little arrogant, but always quite charming.

Scenes from their marriage, scratched and jumpy, flickered through Hattie's mind. The big wedding on the lawn of the cottage in Blue Hill. Friends from Brown and Dana Hall in bright summer dresses. Philip's face in extreme close-up, smiling and attentive. A kiss. A toast. A flying bouquet. Roaring off in that incredible car, Philip drunk and driving like a madman around the small and twisty country lanes. The yellow Lotus, borrowed from Uncle Bish, her mother's rich and careless younger brother.

Fast-forward, two years later, to their tiny one-bedroom apartment in Back Bay, furnished in equal measure from the Salvation Army store in Southie and late-night expeditions along the streets of Beacon Hill, collecting throwaways from the curb.

Now the scene fades into another. The lighting is softer. Hattie sees the two of them standing naked by the bed. She's laughing at Philip, who, for once, is having fun, clowning as

Count Dracula come to suck her blood. She fends him off, turning away to finish folding back the yellow bedspread, her mother's gift, to keep it from getting stained. Philip grabs her. They fall as one, as much from laughter as from lust, onto the sheets, where they make love. Once, and then again. It *was* love Philip was making then, wasn't it? Not simply ejaculate?

Fast-forward three years to the graduation party. The same tiny apartment crammed with Philip's fellow medical students, drinking wine and beer. Smoking a little grass. Celebrating the end of four grueling years of study, the awarding of their MDs. Lucas was there. Late in the party, when they were all high, Lucas pushed her into a corner and kissed her, his tongue probing her mouth. She pulled away. She was married. It didn't matter to Lucas. He always thought he was entitled to whatever he wanted. Even his friend's wives. Even his best friend's wife. Handsome, talented Lucas. So brilliant, everyone said. Destined for great things, everyone said. Even then he was an abuser. Of drugs. Of people. It wasn't just the occasional joint they all indulged in. No, Lucas was much more adventurous than that, much more inventive. Always pushing the edge. With Lucas there was always a sense of something about to happen. Something dangerous. That's what had drawn Philip to him. That's what had drawn Hattie to him as well. Lucas coming into their lives had been both a beginning and an end. It changed both of them.

After Tufts, Lucas and Philip, along with DeWitt Holland and Matthew Wilcox, applied and were accepted into surgical residencies at Bellevue Hospital in New York. Four friends, the Asclepius Society, together for another four years. She and Philip lucked out and got a subsidized apartment for married residents in one of NYU's high-rise buildings just south of Washington Square. Lucas lived way over on the East Side on one of those streets named for a letter instead of a number. Avenue A or Avenue B. She couldn't remember which. The area had already begun its slow transformation from a slum to an artsy enclave.

Those were lonely years. Philip spent most of his time at the hospital, working to exhaustion, sleeping a few hours, then going back and working some more. When he wasn't working, he was often with Lucas. The two of them sitting together, smoking dope, in Lucas's grubby little fourth-floor walk-up. She wondered how many patients they'd cut into, the brilliant young surgeons, both high as kites when they shouldn't have been operating at all. She wondered how many they might have killed.

From her chair, Hattie could see a pair of cardinals on a branch of the large maple just outside their bedroom, barely lit in the last glow of the setting sun. The male preening his fiery plumage. The dull, brownish female, quietly pecking for insects by his side. She'd never known them to be out so late. Finally they flew away.

She remembered seeing Lucas in New York before he left. The winter of 1989. More than fifteen years ago. The city was raw and cold in its covering of sooty slush. The restaurant where they were meeting was a new place—one of dozens of sushi bars springing up all over the East Village. Hattie arrived first, coming directly from her office, and she managed to snag a table for four. The place was crowded, and because she felt embarrassed fending off the waiters as she waited for the others, she drank two large gin and tonics. Finally Philip and Lucas came tumbling in, noisy and laughing. Lucas brought a new friend. A boy with a Spanish name, Carlos or Eduardo or something like that. He was a dancer in the corps de ballet with one of the big-name dance companies—the Joffrey, she thought. He had beautiful dark brown skin exactly the color of the leather sofa in her father's den. She finished her second gin, and they ordered sake. The sake was warm and felt good going down, so they ordered more. Lucas was showing off, ordering and eating esoteric bits of sushi not found on the menu. Revolting-looking stuff, Hattie thought. Leeches and slugs, for all she knew—and there was Philip pretending to love each slimy piece, though she was sure he hated it even more than she did.

Afterward, they all went back to Lucas's place. She remembered climbing the four steep, narrow flights of stairs. The halls smelled of garbage and rotting food. At the top they practically fell into the studio, a tiny single room about twelve feet square with cracked plaster walls and a dirty brown commercial carpet. It was dominated by a huge king-sized bed. Hattie wondered how they'd ever gotten the damned thing up the stairs. Two small filthy windows looked out on an airshaft. The only furniture besides the bed was a chair covered in lime green vinyl, a small bedside table, and two lamps. Most of the light came from a dim overhead.

"Behold!" Lucas drunkenly exclaimed, flopping down on the mattress and pulling the giggling boy, Carlos or Eduardo, down on top of him. "Behold the playing fields of Eton! Upon which the Battle Sexualis is frequently fought and usually won."

Lucas started kissing the boy, but he pulled away. "I want a drink," the boy said, slurring the words.

"Not until you take your clothes off," said Lucas.

Hattie leaned against the door, watching, while Carlos or Eduardo undressed. He had a beautiful dancer's body, long and muscular. He posed for Lucas. "Now do I get my drink?" he said teasingly. He was the first black man she'd ever seen naked. His penis was very dark and uncircumcised. She realized she'd expected it to be huge, but it wasn't, only a little bigger than Philip's. Even so, his body excited her in a way Philip's never had.

Lucas got up and opened a pair of louvered doors, revealing a tiny kitchen a few feet from the bed. Really more of a closet than a kitchen. The small sink was piled high with dirty dishes. He pulled out a bottle of vodka and a glass from a cupboard and handed them to the boy, who poured some and lay down on the bed and began drinking. Then Lucas began taking off his own clothes.

Hattie thought she should leave. Instead, she stood, her back to the door, watching Lucas until he, too, was naked. She glanced over at Philip. He was sitting in the vinyl easy chair, watching her watching Lucas. She felt both nervous and exposed. Lucas opened a drawer in the bedside table and took a joint from a small plastic bag. He lit it, took a long drag, got up, and walked to where Hattie was standing and handed it to her. She took a drag, held the smoke in her lungs, and handed it back. Then Lucas took her hand and put it on his cock. She began stroking it and it got hard. She exhaled the smoke. "I didn't know you still liked it with girls, Lucas," she said.

"With you, Hattie, I think I could like it very much." She felt a tremor rather like electricity. "Besides, Philip and I share everything."

Lucas was staring at her with those extraordinary eyes. He was tall, like Philip, but with a more intense face and a harder body. "Including me?"

"Especially you."

"Have you ever fucked Philip?" she asked.

"Of course," he said. "Many times—and will again. You and I have that in common."

She looked again at Philip. He was enjoying this. Getting off on it. The bastard. "Are you going to take your clothes off, too?" she asked him.

"No. I'm going to watch you take yours off."

The boy on the bed pouted. "Oh, Lucas, you are such a bore. Don't you have anything more interesting than pot? And why are you fooling with that girl? Don't you love me?"

"Oh, yes," Lucas said, "of course I love you, and I have something much better than pot for you. I got these specially from the hospital."

"What are they?"

"Something special."

"Well, let me have them."

He handed the boy some white pills from a gunmetal pillbox on the bedside table. Eduardo or Carlos swallowed a couple, washing them down with vodka.

"Philip?" Hattie said. "Don't you think you should take me home?" She was still leaning against the door, still wearing her red goose-down ski parka, making no move to leave.

"Oh, I don't think so, Hattie."

"But I'm your wife."

"Yes, I know—and a good upright New England girl you are. But, don't you see? That's what makes all of this so interesting. I get to share you with my dearest friend. I get to see you in a whole new light."

A new light? Yes. Why not a new light? Then, as much from the pent-up anger she felt toward Philip as from the attraction she'd always felt for Lucas, Hattie pulled down the zipper on her jacket.

Both Philip and Lucas watched Hattie as she stripped. Eduardo or Carlos was merely bored. She didn't try to make it sexy. She simply took off her clothes and folded them neatly, laying them on the floor in the corner. When she, too, was naked, she walked to the side of the bed, dropped to her knees, and took Lucas's cock in her mouth. She licked it until it was hard again. She could hear Philip breathing heavily behind her.

She looked up at Lucas. "Do you have any condoms?" she asked. "There's no way this happens without a condom. Not with your history."

Silently he pulled a condom from the same gunmetal box that held the pills. "Lucas's magic box," she smiled.

She slipped the condom over him, and then he pulled her up onto the bed and put his head between her legs. His tongue flicked delicately in and out, like a snake's. Her breathing quickened. "Lucas's magic tongue," she moaned softly.

After that she took him deep inside. Even as she approached orgasm, she remained aware of Philip's eyes, watching, probing, never looking away. His hips seemed to be rocking as if he, too, were on the receiving end of Lucas's thrusts, he, too, rising and falling, then rising again toward orgasm.

After she came and Lucas came, Hattie lay there for a few minutes, thinking about what she had done and why she had done it. Finally she got up and walked over to where Philip sat, still watching. "Philip, I want you to know," she said in the same even voice she'd used to announce her decision to accept the presidency of the Junior League, "that that was, by far, the best fuck I ever had." Then Hattie put on her clothes and left. Alone.

She was long gone when Eduardo or Carlos or whatever his name was went into convulsions and had to be rushed to the ER. Lucas, high as a kite, somehow managed to carry the boy, still naked and thrashing, down four flights of stairs and into a taxi for the trip to Bellevue. To his credit, she supposed, he never said anything about her or Philip being in the apartment. Never said anything about what they had done. The boy hadn't died, but it had been close. In the weeks that followed, there was a formal investigation. Hattie didn't know the details, but she did know that, while criminal charges were never filed, Lucas lost his license to practice medicine. After that, he disappeared from their lives. Philip never spoke of him again or said anything about that night. Hattie, too, let the matter rest. She thought she'd never see Lucas again and was content with that. Then four years ago Philip told her Lucas was dead.

Hattie heard the front door open and close. Philip. The downstairs lights flicked on. She looked at her glass. The gin was gone. She wanted another, but she didn't want to see Philip and knew she couldn't avoid him if she went downstairs. Instead, she put the glass on the mantel of the bedroom fireplace, stripped off her gardening clothes, threw them in a pile in the corner of her closet, and locked herself in the bathroom. She turned on the shower. She looked at her naked body in the full-length mirror. Still slim. Still attractive. Or would be, were it not for the scar tissue where her left breast used to be. The other one seemed so small, so lonely, so orphaned by itself. The cancer had been cut out four years ago, a full mastectomy at Philip's urging. She'd acquiesced in spite of her own doctor's less radical advice. "Much the safest course," Philip had assured her. Philip the self-appointed oracle. Philip the concerned husband. Philip the slicer and dicer. "Much the best way to make sure we get it all."

Afterward, angry with herself and with Philip, she decided against reconstructive surgery. After all, only Philip ever saw her naked, and it was important to her that he never again find pleasure looking at her body. That he never forget what he had done.

Hattie climbed into the tub and let the water from the shower, hot as she could stand it, course over her body. She scrubbed herself over and over again with the loofah until her skin felt raw. Then she dried and brushed her hair and dressed in clean jeans and a new sweatshirt.

She went downstairs. Philip sat in the den, reading. Ignoring him, Hattie crossed to the living room and poured herself another two inches of gin. Then she went to the kitchen for ice cubes and added them to the glass. "I'll have a Scotch," she heard Philip call out. "The single malt. No ice." She poured the drink and brought it to him. She sat in the small leather club chair across from him sipping her gin. Philip continued reading. The loudest sound in the room was the ticking of the ancient burled walnut grandfather clock Hattie had inherited from her own grandfather. As she sipped, she felt the familiar easing of tension, the comforting signal the gin was finally kicking in, beginning to do its job. She picked up the half-completed *Times* crossword puzzle, then put it down again.

"That detective was here today," she said. "McCabe?"

"Really? What did he want?"

"I was in the garden and found him peering into the garage. Then he came in and asked me some questions."

"What sorts of questions?"

"Mostly about who drove what car. He asked me about Lucas."

"What did you tell him?"

"That we knew Lucas years ago. That he was dead. That he'd been murdered."

Philip was thoughtful for a moment. "Don't worry," he said. "It's alright."

17

How long had she been there in the dark? Hours? Days? Weeks? Longer? Lucy had no idea, no way to measure the passage of time. Once or twice she tried by counting. "One-one-thousand. Two-one-thousand. Three-one-thousand." Each time, she'd get up to five- or six-hundred-one-thousand and forget why she was counting.

Her throat was parched. Her stomach hurt from hunger. She remembered reading that a human being could last for weeks without food but only three or four days without water. She was desperately thirsty. Her tongue felt like a big dry furry thing stuck in the middle of her mouth, although she didn't think she could be totally dehydrated. Even now she could still make tears. More than once she'd felt the wetness sliding out from under her lids and rolling down her cheeks. She tried catching the drops with her tongue to moisten her mouth, but it never worked.

18

At this hour on a Monday morning, Middle Street was crowded with worker bees on the way to their various hives. McCabe angled past a trio of pin-striped attorneys spread three abreast across the sidewalk. Lawyers and stockbrokers. About the only people left in Maine still wearing suits to the office. A pretty blonde in tight jeans, carrying a briefcase, smiled at him. A fat brown Labrador retriever waddled by her side, apparently on his way to the office, too.

McCabe entered 109 and took the stairs two at a time. The place was already buzzing. Tom Tasco flashed him a greeting. McCabe stopped. "How are you guys doing with the doctors?" he asked.

"Three teams working full-time. We've talked to sixty-two surgeons in the last twenty-four hours. More on tap for today."

"Anything interesting?"

"No suspects yet, but if you ever need a quadruple by-pass, let me know. I've got a lot of connections."

Maggie was on the phone, feet, as usual, propped on her desk. An oversized note from Shockley's admin greeted McCabe at his own desk. *The Chief wants to see you. ASAP!!! Deirdre.* That's all he needed now, more crap from the GO. He held the note in front of Maggie, who was still on the phone, with a "Do you know what this is about?" gesture. She shrugged and shook her head no.

He headed for Shockley's corner office. Might as well get whatever it was out of the way. The door was open. Deirdre told him to go on in. He found Shockley deep in bullshit mode, collar undone, tie pulled down. He was playing to an appreciative audience. Portland mayor Gary Short, who stood nearly six foot five, and Will Hayley, a longtime fixture on the city council, were both seated on his large leather couch. In a city where mayors are selected from the council on an annual basis, Short had no more clout than Hayley, and on issues of public safety Shockley was more powerful than either.

"Sit down, Mike." Shockley signaled to the chair in front of his desk. "You know Gary and Will?"

McCabe continued standing and nodded at the two men. "We've met. What's on your mind, Chief? I've got a busy morning." Short and Hayley exchanged glances and decided they'd rather not be present for what McCabe supposed was intended as a dressing-down. They gathered their things.

"You guys have a lot to talk·about," said Hayley. "We'll leave you to it." Mayor Short closed the door as the two men left.

"I got an unwelcome call this morning," said Shockley, "from Dr. Phil Spencer. He's not happy. Apparently his wife discovered you snooping around their property yesterday. Then you questioned her, according to Spencer, like a common criminal, quote unquote."

"I'm not sure 'like a common criminal' applies, but yes, I was there, and yes, I did talk to her. I also talked to Spencer the day before, at the hospital. What of it?"

"McCabe, Phil Spencer is one of the most prominent men in this community, not to mention one of the top transplant surgeons in New England. He knows a lot of people, and he's got a lot of clout that can impact this department. I would appreciate it if you didn't go crashing around in his affairs. I'd have thought you had more sense than that."

McCabe stood silently for a minute, weighing his response. "Am I or am I not the lead on this case?"

"I beg your pardon?"

"Am I or am I not the lead on this case? If I am the lead, there are a couple of things we'd better get straight before the investigation goes any further."

Shockley eyed McCabe cautiously, a cobra eyeing a mongoose. Nobody talked to him this way. "Really? And what might those 'couple of things' be?"

"For one, as long as I'm in charge of this investigation, I'll go wherever the facts—and my instincts—lead. If they happen to lead to, quote, one of the most prominent men in this community, unquote, so be it. For another, it seems you had an earlier conversation with Dr. Spencer at the Pemaquid Club Friday night. You talked about my private life and revealed confidential information about the investigation, to a man who, by the nature of what he does for a living, might become a suspect. Then, to top it off, you shoot your mouth off to the press about the removal of Katie's heart. We agreed we'd keep that quiet. It's a detail your adoring public didn't need to know."

Tom Shockley stood, placed both hands on his desk, and leaned into McCabe, his pale face turning bright scarlet. "Number one, Phil Spencer is no suspect. I have total confidence that anything I say to Philip Spencer is and will remain confidential. Number two, I also have total confidence he has nothing to do with this murder. Number three, and I believe I've said this before, the public has a right to information about one of the most horrific murders this city has ever seen."

"As for Spencer, maybe he has nothing to do with the case. We don't know. Either way, as lead investigator it's my job to decide how to conduct this investigation. Not yours. As for the public's right to know, all you've accomplished by releasing unknown details is to make it harder for our people to screen out the nut jobs. You know? The whackos who call us every day with bullshit information or confessions. By the same token, you made it harder for us to identify someone as the murderer because he knows stuff he shouldn't. Chief, you may have just doubled our workload. On behalf of my detectives and myself, thanks a bunch."

Shockley was trying to control his rage. "One more word, McCabe. Just one more and you are fucking toast. You got that?"

"You want my shield, Tom? Here. Take it. Go solve the murder yourself." McCabe took out his badge wallet and tossed it on Shockley's desk, wondering if Shockley would call him on it. Wondering if it even was a bluff. Then he jumped in with both feet. "Just remember, Chief, it will make for interesting reading when you try to explain to the press why your star detective suddenly got the ax. The same detective you just bragged about hiring. I'm sure the reporters will find it even more interesting how the chief of police fucked up the investigation."

McCabe paused as if considering the merits of going public. The confrontation was something that had been bubbling beneath the surface for a while. It felt good letting it out. "Y'know, Tom, I've never held a press conference of my own, but I think the public has a right to know. Don't you? I can see the headlines now. 'Ex–New York Cop Quits Job in Maine. Accuses Boss of Shielding Suspect, Hampering Investigation.' Interesting headline, but probably no big deal unless you happen to be running for governor. Of course, you're not thinking about running for governor, are you, Tom?"

"Alright, McCabe, you made your point." He tossed McCabe's badge back to him. "Now get out."

McCabe turned toward the door. For the moment he had Shockley in a corner. Once the case was resolved, all bets were off.

"Good-bye, Tom," he said softly as he left. "Have a nice day."

"Go fuck yourself," said Shockley.

19

Maggie was waiting for him at his desk. "Let's hit the road, partner." She took his arm and steered him toward the elevator. They took a PPD Crown Vic and pulled out into Portland's excuse for rush hour traffic.

"Where are we going?" asked McCabe.

"Well, last night I went to Katie Dubois's wake, y'know, to pay my respects to Frank and Joanne. I figured one of us ought to be there. I also wanted to find out if Katie ever said anything to either of them about our friend in cowboy boots. There were about a million people there. Neighbors. Relatives. At least a hundred kids from the high school. A bunch of teachers."

"Open casket?"

"No, thank God. Seeing her all decked out by some funeral director would have been more than I could bear. Anyway, I couldn't really talk, what with everybody churning around, but I did manage to ask Joanne if Katie ever said anything about being scouted by a soccer coach from Florida."

"And?"

"And she kind of looked at me funny and said yeah, Katie had said something about Florida. Joanne didn't want to talk about it at the wake, what with all the people around. Said we should stop by the house this morning."

"Which is where we're going now?"

"Excellent deductive reasoning, McCabe. You'll make a fine detective someday. By the way, the funeral's this afternoon. Two o'clock. We should go."

"I plan to. Speaking of Mr. Cowboy Boots, any progress finding out if any of Katie's teammates got a look at him?"

"So far no one remembers seeing anyone like the guy Kenney described. I still have a couple of kids to check."

"Anything about the car?"

"Just what Kenney told us. That it was probably dark green."

McCabe nodded. Then he opened his cell and called the PPD Communications Center, which had almost instant access to all motor vehicle information. He asked the woman who answered to check what color Harriet Spencer's SUV was. He hung on while she looked it up.

"It's listed as green."

"Dark or light?"

"Just says green."

McCabe thanked her.

Frank and Joanne Ceglia's house on Dexter Street was a small yellow Cape Cod. It appeared neat and well maintained, though the grass was a week or two overdue for mowing. Maggie parked the Crown Vic in front and walked to the door. It swung open before they could ring the bell. Joanne Ceglia, already dressed for the funeral in a black linen dress and short black jacket, stood with a man wearing a clerical collar. Her eyes looked red. "Oh, Maggie. You're here."

She produced a thin smile. "Maggie, this is Father Wozniak. He'll be assisting at the mass for Katie today. He's just leaving. Father, this is Detective Savage."

The two cops, the priest, and the woman stood for a moment in uncertain formation on the front step, not sure whether to move in or out, forward or back. Finally Mc-Cabe extended his hand. "Mrs. Ceglia, I'm Michael Mc-Cabe. Maggie's partner."

"Her partner in crime?" asked the priest, a practiced smile on his lips.

Everyone laughed uncertainly, and the priest moved off. "I'll see you at the cathedral, Joanne."

She raised her hand in a half wave and invited McCabe and Maggie in. "I'm sorry I couldn't speak to you last night. There were so many people there. Can I get you some coffee or a Coke or anything?"

"No, thank you." They looked around. The room was filled with plates of food, all covered with Saran Wrap. "For afterward," Joanne said. "A lot of the people will be coming back. It seems freaky. Throwing a party because your kid's dead. Food, drink, people. Still, it's what everyone expects."

Maggie started the questioning. This was her witness. "Joanne, you told me Katie said something about a soccer scout from Florida? He's supposed to have talked to her the week she disappeared."

"Yeah. Right. She was so excited. Talking about a free ride, a full athletic scholarship, getting out of Maine, going to school in the sunshine. All that stuff. Yesterday, when I was going through her things, I found this." She handed Maggie a business card. Holding it by its edges, Maggie looked at it, turned it over, and handed it to McCabe.

UNIVERSITY OF WEST FLORIDA, the card read. HARRY LIME, ASSISTANT ATHLETIC DIRECTOR. It featured a logo with a guy in a Trojan helmet. McCabe took out his cell and punched in the numbers. "You have reached an unassigned number at Florida Power and Light. For assistance press zero." He pressed zero.

"Florida Power and Light. How may I direct your call?"

"Harry Lime, please. L-I-M-E."

A pause. "I'm sorry. I'm not showing anyone with that name."

"Thank you."

He hit 411 and got a number for the University of West Florida's Athletic Department. Same result.

"Look at the back of the card," said Maggie.

McCabe, holding the card by its edges, turned it over. The words were written in pencil, stacked in a vertical column:

Lime
Katie Lime
Katherine Dubois Lime
Kate Lime

The writing was round and girlish. Little flowers intertwined the words.

"Was there anything else? A phone number? E-mails? Anything."

"Your people took her computer first thing Saturday morning, so I don't know," said Joanne. "Phone numbers she kept in her cell. She had the phone with her when she disappeared, so I can't check."

"What was her number?" he asked Joanne.

"It's 207-555-6754."

McCabe punched it in. He heard ringing, then "Hi, you've reached Katie. Leave a message." He hung up.

"Do you think this scout is the person who killed Katie?" Joanne Ceglia asked.

"We don't know. We think he might be, Joanne," said Maggie.

"Will you catch him?"

"Yes," said McCabe, "we will catch him."

"Do you mind if we search her room?" asked Maggie.

"You're welcome to, but your people already took it apart a couple of times and didn't find anything. I don't know why they didn't find that card. Maybe it just didn't mean anything to them."

Sloppy police work, thought McCabe. The evidence techs should've picked up on the card.

The two detectives headed up to her room and searched it again. Thirty minutes later they were willing to admit there was nothing else to find at Dexter Street and headed back to 109.

"Tell me about her cell phone," McCabe said to Maggie.

"Tasco checked with Sprint. Ran down all the calls to and from the cell starting two weeks before she disappeared right up till Friday."

"Nothing?"

"Nothing meaningful. Prior calls mostly to friends. A couple to local businesses. Saved messages were mostly from her girlfriends. A couple from Ronnie Sobel. One was pretty sexual. No completed calls at all after she disappeared. Some new messages from Frank and Joanne and some from her friends."

They drove through Deering Oaks Park with its massive two-hundred-year-old trees and headed south on State Street toward Spring. McCabe told her about last evening's visit to chez Spencer.

"Spencer's head of cardiac surgery at Cumberland?"

"Yeah, and a buddy of Shockley's. He called the GO this morning to complain about my going to the house, questioning his wife. Shockley told me to lay off. That's what his come-see-me-ASAP note was all about."

Maggie glanced over at him. "I hope you didn't lose it with him."

"Basically, I told him to go fuck himself."

"Gee, just when I was beginning to like you."

"The good news is Crimes Against People just might get its first female sergeant. Although nothing'll happen until this case is resolved. If Spencer's the bad guy, I'll be a hero. If he's not the bad guy, but I get whoever is, I'll still be a hero. Either way, unfireable. On the other hand, if we don't get him, or somebody else gets him, I get fired. Maybe I'll deserve it."

"Think you've got enough for a warrant?"

"Doubtful. Unless we can find ourselves a nice flexible judge somewhere. One who doesn't belong to the Pemaquid Club. I'll check in with Burt Lund. Maybe he can help."

20

"Ever hear of Dr. Philip Spencer?" McCabe asked as he watched Burt Lund ease his large round bottom onto one of JavaHut's small round bentwood chairs. A prosecutor in the attorney general's office, Lund had a reputation as a bulldog. A chubby bulldog. Once he got his teeth into you, they said, he hung on no matter what.

"The heart surgeon? Sure, I've heard of him. Never met him, though." Lund looked around. They had the coffee-house pretty much to themselves. "Kind of a big cheese, isn't he?"

"Seems to be. He's buddies with Shockley. Hangs out at the Pemaquid Club. There's a picture of him with Bush senior and Olympia Snowe on his office wall."

"He's your suspect?"

"Maybe a long shot, but yeah."

"What makes you think Spencer's cutting up little girls?"

McCabe told Lund about the Lexus turning up in the surveillance video, again at Katie Dubois's soccer practice, and finally in Spencer's garage.

"That's it? His wife owns a Lexus? Even assuming the accuracy of your video manipulation and the coach's re-collection, I hope you have more than that."

"I do. Terri's autopsy indicated Dubois's heart was most

likely cut out by a cardiac surgeon. Spencer's one of the best. He has no alibi for the critical hours, and he matches the description we got from Kenney—"

"From the rear—and from a distance."

"He's also the same height as the guy in the video."

"It's pretty thin, McCabe. There must be a million doctors who own Lexus SUVs."

"Four hundred and ninety. We're checking them out."

"Spencer have any history of sexual kinkiness?"

"None that I know of, but the guy gives off strange vibes. Not exactly sexual, not exactly not. When I was in his office, he described to me how it felt to hold a human heart in your hand. It was strange, like he was getting off on it. Also, I have a feeling he may swing both ways."

"Is that relevant?"

"Probably not."

Each of them sipped at his cardboard cup of coffee. Finally McCabe spoke. "I want a warrant."

"What are you searching for? Even if Spencer's your guy, what do you think he's holding on to?"

"Souvenirs. Serial killers often keep them. An earring was missing from Dubois's left ear. Assuming there were previous victims, and a chat I had with a cop in Florida convinces me there are, Spencer might just be hiding a little collection."

Lund said nothing. Just nodded thoughtfully.

McCabe continued, "I want to go over the Lexus for any trace of the victim. Fingerprints or anything that can give us DNA. Hair, blood, anything else in the back cargo area."

"He'd have cleaned it out."

"Tough to hide blood traces from Luminol. No matter how hard you clean."

"Fair enough. Of course, you might not need a warrant to search the car."

"I will if it's locked in Spencer's garage."

"True."

"You think I've got enough for probable cause?"

"The connection to Spencer's pretty thin. I wish you had more. Although that's not all that's bothering me."

"What else, then?"

"Letting Spencer know he's a person of interest. If the guy was Joe Schmoe, no problem, but he's not. You know as well as I do the minute you show up at Spencer's house with a warrant, he's gonna howl bloody murder. Start calling all of his influential pals. Get himself lawyered up, and it won't be with some court-appointed nobody. You go after somebody with Spencer's resources, you'd better have hard evidence tied down six ways to Sunday or the guy walks."

"Like OJ?"

"For example, and compared to the evidence they had against him, you don't have beans. Why not wait till you have a little more?"

"We can't afford to wait."

"Oh yeah? Why's that?"

"Lucinda Cassidy."

"What about her?"

"I told you I talked to a cop in Florida? A woman named Elyse Andersen was murdered in Orlando in 2002. Whoever killed Andersen used the same alias, Harry Lime, and the same MO as the guy who cut up Katie Dubois."

"Could be a copycat."

"I don't think so. The Orlando cops never released the alias."

"Okay."

"In both cases the killer kept the victim alive for roughly one week before taking out his scalpel and saw. Lucinda Cassidy disappeared early Friday morning. If it is the same guy and if he follows the same pattern—"

"She's scheduled for surgery in four days."

"Give or take."

Lund looked thoughtful. "Unfortunately, not a whole lot of what you've got connects to Spencer."

"At the moment he's all I've got."

"Okay. Write it up. We'll take it to Judge Washburn.

Paula doesn't hang out at the Pemaquid Club, and she's not one to be impressed by Spencer's social standing. I think she'll sign it."

Washburn was an older district court judge, nearing retirement. McCabe had never met her, but her reputation was "tough but fair" and "doesn't suffer fools lightly." He hoped she was the right choice.

Back at Middle Street, Starbucks already had Katie's hard drive wired into his computer. "I'm making some progress," he announced. Maggie and McCabe peered over his shoulder at the screen. "No problem getting in. She always used the same password, SOCCERGIRL07. I checked all her e-mails. Received, sent, and saved at Gmail and Road-Runner. Nothing stood out, but you may want to review them." He handed McCabe a CD.

"In her address books," asked Maggie, "did you find the name Harry Lime?"

"Lime? L-I-M-E?" He reviewed the list. "No. Nothing like that. However, there were a couple of bookmarked Web sites you may want to know about."

"Like what?"

"First, she had a personal profile page on a social networking site called OurPlace. She used it to communicate with her electronic network of friends. A lot of the kids do."

McCabe was vaguely familiar with the site. He wondered if Casey was signed up. Accessing Katie's contacts on the site could widen the circle of possible suspects. Or maybe narrow it.

"Is the site open to predators?" he asked.

"I think so," said Starbucks. "They claim that they offer a lot of privacy protection, but it's not all that tight. We're getting the list of her contacts from the company. She was also registered with a dating service called Heartthrob. com. Do you know it? Anybody looking for pretty young girls could find pictures, a profile, and easy ways to make contact. I know many people who've used it. Including myself. I've met several very nice young ladies."

McCabe imagined the young Somali trolling for dates on the Internet. Odd. He'd never thought of Starbucks as having any social life at all. "How would the wrong person gain access?"

"Easy," said Maggie. "Just register using a phony name and e-mail address and you can contact any target who looks appealing. Exchange e-mails and photos, make dates. Whatever."

"Does anyone keep a record of contacts made?"

"The site is supposed to," said Starbucks. "Again we're trying to get a list, but they, too, have privacy issues, so we'll probably have to wait until that's sorted out."

McCabe went back to his desk hoping to come up with enough probable cause to justify a warrant to search Harriet Spencer's Lexus and the house at 24 Trinity Street. Lund called just as he was finishing up. "Unfortunately," he said, "Judge Washburn's out of town until late tomorrow afternoon."

"Shit. That shoots twenty-four hours. How about trying somebody else?"

"I thought about that, but I think Washburn gives us the best shot of actually getting the warrant. I say we wait."

McCabe wasn't happy with the idea of waiting, but he reluctantly agreed.

"In the meantime, do you have an affidavit you're prepared to swear to?" asked Lund.

"Ready to go."

"Stop by my office and let me eyeball it, see if it needs any changes."

Before going to Lund's, McCabe called Aaron Cahill.

"How you doin,' McCabe?" The deep voice of the Orlando cop boomed out of the phone. It was almost comforting. "Solved your heart case yet?"

"Looks like we're chasing the same whacko, Aaron. Harry Lime's business card turned up in our victim's dresser drawer."

"Well, do tell. Does the card say what Harry does for a living? Aside from cutting up pretty girls, I mean?"

"Assistant athletic director, University of West Florida."

"I assume the card's a phony?"

"Yeah. Nobody named Lime works at the university. The number printed on the card is an unassigned extension at Florida Power and Light."

"Hmm. School's up in Pensacola. Not far from where my mama lives. Fax me a copy of the card. I'll nose around. See what I can find out. Anything else to report?"

McCabe filled Cahill in on the conversations with Tobin Kenney and Joanne Ceglia. "Not much to go on," he added.

"At least you've got a partial ID."

"From the rear."

"More'n we ever got. Anything else?"

"Yeah. Lime was driving an SUV, probably dark green. Same kind of vehicle we caught on video near where the body was dumped. We've got a doctor in the area, a heart surgeon, who owns a similar vehicle. I'm trying to get a warrant to search it. That's it so far."

"Sounds like you're making progress."

"Let's hope so. You busy otherwise?"

"Who me? Hell no." Cahill's voice slipped into sarcasm. "We've just been whiling away the days waiting for the next hurricane to come knock us into next week. McCabe, I'll tell you, it's been a hell of a summer down here, and they're telling us there's more to come."

"Yeah, I've been reading about it."

"You get those case files I sent your way?"

"They're right here on my desk. Haven't had a chance to go through them yet. I'll do that at home tonight. Let's talk in a couple of days."

"Okay, I've gotta run. Keep me posted." Cahill hung up.

21

Monday. 1:30 P.M.

Had Katie Dubois died in any of the ordinary ways teenagers die, from illness or an accident, from an overdose of alcohol or drugs, her funeral would have passed largely unnoticed. As it was, it ranked as one of the major media events of the year in Maine, and the city's press corps and public personages turned out en masse.

Detectives Margaret Savage and Michael McCabe arrived early at the Cathedral of the Immaculate Conception, home of the Diocese of Portland, a massive Gothic Revival redbrick church with a soaring two-hundred-foot spire that was crowned with a golden cross.

As agreed, Maggie positioned herself outside the main door, trying to camouflage herself behind the cluster of reporters and news photographers. She carried an SLR digital camera Starbucks had given her that was fancy enough to look professional. Her job was to shoot head shots of everyone entering or leaving the church. The camera's endless buttons, dials, and levers baffled her when Starbucks first handed it over. He set it on full automatic and told her just to point and click. So far she was doing okay.

McCabe went inside. He'd been in the cathedral a couple of times before, for Christmas concerts with Casey and last year with Kyra as well. Each time the church's soaring, luminous white-and-gold interior briefly seduced McCabe into a fantasy of returning to the religion he'd abandoned twenty years before, something he knew would never happen. He stood alone in a quiet corner, watching the faces of the mourners as they filed in. He felt self-conscious in his only suit, a dark gray pinstripe he once thought pretty dapper. He hadn't worn it since leaving New York and only managed to get the trousers buttoned by sucking in his gut.

The organ was playing something sonorous and sad. People filled the pews, pressing themselves into every corner of the large church. The misnamed Mayor Short seated himself near the front, directly behind Katie's family. The city council came in a group, all in gray or blue suits like McCabe's. A sprinkling of state legislators and local celebrities arrived. Chief Shockley showed up in full dress uniform, Bill Fortier trotting along by his side. McCabe was surprised to see Terri Mirabito. She didn't see him. He'd never seen her at a funeral before.

Teachers and tight clusters of teenagers, many openly weeping, were everywhere. McCabe recognized the boyfriend, Ronnie Sobel, from a photo in the murder book. Tobin Kenney came alone and sat alone. A young woman seated with some students, another teacher, McCabe supposed, beckoned Kenney to join her, pointing to an empty seat next to her. He shook his head and stayed where he was. She shrugged and turned away.

McCabe examined the faces as people entered and sat down, registering those he recognized, studying those he didn't, filing their images away in the hard drive he carried in his head. He wondered if the murderer was among them. There was no way of knowing.

The Most Reverend Leo F. Conroy, DD, ThD, STL, Bishop of Maine, presided over the requiem mass. He greeted Katie's coffin at the door of the cathedral. McCabe was sure the elegant mahogany box had cost the Ceglias more than they could afford. People always pay too much when they bury their child. The bishop sprinkled the coffin with holy water and intoned the words of the *De profundis*.

Then the pallbearers, six of Katie's classmates, carried her coffin and placed it down just outside the sanctuary, feet facing the altar. It was at that moment that McCabe saw the woman's face. She was standing against a wall on the opposite side, her face crossed diagonally by a deep shadow. He watched her stand motionless until he was sure. Yes. It was the same woman he'd followed down Exchange Street and lost.

She sensed his gaze and turned so that she was looking right at him. He nodded, almost imperceptibly, in her direction. She acknowledged the gesture. He glanced around and saw no one else watching him. He moved toward her. The congregation was standing, singing a hymn. She watched him come and didn't move away. The hymn ended, and a voice from the altar echoed through the otherwise silent cathedral. *"For if we believe that Jesus died and rose again, even so them also which sleep in Jesus will God bring with him."*

McCabe stood next to the woman. "Who are you?"

"I can't speak to you here." She spoke with an accent. French, he thought.

"Then where?"

"I'll be in touch. Please don't follow me."

"How do I know you'll call?"

"You don't. You'll have to trust me."

"What's your name?" he asked, but she was already leaving and didn't hear his question. He started after her, then stopped. He'd wait for her call.

McCabe continued scanning faces in the church. But even if he'd known where to look, he wouldn't have seen the tall, dark-haired man looking down at him, eyes peering through a small opening high above the altar, one hand unconsciously scraping the edge of a scalpel along the back of the other, the razor-sharp blade whisking away a dozen dark hairs.

"Let us pray."

22

Every time McCabe turned around, Florida kept popping up. Elyse Andersen. Murdered in Florida by Harry Lime. The University of West Florida soccer scout. Again Harry Lime. Then Lucas Kane, Spencer's medical school friend and maybe lover, also murdered in Florida. Murdered by whom? Harry Lime? Philip Spencer?

Mrs. Spencer, were your husband and Lucas Kane lovers?

Get out.

McCabe booted up his computer and entered the name "Lucas Kane" and the words "murder" and "Florida" in the Google search box. There were thousands of hits. Number one was a headline from the *Miami Herald,* ESTRANGED SON OF ACCLAIMED MAESTRO SLAIN IN SOUTH BEACH CONDO. Turned out Lucas Kane's father was the classical pianist Maurice Kane. At the time of the murder, father and son had apparently not seen or spoken to each other in years.

The murder rated extensive coverage in the *Miami Herald,* most of it written by a crime reporter named Melody Bollinger. McCabe read it all. In the late nineties, Kane was a fixture in South Beach. The article didn't say anything about Kane being a doctor. Or anything else legitimate. He supported himself, apparently well, supplying drugs, mostly coke and meth, and warm young bodies, both male and female, to visiting high rollers from New York and L.A. He lived in an oceanfront apartment, drove a BMW 740, and was a regular on the South Beach club circuit. He frequently mingled with the gay glitterati at the mansions of the rich and famous, including, according to Bollinger, Gianni Versace's.

However, Kane must have pissed somebody off. In March of 2001, somebody stuck a 12-gauge up under his chin and turned his jaw and face into hamburger. His body was found naked and tied to an overturned chair in his apartment. Nobody admitted hearing the blast. Four or five hours after the shooting, Kane's live-in lover, a body builder and hanger-on named Duane Pollard, discovered the body and called the police.

Visual ID of the face was impossible, but the corpse was the right size—six two, 205 pounds—and fingerprint matches were found all over the apartment and the Beemer. Identification was officially confirmed through DNA analysis. No other evidence was found at the scene. Boyfriend Pollard had an airtight alibi. Miami Beach PD looked elsewhere and eventually figured the murder was drug-related since Kane was a known dealer. A detective named Stan Allard theorized the local drug lords killed Kane to rid themselves of a semipro competitor who was becoming annoying. McCabe got the feeling the investigators were just as happy Kane was dead. They let the case go cold after a couple of weeks. The elderly father, Maurice Kane, reportedly suffering from congestive heart failure, refused public comment on his son's death.

McCabe called the Miami Beach PD and asked for Detective Stan Allard.

"I'm sorry, there is no Detective Stan Allard here."

"Allard? A-L-L-A-R-D?"

"I'm sorry, sir, I don't show that name."

"Would you connect me with someone in homicide?"

A male voice answered. "Detective Sessions."

"Sessions? Hi, this is Detective Sergeant Michael McCabe, Portland, Maine, PD."

"What can I do for you?"

"I'm looking for a Detective Stan Allard who worked homicide in Miami Beach a few years back. Is he still with the department?"

"Who is this again?"

"Name's McCabe. Mike McCabe. I'm a detective with the Portland, Maine, PD."

"What do you want with Allard?"

"I just want to talk to him."

"Well, you're going to have a hard time doing that."

"Yeah? Why's that?"

"Stan Allard hasn't done a whole lot of talking to anybody the last four years."

"Are you telling me Allard's dead?"

"They were pretty sure that was the case when they buried him."

Maybe Sessions thought that was funny. "Look, I'm working on a murder that might have a connection with a case Allard handled."

"What case would that be?"

"The murder of a man named Lucas Kane. Do you know who Allard's partner was at the time?"

There was a pause at Sessions's end of the line. McCabe thought this might be like pulling teeth. Finally Sessions spoke. "Yeah, that would've been me. We worked the Kane murder together." Another pause. "How's Kane connected with your case?"

McCabe instinctively disliked Sessions. He decided to keep it vague. "An old buddy of Kane's may be involved in a murder up here."

"Involved how?"

"We're not sure yet."

They danced around for a while. Nobody wanted to be the first to offer substantive information. Sessions blinked first. "Okay, what do you want to know about Kane?"

"I read the press accounts of Kane's murder. Sounds like you guys felt it was a gang hit."

"That was the default option. We never got any decent leads. Nobody saw anything. Nobody heard anything. Nobody knew anything. All we had was a body tied to a chair with its face and head blown half off. Weren't even any teeth left in good enough shape for a dental records match."

"How'd you know it was Kane?"

"Easy enough. Size, weight, and hair were the same. Prints on the body matched prints we found all over the apartment. More prints in his car. Also, Kane's live-in lover officially ID'd him. Said it was Kane's body. Hair, moles, and scars in all the right places. Even made some jokes about the guy's pecker. 'I never forget a penis,' he said."

"So you're sure it was Kane's body you ID'd?"

"Yeah. In the end we proved it with a DNA match. Plus there was no more Lucas Kane swanning around the clubs and the beach. We're sure."

"What do you know about Kane's background?"

"Not much. His father was a famous musician. They didn't have much to do with each other. Kane wandered down here from New York in the late eighties about the time the deco craze and the gay scene were really getting going in South Beach."

"How'd he support himself? Did he have any money?"

"Not as far as we know, but back then South Beach was easy pickings for a good-looking guy like Kane. He lived off sex for a while. Then he branched out. Ended up as a high-end pimp and a dealer."

"You get an FBI match on the prints you found in the apartment?"

"Not on Kane's. Apparently he was never previously fingerprinted. Never arrested for anything."

"That's surprising."

"It surprised me. I figured with his habits Kane would have been busted at least once or twice, but no, not even by us."

"Any other prints in the room?"

"A bunch of partials and smears. Mostly the boyfriend."

"Duane Pollard?"

"How do you know about him?"

"Just reading the papers. Tell me about Pollard."

"He was Kane's bodyguard and muscle as well as his lover. Ex-marine. Basically a gorilla. Liked to beat people up."

"A gay gorilla?"

"Yeah."

"Unusual."

"It happens."

"Any chance he was the shooter? A lovers' quarrel?"

"None. At least six people put Pollard in a South Beach club called the Groove that night. Said he was there the whole time Kane might have been offed. At least two of them said they had sex with him."

"Was there a funeral?"

"Yeah. A small one, hosted by Pollard and a few of Kane's fuck-buddies from the Beach. Kane's father showed up to bid him farewell. So did a few of his old friends."

"Sounds like a fun time. Did the name Harry Lime ever come up during your investigation?"

"Lime? Like the fruit? No, never heard of him."

"So what about Allard? What did he die of?"

"He died of suicide." McCabe's gut tightened. Sessions went on. "It happened a couple of months later, after the Kane case went cold. We were working on some other stuff."

"What happened?"

"He stuck his service weapon in his mouth and pulled the trigger. In a sleazebag motel down on the beach."

"No connection to the Kane case?"

"I don't think Stan's death had anything to do with Lucas Kane. Let's just leave it at that. He was my friend as well as my partner, and I don't feel like chatting about stuff that's none of your business. You want to know more, you submit an official departmental request."

McCabe thought about pushing Sessions a little harder

to talk about Stan Allard's death, but he couldn't see how it would help him find Katie Dubois's killer or Lucinda Cassidy, so he let it go and hung up. He looked again at the byline on the *Herald* stories on his computer. Melody Bollinger. He filed it away for future reference.

23

Even in the blackness of the room, Lucy could feel his presence. She lay perfectly still, holding her breath. She knew he was there, but where? And why? She listened as hard as she could but heard nothing.

Suddenly, unexpectedly, two hands touched her face. Her heart jumped. Her muscles tightened. She stifled a cry as she felt the hands slide slowly and smoothly down her neck, then over her body, exploring, probing. Still she was afraid to move, afraid to speak. One at a time she felt him loosen and release the restraints that held her hands. He took her wrists, rotated and massaged each in turn. Then his hands moved down her legs. He released the ankle restraints, then moved her feet as he had her hands.

He pulled off her gown and washed her all over with a warm, moist cloth that smelled like lavender. She could feel the warmth of his body, the movement of air from his breath. "I think, Lucy," he said, his voice a whisper, "it's time for you and I to get to know each other a little better."

She stiffened and froze, pressing her legs tightly together, balling her fists, waiting for the inevitable.

24

The note was in the mailbox when McCabe got home
around eight. He didn't notice it at first, hidden among
the advertising circulars and bills piled up from deliveries
he hadn't bothered to collect. It was in a plain white envelope with the words DETECTIVE MCCABE, 134 EASTERN
PROM penciled in block letters across the front, as if written by a child's hand. No stamp. No postmark. No return
address. He decided to wait until he was upstairs before
opening it. A blast of music from Casey's bedroom assaulted his ears as he entered the apartment.

"Hello. I love you," he shouted from the doorway, "and
turn that damn thing down."

He heard no response, either verbally from his daughter
or in a reduction of decibels from her room. He crossed to
the kitchen, dumped the junk mail in the recycling bin,
took a bottle of Geary's from the icebox, opened it, and
took a long swig. He was in a foul mood, pissed at Sandy,
pissed at Shockley, pissed at the world. At least the cold
fizz of the beer felt good going down.

McCabe went down the hall and leaned against the
frame of Casey's open door. She was sprawled, tummy
down, diagonally across her bed, feet resting on her pillow,
head hanging over the edge, reading what appeared to be a

science text open on the floor below. He couldn't figure out how she could actually see the words on the page from that position, but it didn't seem to be a problem. She mostly got A's.

"Hi, honey, I'm home," he called from the door, shouting to be heard over the music. Casey looked up and then, without acknowledging his presence, looked back down at her book. McCabe went to the stereo and hit the power button. Silence flooded the room. Casey looked up again. "Isn't that why I bought you the iPod?" he said. "So I wouldn't be subjected to that noise?"

"It's not noise. It's Propaganda."

"What?"

"Propaganda. That's who's singing. They're very hot."

"I can tell. The iPod. Please."

Wordlessly she rolled off the end of the bed, walked to her desk, got the iPod, inserted the earbuds, and resumed her position on the bed. McCabe retreated to the living room.

He tossed the bills on top of the small desk in the corner, where they joined an unopened stack. He sat in the big chair, feet on the glass coffee table. More bills than money. Always. How much longer could he afford being a cop? In a few years there'd be college to pay for on top of everything else he couldn't afford. He could sell the condo. Move to a smaller place away from the water. Move backward. Move down. Maybe Sandy was right dumping him for a rich guy. Maybe the rich guy would pay for college. The idea depressed him.

Maybe he *should* quit the department once the Dubois case was resolved. Shockley might fire him anyway for his big mouth once there was no longer a political price to pay. A guy he knew at NYU who was now CEO of a hot biotech in Boston once talked to him about a corporate security job. The dollars mentioned were a lot more than he was making now. Even so, he wasn't sure it was worth it. Maybe he could become a PI. Spade & Archer? Savage & McCabe? He could do a passable Bogey imitation, but there were damned few Maltese Falcon cases out there. Mostly he'd spend nights sneaking around hot-sheets motels, getting the goods on philandering husbands and wives. Nope. Not a PI.

Fuck it. Snap out of it. Suck it up and deal. He was still a cop. It was a calling McCabe believed in. Go out on the streets and get the bad guys, as many as you could. Then put them away for as long as you could. Simple and honorable. He liked it that way. It was why he dropped out of film school, why he gave up his dream of someday being a director for the simpler dream of being a cop.

He pressed the icy bottle against his forehead, hoping to preempt the headache that was forming. He closed his eyes. Images of New York came tumbling back. Images of his brother Tommy. The big brother. The surrogate father. The hero figure with the feet of clay. Tommy the Narc. Tommy the cop on the take. Images of the drug dealer named TwoTimes. "Some may fuck with me once, but there's none what fucks with me two times."

TwoTimes who shot Tommy dead. They caught the little fucker, but he walked. Wouldn't even cop a plea. Walked right out of court on that bullshit alibi and right back to pushing his shit. "I got an alibi, Your Honor. I was fuckin' my fiancée when the cop got popped," said TwoTimes. "Yeah, she can tell you. Her mama was right there, and she can tell you, too."

"Yeah, Your Honor," said the fiancée, "that's the truth. He was fuckin' me the whole time, so he couldna shot the man. I swear it."

"Yeah, Your Honor," agreed the mama. "TwoTimes was fuckin' my little girl. He was humpin' her ass like hell wouldn't have it. So he couldna shot that cop. No way. No, sir. No way at all."

All of it bullshit, but the cop-killer walked anyway. Never would've happened in the old days. That's what McCabe's father, a retired and highly decorated captain, would've said had he been alive at the time. Never would've gone to trial. A perp shot to death resisting arrest. No questions asked. No answers needed. Simple solution for a simple problem: simple—and honorable. Now Dad was dead and so was Tommy, and the simple solutions weren't so simple anymore.

McCabe snapped out of his reverie. Casey was walking through the living room on her way to the kitchen. "You're not supposed to wear your gun in the house," she said, barely looking at him. "It's a bad influence on an impressionable child."

"You're right," he said. He got up, went to his bedroom, and put the .45 in the locked box in his closet where he kept the shotgun. He felt naked without it.

He heard the fridge door open and close. Then Casey's face appeared in the doorway of his room, a can of Coke in her hand. "I'm not going to see her. I told her that, but she said she was coming anyway."

"Did she call again?"

"Yes. Right after I got home from soccer."

"Casey, you may have to see her. We may not have any choice about that. Have you thought about why you don't want to see her?"

"I don't know. I just don't want to. She's a real bitch, you know." Casey went back to her own room.

McCabe followed. Once again he found himself standing by her open door. "Well, you don't know her very well. Maybe once you get to know her a little better, you'll like her a little more."

"I don't think so, and I don't know why you're even saying something like that."

He didn't know either. He just wanted to make the inevitable meeting more palatable to her. He also wanted to end the discussion, but Casey kept going. "I don't understand you. You hate her as much as I do, but you're making out like she's just some kind of regular mom or something, and you know that's just crap. So stop trying to sell her to me. I'm not buying." She closed the door, leaving McCabe on the outside, staring at wood.

He didn't know if there was anything else to do or say. He wanted to shout through the door that he wasn't trying to sell her anything, and sure as hell not Sandy. Although that seemed a stupid thing: to shout through a door at a thirteen-year-old, even a thirteen-year-old who sometimes sounded like she was thirty. So he didn't. He just went back to the kitchen, got another beer, retrieved the envelope that had been left for him in the mailbox, and sat back down in the big chair.

Inside was a single sheet of lined paper, maybe torn from a school notebook. The message was written in pencil in the same block-letter style as the envelope. He supposed the writer was trying to disguise her handwriting. He assumed it was a her. The woman from Exchange Street and the cathedral. *McCabe,* it said, *meet me Tuesday night at nine. It's about the murder. Drive your red car. Come alone.* The word "alone" was underlined twice. *Take the turnpike north to the Gray exit. Follow Gray Road about six miles. Take a right turn on Holder's Farm Road. Go 1.3 miles and pull over onto the side. Flash your lights on and off twice to signal that you have not been followed. People are watching. When you get there, wait. I'll come to your car.*

The note wasn't signed. He still didn't know who the mystery woman was or if the note was even from her. Whoever wrote it obviously knew where he lived and what kind of car he drove. He considered the possibilities. One, it could be a legitimate meet with someone who felt threatened being seen with him. Two, it could be a crank sending him on a wild-goose chase. Or three, it could be someone setting him up for an ambush. The third possibility, the most dangerous, seemed the least likely. He wasn't close enough to finding his quarry for anyone, including Spencer, to feel threatened enough to take him out.

McCabe went to the kitchen and got a plastic ziplock bag out of a kitchen drawer. He slipped the note inside. He'd have it checked for prints. His own would be on it, but so might someone else's.

He heard footsteps coming up the stairs to their apartment. He wasn't expecting anyone. He heard the sound of a key probing the lock. With his systems on high alert, McCabe's hand went to his hip, where his gun should be and wasn't. Shit. He slipped behind the door, where he wouldn't be seen when it opened. He held his breath. The door opened. A familiar scent. He let the breath out.

Kyra stood in the front hall, arms loaded down with half a dozen plastic bags of groceries. She smiled. "Hello, handsome."

"I didn't know you were coming. I thought you had to be in the studio, quote, half the night, unquote."

"You want me to leave? I can always find someone else to make a delicious dinner for. I don't suppose either of you has eaten."

McCabe had forgotten about dinner. "Oh yeah, food."

"McCabe, you're a parent. You're supposed to see that your kid gets decent nourishment."

"Hey, she has a whole bag of chocolate chip cookies right there on the floor next to her bed."

"Well, that takes a load off my mind." Kyra tried walking around McCabe to the kitchen. He blocked her path, relieved her of the bags, put them on the floor, put his arms around her, and settled his lips on the back of her neck. He slowly nibbled his way around to the front until he found her lips.

"I'm starved," he murmered.

"Me, too," she said, pulling away, "but you'll have to settle for chicken breasts." She picked up the bags and headed for the kitchen. She looked back. "You may get a chance at mine later. If you're lucky."

McCabe loved watching Kyra cook. A foodie in her natural habitat, she moved around the kitchen with ease and an economy of motion. The simple act of chopping a bunch of scallions became performance art, Kyra's fingers manipulating both the vegetables and the finely honed blade with astonishing speed. He poured a Macallan single malt for himself and a chilled Pouilly-Fumé for her. They clinked glasses and sipped.

"Tell Casey we'll be eating in twenty minutes." He slid off his stool and went to deliver the message. Then he came back and climbed onto the stool again.

"Okay?" Kyra asked.

"Yeah, fine. She's in a bit of a sulk right now. Worried about seeing Sandy again."

"I don't blame her. I would be, too, after three years."

McCabe got up, stood behind Kyra, and began kneading the muscles along her shoulders and nuzzling the back of her neck.

"Alright, that feels great, but either I cook or you nuzzle. We can't do both."

"Are you sure—"

"Yes, I'll cut my finger off."

"What I was going to say was, are you sure what you said about us not getting married being the right answer?"

She put the knife down and turned to face him. "Why are you bringing this up again?"

"Because I love you?"

"I love you, too—but it strikes me that your timing, bringing it up right now, just might be more about you and Casey and maybe you and Sandy than it is about you and me. That somewhere in your devious mind you think giving Casey a substitute mother will somehow take the pressure off."

McCabe didn't know if Kyra was right. She might be. He backed away and went to refill his Scotch. "Let's wait until this visit with Sandy is over," said Kyra. "We can talk about it again."

That night, after they made love, he dreamed of TwoTimes.

He dreamed he was climbing the stairs inside the house on Merced Street. Flight after flight of rotting boards wrapped around a central well. His two hands clutching a Glock 17. Pressed against the wall at the side of the stairs. No lights. No backup. Pitch black. Yet somehow he could see through the dark. A stink of decaying flesh growing stronger as he climbed each floor. His foot hit something soft.

"Hey, kid, watch where you're walking."

He looked down. His brother Tommy splayed out on the stairs looking up. Smiling that patented smile no one could resist. Even though Tommy was dead, even though his smile was marred by two large exit wounds where the bullets that entered the back of his head came out the front, carrying with them a spray of brains and bits of Tommy the Narc's oh-so-blue right eye.

Looking down he saw that the dead, but not dead, Tommy had a girl on each arm. Ellie Pearlman to his right. The Jewish girl who lived on the next block. His father's voice rang out. "Tommy, are you still messing around with that Jew girl?" On Tommy's left was Mag O'Connell, her shirt off, her bra unhooked and hanging by one strap. Then Ellie Pearlman was gone and Tommy was standing behind Mag, his arms wrapped around her, one hand cupped under each of Mag's large, soft white breasts with the big pink nipples. Tommy holding Mag's breasts out for the ten-year-old McCabe to admire. "Hey, Mikey, bet you never saw anything like these before." He shook his head. No. No, he hadn't. "Wanna have a feel?" He hesitated before putting his hand out and stroking Mag's soft, pliant flesh.

McCabe looked down. Tommy was dead again, Mag O'Connell gone. He climbed over the body and continued up the stairs. At the top, he saw TwoTimes, a black cigarette, the color of a cigar, dangling from his lips. "I'm tellin' you like I told your brother, you may fuck with me once, but there's none what fucks with me two times."

By TwoTimes's side stood a fat white man with a round pasty face, speaking in a white pasty voice. "Your Honor, we find the drug pusher, pimp, and cop-killer TwoTimes not guilty."

"Not guilty," repeated TwoTimes, still on the stairs. "I told you, hot shot, nobody fucks with TwoTimes two times."

Then TwoTimes reached into his waistband and pulled out a small silver metal pistol, a little .22, shiny like a kid's cowboy cap gun. TwoTimes fired from the hip; the slug whizzed by McCabe's left ear and embedded itself in the plaster wall. McCabe aimed and fired before TwoTimes could fire again. The shot from the Glock, so much louder than the .22, echoed up and down the endless stairwell. McCabe watched the 9 mm slug, visible like a cartoon bullet, traverse the twenty feet between the end of the barrel and TwoTimes's head. It entered TwoTimes precisely at the tip of his wide flat nose.

McCabe continued up the stairs. TwoTimes was gone. Now Sandy stood at the top, wearing a sheer silk nightgown, her naked body gleaming under it, white in the moonlight, her hand out, beckoning him. "Come on up, McCabe." Once again, Sandy as the young Lauren Bacall.

McCabe reached for her, but his hand still held the Glock. The gun brushed against her body. He squeezed the trigger and the image of Sandy shattered into a thousand fragments, images in a broken mirror he could never put together again.

He woke with a start, his body soaked with sweat. He looked across the bed at Kyra, still sleeping. He thought about waking her, but whatever this feeling was, he knew it was not about Kyra, and not about making love. So instead he just lay there, staring into the dark shadows, breathing slowly and deeply until his bad dreams went away.

25

Tuesday. 6:30 A.M.

Kyra and McCabe lay, side by side, holding hands, legs touching, in the queen-sized bed.

"Tell me about TwoTimes," she said.

He glanced over, a frown appearing at the bridge of his nose. "I already told you about that."

"Not everything, I think."

"What do you want to know?"

"I want to know why you're having nightmares and muttering his name in your sleep. His name and your brother's name. And Sandy's."

McCabe stared silently up at the plaster ceiling in the old room, his eyes tracing the route of a crack that had been patched over and had now reappeared for about the tenth time. "Got to fix that crack," he said.

"Look, McCabe, you say you love me. You say you may even want to marry me. If that's true and you want me to be your wife and not just a warm body to get cozy with, I have to know it all."

"You already know most of it," he said. "TwoTimes was a small-potatoes crack dealer in the South Bronx. Just a kid, really. Nineteen when I planted the bullet in his skull. He ran a network of street sellers, other kids, all of them underage, some of them as young as ten or twelve. The idea was if the kids got picked up they'd only do juvie time."

"And Tommy was a narcotics cop?"

"Yeah. Tommy the Narc. Real hotshot. I dropped out of NYU and transferred to John Jay to follow in his footsteps. Tommy knew his way around the trade. Made some big busts. What I didn't know, what I should've known, was that by the time TwoTimes came along, Tommy had turned."

"Turned?"

"Turned bad. Gone on the take. He was pocketing money and drugs from half a dozen dealers in the Bronx. Most of them more powerful than TwoTimes."

"You never told me that."

"It's not anything I like talking about. Anyway, TwoTimes was getting too big for his baggy britches. He was trying to expand his territory and pushing up against some guys who didn't take kindly to being pushed. So they called in their fixer to get TwoTimes out of the way."

"Tommy?"

"Yeah, Tommy. You want coffee? I can make us some coffee."

"No. Thanks. Not until I've heard it all."

McCabe sighed. "Problem was Tommy had gotten greedy. He doesn't want to take TwoTimes out 'cause he figures he'll lose a nice source of income. So instead he decides to talk him out of it. Tommy always figured he could talk anybody out of anything. Anyway, he goes over to TwoTimes's place, a sleazebag apartment on Merced Street, and tells him he's gotta stop crowding the big guys. TwoTimes says, 'What the fuck you talking about? You work for me.' So Tommy tells TwoTimes he also works for a number of other clients, and if TwoTimes doesn't stop horning in on their business, he's gonna have to arrest him."

"Tommy is?"

"Yeah, but TwoTimes is too smart for that. He knows no way in hell is Tommy gonna arrest anybody who can testify in court how he's been paying him off for more than two years. Instead he figures Tommy's gonna kill him. So while Tommy's still talking, TwoTimes takes out this bullshit little twenty-two and puts two slugs into his head. Kills him on the spot."

"How did you find out about all this?"

"Some of it at the trial. Some from Tommy's partner. The rest I got from TwoTimes just before I took him down."

"So what happened after he killed Tommy?"

"Biggest bullshit trial I ever saw in my life. I mean, the DA had TwoTimes dead to rights. They had Tommy's blood all over the apartment. They had the gun—"

"Fingerprints?"

"Not on the gun. He wiped it clean." McCabe paused. "Get dressed," he said. "Let's take a walk. I need some air."

"You'll tell me the rest of it?"

"Yeah, I'll tell you the rest of it."

It took McCabe less than a minute to throw on a pair of jeans and an oversized sweatshirt loose enough to cover his .45. While Kyra dressed, he interrupted Casey's ongoing snooze to let her know it was time to get out of bed and ready for school. Breakfast was Cheerios. They were going out. They'd be back, but not before she left.

Kyra and McCabe walked across the Eastern Prom and down the hill toward the morning light and the water. They crossed the narrow-gauge tracks and then turned north along the joggers' trail toward Back Bay. A few runners passed. Other than that they were alone. "I didn't want to talk about this stuff in the apartment. Casey can hear through walls. She's got ears like a hawk. None of this is for her consumption."

"It's eyes like a hawk. To my knowledge hawks aren't particularly well regarded for their hearing."

"Yeah, I know. I just couldn't come up with an appropriate animal metaphor. How about ears like a rabbit?" He smiled.

Kyra didn't return his smile. She wasn't falling for banter. "Let's stay on subject," she said.

"You're right. Where was I?"

"The biggest bullshit trial you ever saw in your life."

"Yeah, right. TwoTimes's lawyer puts him on the stand, and he comes in with this bullshit alibi that he was having sex with his girlfriend while Tommy was getting shot, and both the girlfriend and the girlfriend's mother swear up and down that it's true."

"He gets off on that?"

"He gets off on reasonable doubt. Nobody denied Tommy was killed in TwoTimes's apartment or that he was killed with TwoTimes's gun, but there were no witnesses. Even though this twelve-year-old girl who lived down the hall told detectives she heard the four shots and then saw TwoTimes exiting the apartment via the fire escape. Unfortunately, she wasn't willing to repeat the story in court. One of TwoTimes's crack crew probably got to her."

"So he gets off, and you, to your everlasting regret, go to his apartment and kill him, what, out of revenge for your dead brother?"

"That's what the Internal Affairs people were trying to prove, but that wasn't how it happened. By the way, I don't really regret it."

"So how did it happen?"

"The problem, as IA saw it, was that I was Midtown North homicide and not South Bronx narcotics. I had no business nosing around in the case, especially after TwoTimes walked."

"But you did?"

"But I did."

"May I ask why, and what you were hoping to accomplish? Assuming, of course, you're telling the truth about not going there to kill the guy."

"I could have done that. I was certainly tempted, but I didn't. I knew he couldn't be tried for the murder again, but I wanted him to admit not only that he killed Tommy but that he was a dealer. That he sold crack to kids for a living. I went wearing a wire. I wanted the truth. I wanted him to do at least a little time." McCabe paused. "Maybe I wanted to rough him up a little."

"So what happened?"

"I go upstairs in this shithole where he hangs out, and I find him in the apartment. He takes me for a cop right off, which is not too hard, but he doesn't know I'm Tommy's brother. I ask him about it, and he tells me what happened. How he'd wasted this narc and walked. He knew he couldn't be tried again. He's laughing his ass off. So I figure fuck it and I tell him who I am. That gets to him right away. I mean, if a dude as black as TwoTimes can turn white, he did. Right away he goes for his piece. He clears his waistband and fires, but the shot goes wide, into the wall. I'm more accurate. My bullet puts a hole in his head. That was the end of it. The whole story."

"There was an investigation?"

"Of course. There always is."

"And you were exonerated?"

"I was exonerated. The bad guy had a weapon, and he fired first. You could hear the two shots clearly on the recorder. First the little plink of his .22 and right after it the louder boom of the 9 mm. Under the circumstances, I used appropriate force. Unfortunately, there was enough lingering doubt about why I was there in the first place to kill my prospects as a detective in New York. It's part of the reason I took the job up here. Part of the reason I met you."

"Casey being the other part?"

"Yeah."

They walked for a while, neither saying anything. Eventually Kyra asked, "Would you have killed him anyway? Even if he hadn't pulled a gun?"

"I don't know. Maybe. I certainly wanted to, but he wasn't too long for this world anyway. He was an arrogant little prick, and there were at least a half dozen bigger sharks out for his ass. They would have gotten him sooner or later."

"You said you have no regrets about killing him?"

"No regrets. He was vermin and he deserved to die."

"So why are you having nightmares about it?"

"I guess because he's the only man I ever killed. Because it was up close and personal. Because it was so fast.

He was alive. Then he was dead. Just like that. In spite of what you see on TV, killing people isn't all that easy."

Kyra stopped and looked up. "That helps."

"What do you mean?"

"Helps me be sure that if I do marry you, my husband won't be somebody who can do something like that easily."

"That's important, huh?"

"I won't dignify that with a response."

"No, if you marry me you won't be marrying a murderer. You'll be marrying a cop. A cop who's a refugee from a failed marriage. Each of those, as you know by now, comes with its own set of problems."

Kyra slipped her arm into McCabe's and moved her body closer to his. He leaned down, pulled her in, and kissed her. She kissed him back. Then, arm in arm, they walked back toward the apartment, marveling, as they always did, at the beauty of the bay and the glory of the sunrise that turned all the clouds pink.

26

Vanessa Redmond sat with her back to the wall at a corner table in the lobby bar at the Boca Raton Club and Resorts, which, at two o'clock on a Tuesday afternoon, was nearly empty. She was dressed casually in a lime green silk shirt and white linen pants. An attractive woman, she'd never bothered to color her naturally gray hair. Her right hand fidgeted with the clasp of a gold Baume and Mercier wristwatch. The only other jewelry she wore was a thin chain around her neck, supporting a gold Elsa Peretti heart, and two small diamond stud earrings. Her makeup was simple and understated. Though she seldom drank much at any time, and never in the afternoon, she ordered a cosmopolitan, hoping the alcohol might calm her anxiety. The man was late. She wasn't accustomed to being kept waiting, and she didn't like sitting by herself in a bar. She picked up her cell phone, thinking she'd check the messages at the house to see if he'd called. Then she closed it, deciding to give him another ten minutes. She sipped the drink.

A man, tall, with broad shoulders and deep-set eyes, entered the room. He wore a well-cut blue blazer over a yellow Izod polo shirt and tan trousers. Glancing in her direction, he walked to her table.

"Mrs. Redmond?"

"Ms. Redmond," she said. "John Redmond is my father. My first name is Vanessa."

"You never married?" he asked, taking the seat opposite hers.

"No. What is your name?"

"Harry. Harry Lime."

"I don't suppose that's your real name?"

"No. My real name is irrelevant."

"You're late, by the way, Harry Lime."

"That, too, is irrelevant."

"Why did you want to meet?"

"I don't want to talk in here. There's a jogging path that winds around the property. We can walk there and talk. Did you only have the one drink?"

"Yes," she said. He took out a twenty-dollar bill and placed it on the table. He pulled out the table to ease her exit. She rose and walked out of the bar first. He followed her to the front door of the hotel, and they went together out into the heat of a late summer afternoon.

They walked down the path, away from the central part of the hotel.

"You're not wearing any recording devices, are you?" he asked.

"Oh, for God's sake, don't be ridiculous," she said, irritation rising in her voice.

"I'm afraid I'm going to have to check. May I have your bag?" Sighing deeply, she handed him her small Hermès shoulder bag. He opened the snaps and rummaged through it. Finding no wire, he handed it back.

"Now I want you to put your arms around my neck and press against me as if we were embracing. I have to check your body."

"The bloody hell I will," she snapped. "Who do you think you're talking to?"

"I know exactly who you are, Ms. Redmond. I know exactly who your father is and what his condition is. I know he was turned down for six different transplant programs because of his age. I know you want him to live. Which means I'm your only option. If you'd rather not proceed, that's your choice. We can conclude our business and I'll be on my way."

"And my father will die?"

"Yes, your father will die. Then again, everyone dies. It's only a question of when. Besides, look on the bright side. You'll inherit a great deal of money."

"I already have more money than I'll ever need. Strange as it may seem to someone like you, I love my father."

"Is that why you never married?"

She didn't answer. She simply turned toward him and, looking up into his face without emotion, placed her arms around his neck and pressed herself, like a lover, into his body. She could feel the bulge of a holster and gun under his jacket as he ran his hands over her in a feigned caress, up and down, back and front.

"Enjoying yourself?" she whispered.

"Not really," he said. "You're not my type." Apparently satisfied she wasn't wearing a recording device, he added, "Okay, you can let go now."

They turned and started walking again down the path. The hotel was to their right, and the vivid green of the golf course fairways lay both to their left and in front of them.

"What did you want to tell me?" She began the conversation.

"We have a healthy heart," he said. "Right blood type. Tissue is compatible. The donor is brain dead. Currently on life support."

"Who is the donor?"

"An accident victim. The precise identity does not concern you. Does your father still want to go through with this? At his age there's no more than a fifty-fifty chance he'll survive even one year, and there's an excellent chance he won't survive the surgery."

"I understand that," she said. "He understands that. But without the surgery he won't last more than another month or two. He's a tough old man, and he wants to live. He thinks this will give him a shot. If that's what he wants, that's what I want."

"The procedure will cost five million dollars. In advance."

"That's a lot of money."

"According to our sources, your father's net worth is more than a billion. For the gift of life, for someone like him, five million dollars is pocket change. In any event, that's the deal. Take it or leave it."

"Who is the surgeon? Is he capable? Competent?"

"More than competent. One of the best. However, for obvious reasons, I can't tell you who he is. Now, do you want to proceed?"

"Yes. It seems I have no choice."

"Very well. From this point on there's no turning back." Harry Lime handed her a slip of paper. "This is the routing number and account number at a private bank in Zurich. First thing tomorrow morning, I want you to wire five million dollars to this account. Then I want you to burn this note. When I receive confirmation from the bank that the funds have arrived, they will be withdrawn, the account closed, and the money placed in another untraceable account. When that has been accomplished, I'll get in touch with you to arrange delivery of your father to the surgery site."

"Where is the surgery site?"

"All I will tell you is that it's in the United States. No passport required. When you are contacted, you will arrange a private ambulance to bring your father to a small airport to be named later. A private plane will pick him up. There will be a pilot, a doctor, and a nurse specializing in cardiac care on board. Other than these, he will travel alone."

"I want to go with him. Since my mother died, I'm the only one who really cares about him."

"I'm sorry, Ms. Redmond, that will not be possible. He will travel alone. During the trip a sedative will be administered to put him to sleep. He won't be told where he's going. An ambulance will meet him at the other end and transport him to the surgery site. The operation will take place as soon as medically feasible. When he is able, he will return home, hopefully in three or four days. He will travel home in exactly the same manner. We will arrange for a nurse to care for him at home and administer antirejection drugs as they are needed."

"Will you send prescriptions?" she asked.

"Your father will need to take antirejection drugs, primarily cyclosporine, for the rest of his life. It's available in tablet form, and what is needed will be sent directly to you. There will be no trips to the pharmacy, no paperwork sent to any insurance company."

"What about side effects?"

"Some side effects are likely. There may be kidney dysfunction. Possibly less output when he is urinating. His hands or feet may swell. He may get tremors in his hands. Swollen gums. Bleeding gums. The list is long, but most are not life-threatening. The nurse will know what to do. If there are any indications of organ rejection, the nurse will let us know and we will arrange for a transplant cardiologist to perform a biopsy. If he needs further treatment, you will be contacted to discuss the options.

"I cannot emphasize strongly enough that you must tell no one of these arrangements. Not your doctor. Not your lover. Not your Aunt Ethel. If you talk in your sleep, sleep alone. If anyone asks why he seems better—if the surgery works—tell them only that's he's had bypass surgery. The scars will look similar enough. If he dies, then contact us at the number you've been given. We will make arrangements for a physician to sign a death certificate and for the body to be cremated."

"Is that all?" she asked.

"One last thing. By accepting these arrangements, both you and your father become complicit in breaking the law. If we discover that you have spoken of it before the fact— and we will be watching and listening—the arrangements are off. We will keep the money, but there will be no surgery. If we find out that you have spoken of it after the surgery, to a doctor, to a hospital, to the police, or to any-one else, the contract, and both you and your father, will be terminated."

Harry Lime spoke these words in a flat businesslike tone, without threat, without emotion of any kind. In spite of the Florida heat, Vanessa Redmond found herself shivering. She knew nothing of this man or the people he worked with. She was taking what he said and what he promised entirely on faith. Yet, because she wanted her father to live, even if only a little longer, she said simply, "I understand."

27

It was late Tuesday afternoon. Four days since Katie Dubois's body turned up in the scrap yard and Lucinda Cassidy disappeared from the Western Prom. Tom Shockley was starting to bitch about the lack of results. Bill Fortier was beginning to worry about the cost of overtime. McCabe was increasingly haunted by the hours ticking down on Cassidy's life.

He spent most of the day huddling with his Crimes Against People unit, reviewing the results of endless interviews, virtually all of which led nowhere. Working round the clock, Tasco and Frazier and four teams of detectives narrowed the so-called Lexus List down from nearly five hundred to fewer than a dozen. Each of these so-called possibles—three surgeons, four other MDs, one nurse-practitioner, and a professor of biology at a small college in New Hampshire—had the requisite skills to remove a human heart. Each lacked an alibi that could be corroborated by a third party. Each was brought in to 109 Middle Street and placed in an interview room equipped with microphones and hidden video equipment. Each was questioned intensively, sometimes for hours, by teams of detectives skilled in ferreting out the slightest inconsistencies in their stories. In Tom Tasco's opinion, the most promising "suspect" was a fifty-five-year-old retired gynecologist from North Berwick. He seemed promising only because he'd lost his license in '02 for allegedly fondling half a dozen patients while their feet were in the stirrups. One was a fourteen-year-old girl.

Unfortunately, the man was only five foot ten, not the six foot plus seen in the surveillance tape and later corroborated by Tobin Kenney. Reviewing the video, McCabe knew there was no way that this man would have been strong enough to carry Katie's body to where she was dumped.

The hunt for Lucinda Cassidy hadn't gone much better. Searches organized in ever widening circles from an epicenter in Portland turned up no leads. Divers explored the waters of Portland harbor and found nothing. Advanced mapping techniques used successfully by Maine Forest Service rangers to find the body of a murdered girl a few years earlier were tried again. This time they failed to produce results. Bill Bacon and Will Messing were running out of places to look.

Perhaps the most promising development came in a report from the state lab in Augusta, which said that Lucinda Cassidy's dog, Fritz, had definitely bitten her attacker and that traces of human blood and hair were found in his mouth. Both samples had undergone DNA analysis, and the results were in. Unfortunately, there was no suspect DNA available to check for a match.

Finally, around six o'clock, McCabe called Burt Lund to find out if Judge Washburn had returned and if Lund had had any luck setting up a meeting with her.

"She just got back," Lund told him. "Meet me in her chambers in ten minutes."

Before leaving, McCabe gathered the exhausted cops in the detectives' conference room. First he encouraged them all to keep their spirits up and to keep going. He told them every suspect eliminated brought them one step closer to success. Looking into their tired faces, he knew they'd heard it all before. He considered telling them about the note in his mailbox, about the meeting set for tonight with the possible witness, but he was afraid to risk a leak either to the press or to Shockley's office. However, he did mention he was on his way to ask a judge for a warrant to search Spencer's car and home. Then he told them to go home and get some rest. Start fresh in the morning.

Judge Paula Washburn's chambers were on the second floor of the Cumberland County Courthouse on Federal Street, less than a five-minute walk from police headquarters. McCabe and Lund were admitted immediately. Washburn was a tall, extremely thin woman with cropped gray hair. She didn't bother with the formality of a greeting, though she did ask them to sit.

"Well, gentlemen, what do we have that's so all-fired urgent it just couldn't wait another minute?" she asked.

"A request for a search warrant in the Dubois case," said Lund. He handed her McCabe's affidavit.

She took several minutes to read it silently. "Well, isn't this interesting," she said finally, peering up at him over the tiny reading glasses perched on her long nose. "I hope this isn't a fishing expedition, Sergeant McCabe. If so, you're going after a pretty big fish."

"No, Your Honor, it isn't. I believe we have sufficient reason to investigate Dr. Spencer further."

"There are other doctors with green Lexus SUVs."

"There are, but so far, at least, Spencer is the only one who is physically similar both to the person seen in the video and the man described by the soccer coach."

She asked several questions about the reliability of Starbucks's video enhancement and Tobin Kenney's memory. McCabe answered them as best he could. Judge Washburn nodded, considering his responses. Then she asked, "Is Dr. Spencer aware that he's about to become a suspect in a murder case?"

"I think he may have an inkling. He called Chief Shockley and complained about my questioning his wife."

"Does Shockley know you're seeking this warrant?"

"No."

"You realize, of course, he's going to be less than pleased."

"I do."

"And you're not bothered?"

"I'm not."

"Are there any other considerations I should be aware of?"

"Yes," said Lund. "Ordinarily, Your Honor, we might wait a little longer, amass a little more evidence, before seeking this warrant. In this case we're rushing it a bit because there may be another life at stake."

"The woman who disappeared?"

"Yes, Your Honor."

"Very well, Mr. Lund, I'm going to grant this request, though I do wish you had some evidence that was slightly more compelling. I'm doing so in the belief that I would have no hesitation issuing a warrant if the suspect were less prominent in the community. However, I do hope this is not going to backfire in all our faces."

"Yes, Your Honor. I hope not as well. Thank you."

Washburn signed the warrant and handed it back, and Lund and McCabe left the judge's chambers.

He called Maggie's cell from the sidewalk. "Let me buy you a beer."

"No can do. I've got company coming. I'm at home in the middle of cooking dinner."

"It's important."

"Okay. Why don't you come over here? You talk. I'll cook."

Maggie had a small two-bedroom on Vesper Street only a couple of blocks from McCabe's own place on the Prom.

"Who's your company?" he asked as she handed him a cold bottle of Shipyard and an opener. She told him tonight was date number three with her new "maybe, might be, might not be" boyfriend.

He popped the top, leaned back against the fridge, and took a long swig. "Whatever you're cooking, it smells great."

"Thanks. Coq au vin."

"Interesting menu selection for a romantic evening at home." McCabe grinned, pleased with his joke.

"Fortunately, my friend doesn't share your sophomoric sense of humor."

McCabe flashed his least sincere smile. "Thanks."

"You're welcome. Anyway, so much for small talk," said Maggie. She poured herself a glass of red wine, sat down at the small kitchen table, and sipped. McCabe pulled out a chair on the other side.

"What's so important we had to talk about it now?"

First he told her about the warrant. She nodded approvingly. "Anything else?"

He showed her the note, saying he was sure it was from the woman he chased down Exchange Street and then saw again at Katie's funeral. He said he was going to meet her alone tonight as requested.

"Why does she want you to drive the T-Bird? Even a Crown Vic would be less conspicuous."

"I don't know. Maybe because she can recognize it easily. Maybe because it doesn't look like a police car."

Maggie said "hmmm" a couple of times as she examined the note, a different intonation on each "hmmm." She drummed her fingers on the table. "Do we know anything about this woman?" she asked. "I respect your instincts, McCabe, but maybe she's a nutcase who just wants to get involved in the case. Or maybe get involved on a lonely country road with a big, handsome hunk of a cop."

"Like me, you mean?"

"Yeah, but don't let it go to your head."

He turned serious. "No. I think it's for real. At the funeral she implied she was being watched. Said if she was seen with me she might be killed."

"She still could be a nutcase."

"I don't think so. I don't know what information she has, but I do think she knows something. I think it could be something important."

"I don't think you going alone is such a good idea. Why don't I follow discreetly in a separate car, give you a little cover? Y'know? Rule number one? Never go anywhere without backup? Aside from anything else, if something did go wrong and you were out there alone, the department'd put your ass through a wringer."

"I guess. The thing is, when she said alone, I think she meant it. She'll spook if she sees anything that looks remotely like a police car. If Cassidy's still alive—"

"Big if."

"Maybe, but if she is, time's running out, and I'm in no mood to lose what could be our best lead yet."

"So fuck rule number one?"

"I guess. Anyway, I don't see why things should get all that hairy. I just wanted you to know where I was going."

"You gonna take a recorder?"

"Yes, but I may not turn it on. Right now she's like a deer in the headlights. One false move and she's gone."

"Mike, I don't like it. I think I should be there."

"Look, you've got a nice evening planned. Go finish making your dinner. And have fun with . . . uh . . . what's his name?"

"Einar."

"Einar? Really?"

"Yes, Einar, really—and no, I don't need any gratuitous wisecracks from you, thank you very much." Maggie stood up and showed him to the door. "Good-bye. I love you. Don't get your ass shot off."

Later, at home, McCabe made a salad and nuked a frozen lasagna for Casey. He nibbled at it himself. Afterward, Casey cleared the dinner stuff and McCabe retired to the living room, where he opened his DeLorme atlas of Maine to the page that included Gray. He located the roads the note instructed him to take, the spot where he was supposed to park. Working outward from the meeting place, he pored over the intricate web of back roads until the entire map was committed to memory. It took ten minutes.

Though he doubted he was going to need it, he pocketed an extra eight-round magazine for his service weapon, a Smith & Wesson 4506. As an afterthought, he also took out the Mossberg 590 pump-action riot shotgun with its eight-round magazine that he kept locked in a case at the back of his closet. He couldn't dismiss the possibility he was walking into a trap. If necessary, he wanted sufficient firepower to blast his way out.

He called Jane Devaney to see if she could come over and stay with Casey. Her machine picked up after four rings. He didn't leave a message. Kyra was in Boston, going to the MFA and having dinner with friends. She wouldn't be back until morning. Reluctantly, McCabe convinced himself Casey would be fine. He didn't think he'd be home all that late. Besides, as Casey often reminded him, other people paid her ten bucks an hour to babysit their kids. She'd be fine for a few hours.

As he left, he told her to double-lock the door. She looked uncertainly at the shotgun case cradled in his arms.

"Where are you going?"

"I'm meeting a possible witness. I shouldn't be late."

"What are you taking that for?"

"I meant to put it in the trunk a long time ago. It's got nothing to do with tonight."

Good question. Lousy answer. He could tell she didn't believe him. Rather than say anything else stupid, he just kissed her and told her not to let anybody in. "Not unless you know for sure it's either Jane or Kyra."

"They both have keys, so I won't let anybody in, period." Then she added, "I'd feel safer if you let me have a dog."

She'd asked for one a dozen times before. "Nice try," he said. "I can see you're a McCabe through and through." He kissed her and left.

He heard the dead bolt slip into place behind him as he turned and headed down the stairs, wondering if a big protective beast hanging around the apartment might not be such a bad idea. Of course, it'd have to be friendly, sloppy, and lovable as well. Probably an unworkable combination. Maybe he'd talk to some dog people when this was all over.

When McCabe got to the car, he put the .45 into a specially constructed holster he'd installed himself on the front of the Bird's single bench seat in a line beneath his right hand. In an emergency, he could get to it a hell of a lot faster than if it were sitting on his hip trapped under the seat belt. He stashed the extra mag and a handful of 12-gauge buckshot shells in the small glove box on the passenger side. He loaded the Mossberg and stowed it in the trunk. Finally, he loosened the bulbs in the car's interior lights. He didn't need the lights making him an easier target each time the door opened.

He slid a Coltrane album into the car's brand-new CD player. The sweet relaxing sound of "Soul Eyes" filled the small space, flowing smoothly, like liquid gold, from the speakers. He turned up the volume, pulled the Bird out of the lot, and headed for the turnpike via Washington Avenue.

28

Tuesday. 8:45 P.M.

There wasn't much traffic on the Gray Road, but McCabe checked the rearview periodically to make sure no one was following him. He found the turnoff onto Holder's Farm Road right where it was supposed to be. He clocked 1.3 miles and pulled off onto the shoulder. He flashed his lights on and off twice, as instructed. Even without them he could see well. The sky was cloudless and the moon nearly full. As his eyes adjusted, he saw the land to his right was open meadow, probably part of a farm. Holder's Farm? He removed the .45 from the seat holster and placed it on the seat next to him, safety on. Then he waited. Five minutes passed. Ten. Apparently the mystery woman was going to keep him waiting. She said as much in the note. He lowered his window and leaned back. It might be a while. The September night air felt cool and fresh on his face. He could smell the composty scent of farmland. He kind of liked it.

That's what he was thinking about when another notion invaded his mind and hung there, refusing to be dismissed. It should have occurred to him earlier, but he'd missed it, and now he couldn't push it away—the idea that the note hadn't been delivered to set up a meeting. It was intended to draw him away. To leave Casey unprotected. He damned himself for not covering his rear. A little paranoia wasn't always a bad thing. Portland was making him feel too safe, too comfortable. That kind of feeling could be dangerous. He grabbed his phone and hit his own number, the fingers on his left hand drumming on the steering wheel as he waited for the line to connect, for Casey to pick up. One ring. Two. C'mon, Casey, answer the goddamned phone. Three rings. Four. Then Casey's voice. "You have reached the McCabes. Leave a message . . ." Shit. He clicked off. Images of dark strangers filled his mind, watching and waiting from hidden places, looking up at Casey's lighted windows, invading his home.

He hit redial. The rings started again. One. Two. C'mon, baby, pick up the phone. "Did you forget something?" Casey's voice again, this time live. McCabe exhaled as silently as he could.

"Where were you?" he asked.

"Where was I?"

"A minute ago. I called. Nobody answered."

"I was in the bathroom."

"Are you alright?"

"Yeah, I'm fine," she said, her voice puzzled.

"Has anyone called or rung the buzzer?"

"No."

"Any strange noises?"

"Dad, you're freaking me out."

"I'm sorry. Look, I'm going to ask Maggie to come over."

"Why?"

"Just because I'm being silly. Humor me. I'll call you back if she can't come. Make sure it's Maggie before you let her in."

"Alright," she said uncertainly. "I'll make sure." She hung up.

Of all the women McCabe knew and trusted, Maggie was the only one who carried a gun. The only one who knew how to tag a stakeout. He speed-dialed her number.

"Hello." Her voice sounded softer, more sensual than the Maggie he was used to. Was he interrupting a moment of passion? Probably. "Hello?" she said again.

"Maggie?"

"McCabe? What is it?" Instantly alert, Maggie the lover morphed into Maggie the cop.

"Listen. I'm up here in hell and gone, and Casey's down there on her own. I think the note may have been designed to draw me away."

"Okay. Any reason you think that?"

"Other than the fact she's unprotected, no, and our friend hasn't turned up yet. I'm sorry. I know you have a date. My mind's playing games with me. I just need to have Casey covered. I'll make it up to you."

A long sigh, then, "I understand. It's okay. You're right. Call Casey. Tell her I'll be there in five."

"Apologize to Einar for me. I'm really sorry."

"It's alright. I'm a big girl. Just remember you owe me." She hung up.

McCabe's anxiety faded. He decided to wait another ten minutes. If the note writer didn't show, he'd head back to Portland and let Maggie get on with her life. The night outside was dead quiet. Not even the chirp of cicadas disturbed the calm—but the sound of a shoe scraping on gravel did. It was coming from the right and rear of the Bird, along the shoulder of the road. So soft that in the city he wouldn't have heard it. McCabe sat still. Moving only his right hand and wrist, he disengaged the safety on the .45 and rotated it so that when the door of the Bird swung open, it was pointed right at the woman's face.

It was a face he knew. The face of the woman he chased down Exchange Street. The woman he spoke to in the cathedral. She was dressed differently, more casually, in jeans and a black cotton shirt, but it was definitely the same face.

"Pulling a door open like that is a good way to get yourself killed," said McCabe. "Get in. Generally speaking, I'd recommend not sneaking up on armed men in the dark."

She ignored both his words and the gun pointed at her and slipped into the seat beside him. She closed the door. "Drive," she said. "We'll talk as we go."

"Where's your car?"

"Hidden. About a mile from here."

He started the engine and pulled out onto the road. "Anywhere in particular you want to go?"

"Just drive. These country roads go on for miles." The accent was French and the woman attractive. McCabe noticed a more than passing resemblance to the actress Jeanne Moreau in François Truffaut's 1962 classic *Jules et Jim*. A little older than Moreau was then. Maybe forty or forty-five.

"You're not wearing a wire, are you?" she asked.

He pulled back onto the road. "No. There's a small digital recorder in the glove box, but it's not turned on."

She opened the box, examined the device, saw he was telling the truth, and put it back. She picked up the extra magazine and some shotgun shells. "Are you planning a war?"

"You never know these days, do you?"

She put the mag and the shells back and closed the door. "*Québécoise?*" he asked.

"*Non. Française. Je suis de Montpellier. Près du Méditerranée.*"

McCabe didn't respond.

"You speak French?" she asked.

"No."

"Okay. We'll speak English." Her English seemed good, though accented.

"You're the note writer?" he asked.

"Of course."

"I didn't think anyone was going to show up."

"I had to be sure you weren't followed."

"Why would I be followed?"

"Because of me."

McCabe checked the rearview again. No lights. He drove faster, turning from one small country road onto another, occasionally doubling back, using the map in his mind to track every twist and turn. The Bird wasn't a Porsche, but with its 312 V8 and a three-speed stick, it had plenty of kick and was more than passably agile. If anyone was attempting to follow, he'd either lose them or they'd reveal themselves soon enough. Unless, of course, they were attempting to follow with lights turned off. Treacherous on these roads. Especially at high speeds, even on a moon-filled night.

"Who are you?" he asked.

"My name is Sophie Gauthier. As I told you, I'm French. French-Algerian, actually. Born in Algiers. My father was in the colonial army. My mother was Algerian. Like most of the colonials, we left after independence in 1962 and resettled in France. I was two at the time. I was brought up in Languedoc. That's in the south of France, west of Provence." Sophie Gauthier kept looking to the rear for signs of a following car.

"Keep going," said McCabe.

"I'm a cardiac perfusionist. Until last year I worked at the university hospital in Montpellier in France, specializing in cardio-thoracic transplant procedures."

Transplant, thought McCabe, Spencer's assurances that it couldn't be done ringing in his ears. It *was* a fucking transplant. "Heart transplants?" he asked.

"Yes, and heart/lung transplants."

"Were you involved in the murder of Katie Dubois?"

"No. Not directly, but I believe I know how she was killed and why."

"And by whom?"

"Unfortunately not."

"Was she killed to harvest her heart for a transplant?"

"I have no proof of that. In fact, I've never laid eyes on Katie Dubois. But yes, that is my suspicion." The glow from the dash lit her face from below in a green light that accented the natural sadness of her expression.

"Tell me what you know."

"I can't. Not until I know I am safe." She looked at him.

"I want immunity from prosecution." Headlights approached from the opposite direction. McCabe slowed the Bird and eased a little over to the right to give the car, an SUV, more room to pass on the narrow road. Sophie Gauthier bent down and shielded her face with her arm as the lights from the oncoming vehicle swept over them.

"Who are you hiding from?" he asked.

"There are people who I'm sure would kill me if they knew I was talking to you."

McCabe glanced at Sophie and then at the clock on the dash with its old-fashioned hands. Fifteen minutes since he'd called Maggie. She'd be at his apartment by now. Casey would be safe. He'd have heard if there'd been a problem.

"It's a little premature to be discussing immunity," he said. "I don't know what you have to offer. I don't even know exactly what you're supposed to have done. Besides, I'm just a cop. It's up to the prosecutors, not the police, to discuss immunity or plea bargains. I can make a recommendation, but that's all it will be. A recommendation."

McCabe downshifted and pushed the Bird hard through a tight curve. Driving fast on back roads was usually a pleasure. Sophie Gauthier's body lurched against his.

By now, McCabe figured, if anybody was following, he lost them long ago. He pulled over to the side of the road and killed the lights. "Listen," he said, turning to face her, "we're all alone here. Nobody is listening, and I need to know more if I'm going to help you. Just tell me what you know about Dubois and what you suspect. I'm not recording the conversation. I haven't read you your rights. Did you ever hear the expression 'he said, she said'? That's all this is. No matter what you tell me, all you have to do is deny you ever said it." McCabe knew the reality wasn't quite that simple, but he needed information fast and this woman had it. "Once I know what you know," he continued, "if you really do need protection, it can be provided."

He guessed Sophie Gauthier was debating how much she was willing to risk. "Do you mind if I smoke?" she asked.

"Just crack the window," he said. She looked puzzled. "That means open it. A little." She did.

He waited while Sophie performed what seemed a practiced ritual of delay. She fished around in her small shoulder bag and found her cigarettes. She tapped one out. She returned the pack to the bag and pushed in the car's electric lighter. She waited for the pop. Finally she lit the cigarette, took a deep drag and exhaled the smoke. A strong familiar scent filled the car. "Gauloise?" he asked.

"Yes. Do you want one?"

"No. I don't smoke anymore. They remind me of when I was a student in New York. We thought smoking French cigarettes was cool."

"Young people are silly about things like that," she said.

"Yes," he agreed.

For a while neither of them said anything. "Alright," she said finally, "I will tell you what I know. As I said, I am French. I am an operating theater perfusionist. That's the person who operates a machine that keeps a patient alive by circulating and oxygenating the blood during thoracic surgery, including transplants of either the heart or of the heart and lungs. I was trained and, until about six months ago, worked at the Hôpital Eduard des Toussaints in Montpellier. It's a major cardiac center. We do many transplant procedures there. Eduard des Toussaints is one of two transplant hospitals in southwestern France. The other is in Toulouse. Anyway, I took my training there and afterward became a member of the staff." She paused as if waiting for him to ask a question. He didn't, so she continued.

"Transplant operations can be long and tiring," she said. "You never know when one is going to start because you are never sure when a heart will become available. So you're more or less always on call."

"It's the same over here," said McCabe.

"I'm sure it is. Anyway, after an operation, before going home, whatever time it was, I usually stopped in at a small café near the hospital to have a glass of wine or sometimes a Pernod and water. Sometimes I'd also have something to eat. Last year, about this time, three or four times in a row, I saw the same man there, sitting at the bar. He was a good-looking man. Early forties. Tall. Dark hair. Expensive clothes. He wore a closely cropped gray beard."

McCabe wondered if Spencer ever had a beard. If there was a picture of him anywhere with a beard.

"Always he sat alone. Like me. Though not so tired as me, I think. Sometimes he'd be drinking wine. Sometimes whiskey. It was easy for me to tell he was not French. I thought English or possibly American. I thought perhaps he was visiting a relative who was in the hospital for a long stay. I'm divorced, and he seemed interested, so we struck up a conversation that lasted several hours. After that we saw each other two or three more times in the café. Once we went elsewhere to dinner."

"Did you become lovers?"

"Yes, but I don't think his heart was in it. I think he may be homosexual. Or maybe not. As a woman who attracts quite a few men, I could tell he was more interested in what I did at the hospital than in me as a woman."

"What did you talk about?"

"Mostly my job. How much experience I had. What kind of equipment we used."

"Did that surprise you?"

"At first, yes, but when I asked him about it, he said what he did for a living was sell medical equipment. Including heart-lung machines. That's what he said he was doing at the hospital, a business deal."

"Did you believe him?"

"Yes. I had no reason not to. He knew a lot about the machines."

"Did he tell you his name?"

"He told me his name was Phillipe Spencer."

"Philip Spencer?" McCabe felt a surge of adrenaline. Here it was. Falling right into his lap. The corroborating evidence Burt Lund was pushing for.

Sophie sensed his excitement. "Do you know him?"

"Let's just say I know the name." He was sitting with a witness who could directly link the sonofabitch to an illegal transplant. Not perfect, but a hell of a lot better than a pair of Bruno Magli shoes. Why would Spencer use his real name, though? Why not Harry Lime or some other alias? It didn't make sense. Yes, it did. Simple. The passport. He was traveling in a foreign country. He didn't have the time, or maybe the means, to get himself a phony. Still, why give her the name? No. It didn't make sense. Then again, lots of things that don't make sense turn out to be true.

McCabe watched her light another Gauloise. With her Jeanne Moreau face, her accent, and the strong smell of the cigarettes, McCabe was beginning to feel like he had somehow landed in the middle of a Truffaut film himself. *Tirez sur le Detective*?

"What happened next?" he asked.

"Phillipe somehow found out, or maybe he already knew, that I had money problems. I'm sure that's why he approached me. I make a good income as a perfusionist in France—not as much as one would make here in the States, but still quite a lot. But I have expensive tastes, and I indulge them. I was carrying a lot of debt at high interest. So when he said he could offer me an assignment that would pay very well, I was interested in hearing more about it. I asked what it was, and he said there was an opportunity for me to take part in a transplant operation in America. I asked him why he'd want me to travel all the way from France when there were already many perfusionists in America. It quickly became clear that this was to be an illegal operation. He wanted me because of my financial problems and, I suppose, because I have no contacts with the medical or legal authorities in America."

"Did he tell you who the patient was?"

"No, not by name. He just told me that a very rich man in his eighties was dying of end-stage congestive heart failure. He wanted a new heart but couldn't qualify for an approved program because of his age. Phillipe said he'd located a resource that could obtain hearts outside of normal channels. I told him I had no interest in breaking the law and even less in going to jail. He said there was no danger of that. He said he and his friends had performed a number of these operations in the past and no one was any the wiser."

"Is that the word he used, friends? Not colleagues? Or associates?"

"I think so. Yes. I'm quite sure it is. Is that important?"

"I don't know. It might be. What happened next?"

"This conversation didn't occur all at once. It took place during the course of two or three meetings."

"I understand."

"Even though he said there was very little risk, I told him I wasn't interested. I didn't want to be involved in any thing illegal, and given the shortage of healthy hearts for transplant, I didn't believe it was ethically right to deprive someone younger of the chance for a normal life to help an old man who'd soon die anyway."

"Did he accept that?"

"He seemed to."

"What changed your mind?"

"Money. Avarice overcame both scruples and discretion. In our final discussion he told me that for one operation, one day in the operating room, he would deposit a hundred thousand euros in a numbered account in my name in the Cayman Islands. That's a hundred thousand euros for one day's work plus a couple of days' preparation and travel. That's more than I make in a year. Even so, I didn't say yes right away. I went back to my apartment and looked at the pile of unpaid bills on my table."

"Sounds familiar."

"Then I drank a bottle of wine and went out and had sex with an old friend I hadn't seen in a year."

"Lucky friend."

She ignored the comment. "The next morning I called Phillipe at his hotel and told him I would take part."

"And you did?"

"Yes. That was three operations ago. The third was last week. It never occurred to me until the Dubois girl's body was discovered that they might actually be killing people to harvest their hearts."

McCabe's mind was racing. Two more transplants. Two more harvested hearts. Whose hearts? Two more young blond female athletes? Where were the bodies? Buried under a golf course like Elyse Andersen? What about Lucinda Cassidy? He was jumping too far ahead. He forced himself to slow down.

"What made you think that's what they were doing?" he asked.

"Timing. We performed a transplant Wednesday afternoon. Katie Dubois's body was found Friday night. Then over the weekend, news reports said her heart had been cut from her body. I didn't know for sure if there was a connection, but it seemed likely. When I saw you at the funeral, I decided I would talk to you."

"When were the other two operations?"

"The first was late December last year, a week or so before Christmas. The second this spring, April sometime."

"Do you know the name of the hotel Spencer was staying in?"

"Yes. The Hôtel du Midi in Montpellier."

"When he was staying there?"

"November last year. I'm not sure of the exact dates. I left my diary behind in France."

McCabe took out his cell and hit Tom Tasco's number.

"Detective Tasco."

"Tom? It's Mike McCabe. I'm in the car, and I can't talk long. Do me a favor and check if Philip Spencer stayed at the Hôtel du Midi in Montpellier, France, spelled M-O-N-T-P-E-L-L-I-E-R, last November. If so, try to get the exact dates he was there. Maybe the local gendarmes will cooperate and check it out. If not, go through Interpol."

"What the hell was he doing in France?" asked Tasco.

"Can't talk about that now. See if you can get any background. Where he flew from and to. Airline and flight number. Anything else that seems pertinent."

"Gotcha."

McCabe hung up and turned back to Sophie. "You said you'd performed three of these operations including the one, when? Last Wednesday?"

"Yes. In the afternoon."

"Where?"

"I don't know."

"You don't know?"

"No. The way it works is I arrive in Boston a day before the surgery. I'm picked up at Logan by a driver and taken to a hotel. A different hotel each time. This time it was a Ramada Inn near Portsmouth, New Hampshire. I check in—"

"Using your real name?"

"Yes."

"Who makes the reservation?"

"I do. Phillipe calls me and tells me to book a flight and gives me the name of a hotel. He also gives me the name of a car service. I book them as well."

"Who pays?"

"I do. With my Visa card."

"Okay, so you checked into the Ramada Inn on what day? Tuesday?"

"Yes."

"Then what happened?"

"It's the same each time. I stay in my room. My meals are sent up. A man calls. Not Phillipe. It's a voice I don't know. This time I was told to be ready by five o'clock on Wednesday morning. I was picked up and taken to the surgery site."

"That's the phrase he used? Surgery site? Not hospital? Not OR?"

"The man said surgery site."

"Who picked you up?"

"A driver. I was made to wear a blindfold the whole time we drove until I entered the building."

"Could you see anything at all?"

"No."

"How long did you drive?"

"About four hours."

Four hours. Maximum radius from Portsmouth about two hundred and fifty miles, give or take. That covered a lot of territory. He needed more to go on. "Try to think back," he said. "I want you to close your eyes and, in your mind, put yourself back in that car. Can you do that?"

She looked at him, not sure where he was leading. "Yes. I can try." She closed her eyes.

"Describe the trip for me as best you can remember from the time you started off."

"I got in the car. The driver closed the door and got in himself. He closed his door. We drove out of the hotel parking lot."

"Did you turn left or right?"

She thought about that for a moment. "Left. Then we drove a little way, a minute or two. Stopped and waited for a moment."

A stop sign, thought McCabe. Or a traffic light. "While you were stopped, could you hear cars passing in front of you?"

"Yes, but only in one direction, left to right." Her eyes were still closed. She was doing well. "Then we turned right and joined the flow of traffic. We drove for a little while, went around a curve and then onto a big road. The driver accelerated fast as we went onto it. A motorway, I think it must have been. I could hear us passing cars and trucks to our right. Sometimes they passed us to our left. We drove on that road for a long way."

I-95, McCabe thought. The guy was driving carefully. Center lane. Not too slow. Not too fast. Probably doing sixty-five. Smart. Why attract attention? "Were you still on the big road when the sun came up? That would've been around six fifteen or so. You would have been driving about forty-five minutes. Could you feel its warmth on your face?"

Again she thought before speaking. "Yes."

"On your left side or right side?"

"Right side. I hadn't thought about that before. We must have been traveling north. It got warmer as we went along."

He wondered about the tolls. "Did the driver slow down or stop at all while you were on the big road? Like for a tollbooth?"

"Yes. I think he must have had a bowl of coins on the seat next to him. I could hear them jingling just as we slowed. Then he opened his window. I could hear it go down and feel the air on my face as we slowed to a stop. I suppose he threw the coins in a basket. Then we accelerated fast again."

Exact change lane. Made sense. No E-ZPass records. No toll takers to notice a woman in a blindfold.

"How long did you stay on the fast road, the motorway?"

"Several hours. I can't be sure of the time."

"How many times did you go through a toll? Where you could hear the change rattle?"

"Three times."

McCabe thought about the pattern of tollbooths along the Maine Turnpike. "After the third toll—this is important—did you start going fast again like on a motorway, or was it more like you were on smaller roads? You know, stops, turns, stuff like that."

"We stayed on the motorway only a little longer, maybe five minutes."

McCabe thought about that and guessed they'd stayed on 95 and probably gotten off around Augusta.

"How much longer did you drive after you left the motorway?"

"A while. More than an hour. Maybe two. We seemed to be going pretty fast with some stops. A two-lane road, I think. I could hear the whooshing sound of traffic coming the other way. Also, several times the driver pulled out suddenly to pass, accelerated fast, and pulled back in suddenly. The last few miles felt like a poorly maintained road. With many bumps."

A couple of hours on secondary roads from Augusta.

Max of what? Seventy-five or eighty miles. Progressively smaller roads at the end. That narrowed things down a bit. "Any sense from the position of the sun or anything else what direction you were traveling in?"

"No."

"At the end of the journey, when you got out of the car, think back to what your senses told you. Put yourself back in that place. Sound. Smell. The feel of the ground under your feet."

Sophie rummaged in her bag for another cigarette. She lit it and inhaled deeply. She considered his question, her eyes open. "I think we were in a wooded area. I could smell pine trees. The ground was soft."

"Could you smell the sea? Or hear seagulls? Or other birds?"

"No. I don't think so. As I was led toward the building, we were climbing up a rocky area. I tripped once or twice. He held me up. When we got to the building, he opened a door. Just inside the door we went down three rather long flights of stairs. Thirteen steps each. I was careful to count them because I still couldn't see. He held my arm and told me when we reached the last step."

Three times thirteen. Thirty-nine. Thirty-nine steps down from the ground level. Thirty-nine steps? Another deliberate movie reference, this time to an early Hitchcock classic? Or was he just being silly? Flights of stairs typically had thirteen steps. Okay. Thirty-nine steps down to what? A basement? An underground surgical center? Somewhere in the woods. With an operating room, a recovery room, dressing rooms. Maybe a prison for the victims.

Sophie began remembering again. "I was led to a small room, no bigger than a closet, really."

"How do you know it was small?"

"That's where I finally took off the mask. I was directed to change into a set of scrubs. I was told to put on a surgical mask and cap before leaving the OR. Then I scrubbed up. There was a sink and antiseptic soap in the room. I didn't see the others until we were all in the OR."

"Could you see the surgeon's face?"

"No. Not really. He entered the room wearing a surgical mask and goggles. So did the assistant surgeon and the anesthetist. Everybody else wore standard surgical masks at all times. We used no names. Each of us was assigned a code name, which was used in the OR. Mine was Catwalk."

"Any significance to the name?"

"None that I'm aware of."

"How many people in the room?"

"Six. The surgeon. An assistant. A nurse-anesthetist. Me. Two other nurses. A very small team for a transplant. I wasn't sure we'd be able to handle it, but the surgeon was very skilled."

"Did you talk to the others?"

"Only to communicate what was necessary during the operations. No names were used. We kept our masks on until we left the building. We were told this was for our own protection."

"It was the same team each time?"

"No. One of the nurses changed."

McCabe considered the size of the team for a moment. That made it a fairly wide conspiracy. A lot of people involved. A lot of possible leaks.

"The team—men or women?"

"Both surgeons were male. The nurse-anesthetist was female. One of the other nurses was a man, one a woman."

"You said one was replaced."

"A female nurse replaced a female."

"How could you tell there was a change if you were all wearing masks?"

"The new one was shorter, fatter. The voice was different."

"Was Spencer one of the doctors?"

"I don't know. He might have been. Right size. Hard to tell about the voice. He didn't say much."

"How about the other surgeon?"

"He seemed more slender. Slightly shorter."

"You were paid a hundred thousand euros for each operation?"

"Yes."

"Who were the patients?"

"They were all nameless old men. I assume they were all rich."

They sat silently for a while, Sophie smoking, McCabe thinking.

29

Tuesday 10:00 P.M.

The bullet from the sniper's rifle traversed the five hundred yards separating it from its intended target faster than the speed of sound. For this reason, McCabe saw the windshield fracture and blood explode from Sophie Gauthier's left arm a millisecond before he heard the crack of the shot. Expecting a second shot, he pushed Sophie down onto the seat and started the Bird's engine. He slammed the gear lever into first, spun the wheel hard left, and floored the accelerator, making the Bird's ancient innards howl with pain. It occurred to him Sophie was alive only because she'd leaned to the right to flick a cigarette out the window just as the shooter pulled the trigger. Chain-smoking, for once, saved a life.

McCabe pushed the big Ford V8 for all it was worth, and the Bird shot forward. On a straightaway, nothing less than a Corvette was likely to catch them. On a winding road in the dark, escape was less certain. In the rearview, McCabe saw headlights flick on several hundred yards behind, then start moving fast in their direction. The shooter was following. He must've seen that he missed and wanted to finish the kill. Still, it'd been a hell of a shot, even with a night-vision scope. McCabe glanced at Sophie.

The bullet had struck an artery, and blood was spurting out of her upper arm in a pulsing arc.

Without saying a word, Sophie pressed her right thumb against a pressure point above the wound. The blood that had been coming out in spurts now flowed more slowly, but not slowly enough. She was lying down on the seat. She'd slipped her head onto his lap. She held her arm across her body. She was shivering, probably with shock, perhaps with cold. He leaned over and switched on the heater. He needed to get her to a hospital. He could drive her there. The bullet had punched a hole in the windshield and there was some spidering of the glass, but he could see through it well enough. The problem was that if he was driving he couldn't apply pressure to the wound, and she'd soon be too weak to do it herself. If he couldn't help, she'd bleed to death.

Option two was to lose the shooter, pull over, and call for help. He had no way to communicate from the Bird other than his cell. Steering with one hand, he punched in 911 with the other. "Officer needs backup. This is Detective Sergeant Michael McCabe, Portland PD. I'm being chased and shot at by a sniper with wheels," he shouted. "I need an ambulance. I have a wounded civilian in my car. Gunshot wound. Arterial bleeding."

"Where are you?"

"Taylorville Road heading toward Bucks Mill. Meet me there. I'm going to try to lose the bad guy."

For the moment at least, they were on their own. "Try to focus," he said. "I figure our friend's about twenty seconds behind us, maybe less. If I can lose him, I'll be able to help you. In a minute I'll be turning fast into a side road. I'm killing the lights before we turn. We'll be moving fast, so brace yourself as best you can. When we make the turn, I'll pull up on the shoulder to the left. I'll get out of the car. When I do, stay low. Keep applying pressure to the wound. I'll help as soon as I can. Do you understand what we're doing?"

"Yes." Her voice was a guttural whisper. She looked

pale. Precious seconds passed. The turn was coming up fast. There were some trees that would provide cover. He glanced in the rearview. The shooter was still following, maybe two hundred yards behind. "We're turning now," he said.

McCabe killed the lights, braked, downshifted, and turned hard, almost blind, to the left. The Bird skidded into a ninety-degree-plus turn. McCabe adjusted, hit the accelerator, narrowly missed a tree to his left, and shot forward onto the side road. He pulled onto the left shoulder and killed the engine.

As he jumped from the Bird, he saw the blackened silhouette of an SUV roar past the turnoff. The car's lights disappeared for a moment. If they kept going, McCabe could help Sophie. If not, he had to be ready for the worst. He opened the Bird's trunk and pulled out the Mossberg. Through the trees he saw the lights of the SUV stopping and then reversing. The shooter was coming back. Sophie was losing strength, blood oozing out. The SUV backed past the crossroads, turned left, and surged forward.

McCabe shouldered the powerful Mossberg and stepped onto the road. The SUV's headlights were closing fast, aiming right for him. He pumped and fired, pumped and fired again. Four shots filled with 12-gauge buckshot slammed straight into the SUV's front end, splintering the windshield, shredding both front tires and shattering the headlights. He leapt out of the way. The crippled SUV swerved first left, then right, finally crashing head-on into a big maple on the opposite side of the road. The air bag deployed. Coolant poured from a hundred holes in its radiator.

McCabe rushed the vehicle. "Out. No weapon. Now."

It was the far side door that burst open. Using the vehicle and the tree to shield him, a man leapt from the passenger side. He was clutching a scoped rifle. He vaulted a low stone wall and ran into the field. Holding his rifle high, he followed a zigzag pattern. Even in the dark, from the rear McCabe could tell it wasn't Philip Spencer. This man was a couple of inches shorter, with a shaved head and weight lifter's shoulders. He was moving fast. By the time McCabe could reach the wall and aim, the man was beyond the fifty or so yards that marked the effective range of the Mossberg. McCabe fired off a couple of rounds anyway. The man ignored them and kept running, disappearing into the darkness.

McCabe rushed back to the Bird, laid the Mossberg on the ground by the driver's door, and climbed in. Raising Sophie's head, he slipped under it and lowered it into his lap. He pushed the fingers of his right hand against her inner arm above the wound, replacing her fingers, allowing her other arm to rest, applying direct pressure, compressing the brachial artery against the humerus. This effectively stopped the bleeding. Sophie was conscious but pale even in the faint light of a moon-filled night. Her skin felt cool and clammy. He hit REDIAL on his cell and told them to hurry.

Following the sniper across the field wasn't an option. Armed with a shotgun and a pistol, he'd be up against a skilled shooter with a sniper rifle and night-vision scope. More important, Sophie would bleed to death. All he could do was wait for help and hope the shooter didn't double back to finish them off.

McCabe leaned down and slipped his .45 out of the seat holster. He laid it on Sophie's chest, where he could reach it in a hurry. He flicked off the safety. Not that it would do them any good. It just made him feel better.

Sophie was still shivering. Without releasing pressure to the wound, he managed to slip off his light summer jacket and drape it over her. They sat there like that for a while covered in drying blood, Sophie drifting in and out of consciousness. He remembered reading it was important to keep a wound victim conscious. So he started singing an old bar song loudly, over and over, his unmusical voice booming out into the night:

She's got freckles on her butt,
She is nice, she is nice.

And when she's in my arms, it's paradise.
All the sailors give her chase
'Cause they love her naval base.
She's got freckles on her butt,
She is nice.

He sang the words over and over. All the while his mind was on the sniper. A shaved head with broad shoulders. Was he doubling back to finish his night's work? McCabe imagined himself lit in the green of the man's night-vison scope, cross-hairs steady on his skinny Irish face, an easy target, even distorted by the fractured windshield. He imagined the man squeezing the trigger. The bullet traversing the distance be-tween them. His head exploding. McCabe scrunched down lower and rolled up the driver's side window.

The rational side of his brain knew the man was more likely running away. He'd have to know his bullet hadn't killed Sophie immediately. Have to know McCabe would call for help. He probably saw Sophie move as he fired, and saw the bullet strike her arm, not her head. Yet he couldn't know how badly hurt she was. She might have died from loss of blood. Or he might have simply nicked her and she was lying low to stay out of sight. McCabe kept singing.

She's got freckles on her butt,
She is nice.

He heard sirens. First in the distance, then closing fast. Less than a minute later, two state police cars and an am-bulance screamed onto the quiet road. The ambulance and one of the cars pulled up next to the Bird. A young trooper sporting a Marine Corps–style buzz cut swaggered over, picked up the Mossberg, and signaled McCabe to roll down the window. He did.

An EMT pushed past the trooper and opened the door. "Are you injured, sir?"

"I'm fine. She's shot in the upper arm. Arterial bleeding. A lot of it."

"If you can slip out of the car without letting go of her arm, I'll lean in and we'll trade places."

McCabe did as he was told. The EMT slid by McCabe in the opposite direction, reaching into the car until his hands could join McCabe's on the wound. McCabe slipped out. The EMT and his partner slid Sophie onto a stretcher and hurried her toward the ambulance.

McCabe turned. The trooper had his service weapon out and pointed at McCabe. "All right, sir. Please turn around slowly and place both hands on the car."

McCabe did as he was told. "I'm a cop," he said to the trooper. "Detective Sergeant Michael McCabe, Portland PD."

Pause. "Where's your shield and ID?"

"Back pocket. Left."

McCabe felt the trooper's hand enter his pocket and extract the wallet. The man opened it and looked it over.

"Okay, you can turn around," the trooper said. McCabe did, and he handed the wallet back. He holstered his weapon. "You're a little off your turf, aren't you, Sergeant? What's the story?"

McCabe gave a weary sigh. He wasn't in the mood to explain his presence in Gray or discuss jurisdictional issues with a gung-ho ex-marine. "Just call Colonel Matthews and tell him I'm here in conjunction with the Katie Dubois murder investigation. It's a Portland PD case. And get reinforcements. There's a skilled sniper with a rifle and probably a night-vision scope fleeing this area. On foot, for now."

The medics were sliding Sophie into the back of the waiting ambulance. "I'm going with them," McCabe announced.

From the driver's seat of the Bird, McCabe retrieved his cell phone, as well as the bloody jacket that had been covering Sophie and the .45. He turned and trotted toward the ambulance. "By the way, take care of that Mossberg for me," he shouted to the trooper. "It's a fine weapon, and I want it back."

The EMTs already had Sophie's good arm hooked up to an IV when McCabe hopped in behind the stretcher. "I'm riding with you," he said. It was a statement, not a question.

The medic looked up and nodded but said nothing. McCabe closed the door and squeezed himself into a corner against lockers filled with medical supplies.

McCabe looked out the back door. He could see the trooper hesitate for a moment, then pick up the shotgun and walk to his car, no doubt to start the radio calls that would work their way up the chain of command to Matthews. The ambulance took off, its lights flashing and siren screaming an unmistakable urgency to the quiet countryside.

Somewhere in the dark, the shooter watched and listened and began planning his next move.

30

McCabe watched the EMT work from his perch in the back of the ambulance. The man placed an oxygen mask over Sophie's nose and mouth. He wrapped what looked like an Ace bandage as tightly as he could around Sophie's wound and resumed applying pressure against the artery above the wound. He looked competent. There was no conversation.

Up front, the driver radioed the ER dispatcher at Cumberland Medical Center. "Cumberland, this is Gray Emergency. We're coming in, lights and siren. We've got a woman. Gunshot wound. Left arm. Arterial bleeding. Kind of shocky. We've got one line normal saline, wide open. Hundred percent O_2. BP soft."

"Eighty-five over sixty, pulse one ten," shouted the man in the back.

The driver relayed the information. "ETA seventeen minutes," he added. "Please advise."

The voice from the hospital crackled from a speaker above McCabe's head. "Open a second line if you can. The trauma team will be ready and waiting. Give us your one-minute ETA."

"Roger that."

McCabe leaned back as best he could. He looked like

an accident victim himself, covered with Sophie's blood. He pinned his shield to his bloodied shirt and used his cell to call Maggie.

"McCabe, what's going on? I thought you'd be back by now." He could barely hear her through the scream of the siren.

He filled her in on the shooting, omitting anything he didn't want the EMT to hear, which was most of it.

"I'll meet you at the hospital," she said. "I'll call Jane Devaney and get her over here before I leave."

McCabe hesitated, trying to figure out if that was the best way to keep the bases covered. He hated waking Jane in the middle of the night but, in the end, figured that was the best solution. "Alright. Can you bring me some clean clothes? I'm a little unsightly at the moment."

"Anything in particular?"

"No. Underwear's in the dresser. Shirts and pants in the closet. Bring some kind of jacket." She said okay. "Also please call Bill Fortier and have him coordinate the search with the staties. Ditto the crime scene people. I want Jacobi working that SUV."

"Sure. Have you had anything to eat?"

McCabe had to think about that for a minute. "No. Not really. Everything good there?"

"Yeah. Casey's a little nervous. She just went to bed, but I don't think she's sleeping. You want to talk to her?"

"Not from here. Just tell her everything's fine, I love her, and I'll see her tomorrow."

They were on the turnpike now. Sophie seemed to be drifting in and out of consciousness.

"BP softening to seventy-five systolic, pulse up to one twenty," the EMT called to the driver. "I'm inserting the second line." The ambulance slowed and pulled over to allow the man in back a steady platform to insert the needle for the second IV. He put it in above the first in Sophie's good arm.

He taped the needle in place. "Okay, go!" he shouted.

The ambulance started back on the road and roared south on 95. What little traffic there was pulled to the right to let them pass. They cut across Washington Avenue and then south on 295. About half a mile north of the Congress Street exit, the driver again spoke to the hospital. "Cumberland, this is Gray. Second line open full. One minute from touchdown."

"See you when you get here."

One minute later they pulled into the ambulance bay at the Cumberland Medical Center ER. The ambulance crew grabbed both sides of the stretcher and exited the vehicle at a run. McCabe followed. Twin automatic doors burst open, and they hurried Sophie directly into the hospital's brightly lit trauma room. A full reception committee, at least ten doctors, nurses, residents, and students, stood in position, ready to receive.

The EMTs and a pair of residents lifted the sheet under Sophie and used it to transfer her to the trauma room stretcher. Someone in scrubs called out, "Trauma room three!" They headed where she was pointing.

As they went, a serious-looking young woman, thin with a long horsey face, checked Sophie's IVs and oxygen, then addressed one of the EMTs. Her plastic badge identified her as Dr. Maloney. "Give me what you've got."

"Gunshot wound to the left arm. Pulsatile bleeding with a lot of blood at the scene. Seems to have missed the bone. BP seventy-five on the way in. Two lines full out. She's taken two liters normal saline."

McCabe waited while she called out to her team, "Okay, start another line in her right groin. I want four units O-negative stat." A group of residents and nurses began to make it happen.

"Are you the husband?" A man in his forties addressed McCabe, who'd come into room three right behind the EMTs.

"No." McCabe indicated the badge pinned it to his bloody shirt. "I'm Detective McCabe, Portland PD. Who are you?"

McCabe could hear the young woman's voice directing

her team from the head of the stretcher. "I want blood sent out for type and screen."

"I'm Dr. Kennedy, emergency attending. I'm afraid you'll have to wait outside, Detective."

McCabe shook his head. "I'm not going anywhere. This woman is a key witness in a murder case and somebody's trying to kill her. She needs protection."

The doctor paused only a second or two. "She'll be alright in here." His tone was friendly. "We're trying to save her life, not end it. There's no room for extra bodies in the trauma room. She'll be going up to surgery in about ten minutes." Dr. Kennedy indicated McCabe's blood-covered clothes. "In the meantime, you can shower in the doctors' locker room. Do you know the patient's name?"

"Put her into your system as Jane Doe, and tell your folks while she's here she's under protective custody of the Portland PD."

The doctor nodded. He turned to a young man, a medical student, McCabe guessed. "Get Detective McCabe some scrubs to put on and show him where to clean up," he said. "You can join her in the ICU recovery room on five when she gets out of the OR, which won't be for two or three hours. Until then she'll have about ten reliable people around her at all times. I'll let you know."

The young man found a large plastic bag for McCabe's clothes and a smaller one for his wallet and keys. He then led him to a small locker room with a row of shower stalls. McCabe stripped down and stuffed the clothes plus his gun and holster into the larger bag. He tied a knot in the bag to seal it and took it with him into the shower stall. He wasn't going anywhere unarmed tonight, and he wasn't leaving any guns lying around untended. As the hot water hit him, rinsing Sophie's blood off his face and arms, he watched the reddened water swirling around and down the drain. The shower scene from *Psycho* played in his mind.

Sophie was in surgery on the fifth floor. About thirty feet from the doors to the OR, along a partially darkened corridor, McCabe sat in a plastic chair in the otherwise empty ICU waiting room. He was dressed in scrubs. He pinned his shield to the blouse. He debated whether to strap his .45 over or under and opted for under the loose-fitting garment. He hooked his cell phone to the gun belt. His hand rested loosely on the weapon.

According to the doctors, the sniper's bullet passed cleanly through her left arm about five inches below her shoulder. It missed the bone but ruptured the brachial artery. A vascular surgeon was working now to clean out the damaged tissue and reconnect the artery itself. McCabe got a little lost in the medical jargon, but the terms "debridement" and "anastomosis" stuck in his mind.

The surgeon said it would take about two hours to repair the arm but she'd probably be just fine, not lose any function. He also said the biggest threat to Sophie's life was infection. McCabe didn't bother telling the doctor that really wasn't the case.

McCabe extinguished the lights and muted the TV, allowing its colorful silent images to remain the only movement in the room, their glow the only illumination. He stared silently through the glass wall at the hallway in front of him. There were few passersby. A couple of nurses, an elderly man pushing a bucket and mop, a young man in scrubs. He watched each for signs of threat. A bank of three elevators stood directly across the corridor from the waiting room. McCabe kept his eyes on the little lighted numbers above the doors, watching for one that might stop at five, though he doubted the shooter, if he was coming, would choose such a direct route.

31

The shooter figured it'd take him about six hours to walk back to Portland. Finding a vehicle he could requisition might prove a little tricky, but he'd keep his eyes open. Where he could, he'd travel cross-country, avoiding the roads. He assumed the cops would be scouring the area, starting where they picked up the woman and working out from there. He wondered if they'd bring in dogs. His scent'd be all over the damaged Blazer. He didn't know if they'd pick up any prints. He'd tried to be careful about that, but he didn't have time to wipe anything down before he flew out the door. He touched his face where he'd banged it against the steering wheel trying to duck when the cop unloaded that shotgun. Then the air bag whacked him again. Fuck it. Too late to worry about that now. Left his favorite Pierotucci leather jacket in the backseat. That pissed him off. It was practically new and set him back four hundred bucks. Looked great, too. He didn't think there was anything in the pockets. Other than that, just a couple of old Billy Ray Cyrus CDs and a DVD of an old movie, *Day of the Jackal.* He'd already seen it a couple of times but was planning to watch it again tonight. Now that was all fucked up.

If they did bring in dogs, he'd be easy to track. Another reason to find a car. Then he wouldn't have to worry about dogs. 'Course, he wasn't real sure about that. A special ops guy he met in Kuwait in '91 told him trained bloodhounds could even track someone driving away in a car. Something about the car's vent system exhausting the interior air out through the back and carrying the smell of the passenger with it. Sounded like bullshit. Probably was bullshit. How the fuck could a dog smell something like that, anyway? Fuck it. He put it out of his mind. Anyhow, they wouldn't have time to organize any fucking dogs. With another six hours of darkness, he'd be to hell and gone before they got anything going.

Just a little hike through the countryside. He was only pissed because he'd missed the bitch's heart. Hadn't accomplished the damned mission. Then that cop unloaded on him with a fucking shotgun. Bastard. Anyway, calm down, be cool, he told himself. Be cool or be dead.

Still, it bothered him that he missed. He shouldn't have missed. Shit, he never missed. It was just because of the fucking cigarettes the bitch kept sucking on, moving around, tossing them out the window. Jesus. Didn't she care what they were doing to her lungs? Didn't she have any fucking respect for her body? And that hairball cop letting her do it. Didn't he know how bad secondhand smoke could be for you? Him a father and everything. Well, he'd give them both something better than butts to suck on. Be cool, he warned himself again. Calm down. Don't let the rage take over.

He walked silently along a line of trees at the edge of a meadow. He didn't know how bad the woman was hurt. The green image through the night-vision scope made things pretty blurry. Specially when they were moving around like she was. He was pretty sure he hit her arm. Couldn't tell how bad the wound was. Might have hit a bone or an artery or maybe both. They would've taken her to the hospital. There were two hospitals in Portland. He'd head for the bigger one.

He held the M24 sniper rifle in the crook of his left arm. Good weapon. Accurate. He stroked it with his free hand.

Shooting someone always got the juices going, and he was getting a hard-on. In fact, he'd had it for a while and it wasn't going away. If you had a hard-on for more than four hours you had to go see a doctor. That's what the TV ad for that limp-dick medicine said. Well, he guessed he'd see a few doctors tonight. He came to a dirt road. Looking both ways he couldn't see much of anything. He was trying to figure out which way to go and thinking about how to get himself a vehicle when he saw a pair of headlights approaching him at a good clip about a half klick away. He squatted down in some scrub. Unlikely to be a cop, but you couldn't be sure. As it drew closer he picked out the shape of a pickup truck. Not a cop. He set the M24 down in the grass by the side of the road and walked into the middle, real cool and casual like, and waved the truck down as it approached. It slowed to a stop. The driver was a kid, seventeen or eighteen years old.

"What's the problem, mister? Car break down?" He was a good-looking boy. Long blond hair. A cute little soul patch growing under his lip. He had broad shoulders and what looked to be a nice body. The shooter nodded and flashed him his best smile.

"Yeah. That's right. My car broke down. 'Bout a mile from here."

"Don't ya have a cell?" the boy asked.

"Nah. It ran out of juice."

"Well, here, you can borrow mine. You belong to Triple-A?" The kid held his cell phone out the open window. The shooter moved closer, as if to take the phone, then, in a single motion, pulled open the door of the truck with his left hand, grabbed the back of the kid's head with his right, and slammed it hard against the steering wheel. Then he slammed it again. Blood spurted out of the kid's nose. The boy was screaming, "You broke my fucking nose. You broke my fucking nose." Still holding the boy's neck, the shooter unhooked his seat belt with his left hand and pulled him hard out of the truck. He threw him onto the road. "You broke my fucking nose," the kid cried again.

"Shut the fuck up!" said the shooter. He kicked the boy hard in the face. "Just shut the fuck up." Then he kicked him again for good measure, this time in the gut. The boy squeezed into a fetal position. He was sobbing and gasping for air, but, shit, that was no reason not to have a little fun.

The shooter knelt down and unbuttoned the kid's jeans and pulled them down. His pink boxers were decorated with little rows of red hearts, which made the shooter smile. Cute, he thought. Maybe he'd get himself a pair like that.

The shooter went back to the truck, turned off the engine, and extinguished the headlights. In the distance he could hear a siren. More than one, in fact, and they were getting closer. Fuck it. He better haul ass. He walked over to where the rifle was hidden. He picked it up. The boy was lying on his side, sobbing quietly. Too bad wasting such a good-looking kid, but he'd seen the shooter's face, and the area was crawlin' with cops. The shooter placed the barrel of the rifle about an inch above the boy's ear. He pulled the trigger.

32

McCabe stared across the room. His mind wandered. He remembered how much he hated hospitals. They were strange anonymous places where the people he loved died. He was fighting off the urge to doze when the sound of a man's voice outside the room jarred him to full alert. The voice was coming from beyond his sight lines, down the corridor to the right. Keeping his hand on his .45, McCabe rose and walked to the door and peered around.

"Fucking sons of bitches, fucking sons of bitches." A dirty man who had bandages wrapped around the top of his head limped in McCabe's direction, muttering the same phrase over and over again. He was a big man. Tough to tell what age. His face was bruised, and it looked to McCabe like he'd come out on the losing end of a bar brawl. He seemed out of place in the hospital, out of place in an ICU, but maybe he had a friend who was hurt worse than he was. He wore a dirty blue sweatshirt with a picture of a lighthouse and the words MAINE, THE WAY LIFE SHOULD BE printed on it. The man glanced at the badge pinned to McCabe's scrubs. It didn't seem to faze him. He leaned in closer. "You got any smokes?" he asked. McCabe noticed a trace of a southern accent in his hoarse voice. He didn't answer.

"I said you got any smokes?" the man repeated. His breath carried the unmistakable smell of Altoids. McCabe hated Altoids.

He shook his head. "Sorry, pal. Even if I had 'em, you couldn't smoke 'em. Not in here, anyway. Beat it. Take off before I have you escorted out of here."

The man looked like he was about to argue and then thought better of it. "Aw, fuck it." He turned and limped off the way he'd come, presumably in search of someone with cigarettes. McCabe watched him leave, wondering how he'd managed to find his way into the ICU unit and if, in fact, there was a reason for him to be there. Had he been looking for Sophie? Maybe, but why come tromping in making noise and dressed in a way sure to attract the attention of every security guard in the place?

A chime sounded to his left and one of the elevator doors opened. Maggie stepped out, carrying a bag from Dunkin' Donuts in one hand and a small overnight bag in the other.

She handed him the overnight bag. "You wear tidy whities," she smiled. "I always wanted to know." She looked at his scrubs. "Cute outfit."

"Thanks," he said, relaxing a little for the first time in hours. "I think the color brings out the blue of my eyes, don't you?" He let out a breath he realized he'd been holding in for a while.

"Oh, definitely. Here. I've brought you some coffee and something to eat." She held out the doughnut bag.

"Glazed chocolate?"

"Of course, and Bavarian crème."

He took a doughnut, and she handed him a large Styrofoam cup. "Why don't you drink the coffee while it's hot? You can change later."

They sat down side by side in the darkened room and began sipping the coffee.

"What's in there?" She pointed at the big plastic bag.

"My clothes."

Maggie unknotted the bag and peered in. "Jesus Christ.

This woman's still alive? How could she possibly have any blood left in her?"

"She probably didn't have a lot. It was a pretty close thing. If our friend had hung around and forced me into a firefight while we were waiting for the ambulance, she'd have bled to death."

"They think she's gonna live?"

"That's what they tell me. I just hope she doesn't clam up. She was pretty frightened before. She'll be terrified now."

Maggie nodded. "The bad guys are going to come after her again."

"I'm sure of it. Either here or as soon as she gets out."

"So we put her in protective custody."

"That's what I'm thinking, but not in a cell. That'd just piss her off and make her less cooperative. Easy enough to organize round-the-clock coverage here at the hospital. This is where she's most vulnerable. Afterward, maybe we find her a quiet, out-of-the-way motel. Register her under a phony name and have a female cop, maybe Davenport, bunk with her."

"She could stay at my place."

"I don't think so. Too traceable. They know you're working the case. Plus I'd rather have you in the hunt than playing bodyguard."

"Tell me again what she told you."

McCabe repeated, more or less verbatim, what Sophie had told him in the car.

"She told you Philip Spencer recruited her?"

"That's what she said."

"Why the hell would he give her his real name?"

"Beats me. The only reason I can think of is it's on his passport."

"He had to show her his passport?"

"No. Yeah. I don't know. It's weird."

McCabe's cell phone vibrated against his hip. The caller was Bill Jacobi.

"You up in Gray, Bill?"

"Yeah, I'm at the site now."

"Anything?"

"Yeah—quite a bit, actually. For one thing, we know how he followed you."

"I wasn't followed."

"Yeah. You were. Only not visually. We found small GPS transmitters attached to the undercarriage of both your car and the woman's car. All the shooter had to do was look at his screen to know precisely where you were and where to go for a clear shot."

McCabe was annoyed with himself. He should have considered the possibility and checked out the Bird before he left Portland.

"We traced the line of fire and pretty much pinpointed where he positioned himself for the kill. A little rise just off the road about five hundred yards in front of you. Looks like he used a post-and-rail fence as a firing platform."

"Any shell casings?"

"No. He only fired once, and he must have policed the brass before he left."

"What else?"

"Well, we won't know about prints till we can flatbed his SUV back to Middle Street and check, but given he left the car in a hurry, my guess is we'll find something, maybe quite a lot. Oh, here's a weird one. There are fresh semen stains on the driver's seat and on the floor under the seat."

"The guy jerked off?"

"Apparently. I doubt he had another consenting adult with him."

"Interesting. I guess he finds shooting people stimulating."

Jacobi didn't respond. Instead McCabe heard some indecipherable chatter. In the background he could hear a siren. Then Bill Fortier's voice talking to Jacobi. Then Fortier's voice on the phone. "McCabe, get your ass up here. We've had another killing."

"Just a minute." McCabe got up and shut the door to the waiting room and put the cell on speaker. "Okay. Maggie's here. What happened?"

Fortier's voice filled the small space.

"A high school kid named Ryan Corbin. Seventeen years old. Body was found in a culvert at the side of the road. Shot point-blank through the head."

McCabe grimaced and wondered if he made the right choice not chasing the shooter across the field. He believed he had. Otherwise Sophie would have died for sure, he probably would have been shot, and the kid might have gotten killed anyway. "Hold on a sec," he told Fortier. "Mag, get some uniforms up here to watch over Sophie. Make sure it's people we know, experienced people and not some rookie. Tell them to make sure nobody, especially Dr. Philip Spencer, goes anywhere near her. We've got to get up to Gray."

Maggie took out her own cell.

McCabe turned off the speakerphone. "Where'd you find the body?"

"Sheriff's deputy found it about a mile and a half from where we found your car and the SUV. I'm headed there now. Come up to where you were. Follow Bucks Mill about a mile, then take a right on Taylorville Road. Go for about a mile and you'll see a whole shitload of flashing lights. State's saying this one's MSP jurisdiction. We're saying it's an extension of the Dubois case so we're still primary. Anyway, we'll work it out with Matthews. By the way, your car's being impounded as evidence. So's the shotgun. Get yourself a rental. We'll pay for it."

McCabe took the overnight bag into the bathroom and changed into the clothes Maggie had brought for him. Jeans. Black turtleneck. Beige windbreaker. Not exactly what he'd choose for a murder investigation, but fuck it. When he came out, two uniformed officers were already talking to Maggie. One was Kevin Comisky, whom he'd last seen leaving the scrap yard on Friday night. The other cop he'd seen a number of times at 109. He didn't know his name.

McCabe skipped the pleasantries. "Detective Savage fill you in?"

They nodded. "Alright, let me reiterate. This woman is

a key witness in the Dubois investigation, and her life is in danger. Someone's already tried to kill her once. He'll try again. I got a quick look at the bad guy from the rear. Shaved head. Big neck and shoulders. Maybe five-ten. Might be him coming for her. Might be somebody else.

"She's listed in this hospital as Jane Doe, and that's the way it stays. When she comes out of surgery, you stick like glue. Walk with the gurney that takes her to her room and park yourselves outside the door. If one of you has to take a leak, the other stays put. When hospital personnel go into that room, doctors, nurses, anyone, you check their ID and then go in with them. Under no circumstances does a Dr. Philip Spencer go anywhere near her."

"If it's Spencer, how do we stop him?"

"Just tell him it's orders, you have no choice—and don't take any shit. He's an arrogant bastard, and he'll try to bully you. Clear?"

"Clear," they said practically in unison.

"Hospital security knows you're here, and they'll back you up. If anyone gives you a hard time, call me on my cell." He wrote down the number and handed it to Comisky. "Let me have your cell number."

"It's 555-6655."

"Thanks. If any cops show up to relieve you, even if you know them, send 'em home. You're on duty here until I personally relieve you."

33

Wednesday, 4:30 A.M.

Maggie drove fast. McCabe sat next to her, pondering their next move. Neither spoke. This thing was metastasizing, McCabe thought grimly. First Dubois. Then Sophie. Now this kid. Next maybe Lucinda Cassidy. They had to move fast before any more victims were claimed. In the dark, Maggie gave McCabe's forearm a reassuring squeeze. "Don't worry, we'll get him," she said.

The flashing light bars of half a dozen police cars, state and local as well as the PPD, lent an eerie glow to the night sky above Taylorville Road. A young trooper flagged Maggie to the shoulder a hundred yards short of the crime scene. He checked their IDs and told them they'd have to walk from there. Terri Mirabito's van pulled in right behind. Terri grabbed her bag, and the three of them approached the yellow crime scene tape cordoning off the area where the boy had been killed. Inside, teams of crime scene techs, Jacobi's and one from the state crime lab, were making measurements and taking pictures.

McCabe and Maggie saw Bill Fortier standing with a senior MSP officer, and they went over to join them. Fortier made the introductions. "Detective Sergeant Mike McCabe, Detective Margaret Savage, this is Colonel Matthews. Colonel, you probably know the assistant ME."

Matthews extended his hand first to McCabe, then Maggie. "Ed Matthews," he said. "I've heard a lot about you two." He smiled over at Terri. "I do know Dr. Mirabito."

McCabe's mind played with the name. "Ed Mathews. Third baseman. Boston, Milwaukee, and Atlanta Braves. Only man to play with the Braves in all three cities. Five hundred and twelve career home runs. Tied with Ernie Banks for seventeenth on the all-time list. Voted into the Hall of Fame in 1978. Spelled with one *T*." What a lot of shit. Sometimes he wished he had a delete button for all the unwanted detritus that lingered in his brain.

"Colonel Matthews and I have been discussing jurisdictional issues," said Fortier. "This could be considered an MSP case because the kid was killed out here in East Hoo-Haa and not in the City of Portland. On the other hand, with the obvious connection to the Dubois case, if that holds up, and we think it will, PPD has a material interest. What we've decided is that Portland will continue as the lead agency, you and Maggie as lead team, but MSP will commit any resources we need—detectives, uniformed assets, whatever. Anybody involved reports to you, Mike, and through you to me and then to Shockley."

"Feel free to call on me for whatever you need," added Matthews. "If we've got it, you've got it."

McCabe nodded, his hands stuffed in his pockets against the early morning chill. "Works for me." Truth was he couldn't have asked for more. He was still running the show, but the new arrangement gave him extra resources whenever and wherever he might need them.

Maggie, Terri, and McCabe all donned latex gloves and paper booties and walked over to where the body lay in a small drainage culvert that ran between the side of the road and an open meadow beyond. In the predawn light, with his pants pulled down and his arms and head turned at improbable angles, the boy looked like an oversized puppet that had been carelessly tossed away. A cop shone his Maglite on the corpse. Dirt from dried tears marked the boy's cheeks just below the eyes. An ugly star-shaped wound, black, red, and orange, shone like a gaping eye an inch above the left ear. The boy hadn't bled much from the wound, but there was a lot of dried blood below his nose on his lips and chin and some spattered on his sweatshirt.

Terri knelt in the culvert and examined the wound. "Not much question about cause," she said. "Contact wound from a rifle. The killer must have held the muzzle up close against the kid's head. This stippling effect"—she pointed with a finger—"was caused by muzzle gases burning and staining the skin." She pointed to a clearly round indentation in the center of the wound. "Muzzle impact." Then, looking up, she said, "It'll match the bore of the weapon." She wiggled the boy's nose with a gloved hand. "Nose is broken. The guy must have roughed him up first."

"Time of death?" asked Maggie.

"Only a few hours ago. Between midnight and 2:00 A.M." She gently moved one of the boy's wrists back and forth. "Rigor hasn't set in yet. Looking at the scrapes on the back and buttocks, I figure he was shot up there on the road somewhere and dragged here postmortem."

"We've found the slug." Jacobi walked over from the road, carrying a small evidence bag. "Imbedded about six inches into the road. Should match the one we took from the seat of the T-Bird."

"It'll match," said McCabe.

"'Course it will," said Jacobi.

Maggie and McCabe drove back to the crash site behind Bill Jacobi. They pulled in behind the crime scene tape about fifty yards away from the damaged vehicles. The shooter's SUV was pretty nearly totaled, its hood smashed in against a two-hundred-year-old maple with a trunk that had to be six feet in diameter. A flatbed driver had positioned his vehicle behind the SUV and was preparing to haul it up onto his truck. Tom Tasco and Eddie Fraser were standing nearby.

"He must have been doing forty at the moment of impact," Jacobi told McCabe. "The air bag deployed. Probably smacked him in the face. I'm surprised the son of a bitch was able to walk, let alone run."

"Anybody run the vehicle?" asked McCabe.

"Yeah," said Tasco. "Rented on September 13 at the Budget counter at Logan under the name of Paul Oliver Duggan. D-U-G-G-A-N. We assume that's an alias."

"It is," said McCabe. "It's another movie character. From *Day of the Jackal*. Paul Oliver Duggan was the name on the Jackal's fake passport. Did Mr. Duggan have a reservation?"

"No. He was a walk-up. No history of renting with Budget before. We've requested passenger manifests on all flights that arrived within three hours of the rental, but we doubt we'll find the name Duggan."

"Let me check the manifests when they come in. The guy likes to use movie names. I may recognize one you miss. How about license and credit card?"

"He had a California license and a valid Capital One Visa card. Both listed his home address as 5333 Zoo Drive, Los Angeles," said Eddie Fraser.

"Let me guess. The L.A. Zoo?"

"You got it."

"These guys are real comedians. Anything in the car?"

"We'll check for prints in Portland. The semen sample is going to a lab in Brunswick."

"He left the car in a hurry. He leave any stuff behind?" asked McCabe.

"Yeah," said Tasco. "A couple of country music CDs and an old DVD, apparently purchased out of the used pile at VideoPort on Middle Street. I guess after killing people, he likes relaxing with a movie."

"Let me guess again. *Day of the Jackal*."

"Two for two. There was also a pricey leather jacket. Nothing in the pockets except one of those tins of breath mints. Almost empty."

McCabe froze. "Altoids?"

"Yeah, Altoids. Also a couple of empty tins on the floor. The guy must have been an addict."

"Shit." McCabe reached for his cell and punched in the number Comisky had given him.

34

The shooter studied his image in the restroom mirror as he unwrapped the bandages from around his head. Nice touch for a hospital, he thought, hiding his shaved head with bandages instead of a hat. He once thought he ought to get a rug. It'd change his look alright. In the end, though, he decided there was no way he was gonna compromise his cool with something that looked so frigging ridiculous. He fingered the bruising under his left eye. It hurt. Fucking air bag smacked him in the face like a punch. Fuck it. Couldn't do much about that now. He pulled off his jeans, rolled them into a tight ball, and hid them as best he could behind the toilet. He put on the scrubs and the little blue hat the cop had left behind in the bathroom. With the scrubs, he'd fit right in.

He checked the Blackie Collins switchblade strapped to his leg. Nice to know it was there, though his two hands were all the weapons he'd need. He didn't have the rifle. That was hidden in the truck, parked two blocks from the hospital and bearing a new set of license plates.

The shooter looked again in the mirror. Blew himself a kiss. Forced himself to breathe in. Breathe out. Slowly. Deeply. Once. Twice. Three times. Keep it cool. Not too edgy. Not too excited. A stealth op. Excitement causes fuck-ups.

Time for recon. If he was gonna get into the bitch's room, he needed one of those plastic ID badges they all hung around their necks. He'd have to borrow one. That was job one. He exited the restroom, turned out the light, and quietly closed the door.

"A lot of people suck Altoids, McCabe."

Maggie and McCabe were heading back down the turnpike toward Cumberland Medical. There was more traffic on the road now, the forward edge of rush hour, and McCabe was weaving around cars, siren blaring.

"Yeah, I know, but I knew there was something not quite right about that guy. I should have seen it. I should have recognized him from his body shape. Didn't fit with an old drunk sailor."

"Well, don't take it so hard. I know you sometimes see yourself as SuperCop, but, like they say, shit happens. We make mistakes. We all do, even you."

"Work homicide long enough and it becomes part of your DNA that mistakes kill innocent people. Even not so innocent ones like my brother Tommy."

McCabe pulled off 95 by the mall and took the connector to 295. A couple of minutes later they were at the Congress Street exit heading to the hospital.

Sophie Gauthier was out of recovery and in a room on the third floor. Finding the room turned out to be easy. When the shooter spotted a cop carrying two cups of coffee and a bag of something out of the cafeteria, he just followed the jerk right to the room. Then he kept walking. No one asked any questions. No one even looked up. Not the cops. Not the hospital security guys hanging around outside the room trying to act like they, too, were the real deal. Assholes.

Okay, so he knew where she was. Now he just had to stop crapping around in the hallways and get the goddamn

ID badge. It had to look at least a little like him. They'd for sure check the picture. It took the shooter a while, going up and down stairs, roaming the halls to find the right guy. Finally, on the fourth floor, a guy walking toward him looked close enough to work. Same shaved head. Same shape to his face. The shooter checked the badge as they passed each other. Charles Lowery, Radiology. Okay, Charles, let's find somewhere we can be alone. The shooter did a quick 180 and followed Charles to the elevator bay at the end of the hall. Charles pressed the down button and waited. The shooter stood next to him. If the car was empty, he'd take Charles right away. When the body was found, it'd cause a commotion. Doctors, nurses, and the security guys, they'd all come running. Maybe the cops, too. Could be the opening he needed.

Charles Lowery glanced at the shooter. Nodded his head. The shooter smiled and nodded back. A little bell rang and the elevator doors opened. The car was empty. They got on. Charles pressed the button for the ground floor. The doors closed.

When the car began moving, the shooter turned to face Charles. In a single swift motion, he swung his right arm around Charles's neck, pushing his head down and under his own left armpit. The shooter's left forearm went under Charles's throat. He pushed forward with his hip, made a quarter turn to the right, and jerked upward with his left arm, instantly breaking Charles's neck. It all took less than three seconds.

With Charles's head still under his arm, the shooter lowered the body to a sitting position against the back wall. He pulled off the plastic badge, put it around his own neck, and took a deep breath.

The elevator bounced to a stop on one. The shooter faced forward as the doors slid open. An elderly woman looked in with wide eyes. She looked down at Charles. Then up at the shooter. "Heart attack," the shooter said. "You stay here. I'll get help."

She nodded. Before leaving the elevator, he reached

back and pressed a button. Then he slipped out through the closing doors, smiling at the woman, who still stood outside. The elevator, empty except for Charles, ascended to three.

The shooter walked to the nearest stairwell and stepped inside. On the landing he examined Charles Lowery's picture. It wouldn't pass close scrutiny. Charles was smaller, skinnier, but that didn't matter. The badge only showed a head shot, and that was close enough. It'd do.

Maggie's Crown Vic squealed to a halt at the main entrance just as the shooter started up the stairs. McCabe killed the engine and siren and bolted out of the car at a run, Maggie right behind. Comisky told him they were putting Sophie, who was heavily sedated, in room 308. She'd be there by now. They entered the hospital and sprinted toward the elevator bay down the hall to the right. An elderly woman with gray hair and a red face stood by the closed elevator doors, shouting, "He had a heart attack. He had a heart attack! He's in the elevator!" A hospital employee was trying to calm her down. McCabe glanced at the lights above the elevator doors. The car she was pointing to was stopped on three. The other was descending from seven. It could stop two or three times before it got to one.

McCabe scanned the area, looking for the nearest stairs. Spotting the sign, he ran toward them.

The shooter exited the stairwell on three and looked down the hall toward the open elevator doors. Pure chaos. Even better than he hoped. Doctors, nurses, and security guys all shouting and running toward the open elevator with Charles's body in it. Even the cops left their posts. One ran from the door of Sophie's room toward the crowd, then stopped ten feet down the hall, his back to the room, looking toward the commotion. The second cop stayed by the door but was out of his chair, watching the action, his back to the shooter.

From what he could hear, it sounded like Charles was

still alive and they were treating him for a broken neck. Tough little bugger. That snap should have finished him off. The shooter grabbed an abandoned meal cart and rolled it toward Sophie's room. He pulled to a stop at the door. As quietly as possible, he opened the door and pushed the cart in. As he closed it, he heard the cop outside the door shout, "Hey, where do you think you're going?" The shooter left the cart in the middle of the room and slipped behind the door, pulling the Blackie Collins knife from its ankle sheath. He snapped it open.

McCabe reached the third floor a full flight ahead of Maggie. He could see people milling around the elevator at the end of the hall. Midway down on the left, Comisky, in a crouch, gun drawn, was entering room 308. The door closed. McCabe sprinted toward the room, pulling his .45 from its holster.

He kicked open the door, holding the automatic in front of him. Kevin Comisky lay writhing on the floor, hands clutching at his neck, trying desperately to hold back gushers of blood spurting from a slashed carotid artery, his life running out. A man in scrubs stood over him, a short-bladed, bloody knife in hand. Surprise registered on his face at McCabe's intrusion. Surprise turned to rage. "Too late, asshole."

The man rushed for Sophie's bed, driving the knife toward her comatose body. McCabe's bullet struck the moving target high, hitting the right shoulder, shattering a bone, driving the shooter backward. Blood spurted out. Like an enraged bull, he turned toward McCabe, managing somehow to hold on to the knife.

McCabe slammed into him, grabbing the wounded arm and twisting it, pushing it back, away from Sophie and toward the wall. The man bellowed in pain. Even wounded, he was as strong as an ox. He turned his body into McCabe and chopped his left elbow hard into McCabe's kidney once and then again. There was a startling explosion of pain and McCabe went down, unable to breathe. The man advanced, now sure of his prey. McCabe raised his arm to fire again and was surprised to find his gun hand empty. Somehow he'd dropped the .45 going down.

He looked around frantically. Left. Right. There. By the bed. He reached for the gun. The shooter was too fast. He kicked it away, turned, and with his good hand grabbed McCabe by the hair. He pulled his head back hard, exposing his throat to the blade. He raised the knife, barely able to hold it with the wounded hand. McCabe made a desperate grab and missed. He was sure he was going to die. Then a sudden explosion, deafening in the confined space, and, to McCabe's amazement, a small black hole, like a ragged ink spot in a Rorschach test, appeared in the shooter's forehead where there had been none an instant before. In the split second it took the shooter to die, a look of utter disbelief spread across his broad face.

A nurse and two white-coated residents ran into the room and began working frantically, kneeling by the still-breathing, bloody form of Kevin Comisky. McCabe's eyes moved to the door, where Maggie was still standing, like Grace Kelly in *High Noon,* still holding her weapon in a two-handed stance, still pointing at the dead man sprawled in the middle of the floor, ready to fire again, as if she couldn't quite believe he was really dead. McCabe fought off waves of pain.

As the medics worked, he felt a tremor of hope that Kevin Comisky might make it. That the doctors might have gotten to him in time. He even found himself praying for it—but his prayers weren't answered. It only took a minute or two for the doctor, who looked to McCabe like he was fourteen years old, to look up, shake his head, and announce, "He's gone."

"You're sure?"

"I'm sure."

"Shit."

Sophie still lay silently on the bed, breathing evenly.

She'd missed the whole thing. McCabe looked back at the body of the shooter. "Too bad we couldn't have taken him alive," he said, as much to himself as to Maggie.

"Fuck you," said Maggie, who'd finally lowered her outstretched arms. She took a deep breath and closed her eyes. "If you have anything at all to say right now, McCabe, just make it a simple thank-you." The words came out tight and controlled. He knew she'd never fired her weapon at a human being before. He knew it wasn't easy.

"Thank you."

35

Outside there would be cars, trees, people, music, but for Lucinda, outside no longer existed. In the beginning she tried singing. College songs, camp songs, rock and roll. Anything she could remember, belted out as loudly as she could. The sound of her own voice was comforting, reminding her she was still alive, she still existed. I sing, therefore I am. Back then she hoped the singing might irritate her captor. It did. He hurt her for it. Once he burned her thighs and breasts. Little round burns that scarred and still hurt. He told her that the next time she made so much noise he would burn her face.

Now she lay silent, using memories, vainly, to drive back the numbing fear, to keep the silence from destroying all reason. She concentrated on reliving her childhood day by day, on remembering every detail. Today was a Sunday In summer. She was four, Patti was seven. They sat at the kitchen table in the white frame house on Keepers Lane in North Berwick. They moved from that house two years later, but that was later. Today, Poppy, always up before Mommy on Sunday mornings, was making blueberry pancakes for breakfast. She loved blueberry pancakes. Saliva formed in her mouth at the thought.

The eternal cigarette dangled from Poppy's lips, an impossibly long ash hanging over the batter, the scent of burning tobacco filling the room. Patti warned Poppy she wouldn't eat the pancakes if the ash fell in. He cupped his hand under it and walked to the sink, plucked it from his mouth, and held the tiny butt under the water to wash away the ash and extinguish the burning tip. The cigarettes would kill him a few years later, but not yet.

This was the year Poppy bought them the pony. She and Patti. "A small thing," he told them, though he looked big enough to Lucy. "Only thirteen hands high. Fifteen years old."

Thirteen of whose hands, she'd wondered. Surely not hers, which were so small compared to his own. Not Patti's, which were only a little bigger.

They named the pony Keener. Poppy said it was because he was always keener to go for a ride than any other pony he had ever known. Patti, who was wise in these things, said it was really because Poppy bought the pony from a farm near Keene in New Hampshire and considered him a Keener, just as they called people from Maine Mainers.

Keener was a leopard Appaloosa, gray with dark spots all over him. As the youngest, Lucinda got to ride him first. Poppy hoisted her up onto the shiny brown leather saddle. English. Not western. No pommel to hold on to, he told her, just the reins. He adjusted the stirrups so her legs would reach. Put a foot in each. Then off they went. Poppy held the pony's harness. He walked alongside as she rode, talking gently all the while, telling her to hold her back straight, telling her to let Keener know who was in charge. After a bit, without her noticing it, he let go of the harness and she rode on her own for the first time. "Nothing to be afraid of," Poppy said. "Nothing to be afraid of."

Nothing to be afraid of.

Only the blackness and the man who came to do things to her body and sometimes to hurt her. No food. Just some disgusting chocolate stuff in a can that gave her diarrhea. For the thousandth time she took an inventory of the things in the room. Things she couldn't see but knew were there. The most important, the bottle of Gatorade on the wooden table by the bed. He told her where to find it. She'd knocked it over once, feeling for it and missing. She'd had to wash the sticky stuff from the floor. He hit her for that.

The only other thing she could find was the bucket in the corner she used as a toilet, and the roll of paper next to it. She supposed he emptied it when he came. The room didn't seem to smell.

He'd led her to it, the first time. Held her hand while she squatted down and peed. So strange, peeing in the dark, her jailer clutching her hand to keep her from falling. He led her hand to the paper, showing her where it was so she could clean herself. The bottle and the bucket, the bed and the chair. All there was. Her entire universe. Beyond them, just the darkness, the memories, and visits from the man.

"When will you come again?" she wondered, longing for sensation. "Perhaps if I do the sex well enough, perhaps if I please you well enough, perhaps you won't, so quickly, quickly, quickly, quickly, quickly, quickly . . ." She repeated the single word over and over again—but couldn't give voice to the word that followed.

36

"They're restricting me to desk duty pending the investigation." Maggie emerged from Al Blanchard's office, closing the door behind her. Blanchard was the PPD's only full-time Internal Affairs officer. He was assisted by a sergeant McCabe didn't know, someone rotated on a temp basis out of Community Affairs. "I'm not supposed to work on the case."

"Shit," McCabe said, more to himself than to Maggie. He was seated outside, waiting his turn with Internal Affairs.

Maggie sat down next to him. "That's the regs," she said. "I fired my weapon. IA gets to say if the use of force was appropriate, if I really needed to kill him."

"You did."

"I didn't announce myself. I didn't yell freeze. I just saw him swinging that knife toward your neck and I pulled the trigger."

"If you hadn't killed him, he would've killed me," said McCabe. "He already killed Comisky."

"I could have wounded him."

"You had to go for a head shot. Any lower and you would have hit me. You did the right thing. The guy was pure fucking evil."

She considered this. "You're right." She nodded uncertainly. "Blanchard said it wouldn't take long. The investigation, I mean."

He supposed she was looking for absolution. A remission of sins. He couldn't offer it. Neither could IA. If she felt any guilt, she'd just have to live it. He put his arm around her shoulder. "You saved my life," he said. "In Chinese philosophy, that means you're responsible for it."

She turned and looked directly into his eyes, forcing a smile. "I guess I should have let him kill you."

A uniformed sergeant named Toomey appeared. "Okay, McCabe, it's your turn."

Al Blanchard was seated behind his desk. Toomey took a seat to Blanchard's right. Bill Fortier stood leaning against the wall behind Blanchard. McCabe hadn't expected him to be there.

Fortier made the introductions. "Mike McCabe. Sergeant Pat Toomey." Each of the men nodded; neither extended a hand. "Pat's been assigned to IA for this inquiry."

McCabe had heard Toomey's name before. He had a reputation for being Tom Shockley's eyes and ears in the department. Most cops watched what they said in his presence, knowing it would eventually get back to the chief. McCabe ignored Toomey and addressed Fortier. "Maggie said you're pulling her out of the investigation, Bill. With one killer still on the loose and Lucinda Cassidy still missing, I think that's crazy. It's obvious she shot him to save me."

Blanchard spoke first. "Sergeant, regulations say we restrict an officer any time a firearm is discharged in the line of duty. Anyway, it shouldn't be for long. The facts seem clear that Detective Savage was justified in using deadly force. We've just got to be sure."

"Alright, Mike," said Fortier. "I want you to tell us everything that happened from the moment you first saw that woman, Sophie Gauthier, right up until Maggie killed that guy in the hospital."

McCabe told it all. They asked questions. He answered them. It took close to an hour. In the end he said, "That's where we are. You want me on desk duty, too?"

"No," said Blanchard.

"Really? Why's that? Hell, I discharged two firearms. Both in the same night. Maggie only fired one."

Blanchard was silent.

"Don't worry about it." McCabe was feeling tired, angry. "We'll just put the case on hold for a couple of days. Hell, I can use the rest. I've got issues at home. Maybe," he said bitterly, "maybe we can get the bad guys to postpone killing Cassidy until the good guys get their ducks in a row. On the other hand"—he shrugged—"maybe we can't."

"You know, McCabe, you're pretty damned arrogant." It was Toomey who spoke. "I heard that about you, strutting around like a New York big shot. Now I see it's true."

McCabe looked at him. "Fuck you, Toomey." The man stiffened.

"Alright, just hold it right there." Blanchard, conciliatory, held up both his hands, the good cop to Toomey's bad cop. "Relax, Pat—and keep personal remarks to yourself. McCabe, you go back to work. You're not being sidelined."

"Really? I thought the regs say we do desk duty any time a firearm is discharged."

"Let's say you've been investigated," said Blanchard, "and cleared. You just didn't notice it 'cause it happened so fast."

"We're stretching the rules in your case, Mike, not breaking them," said Fortier. "For one thing, you didn't kill anyone. Maggie did. For another, we need you right now. When you say we can't count on the bad guys waiting, you're right."

"Are you looking for a thank-you for that, Bill?"

"Stretching the regs wasn't Bill's decision," said Toomey. "If you want to thank anyone, thank Shockley. It was his call. He's the one who'll have to take the heat. 'For the good of the community,' he said."

Blanchard added, "I just hope the department doesn't end up paying for this down the road."

"Does Maggie know about any of this?"

"No."

"When do I get her back?"

"Shouldn't be more than a day or so, maybe less," said Blanchard.

"Personally," said Toomey, "in your case, McCabe, I would've gone by the book. I believe by your actions last night, going to meet that woman alone, without backup, you not only willfully ignored the rules of this department, you also set this whole clusterfuck in motion. It ended in the death of a fellow officer, the killing of one civilian, the wounding of another, and, last but not least, it looks like the guy in the elevator may be permanently paralyzed. But hey, I guess that's how they do things in New York. Bill Bacon could have taken over this case from the beginning and, in my view, should have. Oh, by the way, in case you didn't know it, Kevin Comisky left a wife and three children. The youngest's only two years old."

If Toomey's intention was to induce guilt, he succeeded. "What's the wife's name?"

"Carol."

Carol. McCabe nodded. He'd have to call on Carol Comisky as soon as he could. Beyond that, he knew Toomey might be right about his decision to meet Sophie alone. That would haunt him. He was also surprised Shockley had gone out on a limb for him. Still, he said nothing about it.

"Okay, that's it," said Fortier. "You can go, Mike."

"Try real hard not to shoot anyone else," added Toomey. McCabe let the gibe pass.

37

Maggie dropped McCabe at his condo before heading home herself to shower and change. Jane Devaney met him at the door, index finger pressed against her lips in a shushing gesture.

"What's the matter?" he whispered. She pushed him out onto the landing and quietly closed the door.

"Casey's here. I kept her home from school."

"Why? Is she sick?"

"Not exactly, but she was awake pretty much all night. Crying a little. Worrying a lot. She crawled into my bed around two, but it was after seven before she finally dropped off. I let her sleep in."

"Was it about Sandy's visit?" He started for the door.

Jane put out a hand to block his way. "That's in the mix somewhere, I suppose, but last night it was mostly about you."

"About me?"

"Yeah. You. Last night she sees you leave here carrying a shotgun. Doesn't know where you're going or what you're doing."

"Oh, Christ." McCabe sighed, another kernel of guilt starting to form.

"A little later you call and scare her half to death. You tell her Maggie's coming over. Later Maggie leaves and I turn up. You don't. She asks where you are. I tell her I'm sure you're all right. Then she tells me how her uncle was killed in a shootout when she was ten . . ."

"Tommy."

"That's right. Tommy. Obviously she's worried sick about you getting killed, but she tries not to show it. Wants to be the good girl, the good cop's daughter."

"I suppose me getting killed would mean I was abandoning her in a way, too. Just like her mother did. Was that part of it?"

"Maybe, but I'm not sure it got that far."

"I'd better talk to her—"

"Yes. You'd better. Right now may not be the best time. She's got it under control for now."

"So what do I say?"

"Just be sensitive to how she feels. Make sure she knows you're okay and that you care. You can talk to her a little more deeply when things calm down. Anyway, I'll take her to school in a little while. Let me just grab a shower. I've been up all night, too."

He found Casey in the kitchen eating a bowl of Cheerios. He slipped into the chair opposite her.

"New scrunchie?" McCabe asked, noticing the band of orange fabric holding her hair back.

"Yeah, Sarah and I made them. Her mom showed us how. I've got two more."

"Good job."

"It's easy. You just sew the cloth into a tube and push the stretchy stuff through with a safety pin. Then you sew the ends." She took it off and showed him.

"Cool." He slipped the band around his head. "How do I look?"

"Don't. You'll stretch it." She reached over and took the scrunchie off his head. "You okay?" she asked.

"I'm okay. Did you get any sleep?"

"Not much. Maggie left in the middle of the night. Said she had to go meet you. Jane came over."

"Was that okay?"

"I kind of wanted company. I slept with Jane. Where were you?"

"Up in Gray interviewing a witness. Then over at Cumberland Med."

"Somebody get hurt?"

"Yes." He didn't go into detail.

"Where's your shotgun?"

"I left it down at headquarters."

"Okay."

"It was important for me to be there."

Casey studied him for a minute. "Okay," she said.

He took her hand, the one not holding the spoon.

"Don't," she said and pulled it away.

He realized he was famished. Maggie's doughnuts and a spoonful of lasagna were all he'd eaten in nearly twenty-four hours. He got himself a bowl and spoon and poured out some Cheerios. He added milk and started munching. "Have you thought any more about seeing your mother?"

"Yeah. A lot."

"So what do you think?"

"You said I had to see her."

"I think you do. The judge gave her that right. How do you feel about that?"

"I don't know. She's coming Friday?"

"Yes. She'll meet you here after school. She wants to take you to Boston for the weekend. Probably stay at some fancy hotel. Maybe go see a show."

"Big deal." Silence. "She's really rich?"

"Her husband is."

Casey finished her cereal and took the bowl to the sink and rinsed it out. "His name's Peter?"

"Yeah."

"Peter what?"

"Ingram."

"Is he my stepfather?"

"Only if you want to think about him that way."

"I don't think about him any way. I never even met him. He's not coming, is he?"

"I don't think so. It's just Sandy."

"How come you gave me the same name as her?"

"It's what she wanted when you were born." A little extension of herself, McCabe thought. "Anyway, it's not really the same. You're Casey. She's Sandy."

"Ready to go?" Jane appeared.

"We're both Cassandras," Casey said. "You guys aren't gonna fight about me, are you? You and Mom?"

"I hope not. I'll try not to. I can't speak for her."

"You're supposed to be the grown-ups, you know."

"Yeah, that's what I heard." He hugged her hard. "I love you." He didn't want to let her go. Not to Boston. Not, at the moment, even to school.

"Dad, I gotta go."

"I know. Go break a leg."

"I love you, too," she said and turned and ran down the stairs.

He called Sandy's number in New York.

"Hello, McCabe. Casey ready for my visit?"

He wasn't sure ready was the operative word. Still, he said, "You can pick her up Friday after school."

"I'll be there at four o'clock. I've reserved a suite at the Four Seasons. She should bring a nice outfit she can wear to some good restaurants and maybe the theater. She does have something decent to put on, doesn't she?"

He let the sarcasm pass. "She'll pack something nice."

"Anything in particular she'd like to see?"

"She'll like anything you choose. Or better yet, give her the choice. She doesn't get to go much. You know where we live?"

"I do indeed."

"She'll need to be back early enough Sunday to do her homework. No later than four or five o'clock."

"That's fine."

"Sandy?"

"What?"

"Take good care of her."

McCabe kicked off his shoes and lay on the unmade bed, thinking about Casey and what he might have said to her. Kyra's scent lingered on the sheets. He was exhausted but knew he didn't have time for sleep. He had to go back to the hospital, talk to Sophie as soon as she was compos mentis, but first he needed to sort things out. The list of loose ends was long and getting longer, a Pandora's box of probablys, might bes and what ifs.

He stripped down, got in the shower, and thought about things as the hot water coursed over him. Sophie said they were doing illegal transplants. Most likely somewhere inside a fifty-mile band north or east of Augusta. Unless, of course, they cut south again. He thought about that and rejected it. It'd waste too much time doubling back and forth.

Okay. There were five or six people involved besides Sophie. A transplant surgeon and a second surgeon. One of them Spencer? Probably. Anybody else? Maybe one of Spencer's buddies from the Denali picture. Wilcox or Holland. Who else? A nurse-anesthetist. Identity unknown. Two or three OR nurses. Also unknown. A perfusionist. Sophie.

Sophie said she hadn't known they were killing people to obtain the hearts. Did the others? For sure, at least one of them did. What about the goon Maggie killed last night? Was he part of the surgical team? Unlikely. Finally, there was the fact that Sophie said there'd been at least two other transplants. Jack Batchelder was supposed to be tracking down possible victims. He'd have to find out how much progress Jack had made. Yes, a lot of loose ends. Even so, he felt he was getting closer. What he needed to tie the loose ends around Spencer's neck in a neat little bow might be waiting in the Lexus. They should have searched it already. Unfortunately, events kind of got out of hand. They'd search it today. They'd also bring Philip Spencer down to 109 for a chat.

38

The third floor at Cumberland Medical Center was an armed camp. Dick Cheney's undisclosed secure location couldn't have been closed down any tighter. Uniformed cops were stationed at each of the elevator banks and at the stairwell doors, checking IDs of anyone coming or going including staff. Two additional patrol officers sat at Sophie's door, and a third was in the room. All doctors, nurses, and aides going in or out of her room were checked against an approved list of caregivers. Anyone not on the list didn't go in. Period. Medications and food were double-checked against orders by the floor nurse and the chief resident. Security was as tight as it could be if the hospital was going to function at all. Some comedian put up a sign opposite the elevators, WELCOME TO THE GREEN ZONE. The cops didn't bother taking it down.

Sophie was awake but glum when McCabe entered. Her arm was bandaged and immobilized, an IV inserted in her hand. She didn't look up when he sat in the chair next to her bed. She seemed to be absorbed in an old issue of *Cosmo*.

"How are you feeling?" he asked. No answer.

"You're not talking to me, is that it?" Still no answer.

"Listen, I can't help you if you won't talk to me."

She looked at him and then turned back to the magazine.

"The guy who shot you is dead. He can't hurt you anymore—but there are others who can. I need you to talk to me. If you don't, it's very likely another woman will die. It's just as likely they'll come after you again."

"You swore to me you weren't followed." She didn't look up from the magazine as she spoke.

"I wasn't. They attached a global positioning transmitter under your car. Another under mine. That's how they knew where we were. Sophie, the only safety for you is if we catch the people responsible for all this. The only way we can do that is for you to tell me everything you know."

"I'm going home," she said. "Back to France. As soon as they let me out of here."

"You won't be any safer there than you are here. The man you called Spencer knows where you live. He knows you can identify him. He knows you've been talking to the police, and for all he knows, you've already told us everything you know. For all he knows, you're ready to testify against him in court.

"I spoke to the prosecutor about getting you immunity in return for your testimony. He said he'd do what he can, but I can't promise you that. All I can promise you is that if you don't help us stop him here and now, he will follow you to France, or wherever else you may go—and when he finds you he'll surely kill you."

Sophie sat in her bed staring straight ahead. McCabe saw that she was quietly crying, and it made him feel like a shit. What he told her was the truth of the matter, though, and there was no changing that.

Finally she turned to him. "Alright, what do you want to know?"

He turned on his recorder and spoke into it. "This is an interview between Detective Sergeant Michael McCabe, Portland Police Department, and Sophie Gauthier, a French citizen, recorded at Cumberland Medical Center, Portland, Maine, at 1:30 P.M. on Wednesday, September 21, 2005. Ms. Gauthier, you are participating in this interview freely and of your own volition, is that correct?"

"Yes, it is."

With only a little prompting, Sophie repeated into the recorder everything she had told McCabe the night before on the quiet road in Gray.

When she finished, he handed her half a dozen photographs, including a picture of Philip Spencer he'd printed off Casey's computer. "I am showing Ms. Gauthier six photographs of men who fit the description of the man who contacted her in France. Ms. Gauthier, have you ever seen any of these men before?"

She took the photos and looked at each of them for a minute or two. She finally shook her head. "No."

"None of these photos are of the man who called himself Philip Spencer?"

"No."

"Are you sure?"

"Yes."

"Imagine each of them with beards."

"This one looks like him a little." She picked up the picture of Philip Spencer. "More when I imagine him, as you say, with a beard, but really not so much when you look closely."

He showed her another photo of Spencer, shot from a slightly different angle. "No," she said. "I told you. This is not the man I spoke to."

Okay, so Spencer wasn't the recruiter. He could still be the cutter. The killer. McCabe slid another series of pictures in front of her. "Have you seen any of these men before?"

She pointed at a postmortem photo of the shooter. "Yes. This one was the driver who came for me at the hotels and brought me to the operations. Is he the man who tried to kill me?"

McCabe nodded. "Did he come for you each time?"

"Yes."

"Was he in the operating room during the heart transplants?"

"No."

*   *   *

Tom Tasco and Eddie Fraser were waiting for McCabe as he left Sophie's room. Fraser jumped right in. "We ID'd the shooter, Mike. Jacobi found a couple of usable prints in the SUV, and the bureau came up with a match."

McCabe interrupted him. "Let's go and get some coffee," he said. "Too crowded to talk up here."

They rode the elevator down to the big cafeteria on the ground floor. At two thirty, it was still pretty crowded with a late lunch crowd. They got three cups of coffee and went for privacy to an outdoor area where there were some chairs and tables. McCabe noticed, for the first time, it was a beautiful day. They sat where they could speak without being overheard.

"Who is he?" asked McCabe.

"Name's Darryl Pollock," said Tasco. "Ex-marine. Served as a sniper in the first Gulf War. Won a Bronze Star. Stayed in the marines after the war. Joined Force Recon. That's Marine Corps Special Ops. Apparently he only quit because some of the homophobes in the Corps found out he was gay and made life uncomfortable for him."

"What did he do after the military?"

"Record gets a little sketchy." Tasco was reading from some computer printouts. "Worked as a bouncer in some gay clubs in New York. Couple of assault arrests for getting too rough with some drunks. No convictions. Turns up next in Florida. South Beach."

Tasco sorted through his notes. "In Florida, Pollock does a little time for beating the shit out of a couple of college jocks in a bar fight. He got pissed at them for gay-bashing some aging queen Pollock didn't even know. He told them to lay off. Instead they start in on him. Football players," Tasco said with a snort. "Guess they thought they were tough. Pollock almost killed one of them. That was in '96. He gets out in '98 and disappears. End of story."

Darryl Pollock. Duane Pollard. Initials DP. South Beach. Lucas Kane's lover? McCabe was willing to bet on it. In 1998 Pollock changes his name and hooks up with

Kane. He wondered what, if anything, Detective Sessions would know about that. Or be willing to tell him.

"Mike, are you with me?" Tasco was looking at him. "Hello? Is there something I'm missing here?"

McCabe shook his head. "No. I'm sorry, Tom. Any record of Pollock ever using an alias? Either before he was sent up or maybe after he got out of prison?"

"Not that we're aware of."

"Do me a favor. Dig a little deeper. See if you can find out if Pollock ever used the alias Duane Pollard."

"So who's Pollard?"

"A local enforcer in Miami. My information places him in South Beach in March 2001. At the time, he was the live-in lover of a high-class pimp and pusher named Lucas Kane, who just happened to be an old dear friend of one Dr. Philip Spencer."

"Well, well, well. Didn't know Spencer had such nice friends," said Fraser. "Where's Kane now?"

"Dead. He was murdered back in 2001."

"Really? Was Pollock/Pollard a suspect?"

"No. According to Miami Beach PD he had an airtight alibi."

"Anything to show Spencer knew Pollard?" asked Tasco.

"They could have met at Kane's funeral," said McCabe. Noticing a man nearby eyeing them, McCabe lowered his voice to just above a whisper and shifted his chair so the man couldn't see his lips. Tasco and Fraser followed suit. The line between precaution and paranoia, as always, seemed thin.

"Maybe at the funeral, Spencer asks Pollock to come to Maine to bash any necessary heads in his heart transplant scam," said Fraser. "After all, Kane doesn't need him anymore, what with him being dead and all."

"Possible," said McCabe, considering it. "Pollock/Pollard loses his meal ticket in Florida about the same time Spencer's hatching his transplant scheme in Maine. I mean, why else would a thug like that end up in Portland? Could you find anything about Spencer visiting France?"

"Not much, even though the gendarmes were helpful," said Tasco. "There's no record of anybody checking into the Hôtel du Midi in Montpellier under the name Philip Spencer at any time during November of last year."

"Anything else?"

"Yeah. I checked with the hospital. According to their records, Dr. Spencer performed three heart transplants here in Maine that month."

"So he couldn't have been in France?"

"Technically, he could have, but he would have to have been traveling within a hell of a tight time frame."

"Do me another favor, Tom. Ask your contact in France if anyone checked in using the name Harry Lime."

"Okay, and if he did?"

"Get the passport number and find out where and when it was issued. If it was mailed, find out where it was sent."

"So the guy in France wasn't Philip Spencer?"

"At least not our Philip Spencer. Sophie Gauthier just looked at his photo. She's certain Spencer's not the guy who recruited her."

"Basically you're telling me we have nothing?" said Tasco.

"That pretty much sums it up."

"I've got to tell you Mike, it's getting pretty old running up and down these blind alleys."

"Just hang in, Tom. It'll pay off," said McCabe.

"I hope so. What's next?"

"Next? Next we take a look inside Mrs. Spencer's pretty green Lexus."

39

McCabe hated surveillance, especially from the front seat of a rental car. This one was a Dodge Stratus. About as devoid of personality and creature comforts as a vehicle could get. It wasn't even inconspicuous. In this neighborhood nobody but cops or Jehovah's Witnesses would drive anything so dull—but it was all Fortier would pay for. He didn't know how long the Bird was going to be impounded, but it could be a while. Even afterward, getting the windshield fixed, and maybe some other stuff, too, would take additional time. At least the Stratus had a CD player and a passable, though not great, sound system.

McCabe was parked in front of 24 Trinity Street. He'd already been there two hours waiting for the green Lexus to return. He'd invited Burt Lund to sit with him, and Lund was getting antsy. Tasco and Fraser waited across the street in a PPD Crown Vic. Mostly McCabe passed the time leaning back listening to Marcus Roberts play some very familiar Gershwin on the piano. He alternated the Roberts CD with one by Oscar Peterson, who created similar magic with Cole Porter.

"Any word on what's planned for Kevin Comisky's funeral?" asked Lund.

"Yeah. Memo came down from Shockley's office this

afternoon. Service is scheduled for Monday at the cathedral. Color guard. Bagpipes. Twenty-one-gun salute at the gravesite. The whole nine yards. Cops will be coming in from all over New England to attend. Shockley plans to deliver a eulogy."

"That'll be nice for the widow."

McCabe glanced over at Lund. "Nice doesn't bring her husband back."

"No."

They lapsed into silence. The warrant to search the Lexus waited in McCabe's pocket. Both McCabe and Lund agreed they wouldn't serve it unless and until the Lexus was right there in front of them. Go banging on the Spencers' front door while Phil Spencer was driving around loose and you'd invite some asshole lawyer to hold them up for days while he challenged probable cause.

An ATL for the Lexus had been issued to all patrol units. If the SUV was spotted, officers were to report the sighting and follow the vehicle but not intercept it. McCabe's phone rang. It was Jacobi. "How you doing, Bill?"

"I'm good. What fun and games do you have planned for us today?"

"We're over on Trinity Street waiting on a Lexus SUV. It's the one I think was used to haul Katie Dubois's body over to the scrap yard. I want you to go over it and find what we need to put this asshole away."

"The asshole being Dr. Spencer?"

"You got it."

"Being an asshole is not necessarily a punishable offense."

"Don't start, Bill. I've got good reason to think this guy might have been involved in the murder."

Jacobi sighed. "So you're looking for what? Prints, hair, fibers?"

"Yeah, all that, but mostly blood. I don't see how he could have hauled Katie's body around cut up the way it was without getting some blood on the vehicle. Most likely on the cargo space in back. I don't care how hard he scrubbed it—"

Jacobi finished the sentence. "Luminol will show it."

"Yeah."

"Okay, call me when your pigeon arrives and we'll send over a flatbed. We'll have to bring the Lexus down here to the garage to really go over it. I'll also want to remove the seats and open up the spare tire well."

"That's fine."

Another hour passed before Harriet Spencer drove the green SUV through the gates of the Spencers' inner sanctum. McCabe pulled the Stratus into the driveway behind her, effectively blocking retreat. He called Jacobi to send over the flatbed and then walked up to the Lexus's driver's side window. "Please exit the vehicle, Mrs. Spencer."

"What are you doing here? I thought I told you to leave my property and not come back."

"I'm serving you with a warrant, Mrs. Spencer, signed by District Court Judge Paula Washburn, authorizing us to conduct a thorough search of this vehicle in the police garage. A tow truck's on its way now. We have reason to believe your car may have been used in the murder of Katie Dubois."

"You're out of your mind. How dare you accuse us like this?"

"We're not making any accusations, Mrs. Spencer. We're simply searching the car for evidence. If we don't find anything, it will be returned to you with our apologies. This is Assistant Attorney General Bert Lund."

Lund smiled. "How do you do, Mrs. Spencer?"

"Mr. Lund will verify the validity of this warrant. You may also show it to your own attorney. Now please exit the vehicle."

Hattie Spencer briefly examined the paper McCabe offered, then looked up at him. "May I take my groceries inside, or do you want to search those as well?"

"Yes, but please don't take anything else. I'll have one of my men help you."

"Don't bother, Detective." She gathered up half a dozen

plastic bags from Hannaford's and carried them to the kitchen door McCabe had used to leave the house three days before.

From the kitchen, Hattie Spencer called Philip's cell. "The police are here. That detective McCabe and some others. They want to search my car. The Lexus."

"Oh, for God's sake. Did they show you a warrant?"

"Yes."

"Alright. Don't say anything to them. Nothing at all. I'll call George Renquist. Then I'll come back."

Philip hung up. Hattie stood holding the dead phone for a minute. He sounded so calm. Philip always sounded calm. Finally she, too, hung up. She walked through the house and stood by the big front window watching the scene on the driveway.

She wrapped her arms tightly around her chest. Her world, the one she had so carefully constructed, so carefully cared for, for twenty years, seemed to be closing in on her. The men outside with their cars and vans and official pieces of paper were storming the barricades, and there was nothing she could do about it. Across the street she could see that nosy little suck-up Ellen Markham staring from the front step of her house. She was going to love telling her money-grubbing lawyer husband all about it tonight at dinner. As well as her friends, whoever they might be.

"Imagine!" Hattie could hear them saying. "The police were at the Spencers' half the day. I hear it has to do with the murder of that girl. Katie Dubois? What do you suppose they were looking for?"

Yes, by tonight it would be all over Portland. Hattie went to the burled walnut drinks cupboard and filled a cut crystal water goblet about halfway up with gin. She could take their snide innuendos. She was tougher than that. She walked back to the window with the drink and resumed her vigil as she sipped. She wondered what they were looking for, what they might find. What exactly did happen last week while she was up in Blue Hill? She had a feeling she might know.

Philip's car, the black BMW, turned into the driveway. It stopped behind the car that blocked the Lexus. A uniformed cop directed Philip to park on the street. He did, but when he emerged his face showed that strange, quiet rage she knew so well. He walked over to McCabe and the pudgy lawyer McCabe had with him. Bert Lump. Philip said something. McCabe handed Philip the warrant. He looked at it and said something else. She guessed he was quietly threatening them. That was Philip's way. Letting them know how many important people he knew. Then their attorney, George Renquist, arrived. George looked at the warrant and said something to Philip. Philip and George turned away from the police. George said something. Philip disagreed. He walked toward the house. The front door opened and closed. He walked past the drawing room and climbed the stairs. She called to him. "Philip?" He looked down at her but said nothing. He walked to the bedroom and closed the door. Hattie returned to her post by the window, sipped her gin, and watched a tow truck pull the Lexus up and onto its bed. Then they drove it away.

40

McCabe followed the Lexus back to the police garage, then went upstairs to the detectives' bullpen to wait while Jacobi's team did their thing. He spotted Jack Batchelder at his desk. Jack was holding a half-eaten meatball sandwich in two hands, a paper napkin tucked in his collar to protect his shirt. He looked up, midbite. "What d'ya need, Mike?" he asked.

"Those open missing persons cases I asked you to check? How're you doing with that?"

Batchelder sighed. McCabe guessed he wasn't happy having his dinner interrupted. Jack carefully wrapped the remains of his sandwich in the waxed paper it'd come in, wiped his hands on the napkin, then reached for a file on his desk.

"Your upper lip," said McCabe.

"What?"

"Your upper lip. Tomato sauce." McCabe pointed to the same spot on his own lip.

Batchelder reddened, then swiped at his mouth with the napkin. "Better?" he asked.

"Perfect. Now, what did you find?"

"At first, not a whole lot. I went through all our open missing persons cases for the last three years."

"No young blond female athletes?"

"Nothing even close. So I e-mailed every other department in the state."

"And?"

"We found one. Couple of hours ago MSP sent over the file. Young snowboarder named Wendy Branca turned up missing last December at Sunday River. She was never found. I haven't had a chance to review the whole file yet."

"Blond?"

"Yeah. Blond and beautiful."

McCabe took the file from Batchelder. "Anyone else?"

"Not yet."

"Thanks, Jack. Good job." He went to his own desk, opened the file, and began reading. Wendy Branca was a twenty-four-year-old sales rep for WMND, a Portland country music station. She was indeed blond and beautiful—and an athlete. An expert and avid snowboarder, she was good enough to have been an instructor at Breckinridge, in Colorado, a couple of seasons after college.

Last December, before Christmas, Wendy and a couple of girlfriends went up to Sunday River for a weekend of boarding and prospecting for guys. Saturday night they headed for a place called Giggles, which featured a big bar scene for the twenty-something crowd. All three women started the evening off with a couple of appletinis. The idea of actually drinking something called an appletini made McCabe cringe. After that the women started circulating. They talked and danced with a bunch of different guys. At some point, no one knew exactly when, Wendy disappeared.

Her friends told detectives they hadn't worried. They just assumed Wendy got lucky and left with someone. Not that unusual, they said. Wendy attracted men like flies, and she liked having fun. They figured she'd turn up at the motel either later that night or, if things clicked, sometime the next morning.

When she wasn't back by 10:00 A.M., one of the friends started calling her cell. Each time the message kicked in right away. Still they weren't worried. They figured she'd turned the phone off because she didn't want to be bothered. They left Wendy's stuff with the motel desk clerk, checked out, and headed to the mountain. At 5:00 P.M. they stopped back at the motel and discovered her stuff was still there. That's when they called the Bethel police.

The local cops talked to the motel manager and everybody who worked at Giggles. No one at the bar remembered Wendy except for one of the bartenders and a guy who played guitar in the band. He remembered her because A, she was "a hottie," and B, she kept requesting Dixie Chicks songs. Seems he hated the Dixie Chicks. Neither the guitar player nor the bartender saw who she left with.

After twenty-four hours Wendy still hadn't turned up. The Bethel cops ran out of ideas and called in the state police. Teams of MSP detectives interviewed every male who'd paid with a credit card at Giggles that night. They also showed Wendy's picture around at every other bar and motel in the area to see if she'd been spotted anywhere else. She hadn't. They broadened the search to include men who paid with a credit card either at the ski area for lift tickets or at condos or motels within a twenty-mile radius. Still nothing. They checked with Cingular, who showed no activity on Wendy's phone since early Saturday evening. The phone had been turned off since then. Detectives interviewed every known family member, friend, and acquaintance plus all of Wendy's former boyfriends and lovers. Still nothing.

A massive search of the area yielded no results either. According to a *Press Herald* reporter, Wendy Branca just disappeared "into thin air." McCabe was pretty sure that wasn't the case.

Katie Dubois and Wendy Branca. That still left one heart unaccounted for. Because he knew Darryl Pollock was gay and because he suspected Spencer swung both ways, McCabe pulled the files on missing young men. It took over an hour, but he found what he was looking for. Around the middle of April, just weeks before graduation, a Bowdoin senior from Portland named Brian Henry disappeared without a trace. Henry was blond, handsome, a starting forward on the soccer team, and openly gay. Possibly a sexually desirable target, but, unlike with Branca, there was no obvious time or place where Spencer might have met Henry or picked him up. According to Henry's roommate and partner, they enjoyed a monogamous relationship and neither of them frequented gay bars or other hangouts. It was unlikely Henry had simply taken off. He was a serious student and looking forward to starting medical school in the fall. Tufts Medical School.

It was nearly 8:00 P.M. The Tufts admissions office would be closed. McCabe Googled the name of the dean of admissions, then used Superpages to find his home number. The dean told him yes, prospective students were often interviewed by prominent alumni. McCabe asked him who, if anyone, interviewed Brian Henry. The dean said he wouldn't be able to check the records until morning. McCabe told him why he needed the information sooner. The dean said he'd call back in twenty minutes. He did.

It turned out that Brian Henry had indeed been interviewed and that the interviewer was none other than a "prominent Portland surgeon and Tufts graduate, Dr. Philip Spencer." McCabe stuck both files in his drawer. Brian Henry made victim number three. He knew that unless he made progress fast, Lucinda Cassidy would be number four.

McCabe called Maggie at home. Technically, she wasn't supposed to be working any cases, but he needed her help. He told her what he had discovered about Wendy Branca and Brian Henry.

"Do the dates Henry and Branca disappeared coincide with the dates Sophie gave you for the surgeries?"

"Close enough. We know he kept Dubois alive for about a week after kidnapping her. He probably did the same with them."

"So Cassidy could still be alive?" she asked.

"Yeah, but time's running out. Mag, I want you to do something for me."

"Something like work on the case?"

"Something like that."

"I'm not supposed to."

"I know, but this is important. So just be quiet and listen."

"Go ahead."

"If, as I believe, all three victims plus Cassidy were abducted to use their hearts for transplants, they couldn't have been chosen randomly. At a minimum the donor blood has to be a match with whoever's getting the heart, or the transplant won't work."

"So he has to have access to their medical records."

"Which probably means all four records can be found in one place."

"Cumberland?"

"That's what I'm thinking."

"Someone hacked into the hospital's computer system?"

"Maybe. Or maybe someone already had access because someone just happened to be their number one superstar surgeon."

"Assuming all four victims were ever patients at Cumberland."

"Assuming that."

"There are other places that record blood type. Doctors' offices. Testing labs. Maybe some others," said Maggie.

"Can you check 'em out? Fast?"

"Alright, I'm on it."

"Thanks."

As soon as McCabe hung up, Bill Jacobi called from the garage. "You were right, Mike. We found blood—and something else that'll interest you."

McCabe checked his watch. It was now nearly 9:00 P.M. "I'll be right down," he said.

McCabe locked the Henry and Branca files in his bottom drawer, shut down his computer, and headed for the garage. Jacobi directed him to the cargo area of the Lexus and turned out the lights. Blackness closed in. As Mc-Cabe's eyes adjusted, he could see three small blotches of blue phosphorescence shining on the car's carpet. Then Jacobi opened the spare tire well. The telltale blue glow of more blood. Quite a lot more.

"Okay, you can turn the lights on," said McCabe. He was forced to squint from the sudden brightness. Once again, his eyes adjusted. "When will you know if it's Katie's?"

"We already sent it in for DNA. We told the lab to make it a priority rush."

"Have them check for a couple of other matches as well. A woman named Wendy Branca and a guy named Brian Henry. I have the files upstairs."

"What about Cassidy?" asked Jacobi.

"Her, too."

"We'll get it in the works."

"You said you had something else, Bill. What is it?"

"This." Jacobi held out a small plastic bag. "We found it in the spare tire well. It must have slipped down there. Maybe it caught on something."

Inside the bag McCabe saw a single small gold earring with a dangling heart-shaped charm. The charm was still shining brightly.

41

McCabe fidgeted impatiently, eyes glued to a TV monitor, in a viewing room at 109 Middle Street. He watched a uniformed officer escort Philip Spencer into the interview room next door, where Tom Tasco sat waiting. McCabe was anxious to get as much out of Spencer as possible before a lawyer showed up and shut him down.

The first priority was getting a sample of Spencer's DNA to match against the blood on Cassidy's dog's teeth. Tasco poured himself a glass of water, then offered one to Spencer. Spencer took it and placed it on the table next to him. They needed him to sip so they could check the saliva he might leave on the glass.

A video camera hidden in the emergency light recorded Spencer in medium close-up. McCabe could see Tasco's back and hear his voice-over. "This is an interview at Portland Police Headquarters between Detective Thomas Tasco, Portland, Maine, Police Department, and Dr. Philip Spencer, currently residing at 24 Trinity Street, Portland, Maine. The time is 7:30 A.M., Thursday, September 22, 2005."

Spencer sat back, tanned and confident. He wore a preppy-looking collared polo shirt and had a yellow cotton sweater tied loosely around his neck. Mr. Male Model. Right out of *GQ*. If the sonofabitch was guilty, thought McCabe, he sure as hell hid it well.

"Betcha he talks to us," McCabe said to Bert Lund, who'd asked to sit in.

"You've got to be kidding," said Lund. "He's not gonna say a word."

"Ten bucks?"

"C'mon, this guy knows enough to keep his mouth shut. Why wouldn't he?"

"Arrogance. Spencer's got a congenital need to show off. He's gotta prove he's the smartest guy in the room. Almost can't help himself."

"That's pretty dumb."

Spencer cocked his head one way, then the other, and pushed his dark hair to the side with one hand. McCabe could have sworn he was aware of the camera. Spencer asked the first question. "Would you mind telling me what this is all about? Am I under arrest?"

"No. Nothing like that," Tom told him. "This is just an interview to help us obtain information regarding the murder of Katherine Dubois. Your presence here is entirely voluntary."

Spencer looked around for the camera. "Hello, McCabe," he said. "You *can* see me, can't you?"

Tasco ignored the comment except to say, "Please address yourself to me, Dr. Spencer."

Spencer finally took a sip of the water. Score one for our side, thought McCabe.

"You mean McCabe's not going to ask me any questions?" he asked. "I'm hurt." Tasco showed him the bag containing Katie Dubois's earring. "Dr. Spencer, do you know what this is?"

"It appears to be an earring."

"We found this earring in your wife's car."

"Really?" He didn't seem fazed. Merely curious.

"Do you know how it got there?"

"No, I can't say I do. I suppose it could be Hattie's." He

peered at it again. "Though it doesn't really look like her sort of thing. Maybe it belongs to one of her friends."

"Actually it's Katie Dubois's. Its mate was still in her ear when her body was found." Still no reaction.

"Doctor, where were you last Thursday night between 8:00 P.M. and midnight?"

"I already told Sergeant McCabe. At home. Reading. Then sleeping."

"You also told him your wife was with you."

"Did I?"

"Yes, but she says she was up in Blue Hill visiting her sick mother."

"Really?" Spencer shrugged. "Well, I must have been mistaken."

"She says she drove your BMW."

"Yes. Now I remember. I drove my Porsche that day."

"Not your wife's Lexus?"

"No. I prefer the Porsche."

"Where was the Lexus?"

"I don't know. In the garage, I suppose."

"Who were you with? Thursday night? While your wife was in Blue Hill?"

"I already told you. I was alone. Reading. Then sleeping."

"How about Friday morning between five and seven? Did you happen to go jogging on the Western Prom?"

"No. I was still sleeping."

"Thursday night, what were you reading?"

"*In Cold Blood.*"

"*In Cold Blood?*"

"Yes. Truman Capote's nonfiction novel about a family that gets murdered in Kansas. They're about to release a new movie based on the book. I last read it in college, and I wanted to see how it held up."

"Are you interested in murder, Doctor?"

"Isn't that a little obvious, Detective? My God, the man reads about murder! He must have killed the girl!"

"Are you interested in murder, Doctor?"

"Only as a form of entertainment."

"Entertainment?"

"Yes. You know. Movies. Books. You do read, don't you, Detective?"

Spencer was laughing at them, but neither McCabe nor Lund minded Spencer's attitude. Overconfidence might lead him into a catchable lie.

"Ever heard the name Harry Lime?"

"Well, it seems you do watch movies, after all. Yes. Harry Lime is the name of the Orson Welles character in the movie *The Third Man*."

"How about Paul Oliver Duggan?"

"Sorry. Don't know that name."

"One more, Dr. Spencer. Carol Reed?"

"Never met the lady."

"Did you speak to anybody on the phone Thursday night?"

"I might have. I don't remember."

"Think hard."

Spencer thought hard. McCabe figured what he was thinking about was whether the cops had a record of calls to and from his phones. "Sorry, I don't remember any calls."

"Have you ever met the guy in this picture, the one on the left?" Tasco showed Spencer a picture of a smiling Brian Henry, his arm draped around his partner's shoulder, taken days before Henry disappeared.

Spencer studied the picture. "He looks familiar."

"His name is Brian Henry. A student at Bowdoin. The dean of admissions at Tufts Medical School confirmed that you interviewed Henry last fall as part of the admissions process."

"Yes. I do remember. Bright kid. He came to the house. About a year ago. I wrote him a strong recommendation."

"Have you seen Henry since then?"

"No."

"We have reason to believe Brian Henry was murdered in the same manner and by the same person as Katie Dubois."

This time Spencer did react, surprise showing for a split second, followed by deadpan. "I'm sorry to hear that. He was a nice young man."

"Have you ever been to France? Montpellier?" Tasco pronounced it like the capital of Vermont.

"I've been to France a number of times. The last time was about two years ago. Only to Paris, though." On the monitor they could see Spencer looking at his watch. He was getting antsy. He wanted out.

"Would you excuse me for a moment, Doctor? I'll be right back."

"I'm afraid I have to be leaving, Detective."

"Just one second. I promise. I'll be right back."

Tasco walked back to confer with McCabe and Lund. "Got any bright ideas?" he asked. "He's gonna clam up any minute."

Before McCabe could respond, there was a knock on the door and Jack Batchelder poked his head in.

"Hey, Mike. There's a black dude here says he's Spencer's lawyer. Wants to talk to you. He says now."

The door opened wider, and a tall, slender African American pushed past and entered the room. McCabe recognized him immediately from his frequent appearances on television talk shows. "Gentlemen, Sheldon Thomas," the man said, holding out his hand. "Dr. Spencer's asked me to represent him."

Burt Lund stood up, shook Thomas's hand, and introduced himself. One of the best among a growing cadre of black criminal defense attorneys that included the late Johnnie Cochran, Billy Martin, and Theodore Wells, Thomas worked out of an office in Boston, which, McCabe figured, was why he hadn't gotten here earlier. McCabe clicked off the monitor.

"You must be McCabe," Thomas said.

"How can we help you, counselor?" McCabe asked. Keeping rich guys out of the slammer looked like it paid well, he thought as he shook the proffered hand. The lawyer's hand-tailored pin-striped suit must've cost five thousand dollars, maybe more. Add in the two-thousand-dollar Burberry trench coat slung over one shoulder and the three-thousand-dollar Hermes briefcase hanging from the other and the guy was wearing about ten grand worth of stuff, not counting his shoes and the probable Rolex. Sandy would have loved him.

"I believe you're conducting a noncustodial interview with my client, Dr. Philip Spencer?"

"That's correct."

"A, I'd like to speak with my client, and B, he has nothing more to say." Thomas spoke in a soft, confident voice. "Unless you have reason to detain him, he's leaving now."

"We could place Dr. Spencer under arrest," said Tasco.

Thomas responded, "That's your option, but you'd better have good cause. Also, even if you do arrest him, he's not saying anything more."

"Let him go," said McCabe. He showed the lawyer to the interview room, where Thomas spoke briefly with Spencer. Then the two of them left.

Once they were gone, McCabe rejoined Lund and an agitated Tasco. "Mike, what the hell was that all about? We shoulda charged that sonofabitch and stuck his well-bred ass in a cell. Shit, we've got the car, the earring, the blood, the video. What the hell more do we want?"

"Tom, if Spencer's the guy—and we won't know that for sure until the DNA results come in—sticking him in a cell isn't going to help."

"It'll help keep him from killing Cassidy."

"Only one problem with your logic."

"Yeah? What's that?"

"If Spencer is the guy, he's the only one who knows where Cassidy is. Hell, he could've stuck her in a cave somewhere for all we know. We lock him in a cell, do you think he's gonna tell us where she is? No way. It'd just prove he's guilty. He'll just sit there quiet as a mouse. Meanwhile, Cassidy doesn't have her heart cut out. She just dies of thirst. Or starvation. Or God knows what."

"We could try a plea bargain," said Tasco, uncertainty

creeping into his voice. "Offer him a lesser sentence for letting us know where she is."

McCabe turned to Lund. "Talk to the man, Burt. You're the prosecutor. You seriously think the AG's office would go for a plea bargain that lets a serial killer off the hook, a serial killer who's mutilated and maimed at least five innocent people and, God knows, maybe a whole bunch more?"

Lund shook his head. "No," he said. "Frankly, I don't think Spencer would go for it either."

Tasco turned back to McCabe. "Okay, McCabe, you're the boy genius. What do you suggest we do now?"

"Keep looking. At the same time, keep a loose rein on Spencer. If we don't let him know we're watching, maybe he'll lead us to her."

"Or maybe not." Tasco sounded glum.

"Okay, or maybe not, but right now he's the only connection we've got."

Tasco left. McCabe and Lund followed, just in time to watch Spencer in his preppy sweater and Sheldon Thomas in his pin-striped suit disappear behind a pair of closing elevator doors. "Well, one thing we know for sure," McCabe said, his eyes moving from Thomas to the rumpled Burt Lund, walking by his side, busily munching on a handful of M&M's.

"Yeah? What's that?"

"Their side dresses better than ours."

42

McCabe asked Maggie to meet him for a drink at Tallulah's. Despite the high-toned name, Tallulah's was a neighborhood hangout for the singles crowd on Munjoy Hill. As
usual, the place was noisy and crowded. A couple of off-
duty cops were hanging at the bar, ones McCabe didn't
know very well. They found an empty table in the corner,
far enough away from the cops not to be overheard. An
artist friend of Kyra's, Mandy something or other, took
their order. Like most artists, she couldn't support herself
selling her work, and, unlike Kyra, she had no trust fund to
take up the slack. Everyone should have a trust fund, Mc-
Cabe thought. Of course, then there'd be no waitresses or
dishwashers or plumbers or cops. Just artists and drinkers.
McCabe ordered a Glenfiddich with a Shipyard chaser.
Maggie just ordered the Shipyard. Then, after a brief, losing struggle with her inner demons, she also ordered a plate
of nachos. McCabe could never figure out how she stayed
so slim.

Kyra's friend left to get the drinks and food.

"Okay, I found out some interesting stuff." Maggie went
first. "Number one, Cumberland Medical Center's not the
blood-type connection. Only one of our four victims was ever
a patient there. Number two, they all used different doctors."

Before Maggie could tell him number three, Mandy came back with their drinks. "Your nachos'll be here in a sec."

When she was gone, McCabe asked, "So what is the connection? A testing lab?"

"Nope. The Red Cross."

McCabe considered that for a second. "Blood drive?"

"Yes. Wendy Branca, Brian Henry, Katie Dubois, and Lucinda Cassidy all gave blood within the last year."

"So somebody hacked into the Red Cross computer?"

"No. Here's where it gets interesting. For the past eighteen months, wouldn't you know, a certain doctor's wife has been volunteering at the Red Cross three days a week."

"Well, do tell. With full access to the records?"

"According to my source, yes."

McCabe stirred the warm whiskey with his index finger and then sucked it off. Pieces were falling into place. Pieces he hadn't expected.

Maggie continued. "The way I see it, McCabe, we always thought *one* of the Spencers was involved. Why should we be surprised if *both* of them are?"

The nachos arrived, cheese dripping off. Maggie positioned a jalapeño in the middle of one and managed to lower it neatly it into her mouth.

"Interesting. Just when I was beginning to have doubts."

Maggie stopped munching. "Doubts about what?"

"Doubts about Dr. Phil. About his involvement. At least in the murders. Maybe now in the surgery as well."

"McCabe, if it's not uncool to remind you, yesterday you had no doubts."

"Today I have doubts." He sipped the Scotch.

"So what's changed?" She took another nacho and offered him the plate. He shook his head.

"For one thing," he said, "Sophie seems pretty damned sure he's not the recruiter."

"Okay. He could still be the surgeon. He could still have cut out Katie's heart."

"Yes, he could, but whoever the recruiter was, he told

Sophie his name was Philip Spencer. If Spencer was involved, why would the recruiter do that?"

"I don't know." Maggie shrugged. "To frame Spencer in case the shit hit the fan?"

"Framing Spencer only makes sense if Spencer had nothing to do with any of it," said McCabe. "If Spencer *was* one of the surgeons and he found out 'Harry Lime' was framing him, he'd talk. Anybody would."

"Which means framing Spencer only makes sense if he knows nothing, if he's innocent."

"Right—and there's more. We just had Spencer in for an interview at Middle Street."

"And?"

McCabe signaled Mandy and ordered another Glenfiddich. Maggie settled for a seltzer. "He didn't behave like he was guilty. He was too relaxed. I mean, whoever killed Katie and the others knows we have a witness. He ought to be worried about it. Hell, we *know* he's worried about it. He's already tried to kill her twice and failed both times. His hit man is dead."

Maggie pulled out another cheesy nacho. McCabe waited until it was safely in her mouth, then said, "Spencer wasn't worried. I don't think he had a clue."

"Anything else?"

"Yeah. Jacobi's guys found blood in the back of the Lexus—and Katie Dubois's earring."

Maggie's eyebrows went up. "Incriminating evidence, don't you think?"

"It ought to be, but Spencer didn't recognize or react to the earring when Tom showed it to him. On top of that, I had Tasco ask him about Paul Oliver Duggan and Carol Reed. He never heard of them."

"Who's Carol Reed?" asked Maggie.

"The director of *The Third Man*. The *male* director. Any real movie buff, anyone using the alias Harry Lime, ought to at least know the name. Spencer didn't. I'm sure of it. Anyway, we'll know for sure in forty-eight hours. We gave

him a glass of water and got a saliva sample. The lab's doing a DNA match with the blood on Cassidy's dog's teeth.
That'll prove it one way or the other."

"Okay, let's suppose Spencer isn't the murderer. So how
did the blood and the earring end up in the back of the car?"

"Maybe you just gave us the answer to that."

"What do you mean?"

"Hattie."

"Hattie Spencer?"

"You know any other Hatties?"

"C'mon, McCabe, maybe Hattie Spencer dug up Katie's
blood type, but she didn't rape her or kill her. Or dump her
body."

"No, she didn't—but she probably passed on the information about the blood types to somebody who did."

"Who?"

"I don't know who, but she did tell me she lent the Lexus
to a friend last Wednesday through Friday while she was
up in Blue Hill. At the time, I thought she was covering for
her husband. Now I think she may have been telling the
truth."

McCabe picked up a nacho. The jalapeño slipped off
the top and landed on his shirt. "Shit." He picked it off and
ate it, but it left a greasy ring behind.

Maggie dipped her napkin in the seltzer, went around
the table, and dabbed at the spot on his shirt. He watched
her, a grumpy expression on his face. She looked up and
smiled. "Y'know, you're really very cute when you get all
pouty." She leaned down and kissed him softly on the lips.
"Too bad you're taken."

He glanced over to where the two cops had been sitting.

"They left ten minutes ago," she said, "and the waitress
is in the kitchen. Nothing to worry about." She turned to
go to the ladies' room. "Be right back," she called.

McCabe thought about what Maggie had done. Totally
unexpected, but not totally unpleasant. In fact, he kind of
liked it, wouldn't have minded doing it back. Except he
was taken—and, for now at least, he was happy with that.

Maggie slid back onto her chair. "Sorry about that. Anyway, Hattie lent the Lexus to a friend. What friend?"

McCabe looked into her dark brown eyes and realized, not for the first time, how attractive she was. There was no time to think about that now.

"Mike, what friend?"

He held up a finger.

"What friend?"

"Just give me a minute." He forced his mind back to the picture in Spencer's office. Four surgeons. Four friends. All gazing down from the summit of Denali. *We all went to medical school together. We did residencies together. All but one in cardiac surgery, transplant surgery . . . bringing the dead back to life. The Asclepius Society.*

All but one. Lucas Kane. Lost his license. Murdered in Miami. *A tragic, tragic loss. A great talent. In some ways, the most talented of us all.*

Spencer went to the funeral. Hattie didn't.

Lucas Kane was somebody I knew a long time ago, Hattie had said. *His parents had a summer place not far from ours.*

Was Lucas Kane a friend?

A friend? No, I never would have called Lucas that. If not a friend, then what? A lover?

What about the other surgeons in the picture? DeWitt Holland and Matthew Wilcox. One in Boston. One in North Carolina. Did they attend Kane's funeral as well? Did they all meet the shooter there? McCabe wondered if there was a press photographer at the funeral, if there were pictures. Maybe it was time to contact Melody Bollinger, the *Miami Herald* reporter who covered the case.

"Mike, what are you thinking about?"

He told her about the Denali picture. "Sophie said there were two surgeons in each of the transplant operations. Maybe it's time we talked to Dr. Holland and Dr. Wilcox."

She considered this. "Makes sense. Surgeons. Old med school chums. If Spencer wasn't involved, maybe one or both of them were."

"I'll see what I can find out about Wilcox," said McCabe. "Meantime, you drive down to Boston and talk to DeWitt Holland."

"I'm supposed to be confined to my desk, you know?"

"Holland won't know that."

"Yeah, but Fortier will."

"Call in sick."

"I guess. Anyway, I've got an old pal on the Boston PD. Homicide guy. We used to date. I think he'll help."

McCabe took another nacho.

Maggie looked thoughtful. "McCabe, you said there were three other surgeons with Spencer in that picture. Holland and Wilcox are two. Who's the third man?"

"The third man," he said, "is Lucas Kane—and, like Harry Lime, he's supposed to be dead."

43

Had anyone been watching, the two figures would have appeared almost spectral. A man and a woman, both dressed in white, moving together across a translucent, nearly monochromatic emptiness, where sand blended into sea and sea into overcast sky without perceptible delineation.

For a time, they seemed lost in thought, each looking down, each noting the prints their steps left behind in the sand. After a while they stopped and the woman turned toward her companion. She took one of his hands in hers as if willing him to move closer. He didn't. She let go. A wisp of blond hair blew across her face. She brushed it away.

She spoke, but her words were impossible for anyone but the man to hear. He shook his head. They resumed their walk, legs moving in tandem, as if attached by invisible cords. He slipped an arm around her waist. She leaned in close.

A small bird, a purple sandpiper, ran across their path, flapping furiously with one good wing. The other hung broken and useless. They watched it for a moment. Once again she asked a question. Once again there was a shake of the head. The bird rushed off. The two people continued down the beach.

Finally, where the sand ended, they came to a small

parking lot, which was empty save for a single car. A black Porsche Boxster. The man offered his hand to help the woman up onto the wooden boardwalk that separated the beach from the blacktop. She took it and climbed up. Resting a hand on his shoulder, she stood, first on one foot, then on the other, and shook the sand from her sandals. Then they walked to the car. She leaned against the door, raised her arms around his neck, and pulled him to her. He slid a hand under her jacket to stroke the smooth skin on her back. She leaned into his caress. His hand came around to the front and cupped her small breast, squeezing it gently, playing with her nipple until it was erect. Then it slid to the other side. He stroked the scar tissue where the other breast used to be. She stiffened and moved his hand away. He put it back. She moved it away again and once again he put it back. This time she let it stay.

She looked up and found his lips with her own. "Why are we doing this?"

"Because it feels good?"

"Beside that."

"Because the risk excites you?"

"Yes. I suppose it does."

He slipped his hand down between her legs and probed gently.

"They searched my car," she said, her breath starting to come faster. "They found that girl's earring. The one who was killed in the scrap yard?"

He pulled back, studying her with deep-set eyes, saying nothing.

"O-negative, wasn't she?"

Still he said nothing.

"Don't worry," she said, leaning in to kiss him again. "I won't tell a soul."

"No," he responded after a moment. "No, I'm certain you won't."

His fingers found the top button of her trousers and worked it open. "Not here," she said. "Someone might see."

He pulled down her zipper and slid her pants and panties down over her slim hips.

"Yes. Someone might," he whispered. "Isn't that what excites you?"

They could both feel her heart pounding against her chest as his hand moved back between her legs. Two fingers slid inside.

"Wait," she whispered. She stepped out of the pants and folded them neatly, then placed them through the open window onto the front seat of the car. She watched as he did the same, except he left his in a heap on the ground. She took him in her hand and he grew hard. She leaned back against the car. She let out a little gasp as he entered her.

As they moved together, he studied her face. Eyes closed, lips parted, moaning softly in pleasure. He slipped his left hand around the back of her neck, his right hand into the pocket of his jacket. He felt the handle of the folding knife just where it should be. Hiding the knife behind his back, he pressed its small button, flipping it open. She didn't notice. He rubbed his thumb across the edge of the blade. A minute later, at almost the exact instant Hattie Spencer reached orgasm, her gasp of pleasure morphed into a cry of pain.

Sixteen hundred miles to the south, all sound was drowned out by the screaming twin engines of the Learjet 35 lifting off runway 23 at Boca Raton Airport. The plane's flight plan listed its destination as a private airfield in northern New Hampshire. The Learjet was outfitted as a flying ambulance. In the back, a doctor and a nurse tended a single patient, an old man in the last stages of congestive heart failure. Up front, the crew of two, pilot and copilot, ignored their passengers. They didn't know their names and had been exceptionally well paid not to ask.

44

After leaving Tallulah's, McCabe headed back to his apartment and called Dave Hennings in D.C. His partner for nearly five years, Hennings was a tough, smart cop who'd moved on from the NYPD after 9/11 and was now a player in the federal air marshals program. He had connections with all the major airlines.

"McCabe, my man, how the hell are you? It's gotta be, what? At least a year since we spoke."

"At least that, Dave. I'm okay. How's Rosemary?" Hennings's wife was a breast cancer survivor.

"Still hanging in. Five years and counting. We keep our fingers permanently crossed. You and Kyra still an item?"

"Definitely an item," said McCabe.

"I read about the murder of that girl and thought about how you were so sure things would be nice and quiet up there in Maine. Guess you were a little optimistic." McCabe smiled to himself. Wait till Dave heard the rest of it. "Anyway, that's not why you called."

"Dave, I need a favor."

"I figured. Go for it, partner."

"There's a doctor in North Carolina named Matthew Wilcox. He's a big-deal heart surgeon at UNC Hospital in

Chapel Hill. I need to know if he traveled from Chapel Hill to Portland on any or all of three separate occasions."

"He have something to do with your murder case?"

"Maybe. Maybe not. Either way, I can't talk about it now. So I'd appreciate it if you could just trust me on this one."

"I always trust you, McCabe. Always have."

"Thanks."

"Anyway, back to your doctor. Going out of Chapel Hill, he would have flown out of Raleigh-Durham," said Hennings. "Going to Portland, he'd probably take United. Maybe US Air. Most likely changed planes in D.C. What are your dates?"

"December 2004 and April this year. Last trip would have had him here sometime last week. No firm travel dates. We'll need to check a range."

"You don't want to make a formal request to the airlines?"

"Not if you can get the information quicker. I don't have a lot of time on this one." He didn't tell Hennings there was another life at stake.

"Okay, I'm fairly well connected with senior people at both United and US Air. I should be able to check it pretty quick."

"Thanks, Dave. That's what I hoped you'd say."

As soon as he hung up, McCabe called Melody Bollinger at the *Miami Herald*. He reached the city editor. "Sorry, Detective, Mel doesn't work here anymore. Anything I can do for you?"

"No thanks. You know where I can reach her?"

"She's moved to New York. Got an offer from the *Daily News* a couple of years ago."

McCabe thanked him. He didn't need to look up the number for the *News*.

"Melody Bollinger speaking." Melody's voice didn't live up to her name.

"Ms. Bollinger? This is Detective Sergeant Michael McCabe. Portland, Maine, Police Department."

"Portland? Maine? McCabe?" He might just as well have said he was the chief cop in Siberia. "McCabe? Oh yeah. You're the lead on the murder of that teenaged kid. What's her name?"

"Dubois. Katie Dubois."

"That's right. What can I do for you, Detective?"

"Ms. Bollinger—"

"Call me Mel."

"Mel, then. In Miami, you covered the murder of Lucas Kane in March of 2001."

"Yeah, I worked on that. What's it have to do with you? Or Maine?" She sounded curious.

"Listen, can we meet? I'd like to talk to you about Kane's murder."

"Why don't you just call the cops in Miami Beach?"

"I spoke to Detective Sessions already. I thought you might be able to provide a little more insight. Shouldn't take long." There was a pause at her end. "I might also have something you may be interested in."

"Might and may? Goodness, Detective, you certainly know how to whet a girl's appetite. Why don't you just tell me on the phone what it *might* be that you *may* have? Then I might, or may, bite. I assume it's about Dubois."

"As I said, I'd rather discuss it in person." He was sure he'd learn more from Bollinger if they spoke face-to-face.

"Well, that could be a bit of a problem, Detective, since I'm in New York and you're in Maine. I'm not flying up to Maine without something a little more substantive than mays and mights."

"I'm prepared to come to New York. There's a US Air flight that leaves here at seven tomorrow morning. Can you meet me at LaGuardia around eight thirty?"

McCabe thought for a minute she might turn him down, but her reporter's instincts were too strong. "Okay, what's the flight number?"

He told her.

"I'll meet you at the baggage area," she said. "I'm blond, five foot three, and my friends describe me as zaftig."

"How do your enemies describe you?"

"We won't get into that. I assume you look like a cop."

Casey wandered into the room just as he hung up the phone. "Who were you talking to?"

"A reporter in New York."

He was sitting in his big leather chair, and she flopped down on his lap.

"What am I supposed to call her?"

"Who? The reporter?" he teased.

"No. My mother. Do I call her Mom? Or Mrs. Ingram? Or what?"

"Well, since you call Kyra Kyra and Jane Jane, why don't you just call her Sandy?"

"Am I supposed to kiss her?"

"Not if it feels uncomfortable."

"What if she kisses me first?"

"You can let her know what you're comfortable with. If you don't mind if she kisses you, that's okay. If you don't like it, ask her not to."

"That's easy for you to say."

"I think she'll understand."

"I don't have anything to wear."

"What do you mean? You have lots of stuff."

"Yeah. Right. *Stuff*. We're staying at this fancy hotel and going to these fancy restaurants and a show and everything and all I've got is *stuff*. Yucky stuff."

He thought about that for a minute. "Okay. Let's go shopping."

That got her attention. "Where?"

"How about the mall? They're open for another couple of hours." He pushed her onto the floor and stood up. "Get your shoes on."

She ran off to get them. Meanwhile, he speed-dialed Kyra's cell.

"Hiya, handsome."

"We've got an emergency here. I need your help."

"What's the matter?"

"Can you meet Casey and me at the mall in fifteen minutes? In front of Macy's?"

"I guess so. What's going on?"

"I'll tell you when I see you." He punched END as he and Casey left the apartment.

McCabe felt like he'd been cast in the Richard Gere role in *Pretty Woman* as Kyra and Casey worked their way through five stores in less than two hours. Thank God this was the Maine Mall and not Rodeo Drive. In each store, he tried to find a place to sit while the two of them picked out armloads of clothes and disappeared into the fitting room. Finally they left the mall carrying four shopping bags filled with shirts and pants and shoes and one dressy dress. McCabe thought the dress was a little tarty for a thirteen-year-old. Kyra told him he was totally ignorant about fashion and not to worry his pretty little head about it. He decided not to. His role was to pay the bills. Somehow. They headed across the parking lot to Pizzeria Uno for dinner.

Even at quarter to nine on a Thursday night the place was busy, he assumed with people who'd just left the mall or the nearby Cineplex. The hostess looked about the same age as Katie Dubois. McCabe wondered if the two knew each other. The girl wore too much makeup, and her bare plump tummy flopped out over the waistband of her black pants. McCabe watched it jiggle as she showed them to an empty table in the middle of the room. He figured she wasn't a soccer player.

He looked around. There were a lot of faces he didn't know, and the idea of sitting in the middle of a crowded room suddenly seemed stupid. Too exposed. Too vulnerable. Maybe he was being more paranoid than he ought to be. Hell, they were in Pizzeria Uno. On the other hand, hadn't the day before yesterday started with the murders of an innocent kid and a veteran cop? Hadn't the maniac who killed both nearly succeeded in slashing McCabe to death as well? Maybe it wasn't paranoia.

He spotted a corner booth where he could have his back

to the room. He asked Flabby Tummy if she would seat them there, told her he was superstitious and he thought that was his lucky table. "No problem," she said, adding in a conspiratorial whisper, "I hate Friday the thirteenth myself."

Casey slid in first, her back to the wall. McCabe sat next to her. Kyra took the bench across from them. The girl handed them menus, and a busboy filled their glasses with water. Meanwhile, McCabe scanned the room, looking for anyone looking at them. He checked possible exits. He calculated lines of fire. He brushed his right hand over his .45, making sure it was still there.

As it touched the weapon, his hand started shaking. Kyra noticed. Casey didn't. Delayed stress reaction. He willed it to stop. It wouldn't. He hid the hand under the table. He told himself to relax. That didn't work either. He imagined the headlines. HOMICIDE COP SUFFERS NERVOUS BREAKDOWN ORDERING THIN-CRUST PIZZA. He didn't laugh.

"Your server will be with you in a moment," Flabby Tummy said and left.

Kyra's hand took his, under the table. "What's the matter?" she whispered, her blue eyes registering concern, the familiar little line appearing just above her nose.

"Just a little edgy. Long day."

"Hi, I'm your server, Brian. How are you folks tonight?"

"We're great, Brian. How are you?" Casey was smiling up at him. Damn, she's flirting, thought McCabe. Thirteen years old and she's flirting with a waiter who needs a shave. Twenty's gonna be a rough seven years away. Kyra squeezed his hand tightly, smiled, and winked at him.

"Can I start you folks off with something to drink?"

McCabe ordered a Coke for Casey, a white wine for Kyra, and Dewar's on the rocks for himself. Somehow single malt, even if they had it, didn't go with the ambience.

When the drinks came, he took a long slug of his own. It helped. Alcohol depressing the central nervous system was just what he needed. Maybe he'd just say the hell with it and become a drunk. Not uncommon among cops. Of course, neither was suicide. Okay, he told himself, either balance the traumas of the job with the traumas of your life or you get yourself another job. Another life.

That night in bed, the shaking came back worse than before, and with it the cold sweats. Kyra tried to calm it by laying her body on top of his and rocking him gently. She asked if this ever happened before. Just once, he said, the night after he shot TwoTimes, but that night he had no one to hold him. Sandy was gone and he had slept alone.

They didn't make love. They just rocked until about two in the morning, when McCabe fell asleep. When he woke at five, she was still holding him. The shakes were gone.

45

It was exactly one week since Lucinda Cassidy was kidnapped on the Western Prom, and all McCabe could do was hope she was still alive. His flight to LaGuardia took a little over an hour and, for a change, they landed right on time. Melody Bollinger was waiting for him by the baggage carousel. As it turned out, she was zaftig and then some. She resembled an updated version of Joan Blondell, maybe twenty pounds rounder. She was wearing a pair of tight khaki pants McCabe figured she bought at least fifteen pounds ago. A blue blazer covered most but not all of the bulge. They had no trouble recognizing each other.

"McCabe?"

"Melody?" The terminal was jammed with people. "Let's go get some coffee," he said, looking around. "There's a Starbucks upstairs."

"You know your airports."

"I've been here a few times before," he said. "I'm a New Yorker."

"I know. I did a backgrounder on you. Your career with the NYPD, your little run-in with the drug dealer—and, of course, the Dubois case."

They found a table in the corner, and he bought them

both some coffee. She declined his offer of a pastry. "I'm on Atkins, but thanks anyway."

He handed her the coffee. "Alright," she asked, "what's this all about? What's Kane's connection to your case?" She flipped on her recorder.

He reached over and flipped it off. "Take notes," he said. "I'd just as soon not be on tape or quoted for attribution. Consider me an unnamed source. Plus I'd like you to hold off printing any of this."

"McCabe, you know better than that. I'm a reporter. You tell me something that's news, expect it to be printed."

"Just hold off a couple of days. Say until Monday. You'll have a better story if you do. If we clear it by then, I'll make sure you get details nobody else will have."

"What if something happens in the meantime?"

"In the meantime, print whatever you want as long as it doesn't come from me."

She thought about this. "Alright. Deal." She put the recorder back in her briefcase. "Now, why are you interested in Kane?"

McCabe showed Bollinger a postmortem photograph of the man Maggie had killed in Sophie Gauthier's hospital room. "Do you know this man?"

She picked up the picture and examined it. "Sure. It's Duane Pollard. Lucas Kane's bullyboy. Who killed him?"

"You're sure it's Pollard?"

"I'm sure. Either him or his twin brother. Is this the guy the female cop shot in the hospital yesterday morning? The one identified as Darryl Pollock?"

"You do your homework."

"Story came in from the AP last night. Is this Darryl Pollock?"

"Yes. My partner shot him just in time to save my life. Saved a key witness's life as well."

"Interesting. When did Duane turn up in Maine? And why?" Bollinger started writing notes.

"Let me ask some questions first. Do you think Pollock—

let's call him that, it's his real name—do you think he killed Lucas Kane?"

She looked up. "No. His alibi was corroborated six ways to Sunday. He couldn't have pulled the trigger."

"Could he have recruited someone else to do it?"

"Unlikely. Kane was his meal ticket."

"Maybe they had a spat."

"Yeah, maybe, but I don't think so. I don't know what you're looking for here."

"I'm trying to figure out exactly why this thug ended up in Maine trying to put a bullet through a key witness's head. All I know so far is that Pollock's ex-boyfriend, the late Lucas Kane, was buddies with a doctor in Maine who may be involved in the case."

"What do you want from me?"

"I'd like to know what you know about the murder of Lucas Kane."

"About all I can add to what you read in the *Herald* is a couple of things I've always thought of as weird. Or at least questionable."

"Yeah? Like what?"

"Like whoever shot Kane shot him from an angle and chose a weapon guaranteed to blow away his dentures and turn his face into mincemeat. The only reason I can think of to do that is to make positive ID as hard as possible. Why?"

"I don't know. You wrote that the cops suspected a mob hit."

"Yeah, but that was bullshit. If in doubt, blame the mob. Any mob. Everybody just nods and accepts it. It's a convenient out."

"You think this wasn't their style."

"I know it's not. So do you. If they wanted to kill Kane, they'd just go bang-bang-you're-dead. No reason to hide his identity."

McCabe chewed on that for a minute. "Okay. That's weird number one. What's weird number two?"

"The fingerprints."

"What about the fingerprints?"

Bollinger took a breath. "McCabe, you're an experienced homicide cop. You know better than I do that when you check somebody's house for prints, you generally pick up a lot of extraneous prints from whoever's been there. Not just the people who live there but others. Visitors, delivery people. Whoever. Well, in Kane's apartment there was a lot of that. A lot of partials and smears, here, there, and everywhere, just like you'd expect."

"So what's the problem?"

"I have a good contact, a crime lab tech who examined the room where they found Kane's body. He's somebody I trust. According to my contact, none of those prints belonged to the victim."

"I thought the cops said there were a lot of Kane's prints. That's one of the ways they identified him."

"There were and it is. They found the victim's prints all over the place. On the telephone. On the doorknobs. On tables. On the refrigerator. One on an empty beer bottle in the living room."

"But—"

"Let me finish. These prints were all perfect. Nice fat plump perfect prints. Not a smear or partial among them. It was like somebody walked the victim around the apartment and planted his prints on things just before they shot him. Or maybe pressed his fingers against things just after."

"The FBI didn't have a record of Kane's prints?"

"No. Kane was never fingerprinted while he was alive. Never arrested. Never served in the military, et cetera, et cetera. All they had for a comp was the victim himself."

"How about the DNA? Sessions said they were sure because of the DNA."

"Same sort of thing. The DNA they got was from hairs on the bed right where the techs would look. Saliva in the sink. A complete set of fingernail clippings in the wastebasket in the bathroom. Just seemed to me, and my pal in the crime lab, that it was all too perfect."

"There was no previous record of Kane's DNA?"

"Nope."

"So you're saying the body wasn't Kane's?"

"I'm saying it's a definite maybe."

"So if it wasn't Lucas Kane, who was it?"

"I haven't a clue. In those days South Beach was full of good-looking boys on the prowl. Some selling their bodies. Some just looking for a sugar daddy. If one of them happened to disappear, nobody would even notice."

"He'd have to be the same height and weight as Kane. Same hair color."

"Easy enough."

"How about the car?"

"What about the car?"

"You wrote that Kane's prints—the corpse's prints—matched the prints found in the car."

"They did."

"Same problem of perfection they found in the condo?"

"No. The prints in the car were about what you'd expect. Partials from the victim on the door, the wheel, the gearshift lever, the seat belt lock, and so on. I don't know about DNA."

"Anybody else's prints anywhere in or on the car?"

"Not that I'm aware of. I think it was clean."

"So maybe they wiped it down and then let the victim drive it around?"

"That could be."

"Did you ever ask Allard or Sessions about any of this?"

"Yeah. At first they pooh-poohed the whole thing, told me my imagination was working overtime, but I'm a persistent kind of gal, and I kept asking. After a while they just stonewalled me."

"Kane's father came to the funeral, right?" McCabe asked.

"Yes. The famous pianist. I remember a sad old man. He came with a much younger woman who was supposedly his assistant. Maybe she was. Maybe she was more. I think the mother may be dead."

"Did anybody think to do a Y-chromosomal DNA match

between father and son? That would have confirmed the body's identity beyond a doubt."

"Wouldn't have helped."

"Why not?"

"Kane was adopted. On that note, if you'll excuse me, I'd like to take a short break and find the little girls' room."

Bollinger rose and wandered off. McCabe got them both another coffee and considered the possibilities. Suppose Bollinger was right and the body they buried wasn't Lucas Kane. Pollock would have to have known. He ID'd the body. Said it was Kane. *Hair, moles, and scars in all the right places,* Sessions told him. *Even made some jokes about the guy's pecker. "I never forget a penis," he said.*

Suppose Kane had killed someone else to convince people he was dead. Why? So he could become Harry Lime? In the film *The Third Man,* Harry Lime faked his own death on the theory that the police would never go after a dead man. Had Kane done the same thing for the same reason? The choice of names seemed almost too obvious. Once again the risk-taker? What about the other name? Pollock's alias, Paul Oliver Duggan. The name used by the assassin in *Day of the Jackal.*

McCabe replayed Spencer's words again in his mind. *A tragic, tragic loss. In some ways Lucas was the most talented of us all.* Talented enough to perform transplant surgery on elderly patients after fifteen years of not being a doctor? Seemed like a reach. Talented enough to be someone's assistant? Holland's. Wilcox's. Or even Spencer's. Maybe they were all in on it. The Asclepius Society. Killing healthy young people to bring the dead back to life.

McCabe let his mind range over the possibilities. What about the victims? Katie Dubois. Lucinda Cassidy. Elyse Andersen. Wendy Branca. Brian Henry. All blond. All athletes. All physically attractive. All but one female. The Harry Lime name was linked to both Dubois and Andersen. Dubois was raped before being murdered. Dubois and Andersen had their hearts cut out. The fate of the others remained uncertain.

McCabe wondered about Kane's sexuality. In Miami he lived an openly gay lifestyle. Maybe he was bisexual. Common enough. He remembered reading Kinsey Institute statistics claiming 11.6 percent of white males between twenty and thirty-five were equally attracted to men and women.

Bollinger returned. He handed her her coffee. "What do you know about Kane's sex life?"

"Ah, now we're getting to the fun stuff," said Bollinger.

"Seriously. I know he had an ongoing relationship with Pollard—excuse me, Pollock—but beyond that?"

"Lucas Kane was a sexual predator. Men. Women. It didn't matter. He was vicious and voracious."

"You mean AC/DC?"

"No. That's too gentle a word for it. Sex defined nearly everything Lucas Kane did. He consumed people. Used them and abused them. Most of his targets were young and fit, but lack of beauty never deterred Lucas. If he wanted something, he used sex to get it. He even hit on fat old me on more than one occasion."

"Did he score?"

"Not that it's any of your business, but no. Lucas Kane was physically attractive, very attractive. Beautiful, really, but I found him psychically repellent. Like a snake. Lucas would take you, suck you dry, and throw you away. Darryl Pollock was the only human being I can think of, and I use the term 'human being' loosely, who was tough enough or insensitive enough or sociopathic enough not to care. A match made in heaven. Now, if you don't mind, let's change the subject. Lucas's sex life gives me the creeps."

"Okay. Tell me about Stan Allard's suicide."

"I guess that's weird thing number three. I don't think it was suicide."

"What do you mean?"

"What happened is, a little after Kane's death, Stan's marriage finally broke up and he moved into this grubby little place called the Endless Dunes. Basically a hot-sheets motel a couple of blocks from the beach. The way

Sessions tells it, Stan was so depressed about splitting with his wife that he just wanted to end it all."

"You don't think so?"

"Stan wasn't depressed. He was overjoyed. A few days before the supposed suicide, I had a couple of drinks with him. You know what he said about the breakup? 'Best thing that ever happened to me. I should have walked out on the bitch years ago.'

"Then we started bullshitting about the Kane murder, and I told him about some of my concerns about the fingerprints and DNA. All he said was, 'I'm working on that.'

"I said, 'What do you mean you're working on it? I thought the case was closed?'

"He said, 'It wasn't cleared. It isn't closed. I'm working on it.' Listen, McCabe, Stan Allard was a smart, tough cop. A survivor. I say there's no way he shot himself." Bollinger paused.

"You think it was Pollock and Kane."

"One or the other. Or both. Duane did most of Kane's dirty work, but they both liked hurting people. Probably liked killing them."

"They killed Allard because Allard was getting too close to proving Kane wasn't dead?"

"Yes."

"Sessions didn't do anything about it?"

"I've got some pretty good sources who tell me Sessions was on Kane's payroll. Hired and paid for. He wanted everyone thinking Kane was dead. Again nothing I can prove. Or even print."

"How do you think they did Allard?"

"I think Kane and Pollard, sorry, Pollock, may have been waiting in Stan's motel room. When he gets home, they render him unconscious, sit him in a chair, wrap his hand around his gun, stick it in his mouth, and bang. There were powder burns inside Stan's mouth and evidence of saliva on the barrel of the gun."

"What kind of gun?"

"A Glock 17. It was Stan's."

"Where did they find it?"

"On the floor by the body."

"Nobody heard the shot?"

"Nobody they could find. Nobody willing to talk. Remember, the guest list at the Endless Dunes is mostly hookers and other romantic types who don't want to get caught."

"So Sessions doesn't blow the whistle . . ."

"Because Kane can prove he was on the take."

"He leave a suicide note?"

"Nope."

"Any sign of a choke hold or drugs in Stan's blood?"

"No."

"So you can't prove a thing."

"Damn, you're good, McCabe."

46

McCabe half expected Sandy to turn up on his flight back to Portland. Thank God, she didn't. Sitting next to Sandy, chatting about her coming weekend with Casey, would have been more than he could have handled. Anyway, it was early. Sandy was probably still in her West End Avenue apartment, picking out the perfect wardrobe for parental visitation. Something conservative and motherly. Sandy was good at playing roles, equally good at dressing for them.

The plane was one of those small commuter jobs with undersized seats. He looked around to see if he could snag an empty row before squeezing into his assigned aisle seat. No such luck. The flight was packed. Next to him a distracted businesswoman in full New York chic rummaged through her Ferragamo briefcase. He smiled at her. She smiled back as she extracted a *Wall Street Journal* and stowed the briefcase under the seat. Then she immersed herself in the paper, signaling a lack of interest in small talk. McCabe leaned back in agreement, closed his eyes, and thought about his conversation with Melody Bollinger. Was Lucas Kane dead and buried in Florida or alive and cutting out hearts in Maine? He was ready to bet on the latter.

His cell phone vibrated shortly after the plane bumped

down at Portland International Jetport. Maggie's name appeared in the window. "What's up?"

"Good news, bad news. The good news is I'm back on the case and on my way to search Spencer's house. Thought you might want to join us. Unless you're still in New York."

"No, I'm here. Just touched down. What's the bad news?"

"We don't know where Spencer is."

"He's gone?" McCabe looked out the window. The plane seemed to be crawling to the gate. "Gone where?"

"We don't know. The cop watching his house doesn't know. The hospital doesn't know either. Woman at the Levenson Heart Center said he was supposed to be in surgery this morning. He never showed up."

Spencer would never miss surgery, would he? The plane stopped about a hundred yards short of the terminal. "When was the last time anyone spoke to him?"

"At 6:00 A.M.," said Maggie. "Hospital called him at home. He answered."

Maggie was interrupted by the voice of the captain. "Ladies and gentlemen, I'm afraid there'll be a short delay while we wait for a gate to open up. Shouldn't be more than a minute or two."

"Shit," McCabe said. Too loudly. The woman next to him gave him a look. "Sorry," he mumbled. He looked out the window. Couldn't see anything.

"A teenage boy died early this morning," Maggie continued, "from injuries in a car crash. Spencer was supposed to be installing his heart in a thirty-two-year-old woman named—" Maggie paused. Seemed like she was checking her notes. "—Lisa Lynch."

"He never showed up?"

"You got it. They called Dr. Codman to cover. Almost lost the heart and the woman."

Why would Spencer not show up? There were a lot of reasons, none of them good. "You tried the house yourself, and his cell?"

"Yeah. Voice mail picks up on both. I think we were

wrong about him not being involved. I think he flew the coop," said Maggie.

McCabe doubted it. Even if Maggie was right and Spencer was involved, taking off would practically be an admission of guilt. Okay. They had the earring, and the blood from the Lexus, but even taken together that wouldn't be enough to convict. Not with a lawyer like Sheldon Thomas. Hell, they couldn't even prove Spencer was driving the Lexus. The evidence they had was a lot less damning than OJ and his Bruno Magli shoes. Thomas would have told him that.

The plane inched forward again.

Maggie's voice was in his ear. "I think maybe he's guilty and Tasco rattled him more than you thought during that interview. He decides we're getting close to nailing him and bango, he hits the road."

"Yeah. Maybe," McCabe said. Although he wasn't buying it. The plane reached the gate. The pilot turned off the seat belt sign, and people all around him started getting up. "What about Hattie?" he asked.

"We don't know where she is either. I think they took off together."

The woman next to McCabe was looking at him again. He was still in his seat, and she wanted out. He stood up and banged his head on the overhead. "Where are you now?" he asked, pushing his way into the aisle and rubbing his head.

"We're just leaving 109."

"Have you put out an ATL yet?" He didn't want to use Spencer's name.

"Yeah. For both the BMW and the Porsche. Every department in Maine plus the New Hampshire staties."

The flight attendant opened the door, and the line of people started inching out.

"We've got public transport covered as well. Buses. Trains. The airport."

"Maybe I'll run into them on the way out," said McCabe. The idea made him smile. Grimly.

The line stopped again. In front of McCabe, a girl around twenty, probably a college kid, was blocking the aisle, struggling to release a duffel bag way too big for the overhead space. He slipped the cell phone into his pocket and wrestled it down for her. They started moving again.

He could hear Maggie shouting from inside his pocket. "Hey, McCabe, you still there?"

He pulled the phone out. "Yeah. I'm trying to get off the plane. Call you right back." He flipped it off.

Up ahead, the flight attendant chirped her mandatory farewells. "Bye-bye." Smile. "Bye-bye." Smile. "Bye-bye." Smile. Finally he was free.

He called Maggie back. "Meet you at Trinity Street?"

"I just sent a car to the airport to pick you up," she told him. "Should be there any minute."

By the time McCabe reached the exit, the black-and-white Crown Vic was pulling into a no-parking zone right out front, lights flashing. He slipped into the front seat. "Alright, hit it," he told the officer driving. "Lights and siren, 24 Trinity Street."

Dave Hennings called as they turned out of the airport and onto Congress Street. McCabe asked the driver to silence the siren.

"Howdy, partner, how you doing?"

"Not so great, Dave. A suspect just turned up missing. We're about to search his house. You have anything for me?"

"Yeah, but it's a good thing I love you like family. I had to flaunt my Homeland Security creds big-time on this one. Threaten our nation's air carriers with the Patriot Act. Imply Wilcox was a suspected terrorist. Anyway, it turns out he made three short round-trips between Raleigh-Durham and Portland over the past year. Trip number one was last December. First class out of Raleigh-Durham on United 3281 December fourteenth, changed planes in D.C. He returned on the seventeenth, also on United."

Wendy Branca, thought McCabe.

"Second trip was April nineteenth, return on the twenty-third. Same flights."

Brian Henry.

"Third trip was just last week. Left North Carolina on US Air 621 and changed in Newark."

"What days?"

"Left Raleigh-Durham Tuesday the thirteenth and returned Friday morning the sixteenth. How's that jibe with what you got?"

"You hit the trifecta, Dave. Three dates. Three victims. They all coincide."

"Well, my friend, that means you've got serious cause for concern. Because Dr. Wilcox may be back in Maine as we speak."

Oh, Christ. Lucinda Cassidy.

"He flew out of Raleigh-Durham Wednesday afternoon on American 1560, landed in Fort Lauderdale."

"Lauderdale? I thought you said Maine."

"Hold on. I'm getting to that. His return flight's Sunday morning. From Portland. No info on how he gets from Lauderdale to Portland. Airline calls it 'arunk.' Arrival unknown. Just to be sure we had the right Matthew Wilcox, I called his office at UNC. Assistant said he was out of town. Wouldn't be back until Monday. I asked her if she knew where he was going. She said no. Not real friendly for a southern gal. So I took the obvious tack and scared the bejesus out of her. Told her she might be aiding and abetting terrorist activity."

"Jesus, Dave. You could get your ass in a sling for that."

"Nah. I'll be alright. She didn't sound like she wanted any trouble. Anyway, she finally told me he'd gone to Boca Raton on personal business and then was heading to Maine for the weekend."

"Did she say where in Maine?"

"Said she didn't know. I also checked his cell phone. It's been turned off since he left town."

"Let me have the number," said McCabe. Hennings gave

it to him. "The airline have any information on where he's staying in Maine or possible car rentals?"

"No. None. I called Hertz and Avis directly. Nothing there either. I haven't had time to check the others. Also haven't checked the chain hotels. Of course, there's a million independents up there in Maine. He could be at any one of them."

"Or none, and he could be using an assumed name." The driver pulled up around the corner from Spencer's house on Trinity Street. Tasco and Fraser were already there in one car, Maggie in another. Half a dozen uniformed officers completed the search team.

"Good hunting."

"Thanks, Dave."

"My pleasure. By the way, we're now officially even on favors. You may even owe me a couple."

"Absolutely. Love to Rosemary."

The detectives huddled in the street discussing strategy. Because Lucinda Cassidy might be a hostage, McCabe told the others he wanted to enter quietly and not force a confrontation. They deployed the uniformed officers to the sides and rear of the property to cut off avenues of escape. Tasco and Fraser covered the driveway. Maggie and McCabe headed for the house.

Twenty-four Trinity Street had an empty, forlorn look about it. Windows shut. Shades drawn. On the front step, Maggie stood to one side of the door, her back against the house, McCabe to the other. He rang the bell. They waited. Rang it again. Quietly, McCabe tried the handle. Locked. They could either break in or pick the lock. Again McCabe preferred the quiet option. Less likely to panic anyone hiding inside. The front lock was an Ilco tubular model. Pickable but not easy. Plus you needed special tools they didn't have.

They slipped around to the kitchen door and looked in through the glass. Empty. A coffee mug on the round oak table, nothing else out of place. He tried the knob. Locked, an older-style Schlage pin-and-tumbler dead bolt. He took out the small leather wallet he'd brought from Maggie's car and withdrew a slender tension wrench and one of three stainless steel picks, each shaped like a delicate dental tool, a small hook on the end. He knelt, putting the lock at eye level. Maggie drew her weapon and waited.

McCabe inserted the wrench in the keyhole and turned it a quarter turn to the right. Then he slid the pick in, probed, found a pin, and eased it onto the narrow ledge of the cylinder. One by one, he lifted the remaining pins. When all five were clear of the shear line, he turned the wrench. The lock slid open.

Inside, weapons drawn, the two detectives looked and listened to the silence. A slow drip from the kitchen faucet. The ticking of a clock. A motor turning on in the fridge. The coffee mug on the table was filled about halfway with clear liquid, traces of lipstick marking the rim. McCabe sniffed. The scent of gin. A familiar ploy of drunks the world over. Every morning, for years, Tom McCabe senior sipped his Bushmill's from a bone china teacup. "Pa's tea," he called it. Mom never spoke of it. Never let the kids say anything either. Not to the old man. Not to anyone. She grew angry when Tom junior, Tommy the Narc, brought it up the day they put the old man in the ground. Sixty-one years old. A liver ailment. Mom only forgave Tommy his indiscretion after he himself was dead.

Four interior doors led from the kitchen. The first opened on an empty butler's pantry. The second, a set of back stairs leading up to the second floor. Behind the third, more stairs, this time down to what looked like an unfinished cellar. The last door led into a broad central hall. They decided Maggie would stay in the kitchen to block anyone exiting from either the back stairs or the cellar. McCabe would check the other rooms.

To the right of the hall he found a formal dining room, a gleaming mahogany table and eight Duncan Phyfe chairs in the middle. He had a vivid memory of Sandy coveting a similar set in an antique store in Connecticut. Frustrated and angry they couldn't afford even one of the chairs on a cop's salary, she sulked all the way back to New York. Probably had the whole set now.

Beyond the dining room McCabe found the small den he'd seen from outside on his first visit. It, too, lay silent and empty, the *New York Times* crossword still in the same place, still half finished. He crossed the hall. A pair of massive pocket doors, each weighing several hundred pounds, blocked entry to what he assumed was the living room. He gave one a gentle push. The beautifully balanced door rolled silently and smoothly into its pocket on the far side, revealing another empty room.

An open bottle of Tanqueray stood on a silver tray on a walnut chest. The source, he supposed, of Hattie Spencer's morning nip. On the opposite wall, a pair of tall windows looked out on the front garden. He remembered Hattie's slender form outlined in the far window, seeing him off the property, just days before.

Something soft rubbed against his leg. A small black-and-white cat looked up and purred, then continued past, squeezing itself under the protective legs of an upholstered chair. It peered out at McCabe. McCabe peered back. The animal decided to ignore the man and began licking its once white feet, now stained a dark red.

The trail of cat's prints led out into the hall and up the broad stairs that arched gracefully to the landing on the second floor. McCabe probably wouldn't have noticed them against the dark wood had he not been looking for them. He touched a finger to one at the top of the stairs. Still damp. The paw prints led to a room at the end of the hall, its door open just enough for a small cat to have slipped through. McCabe walked to the end of the corridor, raised one foot, and gently pushed. Silence. He entered and scanned the room, pointing the .45 first left, then right. Sheets lay rumpled on a queen-sized four-poster bed, dark red bloodstains providing a vivid counterpoint to the white lace canopy above. Beyond the bed, McCabe saw a thickening pool still spreading slowly across the not quite level floor. He swallowed hard and walked around the end of the bed to the other side.

Philip Spencer's naked body lay on its back, his smug arrogance gone, his once handsome face contorted in agony. An overturned chair indicated a final struggle. He'd been stabbed half a dozen times. Where Spencer's legs met, there was now only an open wound. On the wall above the bed, written in Spencer's blood, a line from the English poet Elizabeth Barrett Browning.

How do I love thee? Let me count the ways.

McCabe counted the ways and counted again. Each time, the only answer that made any sense was the one that added up to Lucas Kane.

47

McCabe's eyes darted back and forth between Spencer's body and the bloody writing on the wall. In his mind's eye, he saw Lucas Kane standing triumphant atop Denali. Lucas Kane. Spencer's lover. Spencer's betrayer. Spencer's killer. *How do I love thee,* Kane had asked. The only truthful answer was the one Browning had written. *I love thee to the depth and breadth and height my soul can reach.* Assuming, of course, Kane's soul was, as Melody Bollinger described, vicious and voracious, sex defining nearly everything Lucas Kane did. McCabe was sure Bollinger was right about these things. He was now also certain she was right about Kane being alive—and deep down inside himself, in a place of which he was only dimly aware, he knew that was something he was going to have to change.

He heard steps in the corridor. Maggie's long figure appeared in the door. She saw the bloody sheets on the bed. He held up a hand to stop her. Ignoring it, she crossed the room and looked down. She closed her eyes, opened them, looked around, walked to the master bathroom, bent over Harriet Spencer's fancy French bidet, and threw up.

"Sorry about that," she said.

"Not a problem."

He took out his cell and hit Tasco's number. Just as it

rang, they heard the steel basement hatch, outside the back door, clang shut. McCabe moved to the bathroom window. A tall figure, dressed in black and wearing cowboy boots, walked quickly but calmly to the side door of the garage. Then the man turned, looked up, and, for an instant, smiled at McCabe in the window. Before McCabe could get a shot off, Lucas Kane disappeared.

"Mike, Mike, answer me. Dammit." Tasco's voice, shouting from the cell.

"The garage, Tom. He's in the garage. Get him."

"Spencer?"

"No, Spencer's dead. The murderer."

From his right, McCabe saw Tasco and Fraser sprinting up the driveway, weapons drawn.

"Careful, Tommy," he shouted into the cell. Tasco wasn't listening.

An engine roared to life. Garage doors slid open. Tires squealed. Philip Spencer's black Porsche Boxster hurtled down the driveway, spraying gravel. Tasco leapt out of the way. Eddie Fraser stood his ground and fired twice. The car sideswiped Fraser, tossing him into the air. He landed hard on the lawn. The small Porsche just made it past Tasco's blocking vehicle. It turned left and screamed away. Tasco squeezed off two rounds. Both missed. He ran to the radio in his Crown Vic. "This is seven-two-two. Detective down. I need an ambulance at 24 Trinity Street. Hit-and-run suspect vehicle heading west toward Vaughan. Black Porsche Boxster. Maine registration Two-Eight-Zero-One-Victor-Romeo. Repeat Two-Eight-Zero-One-Victor-Romeo. One male subject in vehicle. Consider armed and very dangerous. Over."

"Roger, seven-two-two. MedCU en route, 24 Trinity. We'll be right there. Out." This was followed by the loud electronic signal that would alert all units that a priority transmission was about to be broadcast.

The two patrol units that had been parked around the corner roared by in pursuit, lights flashing, sirens screaming. McCabe and Tasco reached Fraser simultaneously.

Eddie was clutching his side, trying to sit up. Blood poured from a gash on his forehead. "Stay down. Ambulance'll be here in a second," said McCabe.

Tasco opened a first-aid kit, tore the paper wrapping from a bandage, and pressed it onto Fraser's bleeding forehead. McCabe rose, walked toward the house, and stopped, reconstructing the scene in his mind. Had someone been in the car with Kane? Yes. A woman. A blonde. Hunched over in a strange position. Maybe shot. He walked back to Fraser. "Eddie? How many people did you see in the car?"

Fraser held up two fingers.

"You're sure?" asked McCabe.

Fraser nodded and spoke through the pain. "A guy driving. A woman next to him."

"Did you hit either one?"

He shook his head. "Shitty shooting, huh?"

McCabe radioed from Tasco's car. Two people in the suspect car. A dark-haired man and a blond woman, possibly Harriet Spencer, possibly Lucinda Cassidy, either a possible hostage.

He wondered where Kane was heading and if the blonde was, in fact, Hattie Spencer. He'd only seen the woman for a split second as the Porsche sped down the driveway. Had she been restrained in any way? He backed his mind up to the single frame in which her image appeared just as he would a video editing machine. The frame was blurry. It flashed by so fast he couldn't be sure.

He returned to the house.

Upstairs, he gazed at Spencer's mutilated corpse. The sirens faded in the distance. The crime scene techs were on their way. He had to figure out what to do next. For the moment, he didn't have a clue.

Maggie appeared at his side. "McCabe, what in hell is this all about?"

"It's about Lucas Kane."

"I thought Kane was dead."

"Kane faked his own death."

"Why?"

"Lots of reasons. Probably figured being dead would keep the cops from watching his new business venture too closely. Probably thought disappearing into the grave was cool."

"Cool like Harry Lime in *The Third Man*?"

"Cool like that."

"Why'd he have to castrate Spencer? Why couldn't he just kill him . . . well . . . normally?"

"I think it's about power." *Sex defined nearly everything Lucas Kane did.* "In Kane's mind, cutting off the genitals might have been a way of symbolically neutralizing an enemy's power."

Maggie looked dubious.

"That's not a new idea. Balls have been a metaphor for bravery and power for a long, long time."

"Sick."

"Very."

"You're sure it *was* Kane you saw down there?"

"You know me. I never forget a face."

"Jesus, McCabe, doesn't this creep ever take a vacation?" Bill Jacobi called from the door. "My guys can't keep up with the corpses." He looked down at the mutilated body. "Cute. What did he do with the guy's schwantz? Keep it for a souvenir? Terri here yet?"

"Not yet. We'll get out of your way so you can do your job."

Outside, the scene had changed dramatically. An ambulance and half a dozen patrol units were pulled up, plus a couple more unmarked Crown Vics. Crime scene tape surrounded the property. Neighbors and passersby gawked from the street. Rumors of Philip Spencer's violent death brought the media out in force. Flies to honey. News Center 6's Josie Tenant once again in the lead. McCabe had no doubt her reports would go directly into NBC's national feed. He owed Melody Bollinger a call, but that'd have to wait.

A pair of EMTs lifted Eddie Fraser into the ambulance

for the short ride to Cumberland. "Three or four broken ribs and a concussion," Tasco told them. "Maybe some other broken bones as well."

McCabe and Maggie walked over to Shockley and Fortier. "Anybody get the Porsche?"

"Not yet." Shockley spoke first. "Nobody's seen it since it left the West End."

"We'll find him," said Fortier. "If he's still in it."

"He won't be." McCabe told his bosses about Lucas Kane.

"You're sure it was Kane?" asked Fortier.

"I'm sure."

"He's got a hostage?" asked the chief.

"Maybe. Maybe not. We spotted a blond female in the car."

"Harriet Spencer? Lucinda Cassidy?"

"My money's on Hattie."

The call came less than a minute later. A female shopper pulling into a space on the upper level of a garage off Monument Square noticed a blond woman slumped in the Porsche parked next to her. She thought the woman might be sick, so she looked closer. Then she called 911.

Five minutes later McCabe peered through the Porsche's window himself. There was no doubt about it. The blonde was Harriet Spencer, and she was dead. Stabbed in the heart, naked from the waist down, seat belt still engaged, pants and panties folded neatly on her lap. When they looked, the crime scene guys found sand in her panties. Beach sand, they thought.

Kane must have driven into the garage, parked, and driven out in another vehicle. The garage didn't have a surveillance camera. The cashier didn't notice a thing. "Just great," said McCabe. "Now we don't even know what kind of car we're looking for."

"So what now?" asked Fortier, frustration palpable in his voice.

"Beats the shit out of me," McCabe muttered. "I guess we'll think of something."

He checked his watch. In an hour and a half Sandy would be arriving to pick up Casey. He asked Maggie to give him a ride back to the condo.

48

They drove in silence, their minds focused on Spencer's death, needing to figure out what to do next. Images of the city slid by. At the end of Danforth, a bronze statue of John Ford, a Portland native, relaxed in an oversized director's chair. Nearby, giant fish kites fluttered above a Japanese restaurant. Maggie took the half right onto Fore Street and headed into the Old Port. McCabe gazed absently at the passing parade, strategies, angles of attack, taking shape in his mind. He watched a pack of noisy teenagers, boys in baggy pants, girls showing too much skin, pointing and giggling at the silly sex toys in the windows of Condom Sense. A trio of Muslim women, heads and bodies covered, gave the same windows sidelong glances as they passed.

Did you consider Kane a friend? he'd asked Hattie. She'd smiled an ironic smile. *No, I never would have called Lucas that.* No. Kane wasn't Hattie's friend. He was her lover. A lover Hattie helped by fingering candidates with the right blood types. Fingering candidates for murder. Was Spencer dead because Hattie told him about it? Or maybe he figured it out on his own and confronted Kane. Either way he had to be eliminated—and so did she. In the Porsche, Harriet's pants and panties lay neatly folded on her lap, sand inside the panties. Kane must've screwed her on a beach and stabbed her then and there. Death at the moment of orgasm? He imagined Kane getting off on it.

Maggie missed the light at Pearl. While they waited, McCabe watched a group of office workers cross the street in front of them, probably escaping early for a September weekend. He envied them their freedom. When the light changed, Maggie drove across India and up Munjoy Hill, where Fore Street turns into the Eastern Prom. Casco Bay glittered before them.

As she pulled in behind his condo, McCabe broke the silence. "Did you ever talk to DeWitt Holland?"

"On the phone," said Maggie. "Not much joy in it. Said he hadn't seen Spencer in a couple of years. I made a date to interview him in person tomorrow."

"Did he seem nervous?"

"Not especially. Claimed he didn't know anything about the murder, hadn't even seen it on the news. 'I don't pay attention to things like that' is how he phrased it."

"Telling the truth?"

"I'm not sure. He was pretty smooth."

"Maybe you better call your homicide buddy on the Boston PD. If Holland was involved or knew anything about it, he could be next on Killer Kane's hit list."

Maggie reached for her cell and dialed. "His name's John Bell," she said to McCabe as she flipped the phone to speaker mode.

"Hey, Mag," Bell's voice boomed out, "how goes the investigation? When are you coming down?"

"John, I've got my partner, Mike McCabe, with me. You're on speaker."

"Okay, that's fine. What's up?"

"We've had another murder up here. Victim was a top heart surgeon. We think Dr. DeWitt Holland, a heart surgeon at the Brigham, may be the killer's next target."

"Jesus, somebody have something against heart docs? Can you give me a little background on this?"

McCabe slipped a note under Maggie's nose. *How much do you trust this guy?*

She scrawled underneath, *Completely.*

"Mag, you there?"

"Sorry, John." Maggie told Bell what they knew, starting with Katie Dubois's murder and ending with Philip Spencer's.

"How does that connect with Holland?"

"Spencer, Holland, and another transplant surgeon named Matthew Wilcox all did their residencies with Kane in New York in the eighties," McCabe said. "They were big buddies. Called themselves the Asclepius Society after the Greek god of healing. They stayed friends at least through the nineties, climbing mountains together, stuff like that. When Kane dreamed up this illegal transplant idea, naturally he needed a surgeon or two to help. Now we think Kane's closing the business down and wants to get rid of anyone who knows anything. He's already killed Spencer and Spencer's wife. He may have killed Wilcox. We don't know for sure if Holland's involved, but if he is, he's in grave danger. I suggest you get him into protective custody or at least have him covered if Kane comes calling."

"I'll e-mail you what we have on Kane," said Maggie.

"Any pictures?" asked Bell. "Our guys will want to know who they're watching for."

"An old one, taken maybe ten years ago," said McCabe. "Shows the four friends on top of a mountain. We'll have our computer guy age Kane a little and send it down."

"Sounds good," said Bell. "You still coming down, Maggie?"

"Yeah, but not today. How about I let you know?"

"I'd love to see you. It's been what? Five years?"

"Something like that."

Maggie switched off the phone.

"Flame still burning?" asked McCabe.

"I don't think so," said Maggie. "Anyway, like you, he's taken. Married with a new baby." She smiled at him. "Good luck with the ex," she said. "You'll want to spend some time with Casey, and I've got a lot that needs doing."

* * *

Though a good height for her age, five-four and still growing, Casey looked small in his big chair, feet not quite
reaching the floor. Her red duffel, the one for overnights,
waited on the floor by her side. Bunny sat perched on her
lap. Casey fiddled with the animal's remains, mostly just
ragged ears.

McCabe figured he could use something to fiddle with,
too. A bunny for grow-ups. He thought how good a cigarette would taste right about now. It'd even make Sandy
happy. She could report him for secondhand smoke. He
pushed the urge away.

"Hi," he said.

"Hi."

"Ready to go?"

"Yeah."

"You're taking Bunny?"

She looked up, her oval face, framed by dark hair, more
like Sandy's every day. "Yes," she said firmly, as if expecting him to object.

"Okay."

She had on one of her new outfits. He supposed the rest
of the new clothes were packed in the bag. Sitting there
she reminded him of the last kid at summer camp, the one
whose parents always arrived late to pick her up. He sat
opposite on the white couch. "It'll be fine. You'll have a
good time."

She looked at him as if he'd said something stupid, then
looked back at Bunny.

They didn't say anything else for a while. Finally he got
up and knelt in front of her chair. He took both her hands
in his. "Casey, I know how hard this is after three years.
Really. I do. I think one of the reasons your mother wants
to see you is because she realizes how much she's missed
by not being part of your life and how sorry she is about
that. I also think maybe you're feeling that by spending
time with Sandy you're being disloyal to me. You're not.
I think it'll be good for you to get to know your mother

again. When I say I hope you have a good time, I'm not talking about staying at a fancy hotel or going to shows or any of that stuff. I want you to have a good time being with your mother. Not because I love her—that's way over—but because I love you. Does that make sense?"

McCabe kissed his daughter. Then he went back to the sofa and sat down. After a couple of minutes she got up and climbed into his lap and hugged him. They sat together like that until, at five minutes after four, the doorbell rang.

"Hello, McCabe."

"Hello, Sandy." She looked as gorgeous as ever. Wealth agreed with her. He felt his heart beating hard in his chest. He breathed deeply to try to slow it down.

"May I come in? Or are we just going to stand here in the hallway?" He moved to one side, and she walked into the apartment. "Hello, Casey," she said. "I'm glad to see you again."

Sandy offered Casey her hand. Casey took it, and they shook. "Are you all ready?"

"I just have to go to the bathroom."

"Okay. Off you go." Casey went down the hall. McCabe figured she needed a minute to adjust.

"Nice view," said Sandy, gazing out at the boats in the bay.

"That's one of the nice things about living in Portland. The water's never far away. You're staying at the Four Seasons?"

"Yes, the suite's booked under Peter's name. Ingram."

"I remember. Will he be there?"

"No. He's in Europe on business. It will just be us girls."

"Casey will have her cell phone with her, but why don't you give me yours just in case." She recited the number.

"Here's mine," he said. He handed her a slip of paper with the number on it. "Call if there's any problem. Any problem at all. You should get her back by five on Sunday. She'll need Sunday night for her homework."

"That's fine."

Casey returned, unzipped her bag, and stuffed Bunny inside. McCabe looked at his daughter. "Remember what I said about having a good time."

For the first time, she smiled. She was trying to reassure him. "I will," she said.

He watched them from the window as they got into Sandy's rental car. A Chevy Impala. He'd been expecting her to turn up in something fancier. A Mercedes. Or a Jag. Or a Lincoln at the very least. They pulled out of the visitors' parking space and drove off. McCabe went to the kitchen and poured himself a Scotch. Still a little early, but fuck it. He didn't go out for cigarettes.

49

He called Maggie. After leaving his place, she'd driven to Spencer's office, retrieved the Denali picture, and taken it back to Middle Street, where Starbucks produced a high-res scan of Kane's face, then aged it by ten years. Maggie e-mailed the resulting image to John Bell, to MSP, and to every sheriff's department and local jurisdiction in the state. Shockley's office released it to the TV stations and newspapers. Kane was long gone, but at least the searchers would know what he looked like. Aside from that they knew nothing. Not what kind of car he was driving or what direction he was headed in. He could be driving back to Florida for all they knew. McCabe asked Maggie to e-mail the picture to Aaron Cahill in Orlando along with an update.

Next he called Tasco, who was still at 24 Trinity Street. Jacobi and an additional team of techs from the state crime lab in Augusta were going over the place. So far they'd found nothing of significance except Hattie Spencer's cell phone, turned off, in a kitchen drawer under the toaster. Terri Mirabito came on the line, her voice weary. "I've got one Spencer scheduled for tomorrow morning, one for the afternoon. A two-for-one special. No extra charge. I'll e-mail you the particulars."

* * *

McCabe found a Maine road map, a ruler, a piece of string, a red marker, and a yellow highlighter. He spread them all out on the kitchen table and began reconstructing Sophie's ride to the surgery site. From her description, McCabe was certain Pollock headed north on 95. Through the first toll-booth at York. Then another thirty-five miles to Portland, where he could have stayed on 95 or diverted to 295. Slightly shorter that way, but it didn't much matter. Both were four-lane interstates, and they came together again a little south of Augusta. Three tolls either way. Based on Sophie's estimates of time, locations of tollbooths, and the assumption that Pollock was careful to stay at or just slightly above the speed limit, it still made sense that he exited at Augusta and drove maybe forty to sixty miles on local roads.

McCabe lined up the string with the scale of the map and marked it at forty and again at sixty miles. He drew a red semicircle on the map in an arc, west to east, forty miles from the exit and another parallel arc at sixty. He colored the area between the two red lines with yellow highlighter. Hundreds of square miles.

Lucas Kane was someone I knew a long time ago, Harriet Spencer said. *His parents had a summer place not far from ours.*

In Blue Hill?

Near there.

Blue Hill was inside the yellow zone.

McCabe booted up Casey's computer. He went to the Web site for the Town of Blue Hill. On it he found a phone number for Priscilla Pepper, Town Clerk, Tax Collector, and Registrar of Voters.

"Town of Blue Hill." An older woman's voice. Her accent pure Downeast.

"Priscilla Pepper, please."

"This is she."

"Ms. Pepper, this is Detective Sergeant Michael McCabe, Portland Police Department."

"Yes."

"I'm conducting an important investigation. I wonder if I could trouble you for some tax information about a couple of properties in or near Blue Hill."

"Well, I can help you if the property's in Blue Hill. Not if it's near." Priscilla Pepper spoke in clipped, measured tones. McCabe realized she couldn't be hurried.

"Do you have any record of a property belonging to a man named Maurice Kane? K-A-N-E."

"Just a minute." No reaction to the name. Maybe she wasn't a classical music fan. More likely, Ms. Pepper didn't think it seemly to comment on a neighbor's fame.

She returned after a couple of minutes. "I have the record. Mr. Kane owns about twenty-five acres, eight miles north of town off Range Road."

"Not on the water?"

"No. Just a small pond."

"Is there a house on the property?"

"Two structures. One big one. Over three thousand square feet. Also a secondary structure. Supposed to be a guest cottage. Eight hundred square feet. Primarily a summer property. Mr. Kane's not registered to vote here."

"Is it winterized?" Kane would have a tough time transplanting hearts in an unheated building during a Maine winter.

"Nothing in the assessment says anything about either house being seasonal."

"Could you give me directions to the Kane place?"

"Know how to get to Blue Hill?"

"I can find it."

"Take Pleasant Street north out of town. That's Route 15. After about three miles, fork right onto Range Road. Go two, maybe three miles. You'll pass a big farm on your right. After another mile, make a right onto a dirt road. Follow it about two miles and you'll see a mailbox. Says 113. No name on it. Drive another mile or so down a private road to the house. Never been down there myself, but the tax map says the road's unimproved. Turns into a long driveway for Kane. Don't think you'll find any people there this time of year. Folks like that usually clear out right after Labor Day."

"Thanks for your help, Ms. Pepper."

"You're welcome."

"Oh. One last thing. Could you check one more record for me?"

"Well, Detective, I was about to leave. It is after five o'clock, you know."

"Last favor, I promise. Any permits for construction anywhere on the property in, say, the last five years?"

"Just a moment."

McCabe waited again.

"Detective?"

"Yes?"

"I do see one thing. Strikes me as kinda funny, though."

"Funny in what way?"

"Why would anyone want to put a finished basement under a small summer guest cottage? Seems like a big waste of money, if you ask me."

Using the satellite imagery available on Google, McCabe pinpointed the location. He couldn't see any house, but the area appeared heavily wooded. The house might be hidden.

Next he Googled Maurice Kane. Over a million hits. Most focused on Kane's career. Dozens of biographies but no obituaries. The maestro was apparently still alive. McCabe scanned some of the documents. Kane was born in Bath, England, in 1919, which made him eighty-five or eighty-six today. A certifiable prodigy, he played his first public concert when he was seven and studied under some of the most celebrated musicians in Europe. In September of '39, Kane joined British intelligence, working as a translator and interpreter for the duration of the war. For six years, he performed only occasionally, mostly in London. After the war his career blossomed. Critics raved about "the witty, apparently effortless muscularity" of his style. Others extolled his "supreme virtuosity." He moved to New York in 1961. McCabe found dozens of recordings, but no new albums released since the late nineties. Concert tours stopped around then as well. A European tour in 1997 was canceled due to a mild heart attack. Another was canceled two years later, the reason given as "nervous exhaustion." McCabe probed further. Kane was hospitalized early in 2000 for "chest pains." A reference to congestive heart failure. There was no mention of surgery. No mention of anything after 2001.

The phone rang. Maggie. Calling from Trinity Street. "Thought you were coming back here?"

"How's the search going?"

"Still going."

"Find anything interesting?"

"Not a whole lot."

"Lucas leave any prints?"

"Not that anyone's found yet. Back to my original question. You joining us?"

"No. You and Tasco and Jacobi can finish the search. I'm driving up to Blue Hill."

"What's in Blue Hill?"

"Lucas Kane's boyhood home."

"You think that's where he went?"

"I think maybe it's where he goes to cut up people."

"And you intend to go alone?"

"That was my plan."

"A pretty dumb plan, if you don't mind my saying so. You already got your ass in a sling for meeting Sophie in Gray without backup. Why don't you call out the troopers? There's a barracks nearby in Ellsworth."

"For what? So they can come storming in on a possibly empty house with flak jackets and combat gear? Based on what? A hunch? A gut instinct?"

"Based on this being a dangerous guy who's already killed more people than I care to count. Shit, McCabe, you always think you can do everything alone—and you call Kane a risk-taker. Even the Lone Ranger never went anywhere without Tonto."

"Mag, all I know at this point is this is where Kane spent summers as a kid. Absolutely nothing says he's there now. He could be anywhere. If I need help, then I can call in the troopers."

"I'm coming with you."

"Not necessary, Maggie."

"Bullshit. Look what happened the last time you said that. You need some kind of backup, and I guess it'll have to be me. I'm coming with you."

"Suit yourself. Be here in ten minutes."

"I'll stop in at 109. Just to make sure we have everything we need."

50

McCabe drove, following the route he'd constructed on the map. They left the turnpike at Augusta and headed east in slow traffic along Route 3. On a Friday night in September, the roads were still crowded with weekenders, in spite of predictions from the cheery voice on NPR of cool, overcast fall weather. They stayed on 3 through South China and Belfast. NPR was right about cool. The temperature was dropping, and Maggie flipped on the heater. They went through Bucksport, then turned south, leaving 3 and continuing on 15 toward Blue Hill. Nearly four hours after leaving Portland, McCabe found the turnoff from 15 onto Range Road. Five minutes later they passed the dirt road Priscilla Pepper had told McCabe would be there. The night was dark now, and cold, with temperatures in the upper thirties. They passed a mailbox on the left. McCabe stopped, reversed, saw the numbers 113, reversed again, and found a place to leave the car where it wouldn't be seen. He planned to approach the place on foot. They got out of the car into an inky black night without a moon. Too damned cold for the light jacket he was wearing.

"Might get some flurries," said Maggie. She didn't sound unpleased. McCabe believed that Maggie, like a lot of Mainers, took pride in nasty weather the way some New

Yorkers take pride in rudeness and aggressive driving. She pulled two sets of ultralight body armor from the trunk and flipped one to McCabe. He wondered if the Kevlar would help keep him warm. They donned voice-activated headsets, established communication, and left the line open. McCabe stuck a pair of folding binoculars and a digital recorder in his pocket.

They walked without speaking through the darkness. Priscilla Pepper had called it a private road. A dirt track, actually. Road was too grand a word. A mostly quiet night. An owl hooted. Later something bigger crashed through the woods. A deer? McCabe wasn't sure if deer crashed around in the middle of the night. Maybe a bear? He didn't know much about their habits either. A city kid, he'd rather chase bad guys through Manhattan alleyways anytime than through these woods. A low-hanging branch scratched his face, just missed his eye. He swore privately; an accidental injury was the last thing he needed. After that, he flicked the flashlight on and off every ten feet or so to check for more branches at eye level, or branches or holes on the ground that might trip him up. The light revealed fresh tire tracks. A car had passed this way not too long ago.

A hundred yards out, they saw lights from the main house. They moved up another fifty yards and knelt behind a rock outcropping just off the track that gave them a good view of the place. McCabe didn't see any signs of surveillance cameras. Not even an alarm system. Two cars were parked on one side of the house, a gray Chevy Blazer and a black Toyota Land Cruiser. He focused the binoculars on the main building. A large, rustic, Adirondack-style hunting lodge, a log cabin times ten. The porch seemed to go all the way around, its railings crafted from birch limbs. McCabe guessed it had been built in the twenties, maybe earlier. A single dim light shone from an upstairs window. Downstairs, flickering firelight added to the electric illumination. He smelled wood smoke. He couldn't see anyone moving inside. He shifted the binoculars to the guest cottage, which stood in front of a good-sized pond. Dark and quiet. It looked locked up. He searched for an entrance to the "finished basement" and couldn't find one. He decided to check the house first.

McCabe handed Maggie the binoculars and asked her to stay down and cover him. She looked like she was about to argue but instead crouched down and put her pistol and the flashlight on the rock in front of her. Good line of fire to cut off someone fleeing the house, either on foot or by car. It was pretty far out for a handgun, though—and she could only see someone fleeing toward the road, not back into the woods.

Lucinda Cassidy woke up in bed at home, in her room in North Berwick, shivering from the cold. Her quilt, the one Grammy made, must have fallen to the floor. Mommy shook her arm, waking her for school.

"C'mon, Lucy, get up or you'll be late. The bus will be here in half an hour, and I don't want you skipping breakfast again. Get up now."

She tried opening her eyes. No, they were already open. Why couldn't she see? She looked around. No light. She forced her mind to focus. North Berwick was gone. North Berwick was just a dream. Not home. Not with Mommy. Still here in the cold black endless night, alone with her lover. She could feel the light cotton of the hospital gown, again covering her front, tied loosely around her neck, open at the back.

She wasn't on a bed anymore. Beneath her she felt a hard metal table, cold against the bare skin of her back and buttocks. Listening, she heard a piano, faint and far away, playing a vaguely familiar piece. Part of the dream? No. It sounded real, though recently the dreams had become so vivid she no longer knew for sure what was real and what wasn't. He must've moved her to a new place. Drugged her again with the needle and moved her. The only other sound was a white noise like in the other place. Somehow different, though, the pitch a little higher. Nearly imperceptible, but yes, definitely higher. What else? The smell. A hint of antiseptic tinged with pine. Real pine. From trees. Not chemical stuff. The pine hadn't been there before. Maybe the worst thing, she couldn't move her wrists or ankles. He'd put the restraints back on. Why had he done that? Something new was happening. Lucy didn't know what. The terror that over the days, the weeks, had dulled to a constant gnawing anxiety crashed in on her again.

The door opened, the light from the hall momentarily blinding her. She closed her eyes. He shut the door. "I see you've woken from your nap," he said, walking toward her.

McCabe moved in a crouching run, zigzagging toward the house, his darting figure staying in the shadows, less visible, less vulnerable to anyone watching from a window. He climbed onto the porch and backed as far as he could against the wall near one of the lit windows. He drew his weapon, slowed his breathing, leaned forward, peered in. A large room with paneled walls. Bookshelves. Original oils.

Dying embers glowed in the stone fireplace. Above the mantel, a pair of crossed oars from a racing shell were hung to form a large X. Lettered in paint on one of the oars were the words THE HALEY SCHOOL, HENLEY REGATTA, 1980. Underneath were eight names. One of them, L. KANE, STROKE.

Maurice Kane, the great man himself, dozed in a leather chair in front of the fire, a blanket over his legs. A standing lamp beside the chair outlined his face in a mosaic of light and shadow. His skin looked old, worn, paper thin. His mouth hung open in fitful sleep. He needed a shave.

McCabe crossed to the other side of the window. A concert grand piano dominated the far side of the room. He heard music from inside. Bach's Goldberg Variations. Kane's younger, more vital self, playing with what McCabe assumed was the witty, apparently effortless muscularity he'd read about. Hearing the music, he felt a quiet anger he couldn't name, a sense of mourning, of loss building within. Feelings he knew he couldn't afford. He shook them away.

He walked around the porch, staying in the shadows, keeping quiet, avoiding the detritus of summers past. Wicker chairs and tables, the wicker coming unraveled. A porch swing. An antique two-man logger's saw propped in a corner. McCabe continued around to the back of the house, where a door opened onto what appeared to be a small utility room. He tried the door. Unlocked. No picks needed. "I'm going in," he whispered into the headset. He opened the door and entered.

Maggie's voice in his ear said, "McCabe, what the hell do you—"

He interrupted, whispering back, "Be quiet or I'll flip you off."

"Fine," she said, her tone making it clear she didn't think it fine at all.

He stepped inside and flicked on the Maglite. A small room leading to a large open kitchen. He moved the beam of light around the space. Bilious green walls. An electric control panel painted shut. A linoleum floor in a black-and-white checkered pattern. Packing cartons piled in one corner, each marked UNITED VAN LINES. A. JACKMAN AND SONS, MOVERS. 622 EAST 88 TH STREET, NEW YORK, NY 10022. McCabe flicked off the flashlight and walked through the darkened kitchen toward the light and the room where the old man dozed.

In the hall, photographs lined the walls. McCabe could make out images of the famed pianist posing with people even more famous than he was. Fred Astaire and Ginger Rogers. Henry Kissinger. Ronald and Nancy Reagan. There were also several family shots, most in woodsy settings, probably taken here. Two caught McCabe's eye. One showed the elder Kane and his wife with their two sons, one clearly Lucas, one considerably younger. One of the great man's hands rested on each of the boys' shoulders. McCabe wondered briefly what had happened to the younger son. The second shot was of Lucas alone, eight or nine years old, standing on the porch of this house, a serious, unsmiling expression on his face, a cone-shaped birthday party hat perched on his head. His dark intense eyes stared into the camera. In his arms he cradled a small rabbit, perhaps a birthday gift.

McCabe moved into the living room. The old man still slept, his breathing ragged. A droplet of spittle hung at the corner of his mouth. McCabe stood in the shadows, close enough to Kane's chair to be seen and heard but partially hidden from the entrance to the room.

Maurice Kane swatted at something in his sleep, then said something McCabe couldn't understand.

"Mr. Kane? Mr. Kane, wake up. I need to talk to you."

The old man squinted into the shadows, trying to locate the voice. "Who are you? What are you doing in my house?" His voice the rasping whisper of a dying man, the accent more British than American.

"Where is Lucas?"

"Lucas? Lucas is dead. Who are you?"

"No, Lucas is alive, Mr. Kane. I'm a policeman. Detective Michael McCabe. Portland police. I need to know where Lucas is."

"A policeman," Kane repeated. "How did you get in my house?"

"Please, Mr. Kane. Lucas. Where is he?"

The old man looked at him blankly. This was taking too long, McCabe thought. Lucinda's chances of survival were draining away with each passing moment. The hell with it. He'd search the house first. Find out what he could from the old man later.

Lights from a car swept through the windows, its beams crossed the far wall, finally lighting the dark corner where McCabe stood. He went to the window, peered through. He couldn't see anything.

"McCabe?" Maggie's voice whispered in his ear.

"What?"

"An ambulance just pulled up behind the guest cottage. I'm watching it through the binocs. I'm gonna move closer."

McCabe could hear some rustling sounds and Maggie's breathing. He waited.

"Okay, I can see better now. Guess what? Dr. Wilcox is jumping out the back. Now a woman. Now the driver's getting out. He's unlocking a back door to the cottage."

"Is Kane there?"

"No. Just the three of them. They're pulling a stretcher out of the back." There was silence on the line for a moment. "There's an old man on the stretcher. They're heading into the cottage."

McCabe figured it had to be transplant time. Lucinda's heart was nearby, but where? In the cottage? Maybe here in the house? Was it still beating, still in her body? He didn't know.

"I'm calling Ellsworth for backup." Maggie's voice again. "Uh-oh."

"What?"

"Another light just went on. Directly above you in the main house. Third-floor window."

Squinting into the sudden brightness, Lucy saw the man standing by the door, dressed in blue-green surgical scrubs. He locked the dead bolt and walked toward her. In his right hand, he carried a small red-and-white picnic cooler.

Lucinda's eyes darted around. Yes. This was a different room. It looked like a child's attic playroom with a single high dormer window. Toys and games lay stacked in the corner. Three low painted bookcases against the wall were filled with children's books. Beside the window, a large stuffed bear sat upright inside an open cardboard box, its black button eyes peering directly at her. Reflected in the light, she saw a perfect spider's web connecting the bear's arm with the wall. On the other side of the web, a Pinocchio marionette hung, an idiot's smile plastered on its pink painted face.

Closer to the steel platform on which she lay, Lucy could see a large electrical saw, its articulated arm hanging at a strange angle. Even closer, a tray of gleaming stainless steel instruments. The platform itself rose at a slight angle so that her head was higher than her feet. Near the bottom, between her ankles, she could see a round drain. For what? Water? Blood? The terror rose within her. Suddenly the bear and the marionette burst into hysterical laughter, pointing their arms directly at her, laughing at her because she was going to die. The laughter went on and on. She had to stop it. She had to shut it out. She tried to cover her ears, but her hands wouldn't move. She closed her eyes and screamed.

McCabe ran into the open central hall, where the stairs rose up in a broad spiral toward the third-floor landing. He looked up and saw a heavy oak door blocking the entrance to the room where Maggie must have seen the light. His mind was racing. He could rush up the stairs, but the door would be locked. If he tried to break it down or shoot his way in, Kane, armed with a scalpel, if not a gun or a knife, would use Lucinda as a shield or, worse, simply cut her throat. He thought he heard a scream. Sharp. Short. Quickly cut off.

He ran back to the utility room just as Maggie burst in through the back door. He found the circuit breaker box. Removing a heart was easy, Spencer told him—but not in the dark. Not without power. Kane couldn't see where to cut. The surgical saw wouldn't work. He'd have to come out of the room to find out what was happening, to reset the breaker. That might give them the chance they needed. Maybe.

The scream barely escaped her lips. Moving with astonishing speed, the man slapped a strip of silver duct tape against her mouth and pulled it tight, cutting off the sound. She opened her eyes. His face was close to hers, his deep-set eyes shining brightly. She could hear his breathing, feel the breath on her skin. Short, shallow, rapid. He untied and removed her gown, then pulled on a pair of latex surgical gloves. He selected a scalpel from the tray and placed it flat on her chest, between her breasts. He turned on a bright light clipped to a tall silver-colored metal stand, the kind she'd seen in photographers' studios. He adjusted the light until it shone right at her. He picked up the scalpel and, using a sponge, washed her chest with something that felt cold and smelled antiseptic. He smiled at her. Then he leaned over and gently kissed her cheek. "I hope you've enjoyed our time together, Lucinda," he said.

McCabe tugged at the panel door. Shit. Painted shut. He pulled again. Still it wouldn't open.

"What the hell are you doing?" asked Maggie, her voice a whisper, but barely.

He ignored the question. His eyes darted around. He was losing precious seconds. He imagined Kane cutting a neat red line down the middle of Lucinda's chest. He spotted a retractable box cutter on top of the moving cartons, grabbed it, and flipped it open. He ran the blade around the painted edges of the door. He pulled again. Still stuck. This was taking too long. He thought he could hear the whine of the Stryker surgical saw. Nearly frantic, he used the knife again and pulled even harder. The dry paint cracked. Then, finally, it gave way.

Her lover slid a surgical mask over his mouth. He placed the point of the scalpel against her skin at the bottom of her throat. Lucy retreated into the cold steel platform that held her, trying to pull back into its impenetrable hardness. He pushed. She felt a shock of pain as the blade broke her skin. She closed her eyes and prayed to a God she'd never believed in for the peace and redemption that death would bring. The lights went out.

The utility room went black. The Goldberg Variations ceased. McCabe flipped on his Maglite and raced for the stairs that circled the open hallway. He took them two at a time. He was breathing hard by the time he got to the third-floor landing. He could hear Maggie running close behind. Kane was nowhere in sight. Was he still in the room with Lucinda? What was he doing in there? Without power, Kane couldn't see to cut, couldn't use the saw. So what was he doing? The plan was for Kane to come out of the room to investigate the loss of power, to come out where McCabe could get him before he killed Lucy. Where the fuck was he?

McCabe forced himself to calm down. He pressed his body against the wall on one side of the door, his .45 in his hand. Maggie took up a position on the other side. He flicked the Maglite off. An unholy blackness filled the space. Okay, Kane, get your ass out here. Investigate. Don't you want to know why the power went off?

Finally the lock turned, the door opened, and Lucas Kane emerged into the blackness of the hall. He walked three tentative steps.

"Kane," McCabe said. The man turned to face him. McCabe switched on the Maglite. Lucas Kane raised his left hand to shield his eyes from the light. He peered toward the detective.

"Lucas Kane, you're under arrest," said McCabe, his voice flat, hard, matter-of-fact. "Turn around slowly and put your hands behind your head."

Kane didn't move.

"Just so you know, Kane, or is it Harry Lime? I'm pointing my gun right at your heart. I'm going to kill you if you don't do exactly as I say."

Maggie rushed into the darkened room. McCabe could hear Cassidy's muffled cries. She was still alive.

"Lucas Kane," said McCabe, "I repeat, you're under arrest for the murders of Katherine Dubois and Philip and Harriet Spencer. You have the right—"

"Only those three?" Kane interrupted the recitation of his rights. "What about the others? What about Elyse Andersen? She was my first, you know, and in some ways, the best. We used Elyse's heart to save dear Daddy's life."

"Out of love for the old man?"

"Love? Good God, no. It was for the money. I'd already

been written out of his will. There was no love between my father and me."

"You did the surgery? Or was it Wilcox?"

"Only the harvest," he said. "Matt Wilcox did the transplant. He's done them all. A talented surgeon, Matt. Elyse's heart is still beating, right downstairs, inside the old man's body."

McCabe was growing impatient. The longer this went on, the greater the potential for a fuckup. "Alright, Kane. Enough. Lie down on the floor. Now. Hands behind your back."

Slowly, almost imperceptibly, Kane's right hand slipped out of sight. A smile passed his lips. The smile of the hunter, not of the prey. "No," he said.

"No?"

"No. I have no intention of letting you or anybody else truss me up like a pig for the slaughter."

Suddenly Kane lunged. He was fast for a big man, amazingly fast. Something small and shiny flashed by McCabe's face. McCabe dodged the blade and fired, point-blank, into Kane's chest. The slug had to have hit, but Kane kept coming.

"You can't kill me, McCabe," he said. "Didn't you know I'm already dead? Murdered in Florida?"

Kane advanced slowly. McCabe backed away. He felt pain and wetness in his left hand, the one holding the Maglite. The scalpel, if that's what it was, must have sliced the flesh between his thumb and index finger. He let the light fall to the floor, but it stayed on, illuminating the hall in a shadowy semidarkness.

Kane slashed again, this time at McCabe's face. McCabe fired again. Kane staggered but kept coming. Now there was blood leaking from his mouth. "I'm a ghost, McCabe. A ghost that's going to slit your throat." Kane's words came out in a choking cough.

McCabe drew back farther, amazed Kane was still walking, still upright. Either one of those shots should have killed him. McCabe felt the edge of the banister press against the small of his back. Behind him, he knew, there was nothing but air, three stories down to a stone floor. Finally Kane threw himself forward, his arm swinging the scalpel wildly. McCabe crouched, ducking under the slashing blade. Then he lunged forward himself, rising up and under. The camera in McCabe's mind recorded the next few seconds in slow motion. Kane's momentum, aided by McCabe's shoulder as he rose, lifted him up and over the rail. McCabe stared. Freeze-frame. Kane stared back, suspended for an instant, like a cartoon character, in midair. Then he was falling, still clutching the scalpel, his arms flapping as if he could fly. Kane landed headfirst on the flagstone floor below.

McCabe felt blood trickling from his wounded left hand. He holstered the .45, found some Kleenex in his back pocket and pressed it against the wound. He retrieved the Maglite and shone it down on Lucas Kane's body three floors below.

51

"Is he dead?"

McCabe turned and saw Maggie leaning against the door frame, watching, her weapon in her hand. Even in the dim light, she must have been able to see his left hand covered with bloody Kleenex, because she walked toward him and raised it over his head like a child in class who knew all the answers, though he knew he really didn't. "How's Lucinda?" he asked.

"Physically okay, I think. Otherwise? Who knows. The wound in her chest is superficial," Maggie said. "He must have been drawing the process out. Killing her slowly."

"Sadistic bastard," he said. He paused. "Kane's dead."

"I know. I heard the shots and came out to help. Saw him go over the rail."

McCabe looked straight into Maggie's eyes. They were practically the same height. "He came at me with a scalpel," he said. After an awkward moment, he waved his bloodied hand in her direction as a kind of proof that he hadn't done anything wrong.

She touched her hand to his cheek. "You don't have to convince me, McCabe."

Then she took the Maglite, and together they went back into the room where Lucinda Cassidy lay on a steel autopsy table, still naked, her hands and feet still bound to the table, her eyes wild with fear. A thin red line of blood ran neatly from just below her neck to just above her navel. It was already drying.

Maggie bent down and retrieved the hospital gown from the floor. She covered Lucinda's body, tying the strings around her neck. "Lucinda," she said, pointing the light at her own face, "you're safe. I'm a police officer. Detective Margaret Savage." She shifted the beam to McCabe. "This is Detective Sergeant Michael McCabe. Nobody's going to hurt you." She handed the light back to McCabe. "You'll be all right now. You're safe," she said, speaking gently like a mother trying to comfort an injured child. Lucinda's frantic eyes darted rapidly from one to the other of them.

"I'm going to take the tape from your mouth now," Maggie continued, "and unbind your hands and feet."

McCabe watched, sure Lucinda would start screaming and thrashing, as Maggie pulled away the duct tape and untied the restraints. She didn't. She let Maggie take her in her arms and help her to a sitting position. Then Maggie hugged and stroked her and told her over and over that she was safe. That she would be okay. That the nightmare was over. To McCabe's surprise, Cassidy simply closed her eyes, laid her head on Maggie's shoulder, and quietly wept. She babbled a little, the babbles mostly incoherent, except for the word "Mommy," repeated a number of times. For Lucinda it was going to be a long road back. McCabe put the light on the autopsy table next to Maggie and went downstairs.

In nearly complete darkness, he felt his way to the back utility room and flipped on the main power switch. The lights came back on. The Goldberg Variations picked up where they'd left off. In the hallway, Lucas Kane lay in the middle of the floor. Dead once. Now, dead again. This time for good. It was over.

McCabe could hear sirens. He walked to the front door and opened it in time to see three Maine State Police cars and a MedCU unit scream into the compound. Maggie must have called Ellsworth after all. Good for Maggie.

Troopers poured out of the cars dressed for combat. McCabe walked out of the house, hands in the air, holding his shield high over his head for the troopers to see.

"McCabe?" one of them called. A sergeant. Apparently in charge.

"Yes," McCabe shouted and went to join them by the cars.

"Sergeant Bill Dickinson, Ellsworth Barracks." He held out his hand.

McCabe shook it. "Katie Dubois's murderer is inside the big house. He's dead. My partner's upstairs caring for a female hostage."

"The Cassidy woman?"

"Yeah." He turned to the EMTs, one of whom was bandaging his cut hand. "The woman upstairs—she'll need to be sedated. Otherwise she seems okay. Third floor." They nodded and both of them headed for the building.

"What else?" asked Dickinson.

"Some people are holed up in a large basement area under the cottage over there. A doctor. Some nurses. An old man with a serious heart condition. He'll need medical attention, too."

"Armed? Fortified?"

"No. They're using it as an operating room. Just let them know you're here. My guess is they'll come out without a peep."

Two heavily armed troopers rushed the building and tried the door. Unlocked. They slipped inside.

McCabe watched them go, then turned and started walking back toward the house.

"Where are you going?" Sergeant Dickinson's voice boomed out behind him.

McCabe looked back. "Me? I'm getting my partner and going home."

52

Saturday. 1:00 A.M.

They started back to Portland the same way they'd come. Maggie was at the wheel. McCabe stared silently out the window, thinking about nothing, thinking about everything. The road was nearly empty now, and Maggie drove fast, easily overtaking the few cars they encountered along the way. Temperatures had fallen down near the freezing mark, but the promised flurries hadn't materialized. "Get some sleep," she said. "We can trade over in an hour or so." He nodded and closed his eyes, but they wouldn't stay closed. Instead they focused on the center stripe, reflected in the headlights, rushing toward them, then disappearing under the hood of the car.

In the warmth generated by the heater, McCabe's weary brain played and replayed the final seconds of Lucas Kane's life, watching from another vantage point as he and Kane engaged in their slow, final dance of death. He saw Kane, already bleeding from two bullet wounds, lunge forward. Saw himself duck beneath the arc of Kane's slashing blade. Then from his crouching position he saw himself drive forward, his shoulder striking Kane just below the waist. Finally he watched himself as he rose and, using Kane's own forward momentum, lifted the bigger man up and over the railing. He watched the fall. The flapping of the arms. The fatal impact.

Each time he watched, McCabe came to the same conclusion. If he hadn't risen, if, instead, he'd moved straight forward, or angled left or right, Kane wouldn't have gone over the rail. He would have just been knocked to the floor. In all probability, he would have died from the gunshot wounds anyway. Either way, the question McCabe had no answer for was a simple one. Had he flipped Kane over the rail on purpose? Had he, somewhere in the recesses of his mind, wanted to make absolutely sure that there would be no trial? That there would be no Sheldon Thomas finding some slick way to get the killer off? He wasn't certain of the answer—and if truth be told, he finally realized, he didn't really care. Just as he'd told Kyra about TwoTimes, the man was vermin and he deserved to die. Ambiguity. McCabe was comfortable with that.

"Are you alright?" Maggie asked, glancing over at him.

"Yes," he said finally, after thinking about it a little longer. "Yes. I'm fine." He gazed out the driver's side window. They were crossing the Penobscot River east of Bucksport on the old Waldo-Hancock Bridge. The skeleton of the new bridge, still under construction, rose out of the darkness just south of them.

Near Stockton Springs, they stopped for coffee and a couple of candy bars at an all-night gas station. Neither had slept in nearly forty-eight hours. They were both exhausted. The last thing they needed was for one or the other of them to fall asleep at the wheel. McCabe filled the tank. Then they switched around and he drove.

He checked his watch—2:00 A.M. Casey would be asleep in Boston now. In a big bed in a fancy hotel. Anyway, he hoped she was sleeping and not lying awake worrying. He wondered if she and Sandy were sharing a bed. If so, he hoped Sandy had given her a choice about that. He also hoped Sandy hadn't made any remarks about Casey being too old to still be sleeping with Bunny.

His cell phone rang. He glanced at the caller ID. Shockley. He flipped the phone to speaker mode so Maggie could hear. "Hello, Tom. I guess you heard about Kane."

"You're damned right I did. Good work. Great work." Shockley sounded excited. "I issued standing orders for Dispatch to wake me if and when we got this bastard. Can you let me have a few of the details? I'm talking to the press in a little while." McCabe smiled, imagining visions of Blaine House, the governor's mansion, dancing like sugarplums through Shockley's overeager brain. "Mike, can you hear me?"

"Yes, Chief. By the way, you're on speaker. Maggie's here."

"Fine. Can you give me any of the details? I need to get this right."

McCabe took Shockley through the whole thing, starting with his call to Priscilla Pepper and ending with Kane's final fall to the stone floor and Cassidy being found alive.

"Was the scalpel still in his hand when he died?"

"Yes," said McCabe. "It was."

"I saw the whole thing, Chief," added Maggie. McCabe glanced at her, knowing she'd only come out of the room in time to see Kane go over the rail. "Use of deadly force was justified," she said.

"Well, thank God for that," Shockley replied. "The media briefing starts in about twenty minutes. Will you two be back by then?"

"No. We're still the other side of Belfast," said Maggie. "A couple of hours out."

"Okay. I'll handle it. By the way, Kevin Comisky's funeral's scheduled for three o'clock Monday. Full departmental honors. I hope you'll be there."

"We'll be there," said Maggie.

"Can you let me have his wife's address and phone number?" asked McCabe. "I'd like to call on her."

"I'll have Deirdre e-mail it to you."

"Thanks." Then, not wanting to listen to Shockley anymore, McCabe hit the off button before the chief could answer.

He looked over at Maggie. "Use of deadly force was justified? That's what I'm supposed to tell Casey when she asks if I had to kill the guy?"

"Yes. That's what you'll tell her because we both know that's the truth. You had no choice." She looked back at him. "Just like you told me the other day, it was a clean kill. It needed to be done."

He felt Maggie's eyes studying him as they drove on in silence. "Now what are you thinking about?" she asked.

"I don't know. Nothing. Sometimes I just wonder if Casey wouldn't be better off living a life where phrases like 'clean kill' and 'justifiable use of force' didn't enter the lexicon. Where she wouldn't have to lie awake nights wondering if her father's gonna come home dead or alive."

"I can't help you with that."

"I know."

"I would if I could."

"I know that, too," said McCabe.

"I just think you should stop torturing yourself. You're one of the good guys. You always will be."

He reached out from the wheel and took her hand and squeezed it. She squeezed back. He remembered her brown eyes gazing down at him in Tallulah's and smiled. "You know what else I'm thinking about? I'm thinking about a kiss I got from a really good friend of mine the other day in Tallulah's, and I'm wondering what she might have been thinking at the time."

"Oh, that," said Maggie. "That was just an impulsive thing on your friend's part. Don't let it worry you. Like she said at the time, you're taken."

He let go of her hand. "Yup," he said. "I guess I am." He wondered if Kyra would be waiting for him in the apartment. He was hoping she was.

They traded places again at Augusta, and Maggie drove the rest of the way in silence. McCabe snoozed. It was still dark when they reached the Eastern Prom. Maggie turned the Crown Vic into the parking lot behind the condo. McCabe got out and headed for the door. When he got there he looked back to offer a final wave, but Maggie was already gone. He entered the white Victorian and climbed the stairs to the third floor. He knew that if Kyra was there, he would wake her and they would make love. He knew she'd be happy with that. Afterward maybe they'd sleep for a while. After they woke from that sleep, they'd make love again.

McCabe pulled off his shoes on the landing, entered the apartment, and padded silently across to the bedroom. He pushed open the bedroom door. Somehow, in the darkness he could see Kyra, sitting up in bed, waiting for him. Letting the sheet slip from her naked body, she held out her arms. "Welcome home," she said softly.

Read on for an excerpt from

THE CHILL OF NIGHT

the next exciting novel from James Hayman,

available in hardcover from Minotaur Books!

Had Number Ten Monument Square been set among the skyscrapers of New York, or even Boston, no one would have noticed it. In a town like Portland it stood as one of the defining features of the skyline. Twelve stories of reddish brown granite with black windows set between vertical piers, Number Ten towered arrogantly over the east side of the square, a big player in a small town. At its top, large white letters proclaimed to anyone who cared to look that the building was the headquarters of Palmer Milliken, the city's largest and most prestigious law firm. It was also, according to Palmer Milliken's partners, one of the best anywhere in New England, including, they insisted, Boston. The firm's 192 lawyers plus appropriate support staff occupied all but two of the building's twelve floors.

At seven forty-two in the evening, on the Friday before the long Christmas weekend, a young woman stood at the window of her modest office on the seventh floor, gazing down at the activity in the square. Elaine Elizabeth Goff, Lainie to those who knew her well, was one of Palmer Milliken's senior associate attorneys. She'd already finished her work reviewing terms of a pending merger agreement between two small Maine banks. She'd pored over the documents half a dozen times, made a few changes, and sent in her recommendations an hour ago. Now she was ready to begin her winter vacation, a two-week jaunt, away from the bone-numbing cold of Portland, to the small, elegant Bacuba Spa and Resort on the southwest side of ˉAruba. Only two last things remained. A FedEx envelope on her desk that needed to go out tonight, and a phone call that should have come twelve minutes ago. Its lateness was making her edgy.

Six years out of Cornell Law, Lainie was still in her twenties, though, as she recently and frequently began reminding herself, just barely. But even as the dreaded thirtieth approached, she took pride in her conviction that she, Lainie Goff, the scholarship kid from Rockland, Maine, was about to become one of the youngest partners in Palmer Milliken's fifty-seven-year history. The offer, though not certain, was now so close she could almost taste it. She hoped word of the lucrative partnership would come tonight with the call she was waiting for. If only the damned phone would ring. She'd planned her life around that happening. Begun spending money she didn't have. The $500 Jimmy Choo shoes that were a torture to wear. The gleaming $40,000 BMW 325i convertible waiting in the garage downstairs. Not the bright red she really wanted but the platinum bronze metallic she thought more lawyerly. And now the expensive vacation on Aruba. All that money ponied up in anticipation of greater rewards lying just around the corner.

It wasn't that Lainie was such an exceptional lawyer. Her intellectual and legal skills, while formidable, ranked her no higher than half a dozen others among Palmer Milliken's ambitious pack of associates. But in the race for the top, Lainie enjoyed a key advantage not shared by any of her eager competitors. She was not only an able lawyer, she was also an exceptionally beautiful woman with shoulder-length dark hair, a slim athletic figure, and penetrating blue eyes that most people, but men in particular, found impossible to forget. And she was sleeping with her boss.

Lainie glanced at the old-fashioned electric sign atop the Time & Temperature Building. Seven forty-six. Four minutes since the last time she looked. The temperature was fourteen degrees. Down five in the last hour. The cold that had gripped the city for the better part of the past four weeks was showing no signs of letting up. It was a good time to be taking off for the sunshine. A good time to celebrate. Or would be if only Hank would get off his ass and call. Henry C. "Hank" Ogden, managing partner in charge of Palmer Milliken's lucrative M&A practice. Her mentor. Her boss. Her lover. Elegant, rich, fifty-three years old, and very, very married.

Hank told her he'd call at seven thirty. She didn't know why the call was late, but she didn't like it. The Partnership Committee meeting should have been over hours ago. She strummed her long nails on the sill in front of her. Maybe Hank was just stuck in another meeting. He'd call as soon as he got out. Maybe. That was the charitable assumption. The best of three possibilities. The second was that he was keeping her waiting just for the hell of it. To provoke a little extra anxiety. One of the power games Hank liked playing. His way of letting her know who was in charge. Stupid and pointless, like a little boy poking a stick at a hamster in a cage. Well, she could handle his games, she told herself. She was tougher than that. The third possibility, the disaster scenario, was the one she wasn't sure she could handle—that, in spite of Hank's promised sponsorship and strong support, the partners, in their infinite wisdom, had decided not to extend an offer. If that was the case, then Hank wasn't calling because he'd be nervous about her reaction. He hated scenes, public or private, and knew there'd be one. She took a deep breath. She'd give him ten more minutes. Then she'd call him.

She pushed fears about the Partnership Committee from her mind and decided to think, instead, about her upcoming vacation. Far more pleasant to think about that. Two weeks of being pampered in the sunshine. Two weeks to either celebrate her triumph or salve her pride. Massages.

Facials. Mud baths. Hanging out on the beach by herself with a bunch of trashy paperbacks. Well, to be honest, not *all* by herself. She'd find someone to play with. Someone with no connection to Maine or to Palmer Milliken. Someone European might be fun. Maybe she'd have a chance to practice her French. Patti LaBelle's rendition of "Lady Marmalade" riffed through her brain.

> *Voulez-vous coucher avec moi ce soir?*
> *Voulez-vous coucher avec moi?*

If the news was good, she supposed, Hank would want a "performance review." He'd probably want one anyway. He found the term amusing. *Ms. Goff, could you stop by, oh, at five thirty or so? We need to do a performance review. Thank you very much. We'll see you then.* Not an elaborate review either. Just forty minutes of snatch-and-grope on the red leather couch in his office. That was really all there was to this so-called affair. That and the occasional "nooner" back at her apartment or a rare business trip to some out-of-the-way hotel. Lainie wanted more. She wanted a real relationship. If it was with Hank, fine. If not, that was fine, too. There were others she found interesting. One in particular she occasionally spent time with. Either way, she wasn't sure how much longer she could keep this bullshit going.

It started a year ago as a one-night stand after a few drinks on an overnight trip to East Millinocket to do due diligence on the sale of a paper mill, but it had long since become a regular thing. For him, she knew, it was totally casual. For her, things were more complicated. Sleeping with Hank as a means to an end was fine. She'd always been attracted to older men, powerful men, and, when they had enough time, Hank could be a skilled and attentive lover. Intelligent. Charming. Attractive. She knew he liked her. She toyed with the idea that she could somehow close the deal. Wouldn't that be a hoot? Lainie Goff as the second Mrs. Henry Ogden. Elaine Elizabeth Goff Ogden. The trophy wife. It was a role she could play to a fare-thee-well and one she would thoroughly enjoy.

Deep down Lainie knew it would never happen. Divorce for Hank wasn't an option. He was married for good or ill, till death do them part, to the plain, plump, immensely wealthy Barbara Milliken Ogden, the only granddaughter of Edward A. Milliken, one of the firm's founders. Once the partnership was safely tucked away, it would be time to think of a good way to end the relationship without damaging her career. The idea of being free to pursue new adventures pleased her.

Lainie watched the activity below her window. Banks of dirty snow were pushed to the side, and the center of Monument Square was filled with people. Small groups, mostly twos and fours, scurried in and out of the shops and restaurants that lined the pedestrian plaza on the south side of the square. On this last Friday before Christmas, they were open late and busy. In the middle, near the monument, a brilliantly lit, sixty-foot blue spruce commemorated the season. A big, beautiful decorated tree. Not a Christmas tree, though. Lainie remembered reading that in the *Press Herald*. These days calling a Christmas tree a Christmas tree wasn't done. A city spokeswoman told the reporter that Portland was calling it a *holiday* tree. "We want it to sound denominationally neutral," she said. "We don't want to offend anybody." Lainie snorted. She hated such PC stupidity.

At the base of the tree, a troupe of carolers in faux Victorian garb sang. A few dozen people gathered around to listen and sing along. Most were bundled up against the cold and looked, from where Lainie stood, like little round Michelin men and women. Some held the mittened hands of even smaller Michelin children. Down near the entrance to Longfellow Books, she spotted Kyle, the hot-dog man, tending his pushcart, his trademark white apron wrapped tightly around a heavy woolen jacket. On his head he wore a leather aviator's cap with the earflaps pulled down over his gray hair. He seemed to be doing a brisk business selling the gyros, hot dogs, and Italian sausages he grilled over an open charcoal fire.

Lainie smiled. Kyle was her buddy. He always asked how she was doing, when they were going to make her a partner, and, with a wink and a smile, when she was going to go out on his boat with him. He talked about his boat a lot. A twenty-eight-foot Chris-Craft. He'd have to sell a hell of a lot of hot dogs to be able to afford a thing like that. Then again, Lainie knew, because she was a customer, Kyle sold merchandise more profitable than snacks. *Need a little happiness? Need a little joy? Go see the hot-dog man.* Either way, she enjoyed his flirting, enjoyed his easy Irish charm. Sometimes, when she was making a buy, she caught him looking at her a little too directly. Sometimes he looked away. Sometimes he didn't. Once or twice he said with that wry little smile of his that he might let her have a bag or two for free. God, what a thought. Lainie and the hot-dog man. There was no way in hell she would ever let *that* happen. Not now. Not ever. Still, he wasn't bad-looking.

She wasn't sure how old Kyle was but guessed somewhere in his early fifties. It was an age she found attractive. The same age as Hank. The same age as her Contracts professor at Cornell, the one who gave her the A she needed to make *Law Review*. About the same age, she calculated, her stepfather would be today.

Lainie had been thinking a lot about Albright lately, though she hadn't seen him in years. Her mind went back, once again, to that time in their old house in Rockport. A year or so before his career started taking off. Two years before he divorced her mother and moved out. Without his income her mother couldn't afford the old place. She sold it, used part of the money to buy the smaller, crummier place in Rockland, and invested the rest.

She could see that bastard's face now. The handsome, brilliant Wallace Stevens Albright. A lawyer whose parents named him for a poet, though she'd never known a man with less poetry in his soul. He never let anyone call him

Walt or Wally or any other nickname. It was always Wallace. Or Mr. Albright. Lainie was seven when he married her mother and they went to live with him. He wanted her to call him Daddy. She never would, though she knew it made him angry. He wasn't her father. He even wanted her to change her name from Goff to Albright. She didn't want to do that either. Thank God, her mother said no and made it stick. Otherwise Lainie might be carrying that bastard's name even now.

A strict disciplinarian and a stubborn perfectionist, Wallace Stevens Albright held himself, he said, to a higher standard. Lainie smiled bitterly at the memory. Yeah, right. A higher standard. Like pulling down her pants and spanking her when she was little for the slightest infraction. Bastard was getting off on it. But, oh, did he ever put on a righteous show. She was never able to please him or earn his praise, no matter how hard she tried—and, though she hated him, she did try. It seemed important to win him over, to impress him. Important but impossible. She remembered how once in ninth grade, she got a ninety-five on an algebra exam. It was an exam half the class flunked, even a lot of the smart kids. When she told him about it, proudly, he mocked her. *Oh, really? A ninety-five? What happened to the other five points?* She went to bed that night feeling like she had failed. Again. Fuck him.

She was fifteen when the really bad shit started. The day of the Belfast soccer game. Lainie closed her eyes and it all came flooding back, immediate and real. Her sophomore year in high school. Camden Regional, not Rockland, where she had to go after the divorce. It was an afternoon in late October. One of those cold, rainy fall days that in Maine presage the coming of winter. It was an away game, and it had rained on and off all day long. The field was a sea of mud. All the girls were slipping and sliding, and by the end of the game their skin and hair were covered in drying brown gunk. Lainie scored two goals and just missed a third when the ball hit the left upright and bounced back onto the field. She knew, if she told him, Wallace would focus on the one she missed. *Maybe if you'd worked a little harder you would have made it, Lainie. You can always improve. You can always strive to be better.* Yeah. Just like you, Daddy Dearest.

After the game, Annie Jesperson's mom offered Lainie and another friend, Maddie Mitchell, a ride home. Both girls accepted. It was a lot more comfortable than riding in the team bus, and they wouldn't have to stop at school and catch a ride home from there.

"Get in," Mrs. Jesperson told the girls, throwing a tarp across the backseat. "Just try not to get any mud on the upholstery. This car's brand-new, and we'd like to keep it looking that way."

"We won't," they promised and climbed in, shoving Dudley, Annie's dopey golden retriever, over the seat top and into the cargo area. The girls giggled all the way home, pulling monster faces and rubbing mud balls into each other's hair and fending off Dudley's eager efforts to join in the fun. Mrs. Jesperson dropped Lainie off first, in front of her house. The big white colonial with the wraparound porch and black shutters on Mabern Street in Rockport. The house they lived in when they still had money.

It was almost dark when they got there. There were no lights on in the house. That meant her mother and Wallace were still at work. Her mother managing her antiques shop in Camden, Albright tending his growing law practice. He stayed late at the office almost every night. *You'll never achieve anything, Lainie, never amount to anything. Not unless you're ready to put in the hours.* She fetched the key from where it hung under the back steps and let herself in. She pulled off her shoes at the door, stripped down, and tossed her muddy uniform onto the laundry room floor. She walked naked across the semidarkened front hall and climbed the stairs, heading for the bathroom on the second floor.

About halfway down the corridor, the door to her mother and stepfather's room opened, and Albright stepped out. Lainie gasped. She threw her right arm across her breasts and her left hand over her thatch of pubic hair. He'd never seen her naked before, not even as a little kid, and she wasn't sure which way to run. Albright just stood there looking at her, surprise on his face. He was blocking her way to the bathroom door. Blocking her way to her own room as well. She turned and thought about running back down the stairs—but where could she go stark naked? She turned back and saw his expression change, morphing from surprise to something very different. She heard his breathing quicken. She knew she'd made that happen. Not to some boy in sophomore class. To *him*. To Wallace Stevens Albright. The perfectionist. The man guided by a higher standard. For the first time since he'd come into their lives, Lainie felt a sense of power. It was amazing. Intoxicating. It lasted less than a second.

In the instant it took for Albright's mouth to close, for his lips to draw back into a thin, ugly smile, power turned to fear. And then to panic. She darted for her bedroom door, blindly hoping she could get there before him. Hoping she could somehow slip inside. Slam the door. Lock him out.

She never had a chance. As she reached for the knob, he grabbed an arm, turned her around, and wrapped his arms around her waist, pulling her into him, her back against his body. She could feel his erection through the fabric of his pants, pushing, probing at her butt. She tried pulling away but couldn't. He lifted her off the floor and carried her, flailing and kicking and screaming, into her room. Across the oval knotted rug Grammy Horton made for her. He threw her down among the stuffed bears and bunnies that still populated the head of her bed. She tried a sudden bolt for the door. He grabbed her and pushed her down again. She screamed. He slapped her hard across the face. The pain was explosive, shocking. "Don't try that again." He spat out the words in a quiet voice that was, for all its quietness, full of threat. "This is your fault, Lainie. All your fault. You asked for it, and you're going to get what you deserve." He slapped her again. She felt a thin line of blood trickle from her nose.

She closed her eyes and retreated into the corner, more frightened than she'd ever been in her life. She pulled her muddy knees up, wrapped both arms around them, hugged them tight against her chest. When she dared open her eyes, he was unzipping his pants, pulling them down over his high black socks. Her mind froze. This couldn't be happening. Not in her own room. Not on her own bed. He pulled down his underpants. He folded the suit pants along the creases and hung them neatly over the back of her desk chair. She supposed he was thinking he'd have to wear them to the office the next day. He left his underpants on the floor. He didn't bother taking off his shirt or black socks.

From a distance of fifteen years, the adult Lainie could still see Wallace Stevens Albright's hard little cock poking out, peekaboo fashion, from between the flaps of his blue-striped Brooks Brothers shirt. She was crying now. Sobbing quietly. She could still feel his soft white hands grabbing her ankles, pulling her out of the corner, pulling her legs apart. Then he pushed her knees up and apart and knelt between them. He lowered his chest so all she could see was shirt. She remembered that shirt so well. The feel of the starched cotton, the smell of it. All his shirts had a little blue monogram on the pocket. A *W* and an *S* on either side. A big blue *A* in the middle. It was all she could see. She felt him open her with his fingers and push himself up and in. It still amazed her such a little prick could inflict such pain.

Afterward, he smiled and spoke gently. Told her she'd done very well. It was the first time, maybe the only time, he ever praised her. He told her if her eye turned black where he hit her, she had to tell people she'd been hit in the face with a soccer ball. Then he made her to go to the bathroom and wash herself out. He stood at the open door and watched as she did. Finally he told her in the same gentle voice that if she ever breathed a word about what happened, either to her mother or to anyone else, he'd kill them both. "That's a promise," he said. She never doubted he would keep his word.

That night and many nights after that, he came back to her room for "a visit." Each time it was the same. Except sometimes, instead of fucking her, he'd make her get down on her knees and give him a blow job. Each time, before he left, he told her it was her fault. He did what he did because she was a dirty girl who tempted him. Then he would again threaten to kill her and her mother. She sometimes wondered if her mother knew where he was going when he left their bed in the middle of the night. Downstairs for a snack? To read a book? No. Her mother knew—she must have known—but she never had the courage to say or do anything about it. Never wanted to talk about Wallace at all. And Lainie never asked. Finally, two years later, Wallace left her mother. He found a younger woman who was rich and beautiful, and he filed for divorce. He gave her the white house in Rockport as part of the settlement. She sold it, and she and Lainie moved to the little Cape Cod in Rockland. It was over. But the stain stayed with her. It could never be washed away. Her mother was dead now. She committed suicide two years after Lainie graduated high school and went off to Colby. Swallowed a handful of Xanax tablets to still her anxiety and slit her wrists in the tub. But Wallace Stevens Albright was still out there. Still married. With two little girls of his own. Respected attorney. Oft-mentioned candidate for the federal bench. Child fucker. Bastard.

Lainie glanced again at the Time & Temperature Building. Seven fifty-five and still Hank hadn't called. She hadn't eaten since breakfast, and she was hungry. Despite, or maybe because of her usual regimen of plain grilled fish or chicken and garden salads, she found herself lusting after one of Kyle's plump garlicky Italian sausages, covered with sautéed onions and Kyle's own special sauce. She couldn't actually see the sausages cooking from her seventh-floor perch, but she could sure as hell picture them, crackling away in the frosty air on their bed of hot coals. She could almost taste that first spray of hot fat bursting into her mouth as she popped the skin with her teeth.

Lainie realized her mouth was watering. For a brief, tempting moment, she thought about running downstairs and getting herself one of the damnable but delicious things. Maybe score a little coke at the same time. A twofer. A dumb idea, she supposed. But it would only take a minute. No longer than going to the ladies' room. She might miss Hank's call. But then he'd leave a message. Of course, meeting Hank, literally face-to-face, with onions and garlic on her breath might just turn him off. So what if it did? He couldn't take away a partnership on grounds of bad breath, could he? And it might just spare her a session on the red leather couch. Of course, in less than twenty-four hours, she'd be sunning in a skimpy bikini on a beautiful beach where she wouldn't want even the hint of an extra bulge ruining her nearly perfect figure. "Oh, screw it," she finally said. She grabbed the FedEx envelope from her desk to deposit in the box on the square and headed for the elevator. She'd skip dinner.

When she came back from her coatless dash across the square, coke in her pocket and hot sausage in hand, Hank still hadn't called. Lainie lifted her long, slender legs up onto the desk and bit into the succulent snack. She practically moaned with pleasure. This was better than sex. Much better. As she ate, the image of the singers in the square came back, and she felt a sudden longing for a child of her own to celebrate Christmas with. A little boy or girl to love and protect. Like her mother protected her? No. Better than that. Much better. No child of hers would ever go through the kind of hell she'd endured. She'd make sure of that. No child anywhere should ever have to suffer that. Or would if Lainie could help it. Anyway, it all seemed a stretch. Maybe someday, she supposed, but for now she had to be tougher than that. *Ambition should be made of sterner stuff,* Marc Antony told the Romans.

Yes, she thought, *ambition should be made of sterner*

stuff. Did she have what it took to get where she wanted? Lainie Goff from Rockport via Rockland. The overachiever and star student. The valedictorian of her high school class and winner of a nearly free ride through four years at Colby and another through three years of law school at Cornell. Lainie Goff, who everyone, including Hank, saw as a brilliant, tough, self-confident winner. Lainie Goff, who was capable of anything, even fucking her way to the top. Did she have what it took? She wasn't sure. So far at least, she'd fooled them all. Only she knew the truth. Superstar Lainie didn't exist. The real Lainie was a woman unworthy of anyone's love, even her own. A woman who could only achieve the success she so desperately wanted lying on her back, knees up and knickers down. Wallace Stevens Albright would be so proud of his creation. He wanted her to call him Daddy. Once again, he'd gotten his way. She'd become his daughter through and through.

The phone rang. Lainie swallowed the last bite of sausage and picked it up.

Nearly nine o'clock. Lainie Goff's teeth were clenched in quiet rage as she walked toward her car in Palmer Milliken's private underground garage. The clickity-click of her heels against the concrete punctuated her fury in a rhythmic tattoo. He hadn't turned her down. No. He was much too slick for that. In fact, he hadn't said much of anything at first. Just teased her with the possibility until he'd gotten his rocks off. Then, while she was standing there, still half naked, he pulled the rug out from under her.

"Lainie, I'm afraid you'll have to be patient," he said.

She said nothing. Just stood there seething. Staring at him with the same intensity of hatred she once reserved for Albright.

"Just a couple of more months," he said, zipping his fly, pulling up his suspenders. "I'm working on it. It will happen. I promise. It will happen. There are a couple of other good candidates. Janet Pritchard. Bill Tobias."

She wondered if he was fucking Pritchard, too. Wondered if Janet was as good as Lainie at her performance reviews.

"You know as well as I do," he continued, "the committee almost never approves partnerships for anyone who hasn't been here seven years, and you've got a way to go yet. The three of you will probably all be invited at once."

Didn't he get it? She didn't want to wait until the others were invited, too. She wanted her recognition first. She wanted it now. But what the hell was she going to do? Yell? Scream? Hold her breath till she turned blue? She couldn't quit. She needed the job. She had car payments to make. And she sure as hell wasn't ready to give up on her dream of a Palmer Milliken partnership. But she finally figured it out. As long as Hank kept dangling the promise without actually delivering the goods, he had her where he wanted her. Literally and figuratively. Down on her knees with her mouth around his cock. The minute she got it, screw him. He could find himself another eager young associate to fuck.

Her car stood waiting in its assigned spot in the nearly empty garage. Just her Beemer and Hank's Merc remained. Everyone else had long since left for the holiday. She pressed the little button on her key ring. The car's lights flashed. Its doors unlocked. Still distracted, she didn't notice the absence of the accustomed click. She slid into the front seat. She sat there for a minute, still fuming, before she finally turned the key. The engine smoothly hummed to life. She glanced in the rearview mirror.

She froze.

"Hello, Lainie," a familiar voice murmured. "There're a couple of things we still need to discuss."